# Penny Wise

## Neta Jackson
## Dave Jackson

CASTLE
ROCK
CREATIVE
Evanston, Illinois 60202

Published in Evanston, Illinois. Castle Rock Creative.

Scripture quotations are taken from the following:

> The Holy Bible, New International Version®. NIV®. Copyright © 1973, 1978, 1984 by International Bible Society. Used by permission of Zondervan Publishing House. All rights reserved.

> The New American Standard Bible®, Copyright 1960, 1962, 1962, 1968, 1971, 1972, 1973, 1975, 1977, 1995 by The Lockerman Foundation. Used by permission.

"Auld Lang Syne," a poem by Robert Burns in 1788 and set to the tune of a traditional folk song. Public domain.

"Precious Lord, Take My Hand," by Thomas A. Dorsey in response to the death of his wife and infant son in 1932. Inspired by the tune, "Maitland" (original composer unknown).

"He Giveth More Grace," a poem by Annie J. Flint (1866-1932), set to music by Hubert Mitchell. Public domain.

"Your Grace and Mercy," as sung by the Mississippi Mass Choir, credited to Franklin D. Williams, arrangement 2000. Other arrangements by Marvin Sapp and Percy Bady.

"Grace, Grace, God's Grace," words by Julia H. Johnston, music by Daniel B. Towner. Published in Hymns Tried and True (Chicago, Illinois: The Bible Institute Colportage Association, 1911), number 2. Public domain.

"There Is a Name I Love to Hear," by Frederick Whitfield, 1855. Public Domain.

"'Tis So Sweet to Trust in jesus," William J. Kirkpatrick and Louisa M. R. Stead, 1881. Public Domain.

ISBN: 978-0-9820544-6-8

*Printed in the United States of America*

# Windy City Stories
## by Dave and Neta Jackson

### The Yada Yada Prayer Group Series

*The Yada Yada Prayer Group*, Neta Jackson (Thomas Nelson, 2003).

*The Yada Yada Prayer Group Gets Down*, Neta Jackson (Thomas Nelson, 2004).

*The Yada Yada Prayer Group Gets Real*, Neta Jackson (Thomas Nelson, 2005).

*The Yada Yada Prayer Group Gets Tough*, Neta Jackson (Thomas Nelson, 2005).

*The Yada Yada Prayer Group Gets Caught*, Neta Jackson (Thomas Nelson, 2006).

*The Yada Yada Prayer Group Gets Rolling*, Neta Jackson (Thomas Nelson, 2007).

*The Yada Yada Prayer Group Gets Decked Out*, Neta Jackson (Thomas Nelson, 2007).

### Yada Yada House of Hope Series

*Where Do I Go?* Neta Jackson (Thomas Nelson, 2008).
*Who Do I Talk To?* Neta Jackson (Thomas Nelson, 2009).
*Who Do I Lean On?* Neta Jackson (Thomas Nelson, 2010).
*Who Is My Shelter?* Neta Jackson (Thomas Nelson, 2011).

*Lucy Come Home*, Dave and Neta Jackson (Castle Rock Creative, 2012).

### Yada Yada Brothers Series

*Harry Bentley's Second Chance*, Dave Jackson (Castle Rock Creative, 2008).
*Harry Bentley's Second Sight*, Dave Jackson (Castle Rock Creative, 2010).

### Souled Out Sisters Series

*Stand by Me*, Neta Jackson (Thomas Nelson, 2012).
*Come to the Table*, Neta Jackson (Thomas Nelson, 2012).

### Windy City Neighbors

*Grounded*, Neta Jackson, Dave Jackson (Castle Rock Creative, 2013)
*Derailed*, Neta Jackson, Dave Jackson (Castle Rock Creative, 2013)
*Pennywise*, Neta Jackson, Dave Jackson (Castle Rock Creative, 2013)

For a complete listing of
books by Dave and Neta Jackson visit
www.daveneta.com and www.trailblazerbooks.com

# Prologue

CANDY STOOD BESIDE THE PLAYPEN sitting smack-dab in the middle of the room, dangling a rattle in front of her baby brother's scrunched-up face, willing his wails to stop. "See, Pookey? See the rattle? Here, here . . . you can play with it." She tried to push it into the nine-month-old's hand, but he just batted it away and kept on crying.

"Can't you make that kid stop cryin'? Why don' he want that toy?"

Candy narrowed her eyes at the big man sprawled throne-like on the broken-down couch on the other side of the playpen, one arm flung along the back, the other hand holding a beer, one big foot perched on the opposite knee. "He hungry," she said. "He don't wanna play right now."

"Well, see, that what your mama an' I gonna do, go buy some milk for the kid." Raising his voice he hollered, "Renatta! How come it takin' you so long? Let's go, woman!"

"Shut up, Otto! I'll be there in a minnit!"

The baby kept wailing.

Giving up, Candy threw the rattle into the playpen and plopped down in a chair as far away as possible from Big Otto, her arms crossed. Mama was going out again. She always said they'd be back "in a minute," but Candy knew better.

"How old are you, girl?" Otto growled.

"Seven an' a half."

"Oh. Seven *an' a half*." He laughed. "Makes you a big girl, don' it. Well, big girl, go get me another one o' these beers. Long as your mama takes ta get ready, might as well have *somethin'* ta keep me company."

Candy flounced out of the room, into the kitchen, and opened the refrigerator door. Leftover pizza box from Domino's, half package of hot dogs, opened can of refried beans, bag of carrots,

1

grapes in a bowl, an inch of milk in the bottom of a gallon jug, and two more cans of beer from the six-pack.

"Mama?" Candy yelled. "Can I give Pookey the rest of the milk? He hungry!"

Renatta Blackwell showed up in the kitchen doorway, trying to slide big, dangly earrings into her earlobe. "Sure, baby. I'll bring some more when Otto an' I get back."

"Where's that beer you was gettin' me, girl?" Otto bawled from the other room.

"You don' need another beer," Candy's mother called back, disappearing from the kitchen doorway. "Just need to get my purse."

"'Bout time."

Candy quickly fished in the sink for a baby bottle, stood on tiptoe to reach the spigot handles, rinsed it out with cold water, and poured the last of the milk into it. Screwing on the cap and nipple, she ran back into the living room, leaned over the playpen railing, and handed him the bottle. "There ya go, Pookey . . ."

Pookey tipped over onto a scrunched-up blanket in the corner of the pen and sucked noisily on the bottle, his cries silenced.

Renatta showed up in the living room doorway, purse slung over one shoulder, still fussing with an earring. "Thanks, baby. I'll bring some more milk when we get back. He probably gonna fall asleep now. Jus' leave him in the playpen. You okay?"

Candy nodded sullenly. "When you comin' back?"

Her mother glanced at Otto. "In a little while, baby. I'll bring you somethin' nice, okay?"

Candy's head jerked up. "Mama! If you go to Walmart, look at the princess bike. That's the one I want for my birthday."

"A *bike*!" Otto snorted. "Well, ain't you the fancy schmancy one. What you think, girl, money grow on trees?"

Candy ignored him. "Please, Mama! You said when I get eight I can maybe get a bike. That's the one I want!"

"Sure, sure, baby. Next time I go to Walmart, I'll look at it." Renatta headed for the front door. "C'mon, Otto. We ain't got all day. I gotta get back here to my kids."

Pookey was already sucking air bubbles from his bottle as the door closed behind them. Candy ran to the window and pulled aside the sheet that acted as a curtain, knowing it would take a few minutes for them to go down the two flights from third floor. But then she saw them appear on the walk below, laughing and talking as they headed for Otto's car parked across the street.

Running back to the couch, Candy pulled at the square couch cushions and flung them onto the floor. *Yes!* Several pennies, even a nickel and a dime, sat among the crumbs, pull-tops twisted off cans, rubber bands, and other small trash that collected under the couch cushions. *Especially* after Otto was here.

Pulling the couch away from the wall, Candy retrieved a glass jar half full of pennies. Unscrewing the lid, she dropped her new finds into the jar, then screwed the lid back on.

Pookey had pulled himself up to a standing position and was holding onto the side of the playpen. Whimpering, he threw out the empty bottle. Kneeling down until she was nose-to-nose with her little brother, Candy shook the jar of pennies. "Can you keep a secret, Pookey? I'm savin' up these pennies to buy me a bike if Mama don' get it for me. But here . . ." She leaned over and set the jar down in the middle of the playpen. "There. You can play with it for a little while. See? It makes a pretty noise." She shook the jar until the pennies tinkled and clattered.

Pookey dropped to his knees and reached for the jar, momentarily distracted. Huffing, Candy replaced the unwieldy cushions, then flopped onto the couch and sighed. So. How long was it going to be *this* time?

# Chapter 1

M ICHELLE JASPER STOOD IN THE MIDDLE of the living room, eye-to-eye with her thirteen-year-old daughter, trying not to look impatient. They should be going out the door. Why did teenagers always pick the most inopportune times to ask these questions, acting like they're gonna die if they don't get an answer *right now*?

"Tabby, it doesn't make sense to go to cheerleading camp this summer. Stone Scholastic doesn't even have a cheer squad. Why don't you wait until next year when you're ready for high school? You could try out for the freshman squad."

"But Mo-om! All the girls are gonna want to try out for the cheer squad. If I go to camp *this* summer, I'll already know a lot of the good moves and—"

"Honey, can we talk about this later? We're supposed to get over to the Bentleys *before* Mrs. Krakowski arrives. And we'd need to talk to your dad about any camp plans, anyway. It's getting cool . . . you'll need a sweater. But then let's go."

"Oh, all right." Tabitha flounced off toward her bedroom.

Where *were* those boys? Where was her husband, for that matter? They'd just talked about this at supper, joining the other neighbors on Beecham Street to welcome back old Mrs. Krakowski, who'd fallen last winter and broke her hip. The two-flat she'd owned had been in foreclosure. But when the new owners heard the sad tale, they'd had a better idea . . .

Her other thirteen-year-old thundered up the stairs from the basement family room and into the living room. "Can I go over, Mom? DaShawn told me to come early."

"Just wait a minute, Tavis. Have you seen your dad? Where's Destin?"

Tavis jerked a thumb. "Kitchen, I think. Dad's downstairs on the phone."

"Well, tell Destin to get himself in here. Let's go over together."

Tavis headed for the kitchen. A moment later she heard, "Hey! That's Dad's pop. Mo-om! Destin's drinkin' a Dr. Pepper! How come he gets one? Can I have one too?"

"Boys!" Michelle headed for the kitchen.

Her oldest was sprawled in a chair at the tiny kitchen table, right hand wrapped around a can of pop. "Little brother's gonna have to learn not to rat," he muttered. "Not if he hopes to stay alive until high school."

*Patience, Michelle, patience.* "No, you can't have one, Tavis. Too much caffeine. Besides, you both know we save those for Dad to take to work. He *does* need to stay awake on the job. Destin, you know better than that."

Destin lifted the can. "It's the last one. We have to get some more anyway before Dad goes back to work Monday, right?"

The doorbell rang. "I'll get it!" Tavis darted out of the kitchen.

Michelle eyed her oldest. What was going on? He seemed more touchy than usual. "*You* don't need all that caffeine either, kiddo."

Destin rolled his eyes. "Mom, I'm seventeen. Guys on the basketball team drink energy drinks all the time before a game."

"*Hmm.* Don't know what I think about *that.* Anyway, it's time to go over to the Bentleys." She turned to go. "You coming?"

Destin shrugged and pushed the empty can away. "I guess. Sorry I took the last one." He grinned as he stood up. "But at least I saved it from getting pinched by the babies."

"I ain't no baby!" Tavis yelled from the next room. "Hey, DaShawn's here! Time to go!"

Destin followed his mother into the small living room of the brick bungalow. Thirteen-year-old DaShawn Bentley leaned into the open doorway, sounding breathless. Looked like the kid was growing his hair, already a short Afro. "Hey, Pops says they're on their way. If you gonna help me light those whatchamacallits, Tavis, we gotta hurry."

"Wait for me!" Tabitha yelled, heading for the front door with her twin brother and his friend. "I wanna help too." But pausing in the doorway she said, "Promise you'll think about it, Mom! And talk to Dad, okay?" The door slammed behind her.

Destin frowned. "What's *that* about?"

"Oh, she wants to go to cheerleading camp." Where was her husband? Michelle raised her voice. "Jared? You coming?"

No answer.

"Jared! It's time to go!"

"You guys go on without me." Her husband's voice floated up from the basement study. "I'll come as soon as I'm done with this call."

Michelle felt frustrated. "*Hmph.* Pastor Quentin always seems to know the *wrong* time to call your father . . . Sorry. Forget I said that. Let's just go." She took her shawl from the coatrack. "Don't you need a jacket?"

Destin grabbed a jacket and followed her across the porch and down the steps. "Mom, don't forget *I* asked first about that Five-Star Basketball Camp at supper. It's really important—college scouts come to the camp and everything. If I don't register soon, it's gonna be too late! So if you and Dad are gonna talk about summer camps, I get first dibs."

"I know, hon. I'm sorry. We were just in such a hurry at supper . . . oh, look! The kids are lighting those pretty paper bag luminaries along the sidewalk. Looks like a good turnout too."

Neighbors from their block on Beecham Street milled around the sidewalk and small front lawn in front of the Bentleys' two-flat—which used to be known as "the old lady's house" before she fell down the basement stairs last winter, broke her hip, and spent months in rehab. The bank had foreclosed on the two-flat and the Bentleys had bought it. Which was nice for Tavis, since DaShawn lived with his grandparents in the second floor apartment and was in the twins' class at school.

"Don'tcha think the ol' lady's gonna feel kinda weird," Destin muttered as they crossed the street, "movin' back into her own house after somebody else bought it? 'Specially her bein' white an' all and the Bentleys bein' black? Don't remember her bein' all that friendly to *us* before she lost the house."

"She's elderly, Destin. Didn't get out much," Michelle said. "I think it's very kind of the Bentleys to offer to rent her the first floor apartment after they got it remodeled. And I don't want to hear you call her 'the ol' lady.' Her name is Mrs. Krakowski, which you will do well to remember, young man."

Destin shrugged. "At least the Bentleys put up a basketball hoop over the garage. Ol' lady . . . sorry. Mrs. K better not mind."

"Sister Michelle! Destin!" Estelle Bentley, wearing one of those big roomy caftans she was so fond of, swooped between the glowing paper bags lining the sidewalk carrying a tray with a pitcher and steaming hot cups. "So glad you're here for Miss Mattie's homecoming. Hot chocolate?" Beaming, she held out the tray, then glanced around. "Is Jared coming?"

Michelle sighed as Destin helped himself to a paper cup of hot chocolate and sidled away. "Hope so, soon as the pastor lets him off the phone. You know how it is when you're a deacon."

"Oh, honey, tell me about it." With a chuckle, Estelle Bentley moved away with her tray, offering hot chocolate to Farid Jallili and his scarf-wearing wife, who lived next door to the two-flat, as well as the Jewish couple from down the street. The gay couple who lived next to the Jallilis was talking to the man who'd built that huge house on the cul-de-sac at this end of the block. Interesting.

Michelle sipped her own hot chocolate. Beecham Street certainly had turned into a mini–United Nations over the years. Hadn't she read someplace that this whole north end of Chicago was one of the most diverse in the nation? Not exactly a melting pot, though. She barely knew most of the neighbors.

Michelle noticed that DaShawn's grandpa, Harry Bentley, had recruited Destin to pass out sheets of paper with the words to "Auld Lang Syne" to all the neighbors . . . including his father, who was *finally* coming across the street in the deepening dusk. Destin—still two inches shorter than his dad's six-one—ran up and shoved a song sheet into his hands. "Hey, Dad. Mom'll be glad Pastor let you go."

His father ignored the tease as he joined Michelle. "Didn't miss Mrs. K's arrival, did I? Hope she comes soon though. I still gotta go by the church tonight."

"Oh, Jared. Not tonight. How come?"

Her husband shrugged. "The janitor got sick, and his wife forgot to call Pastor that he wasn't able to finish cleaning up after the Mother's Day brunch last Sunday *or* do setup for this Sunday. I'll take Destin with me. With two of us, it won't take too long. I hope."

"Aw, Dad!" Destin groaned. "Do I hafta—"

"Hey, neighbors!" A man with two flaxen-haired children in tow stepped up to them and held out his hand. "Name's Greg Singer. We live on the other end of the block from you, next-to-the last house. And these two munchkins are Becky and Nathan."

Jared shook the man's hand. "Jared Jasper. This is my wife, Michelle, and our son, Destin."

"Becky, why don't you take Nathan and go play with some of the other kids?" The man waved them off.

Michelle nodded toward the two-flat. "Did you know Mrs. Krakowski when she lived here, Mr. Singer?"

"Hey, just call me Greg. No, didn't really know the old lady. I'm gone a lot with my job. But according to my wife, the new people came by our house and invited us to come tonight. Friendly folks, aren't they?"

"Uh-huh . . . You travel a lot?" Jared said politely. "What do you do?"

"Event coordinator for Powersports Expos. You've probably heard—"

"Powersports?" Destin suddenly got interested. "What's that?"

The man warmed to the topic. "We do shows featuring sports vehicles all around the Midwest, though this time of year it's mostly boat shows. Say, you two got any interest in fishing boats, jet skis, stuff like that? Maybe you'd like to come to our next event. Gonna be down at Burnham Harbor, June 3 through 6." He winked at Destin. "It'll be our biggest show this season. I might be able to get you and your dad a ride on a cigarette boat. What would you think of—"

"Here they come!" A shout went up. Two dozen heads turned toward the far end of the street, where headlights had just turned up Beecham. Michelle watched as the nondescript sedan passed them, turned around in the cul-de-sac, and pulled to the curb in front of the two-flat. A middle-aged man came around from the driver's side—Michelle figured it was probably her son—and helped old Mattie Krakowski out of the passenger seat. As the elderly woman leaned unsteadily on his arm, a beautiful soprano voice began to sing, "Should old acquaintance be forgot, and never brought to mind? . . ."

Michelle smiled. The Bentleys must've asked Grace Meredith, who lived next door to the Jaspers—the one who traveled around singing Christian concerts—to kick off the song. But they were obviously supposed to join in.

Squinting at the words on the slip of paper she held in her hand, Michelle realized the words had been rewritten to fit the occasion. Some of the neighbors were singing the traditional New Year's song, and some were singing the new words. But even though the song was kind of ragged, tears slid down the old lady's face, which had a smile on it bigger than the full moon peeking through the clouds overhead.

As the last lines of the revised song died away, people shouted, "Welcome home, Mrs. Krakowski!" and Harry and Estelle Bentley escorted their new renter up the porch stairs and into the newly remodeled first floor apartment. Word was that the place used to be a real dump inside. Not anymore.

Michelle watched, strangely touched. Nothing like this had ever happened on Beecham Street that she could remember—and they'd lived at 7337 Beecham ever since the kids were small. They'd always been grateful for a quiet block, everybody just minding their own business. But that was before the Bentleys moved in. Harry and Estelle Bentley had gone around to every house on the block introducing themselves and handing out cinnamon rolls. The warm, gooey, homemade kind.

And now this homecoming.

But as soon as the door closed behind the Bentleys and Krakowskis, the crowd broke up and began to disperse. "C'mon, Tavis!" yelled DaShawn, and quicker than cockroaches when the light turns on, the two boys disappeared around the side of the house with a basketball. Destin started to follow, but Jared caught his arm. "C'mon, Destin. Let's go."

"Dad!" Tabitha caught up to them as they crossed the street, dancing on her toes. "Did Mommy talk to you about cheerleading camp? I gotta sign up right away!"

"What cheerleading camp?" Her father unlocked the minivan and slid in.

"Oh . . . I'll explain later. Just go." Michelle pulled Tabitha away as Destin glumly walked around to the other side of the minivan. But Michelle called, "Destin! Wait a sec." She caught him before he opened the passenger side door. "Figure it this way, son," she said, lowering her voice. "You'll have your dad all to yourself for at least an hour. Go ahead, talk to him about the basketball camp." She grinned. "See? First dibs."

# Chapter 2

DUSK HAD DEEPENED OVER BEECHAM STREET as Michelle watched the taillights of the family minivan disappear around the corner, heading for Northside Baptist. Most of the residents who'd gathered to welcome Mattie Krakowski back to the neighborhood had already dispersed, disappearing into the various brick bungalows that lined the block.

Saturday night . . . and once again her family was also dispersed here, there, and everywhere. Tavis hadn't even asked if he could go shoot baskets behind the Bentleys' two-flat. He'd just taken off.

She sighed. Why did Pastor Quentin always call Jared when he needed somebody to fill in? *Huh.* Because Jared always said yes, that's why.

"Tabby, honey, you go on into the house. I want to talk to Grace Meredith." Michelle gave her thirteen-year-old daughter a gentle push in the direction of their brick bungalow and called out, "Grace? Do you have a minute?" She did have something to ask the young woman who lived next door, but she was also curious about the good-looking young man who was with her.

The pair halted on the sidewalk and Grace gave Michelle a warm smile as she caught up to them. "Hi, Michelle. That little homecoming for Mrs. Krakowski was pretty special, wasn't it?"

"Amen to that." As if on cue, all three of them glanced across the street at the Bentley's two-flat, where the bay windows of the first floor apartment blazed merrily with bright lights. "Can't even imagine what she must be feeling, seeing her old apartment all fixed up—like a brand-spanking-new house." Michelle turned back and smiled at Grace. "The welcome song was nice. First time I've heard you sing."

"Well, thanks. The Bentleys changed the words, you know. I wasn't sure I got them all right. Oh, I want to introduce my agent. This is Jeff Newman, from Bongo Booking in Denver." Grace glanced up at the dark-haired young man—thirtyish, Michelle guessed, noticing the glance that passed between them. "Jeff, this is my next-door neighbor, Michelle Jasper. She's the one who provided all those brochures we passed out during my West Coast tour."

The young man grinned and shook Michelle's hand. "Delighted to meet you. I hear they kept you trotting to the post office, couldn't keep the brochures in stock. It's wonderful you could support Grace's ministry in that way." He suddenly frowned. "I'm sure postage wasn't cheap. Grace said you had to overnight them a few times. We definitely need to reimburse you—"

"No, no. Already done. Grace's assistant took care of that—for the brochures too. Which basically ended up being a donation to Lifeline Care Center, where I volunteer."

The grin was back. "Should've known Samantha would be all over it. She's a real firecracker."

Michelle tried to keep a straight face. The guy was too darn good-looking for his own good. *Hot*, as the kids would say. Dark, curly hair. A manly five-o'clock shadow. Dimples in his cheeks when he grinned. Grace was no slouch, either. The concert artist was lovely, her dark brunette hair layered in a long shag, framing her peachy-perfect skin and pretty features. If Michelle's female instincts were right, these two had something more going on than just a business relationship.

As if reading her mind, Grace blurted, "Uh, Jeff's on his way to Minneapolis to see another client, had to come through Chicago. He was actually here the day they discovered Mrs. Krakowski had fallen down the basement stairs and broke her hip—during that February snowstorm, remember? He helped your husband shovel a path up to her door so the paramedics could get through. I thought he'd enjoy witnessing the sequel to that little drama."

"That was you? Jared said some guy from Colorado had helped him shovel."

"Yep. That was me. I came to town for a meeting with Grace here, had just been assigned as her agent by Bongo, and it was our first face-to-face. Ended up getting stranded by that snowstorm." He turned his grin on Grace. "Not that I minded."

She whopped his arm with her hand. "Oh, you. Well, there's no snow today, your rental car's not stuck, and there are dozens of hotels within hollering distance, just waiting to take your credit card."

Jeff shrugged and heaved a fake sigh. "So much for Midwestern hospitality."

Grace seemed embarrassed by his teasing, so Michelle got to her point. "I don't know your concert schedule, Grace, but I've been meaning to ask if you want more of the crisis pregnancy and post-abortion brochures when you go on the road again. Lifeline also has one designed especially for guys, and a general one about self-respect and sexual responsibility. If you tell me how many you think you can use, I could place an order ahead of time this time."

"That's a great idea, Michelle. I have another tour coming up in June—and a couple of independent concerts before then too. I'll look at my schedule and ask Sam to help me figure out how many we might need. Can I get back to you?"

"Of course—"

"Mo-om!" Tabitha stuck her head out their front door. "Are you gonna come in soon? You still gotta wash an' braid my hair!"

"In a minute!" Michelle hollered back. Washing Tabitha's hair, which the girl was letting grow out, and then braiding it took at least an hour—and that didn't count the comb-out in the morning before church. "Well, better go. It's nice to meet you, Jeff. Glad you could be here for our little neighborhood celebration. Though"— she glanced again at the two-flat across the street—"I wonder if the Bentleys know what they've gotten themselves into. Mrs. K must be in her upper eighties, don't you think? Oh, well. Not my business." She gave a little wave and headed back to her own house next door.

Whatever was going on with Grace Meredith and Jeff What's-His-Name wasn't her business either. But Michelle couldn't help wondering for a quick minute if that whole song and dance about "dozens of hotels within hollering distance" had been more for her benefit than his.

The faint *thud, thud, thud* of a basketball caught her attention just as she was about to go inside. Uh-oh. Tavis was still in the alley behind the Bentleys' playing basketball with DaShawn. She'd better haul his butt home or those boys would be keeping Mrs. Krakowski awake her first night back in her home with all their thumping and ball bouncing.

"Ow! That's too tight! When's Dad getting home? Can we talk about cheerleading camp when he gets here?"

"Tabby, hold still!" Tabitha's antsy wiggles were getting on Michelle's last nerve. "No, we can't. Dad called, said they'd be late. . . . There. Done. But it's almost ten, so I want you in bed." Michelle raised her voice and hollered down the basement stairs. "You too, Tavis! Shut off that video game. Time for bed!"

"But Mo-om!" sailed up the stairs from the basement family room.

"No buts! Get up here!"

Maybe the twins weren't tired, but she was. It'd been a busy week at her job—DCFS had added four new clients to her caseload at Bridges Family Services. Then they'd gone to the college fair at the high school Friday night, which meant she had to stay up late preparing for the women's ministry committee meeting after church on Sunday, because she knew there'd be no time today. Her Saturday had started with her regular volunteer stint at Lifeline that morning, grocery shopping and laundry in the afternoon, and the welcome home for Mrs. Krakowski this evening—even though all she had to do was show up tonight, but still. And tomorrow, church till one or one thirty, and her meeting with the women's ministry team right after that . . .

Michelle sank down on the stool in front of her vanity mirror in the bedroom. It'd be Monday again before she knew it.

Picking up the wrap she used to hold her hair in place overnight—a short bob, relaxed by a regular perm, with long bangs that framed her large eyes and warm brown skin—she hesitated. Should she wrap her hair yet? Saturday night was often "their" night, and Jared might want to . . . *uhh*. Not tonight. She was too tired. She tied the wrap around her hair, left a bedside lamp on for Jared, and slid between the cool sheets. Should she check if the twins had gotten themselves to bed? . . . No, let Jared deal with them if they were still up when he got home . . .

She must've dozed off, because it seemed only minutes before she was aware of Jared sitting on the side of the bed, taking off his shoes and letting them fall to the floor. "Hi, hon," she murmured, flopping an arm his direction and touching his broad back. "You okay?"

"Yeah." *Thud.* Another shoe.

"How come it took so long?"

He grunted. "You mean besides the regular cleaning? Whole church looked like a hurricane. Found leftover food from last Sunday's brunch that shoulda been thrown out, hymnals scattered everywhere except in the pew racks, Sunday school classrooms with broken chairs—not to mention a toilet that's not working in the ladies' restroom." Her husband stripped down to his shorts and T-shirt, took off his glasses, and crawled into bed. "Gotta talk to Pastor Q about each ministry maintaining their own area. A Saturday workday at the church wouldn't be a bad idea, either."

"Light," she murmured.

"Oh . . . okay." He reached for the light, then threw an arm over her body and pulled her close, spoon style. Michelle relaxed into his embrace, enjoying the press of his sturdy body against her back, glad he was home. She could feel herself drifting back to sleep, now that her whole family was home safe under their roof.

Then his voice in the dark. " . . . Destin . . . basketball camp . . . summer . . ."

*Uh* . . . what? Was Jared talking to her? Or was she dreaming already?

"I said, did Destin talk to you about this Five-Star Basketball Camp he wants to go to this summer?"

"Don't think so," she mumbled. And she didn't want to talk about it now, either. She wanted to go back to sleep. But his voice was directly behind her ear.

"Well, that's all he talked about to and from the church. Said college scouts would be there. Michael Jordan was discovered at one of these camps. They have a camp down in Romeoville, south of the city. At Lewis University, I think. Sometime early July. *Then* he says registration needs to be in by Monday. *By Monday!*" Jared rolled away from her and punched up his pillow a few times. "Why does that boy always wait till the last minute to tell us stuff!"

*And why are you telling me this as we're trying to go to sleep?* "Dunno," she murmured into her pillow, "but maybe we can talk about it tomorrow."

"Yeah. Yeah, okay." Jared punched up his pillow, then settled down again. "Just . . . bugs me when he does that. And, oh yeah, of course he's expecting *us* to come up with the registration fee."

Michelle's eyes flew open in the dark. *Registration fee . . .* She suddenly remembered Tabby's song and dance about cheerleading camp, begging her to talk to her father. But no way would Jared like getting hit in the same weekend with *two* last-minute requests to go to expensive summer camps.

Still, she'd promised Tabby to at least bring it up . . .

Stifling a groan, Michelle slipped out from under the weight of Jared's arm and tried to find another comfortable position, tried to invite the blessed blankness of sleep back into her mind. But now she was dreading Sunday, dreaded having to choose between her children—that, or telling both of them their summer dreams were just that. Dreams.

*O God, what should we do?*

Did that qualify as a prayer? Did God even care about cheerleading and basketball when the whole world was in such a mess?

Jared's breathing slowed and she realized her husband had fallen asleep. But Michelle stared into the darkness for a long time.

# Chapter 3

FINALLY! EVERYONE OUT THE DOOR and into the car.

Michelle let out a long breath as Jared did a U-turn in the cul-de-sac. Getting the whole family anywhere on time was still almost as bad as when the twins were toddlers and Destin in kindergarten. At least when the kids were little she and Jared could wrestle them into their clothes or snowsuits or whatever and cart them out to the car like sacks of groceries. Now, getting three teenagers out the door for church was like trying to herd cats. *"I can't wear this dress! Makes me look fat!"* . . . *"Mom! Destin's taking too long in the bathroom!"* . . . *"Tavis, go back and brush your teeth!"* . . . *"Anyone seen my Sunday school booklet?"* . . . *"Did you talk to Dad yet about you-know-what?"* . . . *"Where did Tabby disappear to?"* . . . At least they'd finally replaced her small SUV with a "pre-owned" Honda minivan, which gave them a bit more room.

"Who's that guy with Miz Meredith?" Tavis asked as the Jasper minivan passed her house. "Saw him last night . . . an' that ain't her car."

Michelle twisted her head and looked back. Grace waved at them as Jeff What's-His-Name opened the passenger door of a silver Camaro. "That's her agent. I met him last night. He's from Colorado, came to Chicago on business. But maybe he's picking her up for church." The couple was dressed in suits—hers feminine, navy and white, skirt skimming her knees; his tailored, gray, with a dark tie. *Were* they a couple? Had he come to pick her up from wherever he stayed last night? Or had he—

"She's got an *agent*? Cool!" Destin sounded impressed.

Tabitha snickered from the second seat. Michelle caught her eye in the rearview mirror and frowned. Had her daughter read her thoughts? She needed to be careful. Like mother, like daughter.

Besides, Grace deserved the benefit of the doubt. Michelle hadn't even known she was a believer until about a month ago. Hadn't really talked much to her next-door neighbor, just the usual pleasantries, "Hello" and "Have a nice day" as they passed coming and going. Until Estelle Bentley moved into the neighborhood and invited Michelle to pray with the two of them that one time. She'd been surprised to find out Grace was a professional singer. Wouldn't have guessed that someone who traveled around the country doing concert tours would live in their modest neighborhood like ordinary folks. But it did explain why the young woman seemed to be gone a lot.

So now there were three Christian families on their end of Beecham Street. Maybe there were others and they just didn't know it. But if Michelle was to guess, their neighbor on the other side—the single guy in the mansion he'd built on the cul-de-sac—looked the playboy type. The wife of the Farid's Lawn Service guy wore one of those Middle Eastern headscarves all the time, so Michelle presumed they were Muslim, though she didn't really know because the family pretty much kept to themselves. And the "two dads" across the street raising the little boy didn't exactly fit the church image—which might be unfair. What did "church image" have to do with anything?

Had to admit she didn't really know any of the families at the other end of the block—though last night she met a mom who said she homeschooled her two children. White family, seemed nice. Why didn't she see them around more if they were home that much?

Michelle sighed. Busy, busy. Everyone was just busy. Life in the big city.

Jared pulled their Honda minivan into the parking lot of Northside Baptist and was out the door seconds after finding an empty space. "Lock the car, will you?" he called over his shoulder, walking quickly toward the side door of the large brick building. "I need to catch Pastor Q before service."

Michelle and the kids climbed out of the car. "He didn't have to run." Destin smirked. "Service always starts late anyway."

Which was true. But she said, "Well, we need to set a good example and be on time anyway . . . oh, good morning, Mother Willa! How are you today?"

By the time Michelle had greeted and hugged and chatted her way into the sanctuary, the kids had settled into the back rows with other teens. Whatever happened to sitting together as a family? But it was hard to insist the kids sit with her when most of the other families let the young people sit together in the back, saying they were just glad the kids were in church. And Pastor usually wanted the deacons to sit up front, either in the row of wooden chairs with red plush seat cushions facing the congregation in front of the platform, or in the stately "thrones" on the platform behind the pulpit. So Jared didn't sit with her either.

Like a good deacon's wife, she headed for the second row near the middle aisle as the choir filed into the choir loft behind the platform. She was glad to see her friend Norma sitting with the altos—she'd been absent last Sunday. Michelle felt a stab of guilt. Should've called this week to see if she was sick or something. Shareese Watson in the soprano section was sporting a new weave halfway down her back, tinted reddish brown. Pretty . . . but good thing she was wearing a choir robe. Shareese sometimes came to church with a bit too much cleavage showing. The young woman seemed sincere enough, though. Eager to serve. Had recently joined the women's ministry team, which was, well, a mixed blessing. Her eager-beaver ideas were a bit much at times—

"Hello, Sister Michelle. Family all doing well?" A matronly figure stopped by her pew and patted her shoulder.

Michelle jumped up. "Oh—good morning, Sister Donna!" She leaned into the aisle and gave Pastor Quentin's wife a "churchy" hug. "Yes, we're all fine. Thank you."

"Good. Good." Northside's First Lady moved on, greeting several other deacons' wives.

Michelle smiled as the older woman, dressed conservatively in a modest black suit, neck scarf splashed with pink roses, and a simple black hat with a matching rose-colored bow, settled down in the first pew. Sister Donna and Pastor Quentin had been at Northside for . . . well, twenty-five years. The last Pastor's

Anniversary, an annual event, had been a big "silver anniversary" celebration.

When the Jaspers first came to the church ten years ago, Sister Donna seemed to be everywhere—heading up the women's ministry, teaching Sunday school, singing in the choir, chairing Women's Day *and* Men's Day committees. But five years ago or so, the First Lady of Northside began to let all that go, encouraging other women to take over those roles. That's when she'd tapped Michelle to take over women's ministry. Now the First Lady basically functioned as "mother" to the congregation, praying for people, spreading words of encouragement.

Took a lot of wisdom and maturity to step aside, Michelle mused. Unlike some pastors' wives she'd known.

A rustling around her clued her that the congregation was standing up as Pastor Quentin walked in from the side room, followed by the associate minister, the minister of music, and the four deacons. Three of the deacons headed for the chairs below the pulpit, but Michelle noted her husband stayed on the platform today. Jared was still a good-looking man at forty-two, hair worn short with just a few flecks of gray at the temples. He'd put on a few pounds in their almost-twenty-year marriage, but he wore them well. The wire-rim glasses and neatly trimmed moustache made him look sophisticated and serious—until he grinned and revealed his dimples.

"Good morning, church!" boomed the rotund minister of music, stepping to the microphone. "Good morning!" bounced back from all corners of the room. "Praise the Lord! Keep to your feet, saints, while we worship the Lord in his sanctuary today." Turning around, he snapped his fingers—*one, two, three, four*—as the gifted young man at the piano launched an intro to Israel Houghton's new gospel song, "Saved by Grace." Michelle wasn't sure of all the words yet, but led by the choir, clapping and stepping side to side, filling the house with joyous music, she let the song carry her into worship. That was why they were here, after all.

"Sister Michelle!" Shareese Watson bore down on her from the choir loft after Pastor Quentin's benediction, her long weave and unzipped choir robe flying. "Is the women's ministry team still meeting on today?"

The open robe revealed a decidedly plunging neckline, barely containing a full, attractive bosom that obviously hadn't nursed three babies. Michelle felt conflicted. Should she say something? She didn't want to embarrass the girl . . . but if she didn't, one of the fussy "church mothers" might—or, worse, one of the male ushers or deacons. *That* made up her mind. No way did she want Jared to feel *he* had to speak to this young woman.

Michelle glanced at the clock on the wall at the back of the sanctuary. It was already 1:20. Church had gone long. "Yes, we are, in about ten minutes in the lounge. But can I—"

"Oh, good! Because I have a great idea for our women's ministry!" Shareese giggled. "See you in ten!"

"—see you for a minute first?" dropped unheard into empty space because the weave, the robe, and the young woman flitted off like a canary released from its cage.

Michelle blew out a breath. Well. She'd take Shareese aside before or after their committee meeting.

But even though she got to the lounge a few minutes early, Shareese was already talking to Sister Norma, who was making coffee and setting out sweet rolls. And then the rest of the ladies on the committee came in, chatting away, making a beeline for the coffee, saying, "Oh, I shouldn't" but taking one of the sweet rolls anyway, and settling down into the various couches and chairs that made up the lounge.

Well, hopefully she'd get a chance to talk to Shareese later.

Michelle shushed the chatter, opened the meeting with a prayer, then asked for reflections about the Mother's Day brunch last Sunday, which had taken the place of their regular second Saturday monthly event. She opened her notebook to take notes.

Heads were nodding around the circle. Most of the committee looked pleased.

"Sister Gleniece, the table decorations turned out nice." Michelle wanted to give credit where credit was due. Heads nodded again.

"Could've used more help," Gleniece pouted. "I was up till two a.m. the night before."

*Decorations need more help,* Michelle jotted in her notebook.

Mavis, the committee treasurer, spoke up. "The food was good. We got compliments. But ordering pastas and salads from Maggiano's this year put us over our budget."

Rolled eyes. "What do you want us to do, cook our own Mother's Day brunch?"

"We could ask the brothers to cook it."

This was met by general laughter. "If they did, you know we'd end up with ribs on the grill and baked potatoes loaded with sour cream."

Michelle wrote, *Increase food budget for M-D Brunch?*

"Speakin' of the mens, don't know why *we* had to plan the Mother's Day brunch. Should've been the deacons or some men's committee." Sister Paulette had been through two nasty divorces and could be counted on to stick it to the men.

The *deacons?* Michelle wasn't going to let *that* happen.

"Um, Sister Michelle?" Shareese was waving her hand. "The Mother's Day brunch was nice and all, but . . . what about us women who aren't mothers? Some of the sisters feel left out."

"Girl, don't be a wet blanket!" Paulette had no qualms about being a wet blanket herself. "What are we s'posed to do? Cancel *Mother's Day?*" The mother of six glared at Shareese. "Ain't gonna happen."

"Um . . ." Michelle scrambled for words. Every few years this complaint came up. "We do have Women's Day, you know, which celebrates the gifts of all the women and girls in the church. So I think—"

"I know, but . . ." Shareese seemed undeterred by Paulette's glares. "I went to this other church once with my girlfriend—one of those multicultural churches—and they put the emphasis on 'everyone has a mother' and gave out boutonnieres to everyone."

"Everyone!" Paulette spouted. "It's *Mother's Day,* for God's sake."

"Now, Sister Paulette," Mavis said sternly. "We don't take God's name in vain."

"Oh, for—" Paulette pressed her lips into a line.

"Just let me finish," Shareese said. "That church gave out red carnations if your mother was still alive, and white carnations if she had passed. So everyone got to be included, but mothers were still the guests of honor. I thought it was real nice."

Michelle nodded. "We'll keep it in mind. Thanks, Shareese." She wrote down, *Red and white carnations for everyone?*

It was time to move on. "Thanks, sisters. These are good suggestions for next year. But we should move on, because we need to decide what to do for our monthly events during the summer. The second Saturday of June is just around the corner."

Shareese was beaming again. "I have an idea. We could start a women's book club!"

Objections immediately peppered the air. "A book club? Who has time to read!" . . . "Would we have to buy a book?" . . . "Don't book clubs go on for months? That could get boring." . . .

"We wouldn't have to do it at our monthly event. This could be something extra, maybe just during the summer on some other night. Could even meet in someone's home. I'd be glad to host it."

"Every week?" someone squeaked.

"No, no. We'd pick a book, maybe something by Beth Moore or . . . or Tony Evans's daughter—Priscilla, I think her name is. Churches all over study their books. We'd all read the book on our own time and then meet at the end of the month to discuss it." Shareese tossed her long weave. "Women really should read more."

Michelle stifled a groan. *Another night gone?* She, for one, wasn't buying it. But as head of the women's ministry, she had to say something. "Well, thanks, Shareese. That's one idea. Let's see if there are other ideas. Anyone?"

# Chapter 4

A<small>LL THREE KIDS HAD SOUR FACES</small> as they piled into the minivan. "Why do you guys always schedule meetings after church? It's so late!" Tabitha could put on a good whine.

"Because," their father said, "everyone's already at church and it saves time."

"*Your* time," Tavis muttered from the third seat.

Michelle took a deep breath. *Be calm. Ignore the grouchiness. They're just hungry.* "Where should we go for lunch? Old Country Buffet?"

"We always go there." Tabitha again.

"Then Old Country Buffet it is!" Jared grinned sideways at Michelle.

"Hey. If we brought both cars to church, I could drive the twins home and you guys could come later," Destin said hopefully. "Yeah?"

"You don't have a driver's license yet." *Praise Jesus,* Michelle thought.

"Well, soon's I finish driver's ed in two weeks, I can get my license."

Jared grunted. "You still need more practice behind the wheel, son. No license until your mother and I think you're a safe driver—and can afford the extra insurance."

"But, Dad! You guys never take me out! You're always too busy!"

Michelle looked out the side window.

"We're all busy, Destin," said his father. "Even you. I know you're just doing track now to stay in condition for basketball, but you've got practice nearly every day after school and meets every other weekend."

"Yeah, I know. But . . . how 'bout this afternoon? We could go over to the cemetery and do some driving."

Michelle glanced at Jared. "Would they let you do that? In the cemetery?" Beecham Street came to a dead-end at the cul-de-sac because of St. Mark's Cemetery, which sat right behind the "McMansion." A section of the cemetery also ran behind their own house along the alley. Made for quiet "neighbors."

"Wait a minute!" Tabitha protested. "Dad! Mom promised we could talk about cheerleading camp today. Did she talk to you yet?"

"Duh. You can't be a cheerleader," Tavis said. "Middle schools don't have cheerleaders."

"Some do! An' anyway, I wanna be ready to try out next summer for high school."

"I need to go to basketball camp *this* summer," Destin cut in. "So wait your turn, twerp."

"Okay, stop it, all three of you!" Jared's voice was sharp. "Mom and I haven't had a chance to talk about *any* summer plans. Let's just go have lunch, *no* discussion in the restaurant, and we'll talk about this stuff later."

"*And* practice driving, right?" Destin added.

Jared's hands tightened on the wheel. "I got it, Destin. Now let it go."

Everyone seemed in a better mood after all-you-can-eat at Old Country Buffet. Getting out of church late even had its advantages, as the usual Sunday line had dwindled and they didn't have to wait long. And when they pulled up in front of the house, Jared said, "Might as well get some driving practice now, Destin. That okay with you, Michelle?"

"Fine. Go." Michelle waved them off and unlocked the front door for the twins.

"Mo-om . . ." Tabitha started.

"Honey, don't worry. We're going to talk about it. Go get your homework done."

Still on the front stoop, Michelle glanced across the street at the Bentleys' graystone two-flat a couple houses down. How was

25

Mrs. Krakowski making out her first day back home in her old apartment? Her son had come earlier in the week with a rental truck bringing Mrs. K's old furniture back, which had been cleared out when the house got sold. At least Michelle presumed that was her son—the same middle-aged man who'd brought the elderly woman back last night.

Should she go over and welcome her back to the neighborhood? Michelle hesitated . . . maybe later. It'd been a long day already. She was ready to get out of her church clothes and into a pair of jeans. And she and Jared still had to talk about these summer camps Tabby and Destin were so pushy about. Besides, she should probably get the clean laundry sorted so the kids could fold and put away their clothes before the school week started. Most of it just got stuffed in their drawers, but she couldn't worry about that. Maybe it was time for them to wash their own clothes too. Now *that* was a good idea. She could assign each a different day, and if they didn't do it on their day, too bad.

Yeah, too bad . . . if she could stick to her guns. Seemed like all three kids knew which buttons to press to get her to make exceptions.

Michelle was putting away the last of her and Jared's clean laundry when he came into the bedroom, tossed the car keys in the tray on his dresser, and pulled off his tie. "Hey. Got any clean sweats in there? I'm ready to get out of this suit."

"How'd he do?"

Jared shrugged as his suit pants and dress shirt came off. "Not bad. He's coming along. Not ready for that license yet though." He pulled on the pair of sweats and sweatshirt she handed him. "Hope there's a good game on. We got any snacks?"

"A game? Jared! Could we talk about Destin and Tabby before you turn on the TV? Or they'll be bugging us the rest of the day."

He groaned. "Yeah, right." He sank into the only chair that fit into their small bedroom. "What about this cheerleading camp? They don't have cheerleaders at Stone Scholastic, do they? And she and Tavis will only be in eighth grade next year."

She took the bed. "Right. But Tabby's got her heart set on trying out for cheerleader at the high school a year from now, and she thinks going to one of the middle school cheer camps this summer would give her some good experience. She says she's found some camps in the Chicago area and wants to talk about them with us."

"Like . . . what? Do these camps go for four weeks? All summer? I have no idea."

"I think just a week."

"A week. How much?"

"I don't know. I haven't seen the information she found online."

Jared threw up his hands. "Seems like we need that kind of information before we can even talk about this. Tell her to print out a couple possibilities and then we'll talk. Though . . . don't know how I feel about Tabby getting into all that cheerleader stuff already. She's only thirteen. You know, all that in-crowd, who's-popular mess . . ."

"I hear you." Michelle sighed. When she was in high school, cheerleading was basically a popularity contest that ended up with a lot of hurt feelings and nasty cliques. "Maybe it's different now. I think a lot of schools treat cheerleading like a regular sport."

"Hmph." Jared didn't sound convinced.

"What did Destin tell you about this basketball camp?"

Her husband leaned forward, elbows on his knees. "Well, sounds like the real deal. One of the Five-Star Basketball Camps they run all over the country. I've heard of them before. And he says there're a couple camps in Romeoville, south of the city, at Lewis University—end of June, first week of July, around there. Overnight camp, so once we'd get him there, we wouldn't have to run him back and forth."

"So it sounds good to you?"

Jared shrugged. "Well, supposedly they send college scouts to these camps. It might be a chance for him to get an athletic scholarship. He's done his research—just, you know, *late* as usual." He grimaced. "Meaning he has to send in the full registration fee *tomorrow* to make the forty-five-day deadline."

"Tomorrow!?"

"Right. Due Monday, remember? I told you when we got back from cleaning the church the other night."

Remember? She'd been half asleep. "Uh, How much?"

"You ready?" Jared snorted. "Five-fifty."

Michelle felt the blood drain from her face. "Five-*hundred*-fifty? Oh dear. We can't—"

"Exactly. Especially since we just paid the first installment of our property tax a few weeks ago."

They both sat in silence for several long moments. Michelle's thoughts tumbled. Of the two camps, the basketball camp seemed the most legitimate and timely. Destin had played basketball all three years of high school so far, had made varsity, and would be a senior next year. Then college. An athletic scholarship would be an answer to prayer—*big* time! But . . . over five hundred out of their bank account all at once, just *bam*, like that? That wasn't in the budget.

And then there were all the related questions . . . like, what were all three kids going to do with the *rest* of the summer? Both she and Jared worked full time, with sometimes crazy schedules. Jared, especially. As an air traffic controller at O'Hare, he usually did two swing shifts, two day shifts, and a night shift—all in the same week. It gave him weekends off, though it messed with his sleep. She supposedly had regular hours as a caseworker at a private social service agency, but they often dealt with family emergencies that rarely fit into eight-to-five. She often had to stay late one or two evenings each week, and getting a call during the night or on the weekend wasn't that unusual, either. Made school holidays and summer break a scheduling nightmare equaling traffic control at O'Hare.

"Unless . . ." Jared mused.

"Unless what?"

"Unless we ask Destin to work off the cost of the camp the rest of the summer. He's seventeen. The kid needs a job this summer anyway."

A smile tipped the corner of Michelle's lips. "Of course! I mean, if he wants to go badly enough, he *should* work for it. Would take care of keeping him busy the rest of the summer too. Only . . ."

Jared's eyebrows went up over his glasses.

"Maybe we could contribute the registration fee. How much is that?"

"A hundred, I think."

"We could do that, couldn't we? Show our support."

Jared nodded slowly. "Suppose so. Except, the deadline for the rest of the fee is tomorrow. Means we'd still have to float the whole wad up front." He ran his hand over his head. "I suppose we could take it out of savings, and Destin could pay the four-fifty back once he gets a job."

Michelle's smile grew. "Good. Let's do it. You want to talk to him? Tell him what we've decided? Oh wait . . . the final payment has to *be* there tomorrow?" The smiled faded. "There's no way!"

"I'm sure we can do an online payment. But I'll check." Jared got up and stretched. "We done here? If so, I'm gonna grab a Dr. Pepper and see if there's a game on." He headed out the door.

*Uh-oh.* "Um, sorry! Destin drank the last one last night!" she called after him.

He poked his head back around the open door and gave her a look. "You're kidding." Then she heard him clomp off, muttering, "The kid's gonna go get me a twelve-pack. Now."

Michelle and Tabitha were at the dining nook table scrolling through cheer camp websites when Destin came in lugging a twelve-pack of Dr. Pepper. "Where's Dad?"

Without looking up from the computer, Michelle tipped her head in the direction of the stairs to the basement. "Watching the game."

"It's still on? He said he was going to talk to me about basketball camp when I got back!"

"Just go watch the game with him. It'll be over soon . . . Okay, Tabby, what's this site?"

But Tabitha was watching her big brother disappear. "Mom! Why is Dad gonna talk to Destin, but not me? I asked first!"

"Honey, it's not about who asked first or second. Dad and I are considering both of your requests—but I told you, in your case we need more information before we can really talk. Let's keep looking . . ."

There weren't as many cheerleading camps in Illinois as she'd thought there might be, much less in the Chicago area. A couple of big-time cheerleading programs turned out to be just for their own school teams, not for the general public. One of the biggest featured cheer squads for "K–8th" . . . What? They started in *kindergarten?*

They surfed some more. "What about that one?" Tabitha said. They clicked on the link for Cheer Illinois Athletics. Photos of cheer squads of different ages rolled across the top of the site. *Hmm* . . . a *lot* of bare skin showing. But Michelle scrolled through the pages of information without comment.

"Hey, Mom, look! It's in Bensenville—that's right out by O'Hare!" Tabitha bounced in her chair. "That's not too far . . . do they have any summer camps?" But most of what CIA offered were weekly classes and weekend clinics, year round, except for one lone link that said, "Summer Tumbling Boot Camps." But that page came up saying "Access Denied."

"Sorry, honey." They kept looking. They couldn't find any more cheerleading camps in Illinois—but they did come across a couple of interesting sites. The Fellowship of Christian Cheerleaders had four-day camps in various states all over the country—some residential, some commuter. And another one called Christian Cheerleaders of America. Same thing—summer camps all over the country. Though neither one had a camp listed for Illinois.

*Too bad,* Michelle thought. Both organizations had youth camps for middle school. And the cost for the four-day camps seemed comparable—in the $190 range for a commuter camper, around $250 for residential.

"Wait, Mom. Look! There's a Christian cheer camp in Fort Wayne!" Tabitha screeched. "That's where Bibi and Babu live! I could stay with them."

*Bibi and Babu*—Michelle's parents, who'd chosen the Swahili names for grandparents back when Destin was born. Michelle would've preferred something more traditional—what was wrong with Gram and Gramps? But her parents were old-school civil rights activists, and she was used to the names now. But the fact that they lived in Fort Wayne might be a divine coincidence. The cheer camp was listed as a commuter camp. Less expensive. Free room and board at the grandparents'.

"Well . . ."

Tabitha bounced up and down. "Oh, please, Mom! I wanna go! That one's perfect!" She jumped up. "I'm gonna go tell Dad."

"Wait, Tabby! Just a moment." Michelle had just noticed something. She quickly took another look at the other cheerleading sites they'd bookmarked . . . and realized she had bad news for Tabby.

"What?" Tabitha said impatiently.

Michelle looked up. "Tabby, honey, all these camps are for *teams* and their coaches. You have to already be part of a cheer squad and come with your coach in order to attend. They don't take individual campers."

The look on Tabitha's face and the slammed door to her room half a minute later shook Michelle as much as the house.

She heaved a sigh and shut off the laptop. Not a good start to making summer plans. At least the Internet search had answered the question for them. She and Jared wouldn't have to be the bad guys saying no.

She should feel relieved. But she would've liked to say yes to something Tabby wanted so badly. Thirteen-year-old daughters and moms didn't have an easy time of it.

Michelle realized the TV had gone silent downstairs, and she could hear the rise and fall of Jared's firm voice. Hopefully he and Destin were having more success.

# Chapter 5

MICHELLE PUT ON HER EARRINGS at the first stoplight and gave her lips a quick coat of gloss at the second. Just once she'd like to be completely ready for the day before having to leave for work! But she couldn't be late.

At least the laundry got done over the weekend so Tavis and Tabitha had clean clothes to meet Stone Scholastic's strict dress code. Not exactly uniforms like a private school, but close, and she and Jared were all for it. The K–8 magnet school offered school gear with the school name, but any solid white or blue shirt or blouse with dark blue or black pants or skirt would do. Solid colors only, no T-shirts with slogans or logos of any kind. Sweaters and sweatshirts had to fit into that category too. She and Jared were not only glad it was a public magnet school with a high academic standard, but they were relieved not to have to deal with bare midriffs, low-slung gangsta jeans, and T-shirts with suggestive sayings—not to mention all the petty who's-wearing-what snottiness.

If only the high schools would follow suit! But at least Lane Tech, where Destin was a junior, made a stab at a dress code—no visible undergarments, no bare midriffs, no shorts or skirts shorter than knee length, no T-shirts promoting drugs or alcohol, no gang paraphernalia, no hats or head coverings of any kind.

Traffic heading south on Western Avenue wasn't too bad that morning, and Michelle got to the offices of Bridges Family Services in the Irving Park neighborhood with ten minutes to spare. Parking was a bear as usual. But as a caseworker for the private social service agency, she had to have a car to visit her clients.

"*Buenas dias*, Michelle!" the perpetually smiling receptionist said as she came in the front door. "You look, ooo, *muy bonita* today."

"*Buenas dias* yourself, Mercedes!" Michelle was sure that smile did more emotional healing for staff and clients who came through the door than some of the professional services the agency offered. "Flattery will get you everywhere, you know."

The older Hispanic woman laughed and went back to her computer.

After checking in with her supervisor, Michelle unpacked her briefcase in the cubicle that passed as her office and tried to organize her workweek. Like other private agencies around the city, Bridges handled a lot of referrals from DCFS—the Department of Child and Family Services—that didn't qualify as hardcore neglect or abuse, as well as families who came to them directly for social services. She had preliminary reports to finish about several new clients she'd been assigned last week. No one at home in one instance, so she needed to follow up today—an eleven-year-old with three curfew violations in one month, hanging out on the street after midnight. The police had notified DCFS, who in turn passed the case to Bridges.

Michelle had a caseload of eighty children and families, more or less, who had to be seen at least once a month. Which meant twenty visits a week minimum, at least four a day. A glance at the calendar reminded her it was mid-May already, and she'd only seen thirty-six clients so far that month. That meant upping her quota for the next two weeks, which probably also meant working a few more evenings when people were more likely to be home.

Resting her elbows on the desk, head in her hands, Michelle felt overwhelmed already, and it was only Monday morning. Didn't Jesus say his grace was sufficient when we're feeling weak? *Could sure use some of that grace this week, Jesus . . .*

She took a deep breath and blew it out. *One day at a time, Michelle, one day at a time.* Today . . . she should check on the new baby who'd been left at Cook County Hospital last week and placed in emergency foster care. Mrs. Dunlap . . . sweetest little grandmother this side of the Mississippi. Still fostering babies after thirty years. Didn't even flinch when Michelle had called to see if she could take the newborn until they found a permanent placement—even though the sixty-something black woman was already caring for two toddlers, ages one and three, needing emergency care.

As long as she was in the Humboldt Park area, she'd check in with the Nigerian family who'd been displaced by that apartment building fire . . . and visit the young single mom of two who'd just taken in two nieces and a nephew when their parents died in a car crash. A working mom with limited resources, she needed urgent assistance obtaining a Link card and applying for aid to assist her application for custody. The court case to determine custody was this week.

Then she'd have to drive to the Near West Side—and if nobody was home for her young curfew violator, she'd have to go back this evening. No, wait . . . Jared had swing shift at the airport today, which meant she needed to be home this evening with *her* kids. She'd have to wait till his shift changed to day hours on Wednesday. Which meant missing Wednesday prayer meeting at Northside, but . . . couldn't be helped.

She was jumping ahead. Maybe the boy's mother or *somebody* would be home. Okay, time to finish these reports and get moving—

Her desk phone rang. "Michelle Jasper speaking."

"Miz Jasper! . . . He showed up at the house last night. Said he just wanted to see the kids. I wouldn't let him in, but he got steamin' mad, said I had no right to keep him from seein' the kids."

Michelle's mind scrambled. The panicky voice was familiar . . . "Tameeka?" Bridges had been working with this family for over a year and had finally recommended the order of protection from her ex because of abuse and threats. "Did you call the police?"

"No, 'cause he left . . . but I got scared Daryl might show up at the school and take Tommy. So I kept him home today, called the school, said he was sick. Didn't take the baby to the babysitter either."

"So you missed work today too?" Michelle rubbed her temples. "Tameeka, this isn't the answer. Look, I'll come by the apartment and we'll work something out. Just sit tight, all right? If Daryl shows up before I get there, call the police. Immediately."

Michelle hung up the phone and stuffed the reports into her briefcase. She'd work on them at home tonight. Some things couldn't wait.

The twins had been home a couple of hours when Michelle walked in the door at six. They'd dutifully called her at four when they got home from school, and she'd rehearsed the usual instructions: snacks and free time till five, but then it was homework from five to six. They hadn't seemed to mind during the winter when it got dark around four thirty, but since daylight saving time, there'd been anarchy afoot to change the schedule so they could go outside while it was light. "Or at least let us have friends over. Why can't you be home like DaShawn's grandmother?" Tavis had complained.

"Because she's retired and I'm not," Michelle had tossed back—even though it was probably only half true. Estelle Bentley was still in her fifties and worked part-time at the Manna House Women's Shelter in North Wrigleyville as the lunch cook, and she'd also mentioned some classes she taught there—sewing or something. But she did seem to be home when DaShawn got home from school.

They'd have to rethink the whole family schedule when school was out in a few weeks. Until then, Michelle had dug in her heels.

After checking on the twins' homework, Michelle pulled open the refrigerator door to study supper options. Destin had track after school four days a week, which his basketball coach had encouraged as a way to stay in shape, and usually got home around six thirty. Jared had swing shifts on Monday and Tuesday in the O'Hare control tower, which began at two and ended at ten. At least that had given him time this morning to do the money transfer from their savings account into checking to make the online payment for Destin's basketball camp.

But it was usually eleven by the time he got home, and he often needed another hour to unwind. And in the morning he would be asleep when she had to leave. Sometimes it felt as if she barely saw her husband at all on days he worked swing shift.

Pulling out some frozen hamburger, Michelle defrosted it in the microwave, started rice in the rice cooker, and began opening cans of kidney beans. A pot of chili served over rice would be easy and the kids liked it. Regular meals . . . something her kids took for granted. Then there was Jeffrey, her curfew violator. What was *he* going to eat for supper tonight? She'd gone by the address just before five, hoping one of his parents would be home. The boy had opened the door two inches, said he wasn't supposed to let anyone in when his parents weren't home. He'd *said* his mom would be home after work, but who knew the real story? What work? And what time would that be? She should've asked for more details.

Michelle had had to skip Mrs. Dunlap because of Tameeka's panicky call, but Mrs. Dunlap was the least of her worries. She'd told Tameeka that her ex showing up at her door was a violation of the order of protection and she should've called the police right then, and in fact, should still report it. It took Michelle a good thirty minutes to talk the anxious mom into taking Tommy to school and going to work herself, even though they'd be late. In the end Michelle had offered to take Tommy to school while Tameeka took the baby to the babysitter, promising to tell the principal and Tommy's teacher not to allow the father on school premises under any circumstances.

Michelle stopped slicing an onion in mid-chop, blinking back tears—unsure whether it was because of the cut onion or the sudden wave of gratefulness she felt that Jared was such a good dad and a good husband. *Never take it for granted, Michelle.*

Squabbling erupted in the basement family room. "If you don't tell, I will."

"Ain't your business, Tabby!"

"Don't care. Gonna tell."

Michelle was just about to yell down the stairs that she wasn't going to listen to tattletales—but just then the front door opened and slammed shut, and Destin appeared in the kitchen. "Man, I'm starvin'! What's for supper?"

"Hello to you too," Michelle teased. "C'mon, give me some sugar."

"Oh, Mom." Destin rolled his eyes but gave her a smack on the cheek, sneaking a peek into the pot on the stove. "Chili? All right! Is it ready?"

"In two minutes. Call your brother and sister, then come back and help set the table—but wash your hands first!" she called after him.

Five minutes later she was dipping chili out of the pot into each person's bowl of rice. "Tavis, wait! We haven't said the blessing yet." While the steaming chili cooled slightly, Michelle bowed her head. "For what we are about to receive, may the Lord make us truly thankful. Amen." Okay, so it was her fallback prayer when the kids were champing at the bit and wanted a short blessing. Jared, on the other hand, always prayed extemporaneously over the food, usually adding a number of prayer requests he considered current, which sometimes got a bit long.

"So, did Dad send in the money for the Five-Star Basketball Camp?" Destin asked between spoonfuls of chili and rice. "It had to be in today!"

"If he said he was going to, I'm sure he did . . . Don't talk with your mouth full, Destin."

"Coach said he was really glad I'd signed up. Said I had the potential to be a starter next year, maybe even get a scholarship."

"It's not fair." Tabitha glared at her big brother, toying with her own chili.

"Whatchu talkin' about, twerp?"

"Why do *you* get to go to *your* camp and I can't go?"

"'Cause you're just a twerp, twerp."

"All right, *stop*." Michelle shot a warning glance at Destin. "Tabby, I know you're disappointed about cheerleading camp, but it has nothing to do with fairness. We found out you have to be part of a cheer squad and go as a team. End of story."

"Still not fair," she pouted. "How are ya s'posed to learn all the moves an' stuff to get on a squad?"

Michelle pursed her lips. Good question. "Don't know, honey. But let's leave it alone for now, okay?" She turned to Destin. "What did you and Dad decide about you getting a job this summer to help pay for this camp?"

Destin shrugged. "I dunno. Dad said he wanted me to start now, applying on weekends. But don't know how that's gonna work. School doesn't even get out till the middle of June, an' then I'll be goin' to camp just a week and a half later. What if I find a job an' they want me to start right away when school's out? I mean, I can't really start a job till I get back from camp, y'know, after the Fourth . . . Can I have some more rice an' chili?"

Michelle's head started to ache. Destin had a point. What kind of summer job could he get that would let him start after the

Fourth of July? And she and Jared still needed to talk about what Tavis and Tabitha were going to do this summer. Maybe a week at a church camp—though they had yet to find one in the Midwest that had a significant number of African American kids, unless it was a special week targeting "urban youth," which kind of set her teeth on edge—like, "Let's have a camp for the poor black kids."

Bothered her more than her kids. Still, even summer camp would just be for a week, two at most. Then what?

It was Tavis's turn to load the dishwasher, which Michelle supervised while putting away leftovers. "You were awfully quiet during supper, Tavis. You okay?"

"That bully's been botherin' him again!" Tabby yelled from the dining room.

"Shut up, Tabby!" Tavis yelled back. "It's *okay*, Mom. Not a big deal. I can handle it."

"Oh, honey. I'm so sorry. I was hoping that meeting we had with the boy's mother and the teacher would stop it. Maybe we should—"

"*No*, Mom. Just makes it worse." He raised his voice. "And you stay out of it, Tabitha!" He gritted his teeth and jammed the next few plates into the dishwasher. "He was messin' with me, an' she got in his face tryin' to defend me. Just made all the kids laugh at me."

"Oh, Tavis . . ." Michelle felt helpless. She wanted to respect his feelings, but her Mother Bear instincts were on full alert. Still, she had to hide a smile. So Tabby came to her brother's defense, did she? *Good for Tabby.*

Tavis disappeared into his bedroom to finish his homework. Destin headed downstairs with the family laptop to write an English paper. Tabby confiscated the house phone until Michelle remembered the flash cards she'd made to help the twins study for the U.S. constitution test coming up next week—"which you need to pass if you're going to get into eighth grade."

It was eight o'clock by the time Michelle hefted her briefcase onto the dining room table and dug out the reports she needed to finish. At nine o'clock she told the twins to get ready for bed, then returned to the dining room table to make notes about today's visits for the reports she needed to hand in tomorrow . . . when her cell phone rang.

*Better not be Shareese with more of her "good ideas."*

"Sister Michelle? Estelle Bentley here!"

Michelle smiled at the buoyant voice on the other end. "Hi, Sister Estelle! How are things going with your new renter?"

"Oh, comin' along, comin' along. I think the poor thing is still in shock. It's her old apartment, but everything's so different. I'm actually callin' a few neighbors to see if we could bring her some meals this week until she gets settled." Estelle chuckled. "That phone list we made up at Miss Mattie's homecomin' is comin' in handy now. Anyway, I took her some chicken an' cornbread this evenin', just made a little extra of our own supper. Would you be able to do a meal sometime this week?"

Michelle's smile faded and she rubbed her temple with her free hand. "Estelle, that is such a sweet idea. I . . . I have some leftover chili if you need something right away—though maybe that's not so good for someone elderly like Mrs. Krakowski. Uh, let me think about what I've got on hand. Can I get back to you?"

"Of course, honey. Like I said, she's just one person, and I don't think she has a big appetite. So just make a little extra of your own dinner. Well, I'll let you go. Just call me with the day that seems good for you."

Michelle clicked End and sighed. Estelle was right. It wouldn't be a big deal, just make a bit more of what she'd make for their own supper. But for some reason, it felt like a puncture in her energy balloon. She still had reports to make of her client visits today, and she didn't want to have to think of anything else. She should've just said she couldn't do anything till this weekend.

"Mo-om?" A plaintive voice floated from Tabitha's bedroom. Lucky girl got her own room in the small three-bedroom bungalow, while the two boys had to share a room and a bunk bed.

Michelle peeked in. Tabitha was in bed, her hair wrapped in lieu of being braided. "You okay, honey?"

"Yeah. Just . . . would you sing a song to me an' rub my back, y'know, like Grammy used to do when I was little? One of her songs."

Michelle slipped into the room and sat down on the edge of the bed. "Sure, sweetie." The request made her smile in the soft glow from the bedside lamp. This house used to belong to Jared's mom, and they'd moved in with her ten years ago when it got too much for her to care for—and "Grammy" and Tabby had especially bonded. But Jared's mom had passed when the twins were eleven. Michelle hadn't realized that her big girl might still miss her grandmother's songs and back rubs.

She slid a hand under the T-shirt Tabby had worn to bed and gently rubbed her daughter's warm, smooth back as she began to sing the old Tommy Dorsey song Jared's mother used to sing:

*Precious Lord, take my hand*
*Lead me on, let me stand*
*I am tired, I am weak, I am worn . . .*

Michelle couldn't remember all the verses, so she hummed through some of the phrases. But Tabby's steady breathing indicated her daughter had fallen asleep before she'd finished the last ". . . *lead me home.*" Michelle turned out the lamp and tiptoed out, heading for her own bedroom.

Maybe that had been a strange song to sing to a thirteen-year-old. *"I am tired, I am weak, I am worn . . ."* More like how *she* felt at the end of a day at Bridges.

But a while later as she slipped wearily between the sheets and turned out her own light, she wished Jared was home to rub *her* back and sing her a song.

# Chapter 6

As Michelle shoveled all three kids out the door the next morning to their respective schools, she saw DaShawn Bentley run out of the two-flat across the street and catch up with the twins. Nice that they went to the same school. Did *he* have trouble with bullying like Tavis did? He was a little bigger than her son . . . maybe she'd talk to Estelle about it sometime.

Making sure she had her car keys, briefcase, and the sandwich she'd packed for lunch, Michelle peeked into the "master bedroom"—which was a joke, since it wasn't much bigger than the kids' bedrooms and didn't have a private bath. Jared was lying on his side turned away from her, but she stepped quietly into the room, leaned over, and kissed the side of his face. Scratchy. Needed a shave.

"Mmm," he murmured. "'Bye, honey. Have a good day."

She hadn't meant to wake him up, but she'd only realized Jared was home and in the bed when she got up during the night to go to the bathroom. Didn't know why she'd been so zonked last night. Yes, it'd been a tiring day, but not that unusual. Tiptoeing out of the room, she knew Jared would fall asleep again soon enough. He'd had to learn to sleep when he could, given his ever-changing schedule.

Once at work, she checked her calendar to see what time she needed to be in family court with Shirley Wilson, the young single mom, to ask for guardianship of her orphaned nieces and nephew. Not till eleven . . . good. She made copies for her supervisor of the reports she'd finished, and then made up a schedule for the day: call Tameeka to make sure her ex hadn't shown up again; stop by Mrs. Dunlap's to see how the abandoned baby was doing; check on two preteens she'd placed in a group home last month; check on the Motajo family, recent immigrants from Nigeria who'd been displaced by an apartment building fire a few weeks ago, to see if they needed more help accessing the resources and benefits available to help them through this loss of their few worldly possessions. Limited English was always a challenge.

As for Jeffrey's parents, she'd wait till tomorrow evening to try again to meet them. At the very least, they were facing a hefty fine.

Jared was at work, of course, when she got home, and the evening was pretty much a repeat of the night before . . . except that she increased the recipe for spaghetti and meatballs she made for supper and packed a plastic storage container with at least two good-sized servings for Mrs. Krakowski.

There. Wasn't that much extra work. Too late for Mrs. K's supper tonight though—it was already seven thirty. Maybe she'd just run it over to Estelle and have her deliver it as needed.

Leaving Destin to load the dishwasher, she hurried kitty-corner across the street and rang the Bentleys' doorbell two houses down. A scratchy voice on the intercom said, "Door's open! Come on up!"

Estelle met her at the top of the open stairway. "Sister Michelle! How nice."

Michelle handed her the plastic container. "I made a little extra tonight for Mrs. Krakowski like you suggested. Spaghetti and meatballs. I know it's too late for tonight . . . could you give this to her for tomorrow or whenever? It should keep for a few days."

"That's great! But you should give it to her personally, let her know the neighbors who are lookin' out for her." Estelle beamed broadly and shooed her back down the stairs. "Go on. Just knock on her door. I'm sure she's still up."

A moment later Michelle stood in front of the apartment door on the first floor. Now what? She hesitated a moment, then knocked. And waited. No answer.

"Forgot to tell you!" Estelle called down the stairs. "You have to knock really loud!"

Michelle rapped loudly this time . . . and heard, "Who is it?" from inside.

"Uh, Michelle Jasper! Your neighbor across the street!"

"Who?"

"Michelle Jasper!"

The door opened a crack, held in place by a safety chain. Mattie Krakowski's pale, wrinkled face appeared in the opening.

Michelle held up the plastic container. "I brought you some spaghetti and meatballs." She suddenly felt foolish. Wished she had brought the food in a more attractive dish. Or maybe the old woman didn't even like spaghetti and meatballs.

The door closed. *Did I blow it?* The chain rattled. Then the door opened again, wider this time. "Well, how nice. Won't you come in?"

"Oh, no, I know it's late. I just wanted to bring you something—"

"Nonsense. Come on in." The lady left the door open and shuffled back into the living room. Michelle had no choice but to follow. Mrs. Krakowski waved a hand around the room. "Did ya see how they fixed up my house while I was in the hospital? Land sakes, hardly recognized the place. Got some renters upstairs now too. Black family, like you. But real nice. Come see the kitchen . . ."

*But* real nice? Michelle shook her head. *Ignore it.* More significant was the old woman's confusion. Did she really think she still owned the two-flat and the Bentleys were the renters? Well, it wasn't up to her to set the record straight. "It's very nice."

"What?"

Michelle raised her voice. "It's very nice!" And it was. All the rooms had been freshly painted, the wood floors refinished, new appliances and cupboards in the kitchen. Mrs. Krakowski's ancient floral-patterned couch and matching rocking chair, both badly faded, looked a bit dissonant but probably helped the old woman feel at home.

"Now that's my boy there . . ." Mrs. Krakowski pointed to a picture of a man on the mantel of the gas fireplace. Michelle recognized the man who'd brought Mrs. K back to the neighborhood the other night. "And those are my grandkids." More framed photos. "That's Billy. And Nell. That one's Susie. But they're all grown now, moved away . . ."

The elderly woman talked on and on like an old Chatty Cathy doll, pointing to pictures, telling stories about where she got that vase, who crocheted the doilies on the back and arms of the rocker, and *tsk-tsking* about all the changes in the neighborhood. "You say you live 'cross the street? Used to know a Mrs. Jasper in the bungalow on the end, but don't see her anymore. Black lady like yourself, real nice."

"My mother-in-law." Michelle smiled, glad to have a point of connection. "I married her son, and we took over the house. But . . . I really do need to go now, Mrs. Krakowski. My children are at home. Uh, be sure to put the spaghetti and meatballs in the refrigerator, okay?"

It still took another five minutes to get graciously out the door, and dusk had settled over the neighborhood as Michelle hustled up her own steps and into the house.

"Mom! Where've you been?" Tavis met her in the living room, clearly upset. "Dad's been calling you, an' you left your phone, an' . . . an' we didn't know where you were! He wants you to call him right away!"

Oh dear. "Honey, I'm so sorry. I dashed across the street to take some food to Mrs. Krakowski, and she ended up talking and talking . . . I told Destin. Didn't he tell you?"

Tavis glowered. "No. He's downstairs somewhere. But Dad called an' I couldn't find you, so then he called your cell, but you left it on the table. You better call him—an' *next* time, tell us where you're goin'!"

Michelle grabbed her youngest—younger than Tabby by five minutes—and gave him a tight hug. "Absolutely. I should've let you know. That's a good rule for all of us, even parents, right?" She smiled to herself as she headed for the phone. Didn't hurt to slip in a teachable moment.

She rang Jared's cell. "Jared? So sorry I wasn't here when you called. Just ran across the street, didn't think I'd be longer than a minute, but . . . What? . . . Yeah, I know . . . Hope you get some good sleep . . . All right . . . Yeah, we're fine. I'll miss you . . . Love you too."

Michelle clicked End and sighed. Tuesday nights were the worst. Jared's schedule switched to a day shift tomorrow morning, which started at six a.m.—but he didn't get off till ten tonight. So he sometimes just stayed at the airport hotel to cut out the travel both ways. Which meant she hardly got to see him from the time she left the house Monday morning till the time she got home Wednesday night.

At least they usually got to see each other Wednesday evening—unless they went to prayer meeting at Northside or she had client visits to make. Thursday was another day shift—six a.m. till two—followed by a night shift starting later that same day at ten. How he managed juggling his sleep with all the switches, she didn't know. By the time the weekend came around, it took Jared a day or two to get his equilibrium back.

"Somebody has to do it, hon," he'd say when she complained about it. "And I'm good at it. People who fly don't think about the guys in the tower, but we get those planes in and out of airports safely. Just be thankful I've got a job."

*Thankful.* Yes, she was thankful. Thankful she had a job too. But sometimes she wished they could just . . . slow down. Life wasn't supposed to be this hectic, was it?

As Michelle left for work Wednesday morning, she noticed the small front porch of the brick bungalow on the southeast corner of Beecham was decorated with huge boughs of greenery. The family who lived there were orthodox Jews . . . Horowitz? Pretty sure that was their name. *Wonder what that's all about?*

Passover had been several weeks back—at least that's when the grocery stores had stocked up on kosher foods. Maybe she'd check it out online when she got home. Seemed like Christians ought to pay more attention to Jewish holidays and what they meant—after all, Jesus and his disciples were Jews and the Old Testament was part of the Christian Bible.

By the time she got home that evening—a little earlier than usual, since she still hadn't connected with Jeffrey's parents and was going to try again after supper—she saw the mother and two of the children at the corner house weaving flowers into the green-ery. "That's so pretty!" Michelle called out as she drove past—then on sudden impulse, she pulled to the curb and got out of the car. Would they think she was being nosy if she asked what was going on? But she was curious.

"Hello!" she called as she came up the short walk. "Your porch is so pretty. Is it a Jewish holiday today? . . . Oh, I'm sorry. I'm Michelle Jasper. I live at the other end of the block." She held out her hand to the woman who stood on the steps weaving flowers into the greenery along the metal handrail.

The woman blushed but held out a slim hand. "Rebecca Horowitz. I saw you last weekend when Mrs. Krakowski came back."

The young mother was quite pretty, her cheeks pink and tendrils of dark strands of hair escaping from the head covering she wore—a black baglike thing enveloping her long hair in back, totally different from the scarf that Farid's wife wore. Like many of the Conservative Jewish women Michelle saw in the stores, Rebecca was also wearing a long, straight, ankle-length skirt, tights, and black shoes. Or were they Orthodox? She didn't really know the difference.

"And these are Jacob and Ruthie." Rebecca nodded at her two helpers. "Say hello to Mrs. Jasper." Both children ducked their heads shyly. Michelle thought Jacob looked about four, his sister maybe five.

"What are the greenery and flowers for?" Michelle waved a hand at the decorations.

Rebecca blushed again. "Shavuot begins this evening. For two days."

"*Sha-voot?* I'm sorry, I'm probably pronouncing it wrong."

Rebecca smiled graciously. "It means Feast of First Weeks, also Feast of Firstfruits. To celebrate the giving of Torah to Moses."

"Abba reads the *whole* Torah," Ruthie piped up. "It takes a *long* time. But Ima reads the story of Ruth. I'*m* named after her."

Michelle smiled at the little girl, dark-haired like her mother. "A pretty name. I like that story too. Well . . . thanks. I hope you don't mind that I stopped. It's very interesting."

"It was nice of you to ask. Stop again sometime."

46

Michelle gave a little wave and returned to the car. It was tempting to stay and talk, but she really should get home and start supper if she was going to go out again.

She had just pulled up in front of the house and got out of the minivan when she saw Estelle Bentley coming out of Grace Meredith's house next door. "Hello!" she waved.

"Oh, Sister Michelle!" Estelle hurried her way. "I knocked at your door a while ago, but the kids said you weren't home yet. I wanted to invite you to the prayer time Grace and I do from time to time."

Michelle nodded. "I remember." Estelle had caught her coming home from work a month or so ago, had sensed she'd had a particularly hard day and invited her into Grace's home to pray. Michelle didn't know either woman well, so it had felt a little awkward at first. She'd just come home from a frustrating meeting with Tavis's teacher and the other parent about the bullying, on top of having to deal with a really difficult foster care situation that day. But there'd been something about Estelle's concern for her challenges that had felt calming and supportive. But now . . . "I don't usually get home till six or later most days—but thanks for thinking about me."

"Well, if there's anything we can pray for, you just let me know. We'd be glad to include you in our prayers. And we'd love to have you join us. 'Cause when women get together to pray, watch out! Things happen." With a wink and a brief hug right there on the sidewalk, Estelle Bentley hurried across the street.

Michelle watched her new neighbor disappear into the two-flat. Of course she believed in prayer. Prayer was important . . . though she had to admit she often resented the Wednesday night prayer meeting at church, which felt like something she "should" do even though it took her away from home on a weeknight. But as she let herself into the house, Estelle's words echoed inside her head . . .

*"When women get together to pray, watch out! Things happen."*

The way Estelle said it . . . made one think God was really up to something.

# Chapter 7

THE HOUSE SEEMED AWFULLY QUIET as Michelle came in and dropped her purse and briefcase. "Hello? Anybody home?" No answer. Where were the twins? She looked at her watch. Not quite five. She was home early tonight. Had they gone out without phoning her?

But as she headed toward the kitchen, she heard the TV down in the family room and followed the sound down the basement steps. Jared was sprawled in his recliner in front of the TV early news, eyes closed, mouth open, glasses held loosely in the hand dangling over the side of the chair. Rescuing his glasses, she kissed him softly on the forehead. "Hey, you."

He awoke with a start. "Oh . . . you're home. Guess I fell asleep. Uh, what time is it?"

"Almost five. Where are the twins?"

"Uh"—he rubbed his eyes and slid his glasses back on— "shooting baskets over at the Bentleys. DaShawn showed up, asked if they could come over for a while." He looked up at her sheepishly. "You're home early, caught me napping."

She sat down on the arm of the recliner facing him. "You get any sleep last night?"

He shrugged. "Six hours, more or less." Then he grinned, caught her off balance, and pulled her down onto his lap. "Say, what've I got here? Empty house, beautiful woman . . ." Brushing her bangs back and wrapping both arms around her, he nuzzled her neck. "Mmm, you smell good. Could give a man ideas. Been a long time . . ."

Michelle laughed and snuggled closer, awkward as it was draped over his lap. *Mmm.* Felt so good to be held in Jared's arms. It had taken her a long time to fall asleep last night, knowing his side of the bed would be empty all night. But tonight would be different—

*Slam!* "Dad? We're home!" Tavis yelled from upstairs.

"Is Mom here? Her car's outside!" Tabitha did a voice-over.

"Down here!" Michelle called, struggling to sit up and barely getting on her own two feet before the twins thudded down the basement stairs.

"I made more baskets than Tavis did!" Tabitha crowed.

"So? It wasn't a real game."

"So? I still got more than you did."

"Enough, you two." Michelle headed for the stairs. "Time to do your homework. I'm going to start supper. We have to eat a little earlier because I need to see a client tonight." She shooed the kids back upstairs.

"What?"

Michelle heard the recliner footrest come down with a thump and Jared's footsteps as he followed her up to the kitchen. She pulled out the chicken pieces she'd left that morning in the refrigerator to thaw and rummaged in the cupboard for a frying pan, aware that Jared was leaning against the kitchen doorjamb.

"You have to see a client *tonight*? But, honey, this is the first evening I've been home since Sunday! I thought . . . you know."

"I know." She busied herself flouring the chicken, heating oil in the pan, and dropping the pieces in. "Hopefully won't be gone too long. But every time I stopped in to see this kid's family, the parents weren't there." She turned and eyed him. "Besides, you usually go to prayer meeting Wednesday nights, right?"

"Yeah, but we could go together."

"Now *that's* a hot date." She tried to keep her voice teasing.

"Aw, come on, Michelle. What would Pastor think if his deacons didn't show up at prayer meeting? And it's only an hour or so."

She didn't answer. *Don't make an issue of this*, she chided herself. She and Jared usually went to prayer meeting together if they didn't have conflicts, leaving Destin at home to babysit the twins—who both insisted they were too old to be "babysat" and could stay home by themselves, thank you, without bossy big brother.

Covering the sizzling chicken with a splatter guard, Michelle turned around. "I'm sorry, hon. I'm sure I'll be back by the time you get home. And then . . ." She walked over to him and slid an arm around his waist, pressing her body against his. Reaching up a finger, she traced his moustache and warm lips—then started to giggle at the flour dust she left on his face.

*Slam!* "I'm home! Somethin' smells good! We ready to eat?"

Destin. Jared rolled his eyes and stole a quick kiss before untangling himself. "Does he come in like that every night?" Then he chuckled. "Ha! Flour's back on you."

Michelle and Jared left about the same time after supper in separate cars. Driving down Western Avenue toward the Near West Side, she half-hoped Jeffrey's parents wouldn't be there so she could turn around and come home again. *No . . . totally selfish thought.* What she really hoped is that somebody besides Jeffrey would be home so she wouldn't have to turn him over to foster care.

As she backed into a parking space on the narrow residential street, she realized the area felt a lot more foreboding in the deepening dusk than it had in the sunshine. The few two-flats and single-family homes looked small and squished between the larger six-flats and twelve-unit apartment buildings that made up the block. Several streetlights were out, the others dim.

A better-lit street a couple of blocks down boasted a 7-Eleven on the corner, a bar, and a laundromat, not to mention a vacant lot and a burned-out building that had been boarded up for months. All of which served as hangouts for the young and unemployed. Mostly male. Gang signs decorated the sides of buildings and the underpass beneath the "L."

Michelle took a deep breath before unlocking the door. *Lord, I hope your guardian angels are on duty around here tonight.* She got out, locked the minivan, and walked purposefully toward the two-flat several houses away, keys clutched like cat claws between her fingers in case anyone tried to bother her.

She made it up onto the wooden porch and rang the doorbell that said 1ˢᵀ FL—LEWIS-COLEMAN without running into anyone. Lights were on in the first floor apartment, so she rang the doorbell again. Soon the front door opened and a slender, brown woman looked out, cigarette in her hand. She eyed Michelle warily.

"Ms. Coleman? I'm Michelle Jasper from Bridges Family Services. May I come in?"

The young woman took a drag on the cigarette, blew out the smoke, and then opened the door wider. "Yeah. Come on."

Michelle followed her into the foyer and through a door into the first apartment. The woman waved a hand at the couch, which was covered with a flowered throw. "Go ahead, sit. You want somethin' to drink? I got Coke. Or you want water?"

"No, thank you. I'm fine." The offer of hospitality was a good sign. She'd been prepared for open hostility. Or a barrage of assurances that everything was fine. In those first moments at the door, the woman had seemed suspicious, but as her face relaxed, Michelle realized the she was quite attractive, her braided hair extensions gathered into a ponytail at the base of her neck. And young. Late twenties at the most.

"This is about Jeffrey, ain't it. You wanna talk to him? I can get 'im."

"No. Actually I need to talk to you."

Jeffrey's mother sank onto an ottoman that had seen better days. "Yeah, I know. We got this." She reached for a good-sized envelope and pulled out the contents. "Hafta pay a fine. *Five hundred dollars.*" The woman shook her head and seemed to fight back sudden tears. "Don't know where in the world *that's* gonna come from. Told Jeffrey I'm gonna take it out of his hide if he ever sneaks out like that again."

Michelle caught a glimpse of Jeffrey peeking around the doorway. "That's why I'm here—to make sure it doesn't happen again. Bridges has a number of support services for families. We'd like to help."

A nod. "Jeffrey tol' me you came by when I was at work."

"What kind of work do you do, Ms. Coleman?"

Another drag on the cigarette and a wry smile. "Not Coleman. Name's Lewis . . . Brianna Lewis. Jeffrey is Coleman, his daddy's name." She sucked in a breath and blew it out. "I work weekends as a hostess at a club in Uptown, four to midnight. But it's legit—no funny business," she added hastily. "Weekdays I got a second job taking care of this ol' lady who's housebound, usually get home by seven or eight.

Michelle nodded. "I see. Is there anyone else in the home?"

Brianna shrugged. "Jeff Senior drives truck—long haul—so he's gone a lot. But my sister lives upstairs. She got four kids. She looks after Jeffrey on weekends till I get home. At least she s'posed to. But Miss . . . what did you say your name was?"

"Michelle Jasper."

"Okay. Miss Jasper, I know what Jeffrey was doin' wasn't right—"

"It was downright dangerous, Ms. Lewis. The curfew laws are there to protect children like Jeffrey."

"I know." Brianna stubbed out her cigarette in an ashtray and shook her head. "It's . . . it's just hard bein' a single mom—single most of the time, I mean, though Jeffrey's daddy an' I are still together. His job . . . you know. I been tellin' Jeff Senior he needs to give it up, get a different job, so he can spend time with his son! Otherwise, we gonna lose him. Like all the other boys 'round here. But Jeffrey's not in no gang!" The young mother's voice suddenly turned fierce. "Jeffrey said he just wanted to go to the 7-Eleven, get some pop an' some chips."

Michelle wondered if that was true. Once, maybe. But three times? Sounded more like the call of the streets, wanting to do what his peers were doing, or trying to impress the big guys, the gangbangers. Her heart ached, but her voice had to remain firm. "Ms. Lewis . . . Brianna. Whatever the reason, if he's picked up again after curfew, the state could make a case of neglect and place him in foster care. I know you don't want that to happen."

"No, no, no." Brianna started to cry, dropping her head into her hands. "He's all I got. An' he's a good boy, comes right home from school. I check in on him by phone every hour. Please . . ."

Michelle touched her arm. "Bridges will do everything we can so that Jeffrey doesn't become a ward of the state." They talked about options for supervision. Afterschool program? Another relative nearby? At the very least, Jeffrey needed to stay upstairs with Brianna's sister on weekend nights instead of getting sent to bed alone in the first floor apartment. And Bridges had a Family Friend program—similar to Big Brother, Big Sister programs—consisting of volunteers who might be able to spend time with Jeffrey on evenings when she was at work.

Before she left, Michelle made an appointment to come back on Saturday to talk with Jeffrey and his mother again—the aunt too, if possible. How she was going to work that into her weekend, she had no idea. But no way did she want this boy to end up in foster care.

She didn't see Jared's Nissan when she parked the minivan in front of their house. Must not be home yet . . . unless he put it in the garage, which he rarely did in nice weather. A block with mostly single-family bungalows usually allowed for plenty of parking—another perk of living on Beecham Street. But she sat in the car a few minutes before getting out, her spirits sagging. Almost nine o'clock. Another "free" Wednesday night gone.

Something was wrong with this picture . . .

Michelle was taking off her makeup in front of her vanity mirror when Jared got home at ten thirty. She eyed him in the mirror.

He sighed, tossed his keys on the dresser, and came up behind her. "I'm sorry, babe." Leaning down, he kissed her on the back of the neck, then sat down on the bed to take off his shoes. "Some young men from the neighborhood showed up at the prayer meeting tonight—not sure they knew it was a prayer meeting, but in they came, gangsta jeans, do-rags, and all. My guess is they needed someplace safe to be tonight, saw the church was open, and ducked in. They were polite and respectful enough. Anyway, Pastor asked me to talk with them after the service. And they seemed open to that . . . could hardly refuse." He dropped his shoes on the floor. "Sorry I'm late."

She fought down the urge to retort, *You had time for those dudes, but weren't here to put your own kids to bed.* "Okay."

Jared shrugged out of his sport coat and polo shirt. "How about you? Find your clients at home?"

"Uh-huh. The mother was actually very cooperative. I'm hoping we can keep this kid out of foster care."

"Well, if anybody can, it's you." Jared pulled on his robe. "I'm gonna go say goodnight to the kids. Don't go anywhere." His voice took on a suggestive note. "I'll be right back."

Michelle finished her makeup removal and stared in the mirror. She didn't exactly look sexy. Didn't feel sexy either. Too pooped after the long day. Should she beg off? Except . . . her period might come any day. Had been kind of irregular the last year or two, made it hard to keep track. And Jared had two shifts tomorrow—his second day shift and a night shift tomorrow night, separated by a mere eight hours in the afternoon from two till ten, two of which were basically spent commuting.

*Quit whining, Michelle.* She knew once they started their lovemaking, she'd get into it. And she couldn't just blame Jared's schedule, crazy as it was. Even if he'd stayed home tonight, she was the one who had to go back to work.

Slipping into the bathroom, she heard Jared in the boys' room talking to Destin, something about the summer job. Doing a quick brush of her teeth, she scurried back into the bedroom and rummaged in the drawer of her vanity for her diaphragm, wanting to put it in before Jared got back.

When he turned out the light and slid between the sheets several minutes later, she was waiting for him, *sans* nightgown.

# Chapter 8

MICHELLE WOKE BRIEFLY when Jared's alarm went off at five, but she didn't move. She needed the extra hour of sleep before she had to get up. But it seemed like only minutes before her own alarm went off at six. *Uhhh.* If only she could sleep in . . .

Forcing herself to throw back the covers and get up, she almost stumbled out into the hall to go to the bathroom, but remembered in time that they'd made love last night and she was still naked. Slipping on her robe and slippers, she headed for the basement. They'd put in a second bathroom a few years ago when trying to make do with just one for a family of five became a major headache. Even though it was farther away, she preferred the newer bathroom for her morning shower—no tub, just a big shower with a glass front and glass sliding door, two sinks, and a large mirror with vanity lights. She wasn't as likely to wake the kids before six thirty either.

Michelle let the hot water run over her head, waking up her brain. Today was Jared's craziest day, working the control tower from six till two, then again from ten tonight till six Friday morning. But at least he'd be home for supper. And the weekend was coming up. Maybe they could even get a night out. And Memorial Day weekend was coming up too . . . If they planned ahead, maybe they could take a couple of days away as a family. Wouldn't that be great?

But she couldn't just stand in the shower. She had to get dressed, get the kids up, throw lunches together, set out breakfast—cold cereal on weekdays—and get out the door herself if she wanted to get to the office by eight.

Even though the day was overcast, the temperature had climbed into the seventies by noon. Made her glad she'd packed a sandwich and could eat her lunch in a park near her next client visit. She dreaded this one. DCFS had received at least five calls from neighbors in an apartment building about a baby crying for hours, what sounded like drunken fights, people coming and going who weren't on the lease. DCFS had passed it on to Bridges Family Services and her supervisor had dropped it on her desk.

"Just check it out. Might not be anything we can do. Use your judgment."

Right. Not serious enough for DCFS to intervene. And the parents themselves weren't asking for help. One of those dysfunctional families that so often fell through the cracks. But . . . she'd "check it out."

Michelle parked on a nearby residential street and found a bench where she could eat her lunch. The park was fairly empty for such a warm day. But it was only late May. Kids were still in school. Most adults were at work. Still, a cluster of young men loitered near the playground equipment, smoking, drinking beer, talking loudly. Walking around like ducks in their low-slung pants. Doing nothing. Why weren't they in school—or at work? She shook her head. *O Lord . . .*

Sometimes the dysfunction in the city threatened to overwhelm her.

But once her sandwich, apple, and snack-sized bag of Fritos were gone, she couldn't put it off any longer. She walked back to her car . . . *darn it!* A parking ticket! She snatched it off her windshield. What in the world for? There weren't any parking meters . . . and then she saw the fire hydrant on the other side of the car. *Oh great. Just great.* How could she have been so stupid? She squinted at the fine print on the yellow ticket. *$100?!*

Now she felt like crying.

By the time she found the address of the apartment building she was supposed to visit—after encountering half a dozen one-way streets—her mood was as sour as spoiled sauerkraut. Standing in the foyer of the apartment building and staring at the names above the two rows of mailboxes—several of which hung open or otherwise looked busted—she finally located the name and apartment number she'd been given. 3B—BLACKWELL. Two other names had been scrawled beside it: *Owens . . . Smith.* She pushed the button. Heard nothing. She pushed again.

Just then a man barged out the inner door, startled to see her in the foyer, but just kept going out. Seemed in a big hurry. Michelle caught the inner door before it wheezed shut. *Okaay.* Not exactly legit, but she'd make one more try at contacting the Blackwells.

No elevator—but she wouldn't trust one in these old apartment buildings anyway. The stairwell smelled musty, stale. She walked up the stairs to the first floor landing . . . then second . . . finally third, feeling out of breath. Was she that out of shape? Locating 3B, she rapped loudly on the door and listened. A baby was crying somewhere, but she wasn't sure from which apartment. She knocked again, even louder.

The lock clicked. The handle turned and the door opened a few inches. But nobody was there . . . until she looked down and saw the cute face of a girl about seven. Nappy hair caught up in three pigtails, one on either side, one high in back. Why wasn't she in school? But Michelle smiled. "Hi, sweetie. Is your mommy home?"

The nutmeg brown face nodded. "But she sleeping."

The sound of the baby crying was louder now. From this apartment.

"What's your name?"

"Candy."

"Is anyone else home?"

A solemn nod. "Otto."

"Who's Otto?"

"Mommy's friend."

*Hmm.* "Can I speak to Otto?"

A shrug. The door opened wider and Michelle followed the little girl into the dim interior. The apartment smelled like urine and cheap alcohol. She tried to breathe through her mouth. The girl pointed into the kitchen. Standing in the doorway, Michelle felt like gagging. Otto was slumped over the table, his face smashed in his plate of food, passed out, dead drunk.

Michelle turned and followed the sound of the crying baby into a dark living room, old sheets covering the windows. A child

57

about nine months old stood hanging onto the side of a netted playpen, wailing halfheartedly. The baby was wearing a shirt and a dirty diaper—full from the way it hung. And smelled.

She turned to the little girl. "Can you go wake up your mommy?"

Candy shook her head. "She tol' me she'd spank me good if I woke her up. Said she gots ta sleep, 'cause she gots ta work tonight."

*Yeah, I bet.* Michelle was unsure what to do. She felt like an intruder, even though she was there on official business and the child had let her in. The one thing she could do she didn't want to do. *Oh, suck it up, Michelle.* "Candy, do you know where the baby's clean diapers are?"

Candy nodded, disappeared, and came back with a disposable. "We only gots one."

*One.* Michelle was on the verge of either laughing hysterically or crying hysterically. The situation was heartbreaking! But she picked up the baby, found the bathroom, wrung out a used washcloth hanging on the tub, and tried to clean the baby's bottom—him, it turned out, when she peeled off the offending diaper. An ugly rash covered his entire genital area. She wished she had some zinc oxide ointment to soothe it.

It took several rinses of the rag to wash the baby, but finally the clean diaper was on. The baby had stopped crying and just stared at her. She picked him up and held him, noticing his beautiful, large eyes as she returned to the living room. "What's your brother's name?"

"Pookey."

"Pookey! Is that his real name?"

Candy shrugged. "That's what Mommy calls him. Just Pookey."

"Do you go to school, Candy?"

The little girl nodded, then shrugged. "But I had a tummy ache today.

"Who are you?" A harsh voice hurtled into the room from the doorway. Startled, Michelle turned quickly. "Whatchu doin' wit my baby? Give 'im to me!" A woman in a rumpled nightshirt stormed across the room and snatched the baby from Michelle's arms. "Whatchu doin' in my house?" She looked Michelle up and down. "You from the school? Kid's got a tummy ache is all. Can't send her to school sick."

"No, I'm from Bridges Family Services. My name is—"

"Don't care what yer name is." The woman thrust her chin forward defiantly. "I wantchu to git outta my house!"

"Ms. Blackwell, DCFS has received calls about possible neglect, and we need—"

"I *said*, Git out! Or I'm callin' the po-lice."

*You do that. Might be the best thing.* But the woman's face was twisted with fury and Michelle wasn't sure what she might do. "All right. But we do need to talk about these children." She held out her card to the woman. "Please, give me a call. Our agency can help. We have resources—"

Parked on his mother's hip, Pookey started to cry again as the woman marched to the door and yanked it open. "I said, git out. *Now!*"

Michelle gave the card to Candy. "Don't lose it," she whispered . . . and a few moments later found herself in the hall with the door slammed behind her.

But as she started down the stairs, she heard the door open again and the mother's harsh voice sailing after her. "How'd ya get in th' buildin' anyway? How'd ya get up here?"

Michelle just kept going and called back, "Good-bye, Ms. Blackwell! We'll be in touch!" By the time she got to the ground floor and headed for her car, she was muttering to herself. Could she make a case for neglect? Turn it over to the state attorney's office? Probably not. She didn't have enough information. But she wished she could get those kids out of that awful situation.

She hardly noticed it had started to rain.

Michelle dragged herself into the house at five thirty and dumped her briefcase and purse on the living room couch. She didn't feel like cooking, but they had to eat. Maybe she'd pull out those frozen burritos she'd bought last week.

Tabby had her face six inches from the computer screen at the dining room table, and Michelle peeked over her shoulder. Looked like her daughter was doing research on Harper Lee, the author of *To Kill a Mockingbird*.

"Doing a book report?" she asked.

Tabby grunted. "Is Daddy home?"

"Yeah . . . sleepin', I think. Said to tell you to wake him up for supper."

Par for the course on Thursdays, trying to catch some z's before going back to work that night. She checked on Tavis, who was sprawled on the top bunk in the boys' bedroom, working on math.

"Hi, Mom. I'm hungry."

"Didn't you have a snack?"

"Yeah, but I'm hungry again."

So what else was new? Their food bill had been climbing with three teenagers in the house—and Tavis hadn't really started growing yet. But after cooking a couple of packages of already-seasoned red beans and rice to go with the burritos and throwing together a quick chop salad, she had food on the table by six thirty. Time to wake Jared.

Destin shoveled in copious amounts of the beans and rice, talking all the while about Saturday's track meet at Lane Tech. "It's the sectionals, Dad—last meet of the season before the state championships! Coach has me down for the 800 since I've been workin' on my stamina, an' he's also got me down as backup for the 4-by-2. One of the guys had an ankle injury a few weeks ago; I might need to sub for him if he's not up to par."

"Will you go to state with the track team if Lane Tech wins?" Tabby was agape.

"Nah. That's not how it works, twerp. Whoever wins first and second of each event goes, just the person, not the whole team. Got ten schools in our league, but we've got some great athletes. Lakewood is one of our biggest rivals, but I think Lane Tech is gonna kick their butt in overall wins."

Jared gave him The Look over the top of his glasses. "Watch the language."

In one ear, out the other. "The meet starts at ten thirty. Can you guys come?"

Jared cleared his throat. "Don't think so, son. The deacon board scheduled a workday at the church Saturday to get some deep cleaning done and repair some broken windows—things that need doing before summer."

"Aw, Dad." Destin eyed Michelle. "Mom?"

Workday? When did that get scheduled? But Destin was waiting. "I'm sorry, honey. You know I lead a post-abortion support group at the crisis pregnancy center Saturday mornings . . ."

"Oh yeah." Destin glumly took another burrito from the serving dish.

"I'll come see your race if someone gives me a ride," Tavis offered.

Jared eyed both of his sons as he chewed his food. Then he wiped his mouth. "Tell you what. Tavis, you come to the workday with me, and if enough people show up, we'll take a break, drive over to Lane Tech, and take in Destin's event at the meet—especially if you can text me, Destin, when you have an idea of when the 800 is. But after this weekend, you need to start on that job search for this summer. We have a deal, remember?"

Big sigh. "Yeah, I know."

Jared pointed his fork at Destin. "You want to go to basketball camp or not?"

"Yeah, yeah, I do."

"Well, then, conversation over. Pass those burritos, please." But after a while Jared looked at Michelle. "You're awfully quiet tonight. Everything okay?"

She shrugged. "Yeah, just . . . ran into an upsetting situation with a family today. I can tell you later."

After supper, Michelle put away the food while Tavis loaded the dishwasher, then she wandered into the living room, where Jared was reading the paper on the couch. She flopped down beside him. "Honey? You got a minute?"

He lowered the paper. "Sure. I guess. Gotta leave for work in a while. What's up?"

"Just wanted to talk about this weekend—and Memorial Day weekend too. I was hoping we could do something as a family if we planned ahead a little. Or maybe you and I could have a night out. You know, after a busy workweek."

Jared took off his glasses and rubbed his eyes. "I'd like to, babe. But don't see how this weekend. You heard what I told the kids at the table. Didn't you see the announcement about the workday in the bulletin? I got it in last-minute Sunday morning. Deacon Jones's wife is heading up a crew of ladies to tackle the kitchen . . . She didn't call you?"

Michelle couldn't remember. Had she? A voicemail she didn't answer? She shrugged. "Don't think so. But even if she did, I volunteer at the Lifeline Care Center Saturday mornings." Oh drat! And she'd made an appointment to go back and talk with Brianna Lewis about Jeffrey on Saturday afternoon!

Jared frowned. "Well, between that and the workday at church and Destin's track meet, that pretty much shoots Saturday. And you know what Sundays are like."

Michelle sighed. "I know. It's just . . . I think we're all working too hard. We need to get away, or at least do some fun things."

"Well . . ." Jared scratched his jaw. "Have you thought about cutting back on how often you volunteer at Lifeline? You wouldn't *have* to go every Saturday."

Why was she the one who had to cut back on something? Irritation crept into her voice. "I'd be glad to get a sub if I knew ahead of time. That's why I'm asking ahead of time . . . about Memorial Day weekend, at least."

"Well, maybe. Though I might have to cover for someone at work since it's a holiday. But I'll check the schedule tonight." The paper went back up.

Michelle stared at the front-page headlines of the *Chicago Tribune* without seeing a thing. She would've liked to tell Jared about the horrible experience at the Blackwell apartment today. But she wasn't about to say, "Can we talk?" again. He'd probably feel annoyed at a second interruption. Besides, he had to leave for work soon.

*Cut him some slack, Michelle. His shifts at O'Hare are intense . . . Let him relax.*

Leaving the room abruptly, she headed for the kitchen. She needed a cup of chamomile tea. But a moment later she stormed down the hall to the boys' bedroom, yelling for Tavis. "You call that loading the dishwasher? Get back in there and do it right. And wash the table too!"

# Chapter 9

THE KIDS WERE EATING THEIR COLD CEREAL on the fly the next morning when Jared got in from his night shift. "Hi, Dad! 'Bye, Dad! Gotta find my backpack!" Tabitha smacked a kiss on her father's cheek as he came into the kitchen.

"It's raining! Wear your windbreaker!" Michelle called after her, hoping she'd also remember to brush her teeth. She gave Jared a welcome-home peck. "You want some breakfast?"

"Nah, that's all right. Not very hungry. Think I'll just hit the sack."

Michelle turned back to the four bag lunches she'd been packing. "Your night shift go okay?"

"More or less. The rain during the night screwed up a lot of schedules—mostly incoming flights from other cities that got delayed where the storm was worse. It wasn't so bad here, but things got stacked up both coming and going. So I'm pretty tired."

"Oh, okay. I've got to leave in about ten minutes, so we'll all be out of here soon." She stepped to the kitchen doorway and raised her voice. "Kids! Don't forget your lunches!"

Michelle decided not to mention the headache she woke up with. She hadn't slept that well . . . never did when he was gone overnight. She'd taken some Tylenol, which ought to kick in pretty soon. But the situation at the Blackwell apartment yesterday had nagged at her subconscious all night. Wasn't much she could do since DCFS didn't think the situation posed immediate danger to the children—not if the mother didn't want any help from Bridges Family Services. Which had been obvious.

But that was the frustration. In her mind she kept seeing Candy's sober eyes and Pookey's tearstained face. Not to mention the baby's angry bottom. And Otto—whoever he was—with his drunken face in his plate.

63

"We can only do so much, Michelle," her supervisor said when she got to the office and reported on yesterday's visit. "You left your card. Maybe the mother will call."

Not likely. But one could hope. And pray.

Most of her day that Friday was spent doing home visits of foster parents where Bridges had helped place children, working on reports, and making calls to find a Family Friend volunteer who might be able to come alongside Jeffrey Coleman. To her relief, Ray Stevens, one of the volunteers from Loyola University, said weekends would be perfect for him. "My girlfriend's doing an overseas program till August, so I need something to fill my lonely weekends," he'd laughed.

Perfect. She asked if Ray could meet her at Jeffrey's home at two o'clock tomorrow. "No problem. Just give me the address."

The rain had stopped earlier that afternoon and Friday going-home traffic wasn't too bad. Her cell phone rang as she headed up Western Avenue but she let it go to voicemail. Then groaned when she checked at a traffic light to see who'd called. *Shareese Watson*. Probably wanted to talk about her book club idea again. So far the committee hadn't come up with any firm ideas for the women's ministry June event coming up in three weeks, which left a vacuum Shareese was only too eager to fill.

Michelle sighed. She really needed to spend some time praying and thinking about that. Ideally, it'd be great to do a summer series with a similar theme, so they didn't have to come up with totally different events each month.

Maybe she'd call her friend Norma, do some brainstorming before Sunday.

As she pulled up in front of the house and got out of the car, she heard her name being called. "Mrs. Jasper! I'm so glad I caught you!"

*Who in the world?* Michelle saw a young black woman come flying out of Grace Meredith's house next door, waving at her. Mid-twenties, perky twists all over her head, a big smile, a clipboard clutched in one hand.

"Hi! I'm Samantha Curtis, Grace Meredith's assistant." The young woman held out her free hand and gave Michelle's a hearty pump. "So glad to finally meet."

Michelle smiled. "Please. Call me Michelle. Guess we've only talked on the phone—and from the West Coast at that." Samantha had called several times on Grace's Just Grace tour in April, wanting more brochures from the Lifeline Care Center. She'd sounded very businesslike on the phone. Hadn't quite expected such a beautiful young lady.

Samantha beamed. "And most people call me Sam. Anyway, Grace said you offered to order some brochures for her upcoming concerts. I'm so sorry I'm just now getting back to you. Grace has a couple concerts over Memorial Day weekend. I know, I know, that's next weekend, but"—she grimaced apologetically—"would it be possible to get copies of all your brochures by next Thursday? We leave Friday morning." Samantha pulled a sheet of paper from the clipboard and handed it to her. "Here's what we think we might need—including a separate order for her upcoming summer tour. But if that's too much all at once, just order enough for next weekend."

Michelle took the sheet of paper and scanned it. "I'll see what I can do. I'm going to Lifeline tomorrow morning. We might have enough in stock, and if there's not enough, I'll call in a rush order."

"Oh, thank you, Mrs. Jasper—I mean, Michelle. We'll cover the cost, of course. Just give me an invoice—including any extra cost for sending it UPS or Priority Mail—whatever's fastest, okay?" She turned to go. "Well, gotta run. And I'm *so* glad I got to meet you in person at last!" The young woman waved good-bye and headed for a car parked down the block.

Michelle headed up the steps onto the small porch, got out her key, and then paused. The porch wasn't very big, but it did cover half the front of their brick bungalow abutting the kitchen. Big enough for a porch swing. Wouldn't that be nice? If they had a porch swing, that's what she'd do right now, just sit on the swing and think about . . . about nothing for ten minutes before entering the fray.

"Ma'am? Did you order pizza?" called a voice. "Looking for Jasper . . . 7337 Beecham."

Michelle turned. A young man in a car with a Giordano's Pizza sign stuck on its roof had pulled to the curb and was calling to her from an open window on the passenger side. "Guess that's us," she said. A moment later he was running up their walk with a large, square insulated bag.

The front door opened and Jared stepped out onto the porch. "Oh! Hi, Michelle. Didn't know you were home yet. I ordered a couple pizzas for supper, hope that's okay." And to the delivery guy, "Yeah, yeah, I'll take those . . . How much do I owe you?" He handed the young man a couple of twenties, told him to keep the change, and followed Michelle back inside the house. "Wasn't sure when you'd get home and I need to eat early so I can head over to the church to get things set up for the workday tomorrow. Thought you wouldn't mind a night off in the kitchen anyway."

"Sure, that's fine . . . but I didn't know you had to go to the church tonight too."

"Yeah, sorry. The whole thing was so last-minute. Have to pick up a rug shampooer I rented this afternoon and get a bunch of other supplies at Home Depot for the workday, so I need the minivan. Then some of the deacons thought we ought to go over tonight and get organized to make the best use of people's time tomorrow." He set the two pizzas on the dining table and raised his voice. "Tavis! Tabby! Pizzas are here!"

"Awriiight!" Tavis came pounding up the stairs from the family room, Tabby hot on his heels. "Didya get pepperoni?"

"But I wanted that tropical one with pineapple!"

"Yuck!"

"Hey, hey, hey!" Jared snatched up the pizza boxes from grasping hands. "Take it easy. We've got two large pizzas here— this one is half pepperoni, half sausage and mushroom . . . and the other one has Tabby's tropical stuff on half, and for *you*, my queen"—he winked at Michelle—"the super veggie."

The front door slammed. "Did somebody say pizza?"

Michelle heard a thud as Destin tossed his backpack on the floor somewhere, sliding into a chair at the table two seconds later. Wagging her head, she headed for the kitchen. "I'll get a knife."

At least the whole family was together for a good twenty minutes.

Jared took the minivan after supper to pick up the rug shampooer and other supplies at Home Depot before heading over
to the church. Destin had picked up a movie at Blockbuster on
the way home from school, and before she could ask about it,
he said, "Yes, Mom"—with that annoying patient tone teenagers use on their parents—"I got *Shrek the Third,* an' it's PG, so
the twerps can watch it too." Tavis ran across the street to ask
DaShawn Bentley if he'd like to come over and watch it with
them.

Fine. Michelle was almost tempted to veg out in Jared's recliner
in the family room and watch it with them. Even she could hardly
resist the loveable ogre and the hilarious donkey. But she decided
she could also use some kid-free time to make her grocery list for
tomorrow's shop, and maybe call Norma to brainstorm some ideas
for the women's ministry.

As Eddie Murphy's "donkey voice" floated up from the basement family room, Michelle pulled out the corn popper and poured
in a little oil. A movie night needed popcorn. As the kernels started
to pop, a wave of gratefulness swept over her. At least the kids
were under her roof, not hanging out on the street somewhere . . .

*Like Jeffrey Coleman had been.* Would Bridges get to the preteen
before the street life in that neighborhood swallowed him up? Her
stomach churned. *Let it go, Michelle,* she told herself. *You can't carry
every situation home with you. Take the weekend off.*

But halfway through popping the corn, she realized the churn-
ing in her stomach was more than an emotional reaction to client
concerns. The pizza obviously was not agreeing with her. Hurriedly finishing the popcorn, she headed for the bathroom, feeling as if
she might throw up . . . but didn't. She just sat on the toilet, head
down, hoping the feeling of nausea would pass.

Finally she took some Pepto-Bismol, went back to the kitchen
and turned the gas on under the teakettle to make some peppermint tea. Jared's mother had sworn by peppermint tea for stomach
upsets when she lived with them.

"Destin?" she called down the stairs. "Destin! Come get the
popcorn!" No response. She finally had to go downstairs with the
popcorn, picked up the remote, and paused the movie. "Kids, I'm

not feeling so good, don't think the pizza agreed with me. Does anyone else have an upset stomach?"

"We're *fine*, Mom. Can we—"

"Okay, good. But I'm going to lie down, so when the movie's done, I want DaShawn to go right home, okay? Everybody . . . okay?"

Heads nodded, then once more eyes and ears were glued to the movie.

Wearily, Michelle pulled herself up the stairs, made the peppermint tea, and headed for the bedroom. She'd just have to make the grocery list tomorrow when she got home from Lifeline. Oh, wait—she'd made an appointment for Ray to meet with Jeffrey and his mother at two. That meant grocery shopping late on Saturday afternoon.

She hated shopping late on Saturday.

Not bothering to brush her teeth or wrap her hair, Michelle crawled into bed, still feeling like she wanted to throw up. *Ugh.* The weekend had barely started and already she felt ground up and spit out.

# Chapter 10

MICHELLE WOKE EARLY—not surprising since she'd been in bed since eight thirty last night. She'd awakened briefly when Jared got home, told him she had an upset stomach, and asked him to supervise bedtime. He got her some more Pepto-Bismol . . . and that's the last she remembered until she awoke at ten to six.

She rolled out of bed, pulled on her robe and slippers, and padded out to the living room. The house was blessedly quiet. She wasn't sure if Jared had set his alarm, but he said he had to be at the church by eight thirty. If he wasn't up by seven, she'd wake him. Until then . . .

She pulled aside the front window curtains to check the weather. Beyond the porch a thick morning fog wrapped the neighborhood like a scene from *Sherlock Holmes*. Hopefully it would burn off soon. But a figure emerged through the fog . . . no, two figures, a man and a dog. Could be Harry Bentley walking his black Lab—some kind of police dog, if she remembered correctly. Estelle's husband did security for Amtrak and the kids said he had a dog kennel in the back of the SUV he drove to work, though it wasn't obvious through the tinted windows of the Dodge Durango.

Putting coffee on to drip, Michelle perched on a stool at the counter separating the compact kitchen from the dining area and read a few psalms from her Bible—something she rarely had time to do most mornings. A verse in Psalm 5 caught her eye and she read it aloud softly. "Let all who take refuge in you be glad; let them ever sing for joy. Spread your protection over them, that those who love your name may rejoice in you . . ."

*Refuge* . . . The word kind of summed up why she worked as a social worker for Bridges Family Services, and why she volunteered at Lifeline Care Center. *Providing a safe place for families and women in crisis—offering whatever protection she could.* But of course this verse was talking about finding refuge in God . . . Did she think of her relationship with God that way? A place of refuge for herself? Most of the time she felt as if she was always running, trying to juggle home and kids and church and work and clients. Wasn't too often that she just "sang for joy" either—unless it was Sunday morning and she let the worship carry her away.

The coffeepot dinged, signaling it was done. She poured a fragrant cup and glanced at the clock. Six thirty . . . the household would be stirring in half an hour. But maybe she had time to get her grocery list together so she could shop on her way home from her appointment with the Lewis-Coleman family this afternoon.

The list was almost done when Jared wandered into the kitchen in bare feet, sweatpants and T-shirt, scratching his head sleepily. "Hey, hon." He kissed the back of her neck and then poured himself a cup of coffee. "You feeling any better this morning?"

"Mm-hm. Should've stuck with the veggie pizza last night. I had a slice of the pepperoni too, don't think it agreed with me. But I'm okay now. The extra sleep did me good, but I could use another shot of that coffee." She held out her cup and Jared refilled it. "So you're taking Tavis with you to the workday, and Destin's taking the bus to the track meet. That leaves Tabby . . . don't really like to leave her home alone all day. Any chance you could take her with you to the workday too?"

Jared frowned and glanced at the clock. "Guess so. As long as she knows she needs to be a help, not a hindrance. I can't be supervising kids and the work crew at the same time. We should've told her last night though, let her get used to the idea."

"Sorry about that. Wasn't thinking too good last night . . ." Pushing the grocery list aside, she slid off the stool. "Guess I better go wake her up, let her get used to the idea now. I'll make pancakes when I get back—oh! Did you look at your work schedule for Memorial Day weekend?"

"Yeah, I did. Don't have the holiday off, but it's my usual Monday schedule—don't have to be at work till two, so guess we could do something, as long as I'm back in time."

"Oh, Jared! That's great." Michelle gave her husband a happy hug. "Let's talk about it tonight, ask the kids what they'd like to do. But we better get moving now if you and the twins need to be at the church by eight thirty." And get herself to Lifeline by nine. She zipped toward Tabby's room, suddenly feeling energetic.

"Just can't spend a lot of money!" he called after her. "We're out Destin's basketball camp fee until he pays us back—and whatever we work out for the twins this summer is gonna take some bucks too."

"I'll remember!" she called back. There were a lot of things they could do that didn't cost very much . . . she hoped.

Michelle pulled Jared's Altima into the parking lot of the Lifeline Care Center a little before nine. They'd traded cars so that Jared could use the minivan in case he needed to haul more supplies—or people—for the workday at Northside. Nice little car, the Altima—a two-door coupe, dark slate metallic on the outside, charcoal black on the inside. Clean as a whistle, but that was Jared. Definitely a Type A. Had to be, she guessed, to do his kind of job, all senses on alert watching blips on a screen that represented hundreds of lives in each plane, getting each blip in and out of O'Hare safely.

She sailed through the glass doors into the cozy lobby of Lifeline. The crisis pregnancy center had started in a church basement, then moved several times before a yearly fundraiser enabled them to purchase their current space in the Humboldt Park neighborhood and support two staff persons and a legion of volunteers. The new center not only offered pregnancy testing and counseling, but housed a Wee Welcome Shop with new and gently used maternity clothes, baby clothes, cribs and car seats. The most recent addition was post-abortion support and healing—which was Michelle's passion.

In her job as a caseworker for Bridges, she'd encountered too many women who'd had an abortion and were then ignored once their "crisis pregnancy" was ended. But many suffered from post-abortion syndrome or simply needed nonjudgmental aftercare.

She'd advocated that Lifeline offer a post-abortion support group—called Hope and Healing—and offered her services free of charge.

"'Morning, Bernice! Do I have any new appointments this morning besides the support group?"

"'Morning yourself, Michelle. What you all perky for today?" The volunteer receptionist was in her fifties, a grandmother six times over, a tad on the plumpish side, and fairly light-skinned for an African American.

Michelle laughed. "We're going away for the holiday next weekend—so don't make any new appointments for me, okay? The Hope and Healing group already agreed not to meet on the holiday weekend."

"Lucky you." Bernice was running her finger down an appointment book. "Nothing till your support group at ten—but you have a new client, Hannah West, at eleven. I blocked out an hour for her since it's her first session."

"Thanks, Bernice. Perfect. I have another favor to ask . . . do we have a lot of brochures in stock?" She briefly explained about her neighbor who did concerts for young people and wanted the brochures to be available. "They're willing to purchase them, but she's got a couple concerts next weekend."

Bernice shrugged as the telephone rang. "Check the cabinets just outside the Wee Welcome Shop . . . Hello? Lifeline Care Center. May I help you?"

Michelle poked her head into Margie Sutton's office to say she wouldn't be in next weekend, but the director's office was empty so she left a note on her desk. Voices and laughter spilled into the hallway from the large, brightly painted room housing the Wee Welcome Shop, and as she passed she waved at the handful of high school volunteers and their youth group leader who'd come in early to sort and fold donations. Opening the first cabinet lining the hallway, she was grateful to see large stacks of brochures on the shelves. Checking the list Grace's assistant had given her, she grabbed packets containing fifty of the four brochures Lifeline kept on hand until she had 250 of each. Seemed like a *lot* of brochures—but then, Samantha had said Grace had a couple of concerts

Memorial Day weekend, plus a few other concerts before her tour next month. If they were going to use so many, maybe they ought to order them directly instead of through Lifeline . . . not that she minded helping out, but still.

Making a note of how many she'd taken, she asked Bernice to figure the cost and make an invoice she could give to Grace. And by the time the five young women in the support group showed up, a few others were getting pregnancy tests, two very pregnant young women were browsing in the Wee Welcome Shop, and two of the counseling rooms had closed doors.

Michelle met her group at the door of one of the larger rooms, giving each one a warm hug before they settled into the circle of comfy chairs. She let them chat with each other a few moments, knowing the group had bonded pretty tight during the six sessions they'd spent together so far. After an opening prayer, she asked, "How many of you wrote letters this week?" Four of the five girls raised their hands. Michelle smiled. "Remember, these letters aren't necessarily for mailing—you can decide what to do with them later."

"Well, I couldn't mail mine anyway." Ellie Baker, a dental technician, pulled a folded sheet of paper from her purse. "'Cause I wrote to my baby."

Murmurs and sad smiles went around the circle.

"Would you like to read it to us?" Michelle asked gently.

Ellie shook her head shyly. "It's just between me and Baby. But I asked forgiveness for not having the courage to bring her into the world . . . or him. I didn't know the sex, it was too early in the pregnancy. But it felt more personal to use 'her.' I imagined my little girl in the arms of Jesus, and they both forgave me." Ellie's eyes teared up and Michelle passed her the box of tissues. Maria Gonzales, the girl sitting next to her, scooted her chair closer and put an arm around her shoulders.

"Hang onto that letter," Michelle encouraged. "You might want to use it at our memorial service at the end of our sessions." She looked around. "Anyone else want to share their letter?"

Maria had written a letter to her boyfriend, who'd threatened to disappear if she had the baby—and then disappeared anyway after her abortion. Denise Martin, who'd had an abortion fifteen years ago as a teenager, wrote a letter to her former church, wishing they had modeled Christ's forgiveness and restoration toward people like her who'd messed up. "I couldn't bear the rejection and gossip that got dumped on anyone who made a mistake," she wrote. "A secret abortion seemed the only way to remain in good standing."

LaVeta Gates addressed her letter "to other young women," encouraging them that they weren't alone, that there were people like the ones at Lifeline Care Center who would walk through a crisis pregnancy with them—before and after the baby was born.

"What about you, Linda?" Michelle asked the last young woman.

Linda Chen, a twenty-something from Taiwan, just shook her head. "It is too hard. I am still too much angry—but I don't know who I'm angry at. Myself, I guess. It is all my fault. If my parents knew . . ." More tears, more tissues.

Several of the girls gathered around and prayed for Linda. Lifeline didn't require that women had to be Christians to be in the group, but all knew that LCC was a Christian ministry and Michelle had told them the post-abortion support group would use Scripture and talk about God. If they were okay with that, they were welcome to participate. She'd seen most of them begin or renew seeds of faith as they experienced the love of God.

But not all. Linda couldn't seem to get beyond anger and self-hatred.

Before the young women left, Michelle told them to begin thinking of some creative expression they could present at a memorial service for their aborted babies in a few weeks. "Could be a poem, something you make, some kind of memorial or remembrance . . . just be thinking about it. If you get an idea, you can get started."

Michelle felt wrung out after the girls left. She wished she could just go home, but Bernice poked her head in the door and said, "Your appointment is here."

Michelle met her new client at the front desk. A plain girl, mousy-colored hair long and shapeless, black skirt, socks with sandals, glasses. Looked as if she grew up in a small town and hadn't adjusted to urban life. "Hannah? I'm Michelle Jasper. I'm so glad to meet you. Let's go somewhere where we can talk privately, okay?"

She ushered the girl—maybe nineteen? twenty?—to one of the smaller rooms. Today what she needed to do was just listen to Hannah's story . . . but she was afraid she already knew the gist of it. Sheltered girl moves to the city, gets swept off her feet by some cad who sweet-talks her into bed because she's never had a boyfriend, no guy has ever paid attention to her, and she believes him when he says she's so special, he loves her, and if she loves *him* she'll "prove it." Gets pregnant, then gets an abortion because she can't face her family. Now overcome by guilt.

Michelle's heart melted as she sat down across from the nervous young woman. *No son of mine will ever,* ever *treat a woman that way— black* or *white!* Come to think of it, Tavis and Tabitha were thirteen now. High time for the mother-daughter, father-son talks. Maybe past time. And wouldn't hurt to have "the talk" with Destin again too.

But Hannah's story was worse than she thought.

# Chapter 11

SLAMMING THE CAR DOOR AS SHE GOT IN, Michelle headed for the nearest fast-food drive-through. She'd driven several blocks before realizing her foot was heavy on the gas. Better slow down or she'd end up with another ticket—wouldn't that be a fine mess. She turned in at the first Golden Arches she saw, even though she didn't feel hungry. In fact, her stomach was in knots after listening to Hannah's story, but she probably ought to eat something. It'd be another couple of hours before she got home.

Waiting for her grilled chicken sandwich and mango smoothie at the drive-through window, Michelle hit the steering wheel with her fist. People like Hannah's so-called uncle—Hannah's mother's cousin to be exact—should be locked up for life . . . or branded with a big R on the forehead.

*R for Rapist.*

Hannah had twisted a tissue into a hundred pieces as her story came out bit by bit. "Uncle Ned" had always teased Hannah that she was his favorite, which gradually became more sexual. He'd molested Hannah from age ten on and finally raped her at fifteen. Pregnant and horrified, she'd had a secret abortion. The family was very religious and would never believe sweet Uncle Ned could do such a thing. None of her family knew to this day what had happened.

That was five years ago. Hannah's grades went down, she barely graduated high school. Didn't even apply for college. Her parents threw up their hands. She was such a disappointment to them. Hannah finally moved out, moved away from the small Indiana town where she'd grown up, got a job as a waitress in Chicago. But she felt frozen. Afraid. Had a hard time making friends. Saw the Lifeline Care Center ad on a bus, the one that said, "There's hope after abortion . . ."

*O God, that girl needs your healing in a big way, and I hardly know how to—*

"Here ya go, miss." The window clerk with the microphone clamped on his head handed her a paper bag and the smoothie, which Michelle stuck in a cup holder. Maybe she'd eat it later. Should she go home? No, she'd just have to turn around and drive back to the Near West Side for her two o'clock meeting with Jeffrey and his mom. She'd find a parking space on their block where she could sit and make some phone calls. Maybe Norma would be home and they could talk about women's ministry.

But first she ought to check in with Jared. He didn't pick up the first time, so she tapped his number again. This time he answered. "Michelle?" She could hear lots of commotion in the background. "Everything okay?"

"Yes, yes, I'm fine. Just wanted to know if you and the twins got to see Destin run at the meet."

"Yeah, yeah. He called about eleven thirty, said his event would start about twelve. We got here just as he was lining up. He did real good, came in fourth out of ten schools. He won't go to state, but . . . maybe that's just as well."

"Fourth? That's amazing for the 800 meter! So glad you and the twins were there to see him run."

"His coach has him down for the 4-by-2 relay too, but that's not for another hour. I really can't stay that long, so I'm getting ready to leave, soon as the kids get back here with some hot dogs and pop . . . oh, here they are. Gotta go. You good?"

*Not really.* But now wasn't the time to talk about her new client at Lifeline. "I'll see you at home. What time do you think the workday will be over?"

"By suppertime, hopefully. But who knows. I'll call you."

Michelle shut her phone and looked at her watch. One thirty . . . half an hour to go. Might as well eat her lunch. She sucked on the smoothie, then opened the bag and took out the chicken sandwich. But after a few bites, she wrapped it up again. Maybe she'd be hungry after her meeting.

The Altima wasn't as convenient for loading and unloading groceries as the minivan, but a couple more trips ought to do it. Michelle hefted a twelve-pack of Dr. Pepper from the front seat, stuck it under one arm, hooked a few plastic grocery bags with her other hand, and headed into the house.

At least the meeting with Jeffrey Coleman and Ray Stevens had gone well. In fact, the Family Friend volunteer had agreed to come over tonight and tomorrow night to "hang out" with Jeffrey while his mom went to work. *Ha.* They'd all avoided the word *babysit* like the plague. She still wanted to meet Brianna's sister upstairs to see about covering other times, but they'd made progress.

When she came back out for the last of the groceries she heard, "Hellooo, Sister Michelle!" Estelle Bentley was waving at her from her front steps across the street. "Where are those strapping young men you're raising? They should be carrying those groceries for you!"

"Not home right now!" she called back, and grabbed the last three plastic grocery bags from the trunk.

"Come join us!" Estelle beckoned again. "I've got iced tea!"

*"Us,"* Michelle realized, was Mrs. Krakowski, sitting in a folding lawn chair on the tiny front stoop, and Estelle, who was sitting on the top step leaning against the white iron grillwork of the railing.

Iced tea sounded good. The day had turned fairly warm, somewhere in the low seventies. But she needed to get the frozen stuff put away. "Give me a few minutes!"

Five minutes later she walked across the street and down the sidewalk to the two-flat and greeted the two women. "Sit! Sit!" Estelle said, pouring a large tumbler of iced tea from a picnic jug and handing it to her.

Michelle sank down on the steps against the other railing and took a good drink. "Mmm. Just sweet enough. Thanks."

"Everything all right at your house? DaShawn was lookin' for Tavis, kept ringin' your doorbell, but came back sayin' nobody's home."

Michelle rolled her eyes. "Oh, it's one of those Saturdays. Destin had a track meet at Lane Tech. Jared took the twins to a workday at the church. And I volunteer at Lifeline Care Center most Saturday mornings. Also had a client I had to see this afternoon, which made me late getting to the grocery store—and you know what crowds are like this time of day. But . . . hopefully that's it. I'm done in."

"Well, take a load off. It's such a pleasant day, I persuaded Miss Mattie here to come sit outside with me—right, Miss Mattie?" Estelle looked up at the elderly woman, and then chuckled softly. Michelle followed her gaze and smiled too. "Miss Mattie" had nodded off, her chin on her chest.

They sat quietly on the stoop for a few minutes—the first time all day Michelle had slowed down. Sparrows and finches flitted between trees, chirping and trilling. Any traffic noise on the main streets—Ridge Avenue to the east, Touhy to the south—sounded muted and far away. A slight breeze caressed her skin, and stray clouds floated lazily overhead. Now if they had a porch swing, she could do this more often, invite Estelle to come sit on *her* porch . . .

"So tell me about Lifeline." Estelle interrupted her daydream. "That's the crisis pregnancy center where you volunteer, right?"

Michelle nodded. "Though some women come in who've had abortions. That's what I do, facilitate a post-abortion support group. Usually a nine-week process. Some of the stories are heartbreaking . . . like a girl I met today." She cast a quick glance at the dozing Mrs. K. Wasn't sure she should say more around the old lady.

"I can only imagine." Estelle heaved a big sigh. "Sure wish some of the girls who end up at Manna House would make use of those resources. Mercy me, some of them havin' babies left an' right, most of 'em with different daddies. Then they end up homeless with the kids in foster care or farmed out to Grandma or Auntie . . . or they're using abortion as birth control, Lord help us. Don't get me wrong. All kinds of reasons people end up homeless, some through no fault of their own." She chuckled. "I was homeless once myself, don't ya know. Still, we got a couple girls now—"

Estelle suddenly slapped her knee and laughed, which made Mattie Krakowski jump. "What?" she mumbled.

Estelle didn't seem to notice. "Sister Michelle, there you sit like God just dropped you into my lap, tellin' me you volunteer at Lifeline. An' we have girls who need the kind of resources Lifeline offers. It's not enough to hand them a brochure. What I'm thinkin' is . . . would you be willin' to come talk to our young ladies sometime? Sooner the better, far as I'm concerned."

"Well, I . . ." She was already so busy. Should she add something else? Yet letting homeless women at the shelter know they have positive, life-affirming options in a crisis pregnancy fit hand-in-glove with the kind of work she did every day. "Let me think about it, Estelle. We're going away for Memorial Day weekend, but maybe after that I could find a time."

By the time Jared and the kids arrived home for supper, Michelle had laid out all the makings for tacos. Supper felt a little crazy with everyone reaching for favorite ingredients and talking all at once. Destin crowed about the track meet, excited that Lane Tech had qualified to go to state finals, and Jared ticked off all the work that got done that day at Northside Baptist. "Gotta say Tavis and Tabby did their share too."

"Yeah," Tabby moaned, mouth full of taco, "'cept when Deacon Jones made me take the little kids into one of the Sunday school rooms and play games with them. Woulda rather helped paint or somethin'."

"Still, that was a *big* help, young lady. The Winthrop kids were tearing around with no supervision. Next time we'll have to provide more childcare—"

"Or just tell people to leave the little kids at home!" Tabby pouted.

"Well, I'm proud of all of you," Michelle said, uncovering the lemon meringue pie she'd picked up at Baker's Square—Jared's favorite. "The good news is, *next* weekend is Memorial Day weekend and your dad and I agree we should do something as a family. So . . . how about driving to Fort Wayne to visit Bibi and Babu for the holiday? We haven't been there for a while, but I seem to remember somebody—somebod*ies*, I mean—begging to try out that laser tag place, Lazer X or something, last time we visited your grandparents."

The table erupted in a three-way chorus of cheers and "Awriiight!" and Tabby bounced in her chair. "An' Bibi told *me* that next time we came, she'd take us to that chocolate factory place, 'cause they give you free chocolate if you take a tour."

Michelle eyed Jared to see if he approved. He ought to, since going to her parents meant free lodging and meals—which meant they could spend some money on activities for the kids. He shrugged and nodded. "Sounds fine to me. Just so everybody knows we gotta be back on Monday in time for me to get to work by two. I don't actually have the holiday off."

So it was settled. As soon as she called her parents and asked *them* if it was okay.

Michelle never did get a chance to call Norma and brainstorm ideas for the women's ministry summer events, and found herself dreading their committee meeting after worship the next morning. She was falling down on the job. She should have a recommendation to present to the committee and she didn't.

"Aw, Mom, you don't have a meeting after church today too!" Destin complained. "Church was already longer than usual an' I'm hungry!"

*True.* Today was Pentecost Sunday, fifty days after Easter—which she'd totally forgotten—and besides several special selections by the choir, receiving some new members into the church, and a report on the workday yesterday by the deacons, Pastor Q had preached longer than usual about the power of the Holy Spirit available to us. Michelle had actually taken notes about the ways that power has been used and abused and—for many Christians—simply ignored or explained away.

Maybe the women's ministry should do a study on the Holy Spirit this summer.

"Sorry, Destin. I'll try to keep it short." She hurried away.

"Sister Michelle!" Shareese Watson caught her at the door to the lounge where they met. "Did you get my voicemail Friday? I really wanted to talk to you before today, because I have a great idea—"

Michelle held up a hand. "I'm sorry, Shareese. I did see that you called, but it's been a really hectic weekend. Is this about the book club idea? Because I don't think that's going to work, not if it means adding another night to everyone's week." There. She'd said it.

Shareese nodded eagerly. "I know. That's why I called. Because my girlfriend told me about this really great video series they're doing at her church about listening when God speaks, something like that. Here, she gave me this." The young woman dug in her big bag and pulled out a flyer. "It's by Tony Evans's daughter—my girlfriend says she's really good. It's based on a book she's written, but I don't think everybody has to buy the book in order to do the video series. That's why I thought it might work for our monthly women's meetings."

Michelle took the flyer. *Discerning the Voice of God—Leader Kit.* Contained DVDs for seven group sessions, plus discussion questions and interactive exercises. Michelle nodded slowly. "Well, it does look interesting. But not sure we're looking for something that would go for seven months."

Shareese shrugged. "Well, maybe we could just do the first three sessions of the study during the summer—that would take care of June, July, and August. In the fall we could decide if we wanted to continue or do something else. So . . . what do you think?"

The others were arriving. "Well, I haven't looked at the material but . . ." Frankly, it was the only solid idea they had in hand. Maybe they should look into it.

The moment Shareese proposed the video series, the committee pounced on it. "Love it!" "Oh, that Priscilla Shirer—she's great!" "If we do a series, we won't have to come up with something new every month." And . . . "Having to meet every Sunday after church is a pain in the you-know-what. Let's do it and be done. I'm hungry." Sister Paulette was on her feet, ready to go out the door.

"Wait just a moment." Michelle felt she needed to regain some control of the process. "We haven't decided to *do* it yet. We're just deciding to look into it." Shareese's enthusiasm was contagious, but there was still a proper order to making decisions. "Norma, would you be willing to do some research, maybe check out a few churches who've used this series and how it worked for them?" She could count on Norma to have a level head. "Don't mean to rush you, but can you get back to us by next Sunday? That still only gives us two weeks to order the materials and advertise the event here at Northside."

Fifteen minutes and they were done. That part was nice. Until Michelle remembered that she'd be gone with the family next Sunday. *Ouch.* Well, she'd stay in touch with Norma and communicate to the committee by e-mail if necessary.

Jared and the kids were ready to go and, as usual, they headed for Old Country Buffet for their Sunday lunch. The balmy May temperatures had suddenly soared into the high eighties and they were all glad to get into the air-conditioned restaurant. But Jared seemed preoccupied and didn't head back to the buffet stations as he usually did when the three kids scurried back for seconds

"Honey, everything okay?"

He nodded. "Yeah, just . . . Pastor Q told me his brother-in-law passed yesterday. Not Donna's brother, but her sister's husband. Cancer, I think."

"Oh. I'm so sorry. They should've said something from the pulpit."

He shrugged. "They just found out this morning. Guess they're still getting used to the news. But . . ." The twins and Destin came back just then, comparing plates and noisily slurping their refills on lemonade and soft drinks. "Never mind," Jared finished. "I'll fill you in later."

As they pulled up in front of the house forty-five minutes later, Jared put a hand on her arm as the kids clambered out of the minivan and headed for the house. "Wait," he said. "I need to tell you something."

Michelle raised an eyebrow and waited.

"Pastor Q said their brother-in-law's funeral is next weekend down in Rantoul. They're going of course and he, uh, asked if I would bring the message next Sunday."

She stared at him. "*Next* Sunday? Jared! That's Memorial Day weekend. You told him we're going to be gone, didn't you?"

He shook his head. "I . . . didn't. I mean, it's a family emergency for them, seemed like I ought to support our pastor by covering for him."

For a moment, Michelle was so steamed she didn't trust herself to speak. But then the words tumbled out. "So. Pastor Q and the church come before your family, is that it?" Without waiting for a reply, she opened the car door and slammed it shut behind her as she stormed up the walk to the house.

# Chapter 12

U NBELIEVABLE! HOW *COULD* HE?

Michelle marched straight to their bedroom and banged the door shut. The kids were going to be so disappointed! *She* was disappointed. She'd actually thought they were going to pull off a short family vacation. *Huh!* Should've known better. If it wasn't Jared's ATC schedule at O'Hare, it was something at Northside Baptist. The tail wagging the dog as far as she was concerned.

She had just stepped out of her Sunday dress and kicked off her heels when the bedroom door opened and Jared came in. Turning her back, she pulled on a pair of khaki capris and a lightweight cotton blouse.

"Michelle? Look, honey, let me finish, okay? I want to explain."

A few choice retorts leaped to her tongue but she kept her mouth shut and strapped on her good walking sandals. It was hot out there, but she needed to go for a walk. Something. Anything. Just get out of the house.

"I understand you're upset. But this doesn't mean you and the kids shouldn't go. I'm really sorry this happened, but—"

"Fine. We'll go without you." Her words were clipped. "I don't plan to disappoint the kids just because you don't know how to say no."

Jared peeled off his tie. "It's not that. I . . . I've actually been praying for a chance to bring the Word some Sunday, feeling a little limited in my role as deacon. I think I have more to offer the church, but I didn't want to push myself—you know, don't think more of myself than I ought to think, like that verse says. And then, God just drops the opportunity in my lap! It seemed like a God-thing! Honestly, Michelle, it seemed like I was supposed to say yes."

Michelle buckled the last sandal. Oh great. Now Jared was playing the "God card." How could she fight against "God told me to"?

She paused . . . and then sighed and flopped down into the chair by the window overlooking their backyard. Such as it was. Hardly bigger than a postage stamp, especially since their garage took up part of it. Flowers. They needed some flowers both front and back to spruce things up. She should've asked for a hanging basket for the front porch for Mother's Day instead of the cut flowers that were gone by midweek.

They were both quiet for several minutes as Jared finished changing into a pair of cargo shorts and a Bulls T-shirt. Her anger was gradually dissipating. She didn't want to fight with Jared. She knew he was sincere. Serving God in the church was deep in his heart. "It's just so disappointing!" she blurted.

"I know." He sat on the edge of the bed nearest her.

"Can't you come for part of the time at least? If we go down on Friday, you could come back Saturday night. We'd have one day together at least."

He shook his head. "Honey, you know what traffic is like Friday night—*especially* on holiday weekends. A madhouse! That's why we usually drive to your folks' early Saturday morning. I'd no sooner get there than I'd have to turn around and come back. Though that's not the only reason. I work all week . . . so I know I'm going to need Saturday to prepare a sermon. I don't do this every week, you know."

Her eyes teared up, and she had to reach for a tissue and blow her nose. "Well, you're going to have to be the one to tell the kids. I don't want to."

"Okay." Jared took off his wire rims and cleaned the lenses. "Actually, I've been trying to think of a way to make it up to the kids, and remembered the guy I met at the neighborhood thing for Mrs. Krakowski—Singer . . . Greg Singer, I think. They live next to the corner house at the end of the block. He works for Powersports, puts on big sport vehicle expos. Anyway, he practically offered Destin and me a ride on a cigarette boat—"

"A what?"

"Ha, ha. A cigarette boat, one of those really fast powerboats you sometimes see in the lake. Anyway, his company's putting on a boat show down at Burnham Harbor June 3 through 6, I think he said. Thought maybe I'd walk down to his house, tell him I'm interested. Destin seemed excited about going, and I'm sure Tavis would too. Maybe even Tabby. It might be something special I could do with the kids to make up for this weekend."

"I guess." Michelle frowned thoughtfully. "I met his wife that night—her name's Nicole. She's a stay-at-home mom who homeschools their two kids. Been thinking I should try to get to know her a little. She was all dolled up as if the little neighborhood event was a major outing. Must be kind of lonely staying at home with her kids all the time since everyone else in the neighborhood goes to work or school." Well, maybe not everyone. She wasn't sure about Rebecca Horowitz, the Jewish mom she'd talked to last week. Rebecca had young kids, even a baby. Maybe she was an at-home mom too.

Jared looked hopeful. "Would you like to walk down to the Singers' with me? Might be nice for both of us to show up." He looked sheepish. "Actually, that would make it more of a social visit, instead of just me showing up with my hand out for a free boat ride."

"Uh huh. So now you want me to help bail you out of bailing on us this weekend? Shame on you, Jared Jasper." But she allowed a small smile to tip the corners of her mouth.

He reached out with one hand and pulled her out of the chair onto the bed, making her shriek. "That, or we could forget the Singers and generate some hanky-panky right here in the bedroom."

"Oh you!" Michelle wiggled out of his grasp. She wasn't ready to go from Angry Wife to Lover Girl *that* fast. "Give me five minutes to repair my face and I'll walk down to the Singers with you."

It felt good to get out in the fresh air, even if the temperature had hiked up just shy of ninety degrees. "Typical Chicago weather," Jared groused as he and Michelle walked toward the Singers' house. "First it's winter, then it skips over spring and suddenly it's summer. It's not even Memorial Day yet!"

"At least the humidity isn't too bad . . . oh shoot!" Michelle slapped her forehead.

"What?"

She pointed at Grace Meredith's house as they passed. "Grace ordered a whole bunch of brochures from Lifeline for her concerts next weekend, and I totally forgot to give them to her. They're still in the trunk of your car. Help me remember to get them out when we get back, okay?"

Jared grunted. But he'd probably forget. What she should have done was write it down on her to-do list.

The next yellow brick bungalow they passed had a large, curved bay window that took up three-quarters of the front of the house. Lacy curtains peeked through its four tall windows, which were arched at the top. The mixed couple who lived there—he was white, she was black—rarely seemed to be home, even on weekends, and when Michelle did see them coming and going, both of them were always dressed in suits or other office attire. Professional types. "DINKS"—Double-Income-No-Kids. Eyeing the lacy curtains, she was sure the house must be decorated to the nines.

A couple of men were sitting on the steps of 7323–7325, the only other two-flat on the block besides the Bentleys'. "Hola!" One of the men waved at them. Michelle and Jared waved back. The family on the first floor had a couple of cute kids she saw from time to time, but they were much younger than the twins. She was pretty sure the name was Alvarez—at least they'd gotten mail with that name and address by mistake from time to time, and she'd had to put it in their mailbox.

They turned in at the next-to-last house before the corner. This was a more typical brick bungalow, considered one and a half stories, probably a remodeled attic because a café curtain covered the single window under the pitched roof. Walking up onto the small porch, Jared rang the doorbell.

A pale woman with longish blonde hair opened the door. "Oh! Uh, hello."

"Nicole?" Michelle smiled. "We met last weekend when Mrs. Krakowski came back to the neighborhood."

"I remember . . . Michelle Jasper, right?"

"And I'm Jared." Jared held out his hand. Nicole shook it tentatively. "Is your husband home? I actually came down to see him, and my wife wanted to come along to say hi."

*Well,* Michelle thought, *as good an excuse as any.*

Nicole Singer opened the door a bit wider. "You want to come in?"

Stepping into a foyer of sorts, Michelle took in the layout at a glance—living room off to the right side, dining room off to the left and a glimpse of the kitchen beyond that in back. Directly in front of them were stairs going up to the floor above, and beside it a hallway leading to, she supposed, one or more bedrooms and a bath.

"Greg?" Nicole stepped to the living room archway. "Someone to see you." She beckoned at Jared. "He's in here." But instead of going into the living room with them, the woman turned to Michelle and asked, "Would you like some iced tea?" Without waiting for an answer, Nicole headed the other way through the dining room. Leading the way into the kitchen, she waved at a little breakfast nook along the back wall with a window overlooking the backyard. "Have a seat. The tea's unsweetened, but you can add sweetener if you like."

*Never the same,* Michelle thought, scooting into the breakfast booth, but she smiled. "That'll be fine."

Michelle heard feet pounding down the uncarpeted stairs, and the next moment two blonde tornados swept into the kitchen. "Who's talking to Daddy?—Oh." The girl and boy—about eight and six—stopped and stared at Michelle.

She smiled at them. "Hi. I'm Mrs. Jasper. We live down the street, right next to the big house at the dead end."

"You live next to Mr. Paddock?"

Michelle was surprised they knew the man's name. "That's right. On this side of the street."

"Danny and his two daddies live next to Mr. Paddock on the other side of the street," the boy piped up. "But we're not s'posed to talk about that."

Nicole seemed uncomfortable. "Kids. They seem to know everybody."

The two children clambered onto the breakfast nook bench across from Michelle. "Nuh-uh!" The boy shook her head. "We didn't know Mr. Paddock before, but now we do 'cause he gave us a ride in his big limo. It has a TV!"

"Yeah. An' a refrigerator and stuff to drink!" his sister chimed in.

"All right kids, that's enough." Nicole handed them two plastic kid glasses with straws sticking out of the snap-on covers. "Why don't you take your iced tea into the backyard?"

"Aw, we wanna stay here."

"Out. Now."

The two kids slunk out the back door. Nicole smiled apologetically as she brought two glasses of iced tea to the nook and pushed the sugar bowl toward Michelle. "I'm with the kids 24/7, so they think they belong in the middle of every conversation. But I don't often get to visit with another adult."

Michelle tried not to show her surprise. The woman really did seem lonely. "I didn't catch their names."

"Oh. Sorry. Becky is our oldest, she's eight, and Nathan is six. I homeschool them. We have a school area set up in the basement. Been doing it now for four years, ever since Becky was in kindergarten."

"Sounds like a big commitment. How did you and your husband decide to homeschool?" Michelle stirred two heaping teaspoons of sugar into her tea, studying her hostess as the woman chatted. Nicole was a natural blonde as far as she could tell, with blue-grey eyes and pleasant features. She carried a few extra pounds—Michelle had gained a few herself after three kids—but was still very attractive.

"—What about you? What do you do?" Nicole was asking.

Michelle told her a little bit about Bridges and Lifeline. "Together they keep me so busy, I hardly know if I'm coming or going. At least Sunday's a day of rest. Or supposed to be."

"Your husband?"

"Jared? His schedule is even nuttier than mine. He works at O'Hare Airport as an air traffic controller. Crazy hours. His shift changes every two days. What about your husband? Jared says Greg puts on these sport expos or something like that."

"Did."

Michelle wasn't sure she heard right. "Did?"

"He *did* work for Powersports Expos. But he, uh . . ." Nicole picked at a stray spot of food stuck to the nook table. "Greg says he wants to, um, move on, explore some new opportunities."

"Oh. That's . . . interesting." Michelle wasn't sure how to respond. Was this good news? Or bad news? Didn't sound like he had anything in place.

She was just about to ask what kind of opportunities Greg was exploring when she heard Jared calling from the foyer. "Michelle? You ready to go?"

"Coming!" She slid out of the breakfast nook bench, but turned back to Nicole. "Making a job change can be challenging, I'm sure. A brave thing to do—maybe scary too. I'll be praying for you both."

Nicole nodded but didn't follow her out to the foyer.

Greg Singer showed them to the door. "Thanks for stopping by, Jasper. Sorry I can't get you those tickets." The two men shook hands. Greg was several inches shorter than Jared, clean-shaven, face slightly tan, hazel eyes and brown wavy hair, nice-looking. Still in dress slacks and an open-necked, short-sleeved shirt.

"Not a problem. Best wishes on your new venture."

The door closed behind them.

Michelle waited until they got out to the sidewalk. "So, no tickets. Guess he told you about the job."

"Uh-huh. Said it was time for a change. He seemed pretty upbeat about it. But to tell the truth, I can't imagine why a guy would up and make a change like that without something already in his pocket."

"Me either. I mean, his wife is a stay-at-home mom. So it's his income, period."

"Well, Greg seems like an enterprising kind of guy. Hope it works out for them."

Michelle walked silently up Beecham Street beside Jared, lost in her own thoughts. A one-income family with two kids? Giving up a sure thing to try something new? If she was Nicole, she'd be scared spitless.

# Chapter 13

MICHELLE WAS HEADING INTO THE HOUSE when she realized Jared was no longer beside her. He'd stopped by the Altima at the curb and popped the trunk. "Where are you going?"

He eyed her patiently. "Nowhere. You said you wanted the stuff for Grace Meredith that you left in the car."

"Oh, right." She scurried back to the car. "Thanks for remembering," she added, hoping sincerity would cover her first assumption that he was going off somewhere. Guess she was still kind of mad about Memorial Day weekend.

Might as well take them over to Grace's house now, while she was thinking about it. The invoice was in the plastic bag with the brochures, all four sets. "Be back in a sec," she told Jared.

She rang the doorbell at 7333 and the door opened mere seconds later.

"Oh!" Grace seemed surprised. "I thought you were—" She laughed and looked over Michelle's shoulder. "Never mind. Here she is now." Grace waved and Michelle turned to see Estelle Bentley bustling across the street.

"I'm sorry. Looks like I chose a bad time to bring these to you. I can just drop them off." Michelle held out the heavy plastic bag, then stepped aside to make room for Estelle as she came up the steps.

"What's this?" Grace took the bag and peeked inside. "Oh, great! The brochures from Lifeline. Thanks so much!" She looked up. "No, no, it's not a bad time. In fact, it's perfect. Look, Estelle . . ." The young woman reached into the bag and pulled out one of the brochure packets to show their new neighbor. "Michelle brought the brochures I need for my Memorial Day weekend concerts."

Estelle Bentley, clothed in a lightweight caftan with a big swirly purple-and-white print, chuckled. "Just in time to pray over them. Can you stay, Sister Michelle?"

"Stay?"

As Grace stepped back inside, Estelle took Michelle's arm and ushered her into Grace's house. "Mm-hm. Was just comin' over to pray with Sister Grace about her concerts next weekend, and to my way of thinkin', two is good, but three is even better." But she paused before closing the door. "If you can stay, that is."

"Well . . . sure. I guess. Better let the family know where I am." Well, Jared knew, but she'd said she'd "be back in a sec." Pulling her cell phone out of the pocket of her capri pants, she sent a quick text. *Staying to pray. Be back*—she hesitated, then typed—*when we're done.*

Grace had a frosty pitcher of iced tea and two glasses on the coffee table. Disappearing into the kitchen, she came back with a third glass, looking a little sheepish as she poured out the tea. "Okay, Estelle, I tried to make sweet tea the way you make it, but I'm not sure it tastes like yours."

They all laughed and Michelle accepted a glass, even though she'd just had some at the Singers. "Feel like I'm barging in here."

"No, no. I'm glad you came." Grace, dressed in casual white slacks and a sleeveless black tank, curled up with her iced tea in the lone living room chair, leaving the couch for her guests. Her black-and-white kitty wandered into the room and hopped up into Grace's lap. "I know everyone gets busy during the week, so I asked Estelle if she'd come pray with me this afternoon about the upcoming concerts. And having you show up at my door with the brochures at the same time—well, I think Estelle would say—"

"Ain't no such thing as coincidences," Estelle chuckled. "So how can we best pray for you, honey?"

Grace absently stroked the fur of her cat. "Well, safety for travel on a holiday weekend, first of all. I . . . I still haven't flown anywhere since my January tour, and the train to Indianapolis gets in too late at night. So Sam and I are driving Friday, will meet the band there. Then I have two concerts in Louisville the same weekend—well, a Saturday night concert and then Sunday morning worship in the same big church—but that's only a two-hour drive from Indy. Then we'll drive home on Monday, which means we'll be hitting holiday traffic." She made a face. "But my tour in late June starts in Denver, so I need to decide whether to take the train, like I did for the West Coast tour a few weeks ago, or . . . whether I'm brave enough to fly again. Would appreciate prayer for *that*."

Michelle looked from one to the other. Grace was afraid of flying?

Estelle caught her glance. "Grace had an upsetting experience last time she flew." The older woman reached out and squeezed Grace's hand. "But God is healing you in his own good time, isn't he, baby."

Grace nodded, giving Estelle a grateful smile. "I know I can't live in fear. So . . . just keep praying about that, okay? Besides"—the singer reached across the cat for the bag of brochures she'd set on the coffee table—"I like Estelle's idea of praying over these brochures. That God will touch the hearts of young people who pick up one of these after listening to the Just Grace concert, and give them whatever encouragement or courage they need since we don't know each one's story."

"Amen to *that*!" Estelle waved a hand in the air, then raised her eyebrows at Michelle. "And how can we pray for you, sister?"

Michelle was taken off guard for a moment, then blurted, "Well, to be honest, I'm struggling with disappointment right now. We were supposed to go visit my parents in Fort Wayne for the holiday—and then our pastor asked Jared to fill in for him next Sunday because of a family funeral on the weekend." She grimaced. "Maybe I shouldn't say this, but I think my husband should've stood up to the pastor, told him no, his family comes first. I mean, let someone else bring the message!"

"Oh, Michelle. That's a real bummer." Grace looked genuinely distressed. "Can you and your kids still go to your folks?"

Michelle nodded. "We are. It's just . . . it's so hard with our busy work schedules to ever get away or do things as a whole family! I'm having a hard time not being mad at Jared . . ." She stopped. She shouldn't have said that. It was true, but not very loyal to her husband in front of these women. "But he does have his reasons," she added hastily. "I need to respect that."

Estelle patted her knee. "Don't worry, honey. These family tensions are not always right versus wrong. Sometimes it's two good things competin' for the same time an' space! But that's a good reason to pray about it, that God would work this out for the good of all of you."

Michelle wasn't quite ready to give up the right-versus-wrong version, but didn't say so.

"What about you?" Grace asked Estelle. "How can we pray for you?"

Estelle gave a little snort. "Hmph! Don't get me started! But . . ." Her eyes got a troubled look. "Guess I'd like prayer for my Leroy. Oh, he's grown an' all, but he has his struggles, dealin' with some serious mental health issues. Had to put him in a home to keep him safe from himself, but I still feel guilty sometimes not havin' him with me, like I'm not being the mother I should be."

"Oh, Estelle." Michelle's social-worker genes fired up. "I'm sure you've done all a mother could do. And you and Harry are raising DaShawn—"

"I know, I know. It's just . . . sometimes I can't help thinkin', if we can raise Harry's grandson, why can't I be takin' care of my boy?" The older woman's eyes glistened and she fished in the roomy folds of her caftan for a tissue.

*Harry's grandson . . . my boy . . .*

Michelle realized those few words hinted at complex family dynamics. Whatever their history, the Bentleys were dealing with a blended family with all its complications.

Estelle blew her nose and took a big breath. "Now, there, I'm fine. Anything else we should pray for? Let's keep our Beecham Street neighborhood covered in prayer—'specially Miss Mattie, now that she's back. Harry an' I thought she'd enjoy havin' her old apartment remodeled, but I think it confuses her. Not her ol' familiar space. Plus she's got some dementia goin' on, makes it hard to have a straight conversation sometimes." Estelle wagged her head. "Just pray for her, sisters. For Harry an' me too."

Well, if they were going to pray for the neighborhood . . . "We should pray for the Singers," Michelle offered. "Greg and Nicole and their two kids, in the house second from the corner. Greg is making a job change, but it sounds like he quit his job without knowing exactly what's next, and Nicole's a stay-at-home mom, homeschools their two kids. I think it's kind of a shock for her."

Both Grace and Estelle stared at her. "She told you this?"

Michelle nodded. "Just this afternoon." She suddenly wished she'd kept her mouth shut. Their news wasn't hers to share with the other neighbors! In fact, the Singers probably wouldn't have told *them* if Jared hadn't gone there to accept Greg's offer of tickets to one of his expos. After all, they barely knew each other. "Uh . . . I'm sorry. I may have spoken out of turn. Please don't say anything to them."

Estelle patted her knee. "I know you're just concerned about them, but we need to be careful not to pass on this kind of news without their permission. 'Holy gossip,' my pastor calls it."

Michelle groaned. "I know, I know. I should've known better."

"But since we *do* know, we should certainly pray for this family. Father God, you know our every thought, our every word, so you already know the burdens and concerns we have on our hearts . . ."

Estelle had moved right into a prayer without even closing her eyes, as if God was the fourth person sitting in Grace's living room with them. Michelle wasn't sure whether to shut her eyes or keep them open, but she was used to closing her eyes when she prayed, so she quickly bowed her head. It touched her when Estelle prayed for "the Jasper family" and the upcoming weekend, as if they really mattered to her. While the older woman was praying, Michelle mentally threw in all the other "Jasper concerns" she hadn't even mentioned—summer plans for the kids, Destin needing a summer job, their tight finances, all her clients at Bridges she worried about, the girl she'd met that morning at Lifeline who'd been sexually abused by her relative, feeling overwhelmed and tired too often . . .

How long they prayed, Michelle wasn't sure, though between the three of them they eventually covered all the requests that'd been mentioned. It felt good to pray. Felt right. Maybe she needed something like this, sisters getting together to help each other pray. Sharing their burdens. Being honest about their struggles in a safe environment . . .

*Huh.* No way could she share the struggle she was having with Jared at the prayer meeting at church. Talk about feeding the "holy gossip" machine!

"Amen!" Estelle heaved herself up from the couch. "Guess I better get on back an' feed my menfolk." But at the front door she turned back. "Oh, Sister Michelle, did you have a chance to think about comin' to the shelter an' talkin' to the young ladies about the Lifeline Care Center an'—oh!" Estelle put her hand to her mouth—and then started to laugh. "Here I am, starin' at a pot o' gold in the middle of the room without even seein' it!"

Grace and Michelle exchanged glances. What in the world was she talking about?

Estelle was still chuckling. "See, a couple days ago I asked Sister Michelle here if she'd come to Manna House and talk to our young girls—and some not so young—who are either poppin' out babies left an' right with no means of support, or else usin' abortion as birth control. Either way, we got some sad cases who don't know about the resources available to them. But"—she wagged her head—"crisis pregnancy centers like Lifeline provide help for young women who are already in trouble. What I'm realizin' is, these girls need to catch a vision for who God created them to be, so they don't just keep repeatin' the same ol' destructive cycle. You know, that thing you told me you like to say at your concerts, Grace . . . 'You're worth the wait,' or somethin' like that."

Grace smiled, but it seemed like a sad smile. "*Used* to say. I changed the theme of my concerts, remember? Now I tell them about God's gift of amazing grace, even when they mess up."

Michelle felt slightly bewildered. Obviously, more was going on here than she knew about.

"I know, honey, I know," Estelle said. "All I'm sayin' is, can you *both* come to the shelter one of these days soon? Maybe you could sing for the ladies, Grace, and share a bit of your own story, the way you encourage those young people who come to your concerts. An' Michelle, *you* could tell them they've got choices, an' there are people willin' to stand with 'em if they choose life. And there's healin' to be had if they do make a bad choice. So many of these girls just let life happen, don't feel they've got a choice. Then they drown their guilt and shame with drugs and alcohol or a series of johns."

"I . . . well, I guess I could." Grace went to the secretary desk and picked up her DayTimer. "Next weekend is out obviously. It'd have to be sometime in June before I leave for my next tour. Are you thinking during the week or on the weekend?"

Estelle tossed the question to Michelle with a raised eyebrow.

"Would have to be a weekend for me. Maybe the first weekend in June? That's two weeks from now." She'd work it out somehow.

Grace shrugged. "I don't have any concerts that weekend. But . . . let me think about it a little more, okay? I haven't shared my personal story with very many people. Not sure I'm there yet."

"Absolutely, honey." Estelle wrapped Grace in a big hug, her caftan wrapping up the slender woman like a cocoon, then unwrapped her and gave Michelle a hug too.

But as Estelle and Michelle started for the door, Grace said, "Wait. Actually, I would like to come to Manna House sometime soon—especially if Ramona is still there. I'd really like to see her again. Our last interaction was so . . . unfinished."

Estelle nodded with a knowing smile. "She's still there. Will be for a while."

They said their good-byes and the door shut behind them. Estelle headed across the street and Michelle cut across the tiny front lawns to her own house next door. Who was Ramona? And why did Grace know someone staying at the Manna House shelter?

Well, guess she'd find out.

# Chapter 14

ONLY TWO DAYS INTO THE WORKWEEK and Michelle already felt desperate for the weekend. She'd spent most of Monday in court on behalf of a child in a custody dispute, half of Tuesday at a group home trying to calm a staff member who was threatening to remand one of her boys back to the juvenile justice system for rule violations, and she missed her lunch hour trying to set up a meeting between the principal, homeroom teacher, and foster mom of a kid who'd been skipping school. Not to mention the temperature had hiked up into the low nineties, dragging the humidity with it.

On top of all that she got a call Tuesday afternoon from the assistant principal at Stone Scholastic saying Tavis had been sent to the office for improper school attire, and since this was his third warning, he was contacting the parents.

"Improper . . . ? Improper how?" Michelle was incredulous. "He went to school in a pair of black pants and a plain white polo shirt we got from the school store."

There was a pause on the other end. "Well, the pants he's wearing right now are at least three sizes too big, no belt, and pulled down around his butt, gangbanger style."

"*Tavis?*" She was about to say, Put that boy on the phone! But this wasn't the time. "All right . . . I appreciate you calling me. I don't know what's going on, but we'll deal with it." Michelle hung up and massaged her temples. Not *we . . . she'd* have to deal with it. Jared didn't get home till eleven on Tuesdays—if he came home at all. His day shifts started on Wednesday at six, so he either slept at the airport or had to leave the house by five. Either way, it'd be tomorrow night before Jared could deal with it.

Tavis was holed up in his room when she got home. "Are you gonna tell Dad?" he asked sullenly when she found him.

"You bet." But she wasn't going to tell his dad until tomorrow night. No point upsetting an air traffic controller on duty. As empathetic as her husband might be toward those kids who'd come off the street during prayer meeting last week, she'd also heard him verbally blister a few church kids. "Pull those pants up, boy! Don't let me see you dressing like some fool gangbanger!" He had a thing about giving the wrong impression by the way a kid dressed and carried himself.

Michelle pulled out the wooden chair from the boys' desk and faced her youngest, who'd flopped on his brother's lower bunk. She noticed he'd changed into his usual afterschool clothes— athletic shorts, T-shirt. "What's going on, Tavis? Where'd you get the clothes you were wearing at school today? And sit up when I'm talking to you."

He swung his legs over the side of the bed and sat up but didn't look at her.

"Tavis!"

"Okay, *okay*. They're . . . Destin's."

"Destin's!" Michelle threw up her hands. "For heaven's sake, why?"

Tavis shrugged. "I dunno."

"Not good enough. Why? You know the rules. Even if the school didn't have a dress code, you know your father and I don't want you dressing 'street.'"

A mumble. "You wouldn't understand, Mom."

"Try me."

Tavis just shook his head sullenly. The alarm clock ticked on the desk.

Finally she sighed. Maybe she should've left the whole thing for Jared to sort out. But she'd started this, had to finish it now. "Well, this conversation isn't over. But you're grounded for the rest of the week. No TV, no video games, no playing outside with DaShawn or any other friends."

Tavis looked up, alarmed. "The rest of the week? But we're going to Bibi and Babu's house this weekend!"

Michelle pursed her lips. She didn't want this hanging over the holiday weekend either. She drummed her fingers on the bedroom desk for a moment. "The weekend's on probation. If you cooperate with the grounding until we leave and I don't get any more calls from the school, I'll cancel the grounding for the weekend. But you still have to answer to your dad."

She stood up, but before leaving the room, she laid her hand on his nubby head for just a moment. Her baby . . . only thirteen. What was going on in his mind? *I don't want to lose my boy, Lord!*

Jared got home late and crawled into bed. Michelle had had trouble falling asleep and was grateful he came home instead of staying out at the airport. She snuggled up to his broad, firm back in spite of the warm evening and sweaty sheets. How she wished she could talk to him about Tavis! But she could tell he was exhausted after his swing shift and knew he had to get up early.

And . . . maybe she was worried about nothing. Teenagers in every generation annoyed their parents with their ideas about what was cool, didn't they? Even her mother had told stories about rolling up her waistband to look like a miniskirt back in the sixties. And Michelle herself had worn baggy sweaters off her shoulder and garish neon tights with bulky leg warmers—the mismatched eighties look—when she hit thirteen.

Well, tomorrow. She'd talk to Jared tomorrow. Maybe he'd know what to do . . .

The alarm cut into her consciousness in what felt like mere moments after she fell asleep. Daylight had already brightened the bedroom in spite of the closed blinds and the digital clock said 6:01. She flung out an arm—but Jared's side of the bed was empty. Already gone and starting his new shift at the airport.

Michelle sighed as she stuffed her feet into her slippers, pulled on her robe, and headed for the bathroom in the basement. Three more days to plow through and then they'd be on their way to Indiana. A three-day vacation! Except . . . knowing Jared wouldn't be going took a lot of the air out of her joy.

So did finding out that Jared had to lead prayer meeting that night at Northside, since Pastor Q and First Lady Donna were already on their way to Rantoul to help Donna's sister with funeral arrangements. Well, if you can't beat 'em, join 'em. Setting Tabby to work loading the dishwasher after supper and reminding Tavis that he was grounded, she left Destin in charge and told Jared she was coming with. It'd be a chance anyway to check in with Sister Norma about her research on that video series they'd discussed for the summer women's events. And she'd at least have the ride to and from church to catch Jared up on what was going on with their youngest son.

"He what?" Jared snorted in disgust when she told him about the assistant principal's phone call. "Sounds like that boy needs his britches warmed."

Michelle flipped his arm with the back of her hand. "Oh, right. He's too big for a spanking. But I did ground him for the rest of this week—including no TV or video games. But what bothers me, Jared, is he wouldn't say anything when I asked him *why?* He was sure to be noticed at Stone, which has a strict dress code just a hair shy of uniforms. I mean, it doesn't make sense!"

Jared drove silently for a few minutes. Finally he said, "Okay. I'll talk to him tonight when we get home. Did you ask Tabby about it? She probably knows what's going on."

"Believe me, I was tempted! But I don't want to put her in the position of being a tattletale on her brother. And for some reason she hasn't said anything, which isn't like her. She's usually quick to spill the beans about stuff that happens at school, whether Tavis wants her to or not—like when that bully was messing with him."

"Hmm. You think it's related?"

Michelle shrugged. "Wish I knew."

Jared turned into the church parking lot. Only a few cars. And to her husband's credit, he kept the meeting to an hour, spending the first fifteen minutes giving a short devotional on God's never-failing presence even when we go through tough times. "The psalmist included this promise in the Twenty-Third Psalm: 'Yea, though I walk through the valley of the shadow of death, I will fear no evil: for thou art with me' . . . "

Michelle smiled to herself. A number of Northside members still preferred the old King James Version with its "thees" and "thous," even though she and Jared and others used modern versions. Still, there was something lyrical and beautiful about the old English language for those old familiar passages.

Jared passed out blank index cards—there were only about twenty people in attendance—and asked everyone to jot down a prayer request, which they could sign with their names or not. He then asked everyone to gather in groups of three or four, trade cards, and pray for one another.

*Nice*, Michelle thought as she scooted over in the pew to pray with Mother Brown and Sister Mavis. Pastor Q always did prayer meeting the same old way—stand up, state your prayer request (some of which often bordered on "holy gossip"), while Pastor Q jotted down a list. Then he'd appoint someone to pray for each request. And sometimes those prayers got long and fervent, almost as if each person was trying to outdo the previous one.

"I liked that," she told Jared on the way home. "It was more personal." Made her think of the prayer time she'd had at Grace Meredith's home last Sunday.

He glanced at her and grinned. "Glad to hear it. Didn't hear any complaints—yet. But I've been thinking we need to change something about these midweek prayer meetings. Seems like fewer people come every week."

She poked him playfully. "Mm-hm. So the mouse comes out to play while the cat's away, is that it?"

Jared chuckled. "Something like that."

But as he parked the Altima in front of the house ten minutes later and shut off the engine, he just sat for a few minutes before getting out, shoulders sagging. "Think I'll get to bed. Had a really short night last night and have to get up early again. And then it's night shift tomorrow night."

So what else was new? He did this crazy 2-2-1 schedule every week. Barely caught up on normal sleep over the weekend and then it started all over again. "Thought you were going to talk to Tavis when we got home. Find out why he'd do such a stupid thing, knowing he was just going to get in trouble."

Jared snorted as they got out of the car and walked toward the front door. "*Why?* Huh! Don't see any reason to make a big deal about 'why.' He broke the rules, he's grounded, that's the way it is. Period." He opened the front door with his key, then muttered, "Don't worry. I intend to talk to him. I'm going to read him the riot act for trying to dress like some gangbanger. No son of mine is going to feed the negative stereotype of young black males as thugs and hoods!"

# Chapter 15

BY THE TIME FRIDAY ROLLED AROUND, Michelle was tempted to throw the kids and suitcases into the minivan and head out of town as soon as she got home. Which was ridiculous, she told herself, because she hadn't even packed yet—in fact, she still had a few loads of laundry to do tonight so they could take clean clothes to her parents' house. Not to mention the usual holiday traffic tying up the interstates on Friday night, and the fact that she felt tired. Really tired.

A better idea. She'd phone Jared and suggest they all go out to eat tonight, something special to do together before leaving him alone for the weekend. And she wouldn't have to cook. Michelle glanced at her watch . . . three thirty. Jared had gone to bed almost as soon as he got home that morning from his night shift, but if he wasn't up by now, he should be or he wouldn't sleep tonight.

Pushing aside the reports she was filling out, she called the house. No answer. She tried his cell phone . . . and got a sleepy, "Jared here."

"Hi, hon. Sorry if I woke you. Hope you had a good sleep."

"Yeah, it's fine. Uh . . . . Need to get going anyway. What's up?"

She heard rustling and movement as if he was getting out of bed and pulling on some clothes. "Thought it might be nice for the five of us to go out together tonight for supper since you're not going with us to Fort Wayne. Wanted to run the idea by you before the kids got home. We can decide where later."

"Yeah, okay, I guess . . ." More rustling and grunting. "What about Tavis being grounded?"

She felt a twinge of annoyance. Couldn't he be more enthusiastic? As for Tavis . . . "Dinner out with the family is different. Especially in view of the circumstances."

"What circumstances?"

Now she heard the unmistakable sounds of the coffeemaker starting to drip.

"Us going away for the weekend," she said, trying to sound patient.

A long pause on the other end.

"Jared?"

"Wish you weren't going. The timing is lousy."

Now she was the one who let silence sit between them. Anything she said at that moment was going to come out wrong. Or nasty. Finally she said, "The timing. Uh-huh. It's *never* a good time, Jared."

He sighed in her ear. "Look. I know going to see your folks is a good thing. But maybe Destin should stay home with me. The boy *should* be spending the weekend looking for a summer job. We made a deal, remember? And he hasn't done squat to look for work."

The twinge had grown to full-fledged irritation now. "Don't put this on me at the last minute, Jared. You've already pulled yourself out of our family trip. I'm not going to let you pull Destin out too."

"I'm just sayin' . . . it's lousy timing."

"No. The pastor asking you to fill the pulpit this weekend was the lousy timing." Okay, she knew that didn't help anything, but it came out anyway.

"Yeah, you made that clear." Another pause.

*Argh.* Did she even want to go out to supper with Jared and the kids now? She took a deep breath. "Look, I gotta go. I have a few more reports to do before I can leave the office." She hung up before she said what was *really* on her mind.

But as she drove home a couple of hours later, she had to admit Destin needed to take more initiative. There weren't *that* many summer jobs for teens out there, and it was usually the go-getters who got hired. School would be out in a few weeks and it'd be great to have something lined up. But keeping Destin home this weekend only penalized the whole family.

*Oh Lord . . . !* Sitting at a red light, she almost closed her eyes, feeling an urge to cry out to God to work out all the details they were trying to juggle—but a car horn behind her reminded her she'd better pray with eyes open. She had a green light. *Lord, I really want to go to my folks this weekend . . . really need a break . . . and I want the kids to come with, so we can just spend some fun time together. So, please, Lord, provide a job for Destin even if he's not out looking this weekend.*

By the time she parked the minivan in front of their house on Beecham Street, her irritation had dissipated, and she was able to give Jared a genuine glad-to-be-home kiss and get the laundry started before they headed out to the Flat Top Grill—the kids' choice, which won three to two over Red Lobster. The kids were excited about leaving early the next morning, and she sat back, enjoying the everyone-talking-at-once banter and laughing at their bungled attempts to use chopsticks to eat the big bowls of made-to-order stir-fry . . . though she noticed that Jared seemed somewhat subdued.

Only later as she fell into bed—laundry finally dried and folded, suitcases packed—did it occur to her that maybe there was something else behind Jared's "lousy timing" comment. This was the first time her husband would be preaching in front of the whole church . . . and she wouldn't be there to give him moral support.

"Honey?" she whispered, laying a hand on his bare chest. "I'm really sorry I won't be here when you preach on Sunday. I'd love to hear your sermon." But all she heard from the other pillow was a soft snore.

Hot coffee in her travel cup. Bottles of water and snacks in the picnic cooler. Three sleepy teenagers belted into the minivan. A promise to stop at the first McDonald's they came across once out of the city limits for Egg McMuffins. Cheery waves to Jared, standing on the curb in the cool, early morning sunshine to see them off.

Hopefully he'd find the note she'd written to him, saying she was sorry to miss his sermon on Sunday and would be praying for him, which she'd tucked into his underwear drawer.

Michelle was grateful they'd waited till Saturday morning to make the drive to Indiana. She felt more rested. Traffic was minimal.

They sailed through the city along Lake Shore Drive, the magnificent glass and steel buildings of the Loop catching brilliant flashes of the early morning sun rising higher over Lake Michigan. Only scattered clouds, no rain in the forecast. A perfect day for driving.

"I can drive if you get tired," Destin offered hopefully from the front passenger seat.

"Sorry, buddy. Your permit says you can only drive with one adult. You haven't driven on the highway yet." And frankly, she'd rather he not practice with the twins in the car. But she playfully punched his arm. "Maybe your grandpa will take you driving this weekend."

Michelle slid a mix of favorite gospel music into the CD player and the minivan rocked as the kids bounced in their seatbelts and clapped to the music. But after their breakfast stop, all three kids retired behind their own earbuds and iPods—Christmas gifts from Bibi and Babu, of course.

Near Valparaiso, she got off the toll road and took Route 30, the most direct route to Fort Wayne, though a little slower than the interstate. Both routes took about the same time, however, and she pulled up in front of her parents' home in the southeast part of the city by ten thirty—though with the time change it was already eleven thirty in Indiana.

"There they are!" The screen door of the two-story, white-frame house slammed behind Michelle's parents as they crossed the porch and came down the steps. All three kids piled out of the minivan to give their grandparents hugs. "Come in, come in. Got some lemonade ready, bet you're thirsty . . . Now, now, what's this?" Coral Robinson held Tabitha at arm's length, eyeing her critically. "You letting your hair grow out, young lady? You better learn how to take care of it then. None of this bushy stuff. Mm-mm."

"Will you braid it for me, Bibi? It's long enough now. I like how you do it." Tabby tucked her hand into the crook of her grandmother's elbow and happily disappeared with her through the screen door.

Martin Robinson grabbed Destin to help unload the suitcases from the back of the minivan. "Don't mind your mother, Micky," he muttered to Michelle. "She's just looking for an excuse to do the hair thing with Tabby like she used to do with you."

Michelle grinned at the childhood nickname and glanced up and down the street of older frame houses, mostly painted white or yellow, with the occasional pale blue or weathered green thrown in, plus the one with the daring red trim. Across the street a couple of older folks sitting out on their wide porch waved. Here and there bicycles and riding toys had been left sprawled on the grass or parked on the cracked sidewalks.

The old, familiar neighborhood. Probably still mostly African American. Some things never changed.

She followed her dad and Destin into the house, pulling her own carry-on suitcase. Warm, savory smells drifted from the kitchen. Her mother probably had a pot of greens and smoked ham hocks on the stove already for tonight's supper. Frosty glasses of lemonade in hand, Tabby and Tavis were helping themselves to homemade oatmeal cookies cooling on the kitchen counter.

"I said they could take a couple since it's not quite lunchtime yet," Coral Robinson said, daring anyone to contradict her.

"Mom, they'll be spoiled rotten by the time I take them home."

"That's the idea." Her mother winked. "What else are grand-folks for? Now come here, Micky, and give your mother some sugar. Haven't had a hug yet from my baby."

Michelle realized it only took about five minutes of coming home before she felt about twelve again. Still "Micky." Still their little girl. Not that she minded totally. Maybe, she admitted to herself, that's what she came home for. Being Mom-in-Charge at home and Caseworker-on-Call at work felt overwhelming at times. A little motherly TLC might be just what the doctor ordered.

As usual, Michelle settled into her old room with the full bed, while the boys took over her brother Martin Jr.'s old room and Tabby got the guest room that doubled as her mother's sewing room, all on the second floor. She texted Jared telling him they'd arrived safely, and then flopped back on the faded flowered bedspread.

Her folks looked good. She got her own warm, caramel complexion from her parents. In their early seventies, both Martin and Coral Robinson had let their hair go silvery-grey, though her mom probably used a silver rinse too, making her short "natural" look perky and elegant, especially with the big silver hoop earrings she liked to wear. Dad's hairline had receded, but his wrinkles were all in the right places, laugh lines crinkling at the sides of his eyes and creating long dimples on either side of his mouth.

"Bibi says lunch is ready!" Tavis yelled up the stairs. "Hurry up! I'm hungry!"

Over gooey toasted cheese sandwiches, pickles, potato chips, and apple wedges, the grandparents wanted to hear all about Destin's track meet and what kind of plans they had for the summer.

"I'm going to one of the Five-Star Basketball Camps!" Destin enthused. "That's where Michael Jordan was discovered. College scouts come there an' everything, Babu."

"Great! What about you, sport?" Babu pointed a pickle at Tavis. Tavis shrugged. "I dunno. Nothin'."

"What? That's a good recipe for trouble, young man. Don't you usually go to day camp?" He sounded stern but he winked at Michelle. "Send him down here, Micky, and we'll keep him busy mowing the lawn, painting the porch, picking up trash—"

"Babu!" Tavis protested. "I'm a kid! Kids don't have to work."

"Hmph. They did in my day."

"Well, I wanted to go to cheerleading camp, but I can't. It's not fair." Tabby stuck out her lower lip.

"Why not?" Michelle's mother aimed the question at her. "Why, there's an excellent Christian cheer camp right here in Fort Wayne. Tabitha could stay with us if it's too expensive to stay onsite."

"See, Mom?" Tabby said.

"Tabby, you know that's not it." Michelle gave her daughter The Look before turning back to her mother. "Mom, all the cheer camps we researched—including the one here in Fort Wayne—require that participants come as a team with their coach. Tabby's school doesn't have a cheer squad, so she needs to wait till high school."

"Yeah, but it's still not fair," Tabby muttered.

"Well, I agree with Tabitha." Bibi looked offended. "You'd think these camps would help prepare young ladies like Tabitha who want to try out for high school teams."

"See, Mom?"

"In fact"—Michelle's mother was on a roll—"I happen to know one of the administrators of that camp. She goes to our church. Maybe she'll make an exception."

"Oh, Bibi, would you?" Tabby's eyes went wide.

"*Mom*. Please don't. We don't need any favors. And don't raise Tabby's hopes like that. She can try out for the high school team next summer after she graduates from eighth grade."

"It never hurts to ask. Tabby, get that plate of cookies for dessert. Now . . . what do you kids want to do this afternoon? There's a beautiful botanical garden downtown—"

"The chocolate factory!" yelled all three kids in unison.

Babu chuckled. "Gets my vote."

"And Mom said we could go to that laser tag place while we're here," Destin added. "Can we go tonight?"

Michelle made a face. "I did kind of promise we'd check it out.

"Awesome!" Tavis pumped the air with the cookie he had in his fist.

"But if we do," she added, "Bibi and I get to choose what we do tomorrow after church, right, Mom?"

# Chapter 16

*U*GH. WHY DID SHE FEEL SO LOUSY? Michelle opened her eyes to the morning light, taking a few seconds to remember that she wasn't in her bedroom at home, but her old room on Drexel Avenue in Fort Wayne. It wasn't like she'd played laser tag herself last night. Lazer X had a lounge area of sorts where parents and nonplayers could wait, with fountain drinks and hot snacks like pizza, nachos, and soft pretzels. There was even a table looking into the laser tag arena from which she'd been able to spot her three teenage terrors from time to time, though the flashing strobe lights soon gave her a headache.

Michelle's mother had elected to stay home, but her dad had gamely accompanied Michelle and the kids to the gigantic laser tag building near the Glenbrook Mall. She was prepared for the laser tag tickets—but of course the kids wanted to do the "LazerMaze" and play the video games in the arcade as well. Oh well, this weekend had one objective as far as she was concerned: letting the kids have fun. Her dad had generously footed the bill for soft drinks and nachos for her brood, who'd insisted they were "starving," even though her mom had stuffed them all at supper with ham and fried chicken, as well as mac 'n cheese, savory greens, and strawberry pie.

It was eleven by the time they got back to the frame house she'd grown up in, and even though she'd taken a pass on the nachos, the soft pretzel she'd eaten didn't sit well in her stomach. She'd had to get up twice to go to the bathroom.

Pulling on a bathrobe, she woke the kids, swished the blahs out of her mouth with mouthwash, and made her way downstairs to the kitchen. Her mother was pulling a large egg-sausage-bread casserole out of the oven.

"Good morning, Micky! Fresh coffee in the pot."

"Uh, thanks, Mom, but think I'll make some tea this morning. Do you have some herbal peppermint?" Michelle turned the flame on under the teakettle.

"What? Tea for breakfast? You aren't sick, are you?" Bibi bustled over and put a hand on her forehead.

Michelle made a face. "No, I'm not sick. You'd want tea too if you'd spent four hours at Lazer X last night."

Her mother chuckled. "Knew I made the right decision to stay home. Are the kids up? We need to leave for church in an hour."

"I woke them. I'll check again after I call Jared. He's giving his first sermon this morning." She foraged for a mug and the box of herbal tea, then sat down at the kitchen table with her cell phone. They'd gotten home too late to call last night.

"Well, you tell that husband of yours we'll forgive him this time since he's preaching. But I don't take kindly to him missing my cooking."

Michelle laughed. "You spoil him as much as you spoil the kids, Mom."

She dialed Jared's cell number, but after four rings the call went to voicemail. *Rats.* "Hi, honey. I was hoping to catch you before church this morning. Just want you to know I'm thinking about you and praying for you. I want to hear what you decided to preach on this morning. Will anyone record it? Okay, talk to you later. Love and kisses." Disappointed, she ended the call. She should've called him last night, even if it was late.

Getting the kids up and ready on time for church was like pulling taffy on a cold day, but they were finally in the car, following her parents to the large Baptist church they attended. She'd begged off the rich breakfast casserole, saying her stomach was a little upset—which was true, but she also wanted to avoid all those calories her mother mixed into everything. If she weren't careful, she'd end up waddling home to her husband like plump penguin.

A few of the "old folks" at St. John the Baptist Tabernacle remembered Michelle, but she'd been gone twenty years and the congregation had seen one pastor retire, another move on to "bigger and better pastures," and the current pastor was barely thirty and looked like an NBA basketball player. "He's attracting more young people, which is a good thing," Michelle's father said in an undertone as the six of them filled a pew. "But with all this newfangled music, just hope we don't lose all the good ol' gospel songs."

"Not that your father can carry a tune," her mother said with a wink.

Growing up at Baptist Tab, all the kids stayed during church. But the new pastor had instituted children's church and a teen group during the sermon time. *That* was different. All three Jasper teens elected to stay in the worship service rather than go to the teen group, which didn't surprise Michelle. They didn't visit Bibi and Babu often enough to know any of the kids at Baptist Tab. But they seemed to enjoy the spirited choir in their black robes and African-print stoles, even though they smirked at the young pastor's animated pacing and arm flailing during the sermon.

Michelle was distracted. How was Jared's sermon going? She didn't even know his sermon topic. In fact, had to admit she'd been pretty selfish about the whole weekend, looking at it only from her point of view, not his. If she could "Beam me up, Scotty," she'd love to be sitting in her regular pew at Northside Baptist at that moment listening to Jared's first sermon.

After the service, Michelle noticed her mother talking to a tall, willowy woman and pointing out her visiting family. Oh no, was this who she thought it was? Sure enough, her mother waved her over and introduced her. "Michelle, this is Trisha Burns, the woman I was telling you about who's one of the administrators of the Christian Cheer Coalition here in Fort Wayne." Bibi craned her neck, looking around the sanctuary. "Where did Tabitha go? I wanted Sister Trisha to meet her."

Michelle felt her face flush. "I'm sorry, Ms. Burns. We know participants who come to your camp need to be part of a cheer squad, and Tabby's not—"

"It's all right." The woman smiled graciously. "In fact, Sister Coral's call last night was the third call I've had this week about girls wanting to come to our program who aren't part of a cheer team yet. I've been thinking about possibly putting together a temporary 'team' of unattached girls for camp week. But that's not a promise," the woman added hastily. "I'll need to talk to my staff and get their input."

Coral Robinson patted her arm. "Well, it's a wonderful idea. You can put my granddaughter Tabitha down as a 'for sure' if you put together a temporary team."

As they walked away, Michelle said under her breath, "Mom, don't get ahead of me here. She didn't promise anything. I'd hate for Tabby to get all excited and then be disappointed again."

"Oh, Micky, I'm perfectly confident Sister Trisha will make this happen. When is the camp? We'd love to have Tabitha stay with us that week. In fact, I'm sure your father and I will be happy to help with the tuition fee."

"Well, don't say anything to Tabby until we hear something more definite—"

Too late. Tabby was making a beeline for them. "Mom! Bibi! I saw you talking to that lady! Is that the cheerleading person you know, Bibi? What did she say? Can I go?"

"She just—" Michelle started.

"She's working on it, sweetheart," Bibi cut in. "Just be patient. Come on, let's go home and put our picnic lunch together. We've got lots of cold chicken left from last night's supper and we can pick up some deli potato salad on the way. It's a day of rest, right? Even grandmothers get *one* day off from cooking!"

The kids didn't complain too much about going to the botanic gardens since it involved Bibi's large picnic basket—but once they arrived, even they seemed mesmerized by the incredible butterfly exhibit in the indoor showcase garden. "Mom, Mom! Look at this one that looks like it's got owl eyes on its wings!" and "Ohhh! That one's so blue!" African drums and other percussion instruments lent an exotic air to the annual display . . . and that was only one of the many gardens they wandered through.

While her parents and offspring wandered through the tropical display, Michelle found a quiet corner to call Jared. Almost two o'clock; he should be home by now. But again her call went to voicemail. Strange. Was he mad at her for being gone this weekend? No, not mad—that wasn't like Jared. Disappointed, maybe. *She*, on the other hand, *had* been angry at him for putting church before the family but had finally realized it didn't help anything to stay mad.

She was relieved to see his caller ID when her phone rang an hour later as they strolled through one of the outdoor gardens, full of blooming azaleas, rhododendrons, and lovely purple heather. "Hey, Gumdrop. Sorry I didn't answer the phone a while ago. Mother Willa dragged me home after church to feed me when she realized the family was gone this weekend." He chuckled. "Your call came right in the middle of chowing down on jerk chicken, black beans, and plantains."

*Gumdrop* . . . Michelle smiled at the pet name, something he used to call her all the time. Maybe she should go away more often. "I better not tell my mother you're being fed by Miss Willa's Jamaican cooking. She thinks your biggest loss this weekend is missing out on her soul food."

"Well, your mom can cook, that's for sure. Did she make strawberry pie?"

"She did."

"Hmm. I don't suppose—"

"The kids finished it off. Sorry."

He sighed. "Dang. Oh well. Hey, your voicemail this morning said you wanted to hear about my sermon. I—"

"Honey? I . . . I do. But right now I'm standing in the middle of the botanic gardens here, and I've lost sight of the kids. Can I call you later when we get back to the house?"

"Oh. Okay. Talk to you later. Give my love to the kids—and to your folks too."

Michelle pocketed her phone and hurried along the path where she'd last seen her parents and progeny. Playing phone tag wasn't any fun . . . though sometimes it wasn't any better back home, what with Jared's crazy schedule during the week and their weekend commitments. She brushed away an involuntary tear. Passing like ships in the night—more like ships in a fog—pretty much described their marriage right now.

She intended to lie down for just a few minutes after they got home from the conservatory and then call Jared . . . but the next thing she knew she heard Tavis yelling up the stairs, "Bibi says supper's ready in two minutes!"

What? She looked at the bedside clock. Six thirty already? She hadn't realized she was so tired. Stumbling into the bathroom, she dashed cold water on her face, touched up her lipstick, and then made her way downstairs. "Supper" consisted of a big bowl of popcorn, chips and salsa, raw veggies and hummus, pizza rolls straight from the freezer to the oven to the table, and cans of pop—all of which the kids were loading on sturdy paper plates before heading into the living room to watch the *Survivor* reality TV show with Babu.

"Told you I didn't cook on Sunday," her mother teased, but her eyes gave Michelle a good once-over. "Are you okay, Micky? You don't look so good."

"Just tired, Mom. Told you I needed a vacation! You know what my job's like—can be really stressful. Now that I have a few days to relax, it's catching up with me is all."

"Hmm. Stress can take a real toll on your body, sweetheart. When was the last time you had a checkup?"

"Oh, a year or so ago. Don't remember exactly." Michelle filled the teakettle and turned the gas burner on under it. She didn't feel like chips or pizza rolls. Tea. Maybe some toast.

Going out on the front porch with her tea, she called Jared, all set to apologize for not calling when they first got home—and again got voicemail. She left a message for him, but he still hadn't called back by the time she climbed the stairs to her old bedroom at nine thirty.

Where in the world was he? Probably had the TV on, didn't hear the phone.

Okay. She'd call in the morning before they started for home. His Monday shift didn't start until two—morning ought to be a good time to talk. She hadn't planned to leave Fort Wayne until after lunch, but what if they left right after breakfast? Maybe they'd get home in time to see him before he left for work . . .

No. The kids were still downstairs playing a cutthroat game of Monopoly with their granddad, which might go till midnight, and they were counting on sleeping in at least *one* day of the holiday weekend, especially since they'd had to get up early the last two mornings. And even if they did arrive home before Jared left for work around one fifteen, there'd only be time for hi and good-bye.

Michelle turned out the light and crawled into bed. Better just stick with the plan. It took her a long time to fall asleep, even though she felt exhausted.

# Chapter 17

THE KIDS WERE STILL ASLEEP when Michelle came downstairs the next morning. Her mother was alone in the kitchen, oiling the old waffle maker. "Morning, baby. How'd you sleep?"

"Okay, I guess." She made a face. "Don't sleep so good when Jared's not in the bed. You going to make waffles?"

"Whenever those kids get up . . . and by then it'll be brunch instead of breakfast. Here, you want to cut up those strawberries to go on top?"

"Sure, after I make some tea. Where's Dad?"

"Oh, puttering around in the garage. Who knows what he's doing." Coral Robinson frowned. "You still off color? Baby, you've been working too hard. You need to see a doctor."

"Mom, please . . ."

"Now, you listen to your mama. Stress can elevate your blood pressure, sap your energy, give you headaches, ruin your digestion, mess with a good night's sleep, and . . . oh, you name it. I'm sure it's on the list."

Michelle rolled her eyes. "Thanks, Mom. I feel better already."

"Oh, don't be so stubborn. I'm serious." Her mother's voice softened. "Just make a doctor's appointment and get a checkup."

Michelle didn't argue, finished making her tea, then picked up a paring knife and started taking off the stems of the washed strawberries and cutting them in half. Maybe she should make an appointment with her doctor. A checkup wouldn't hurt. It'd been a year or two. Should probably schedule a mammogram too, now that she was over forty.

Strawberries finished, she glanced at the kitchen clock. Nine thirty. Perfect time to call Jared. Taking her phone out to the front porch, she settled into a plastic chair. Ugh. Plastic. This porch could sure use a nice wooden porch swing too.

118

She heard the phone pick up. "Jared? Hi, honey. Sorry we missed each other last night. Everything okay?" She heard what sounded like the TV in the background.

"Last night? Oh, yeah, yeah, everything's good. It was such a beautiful evening I went for a run along the lakefront. Had to work off Mother Willa's big meal, you know. Been awhile since I've been over to the lake. It felt good—real good. But when I got back, wouldn't you know it, I fell asleep in front of the TV . . . Say, are the kids around? I'd like to say hi. It's too quiet around here."

"Sorry. The kids are sleeping in this morning. It's quiet here too, for a change. Thought it might be a good time to hear about your sermon yesterday."

"Okay, sure. Let me get my notes . . ." The TV noise in the background shut off and in a minute Jared was back. "Well, since it's Memorial Day weekend, I thought we ought to acknowledge it somehow, especially since we've got several veterans at Northside, but without getting all political—you know, God and country and all that."

That sounded like Jared. Like many black men, he'd experienced his share of discrimination growing up, even after the civil rights movement of the sixties. As grateful as he was for the progress we'd made as a nation, he didn't have too many romanticized notions that we'd arrived at the promised land.

"But after you guys left on Saturday," he was saying, "I had the house to myself and all day to prepare . . . but I didn't seem to be getting anywhere. To tell you the truth, Michelle, I was starting to worry. Yeah, my first solo sermon, and I was going to fall flat on my face."

"Oh, Jared."

"So I went out for a walk in the cemetery—there's that gate behind Lincoln Paddock's big house, you know. Wandering around the gravestones reminded me that Memorial Day—unlike Veteran's Day, which honors our service men and women who made it back—is really for remembering those who gave their lives to preserve our freedom. And suddenly it felt like God dropped this thought into my spirit: 'I sent my Son to die for your freedom.'"

The way he said it took her breath away. "Oh, Jared. That's perfect."

"Right. I practically ran back home, and started looking up scriptures having to do with the freedom God gives us because of what Jesus did. You know, Isaiah 61:1, the scripture that Jesus quoted in the synagogue—"

"The one about proclaiming freedom for the captives and release for the prisoners?" She could feel his excitement.

"Exactly. Spiritual freedom as well as physical. And then I came across the first verse in Galatians five . . . here, let me read it in the NIV version. 'It is for freedom that Christ has set us free. Stand firm, then, and do not let yourselves be burdened again by a yoke of slavery.' Paul was talking about circumcision in particular, but he meant anything people try to add to the gospel—you know, all the extra rules and expectations we set up to judge whether somebody's *really* saved."

She squirmed a little, thinking about Sister Shareese's plunging necklines and her doubts about the young woman's salvation at times.

"But that's not all. Same chapter, verse thirteen: 'But do not use your freedom to indulge the flesh; rather, serve one another in love'—oh, hey, can you hold on? I've got another call—it's the tower, I better take it . . ."

The phone seemed to go dead as he switched over, but she felt breathless. Really wished she'd been there to hear Jared's sermon. *Use our freedom in Christ to serve one another . . .* It sounded so powerful. She wondered how the folks at Northside had received it.

Her mother pushed open the screen door. "You still on the phone? Trisha Burns just called and—"

Michelle waved her away. "Can't talk right now, Mom. Later." The door banged shut.

Jared came back on. "Uh, gotta go, Michelle. Bucky just got a call that his wife's in labor. Boss says he's totally useless, asked if I can come in early and finish his shift."

"Oh . . . of course. Tell Bucky congrats. It's his first baby, isn't it?" *Bucky* . . . All the guys in the tower ended up with nutty nicknames. Jared's was "Jazz," a takeoff on Jasper she supposed, and he only tolerated it from his buddies at work.

"Yeah. Sorry, gotta run." Now the phone went dead.

Well, of course he had to go. But she felt a little cheated. She wanted to hear more about Jared's sermon—but given his schedule that bounced all over the place, it might be next weekend before he had a chance to tell her any more.

Michelle wandered back into the house. Her dad had come in from the garage and was eating a bowl of cold cereal at the kitchen table. "Can't wait for those sleepyheads," he muttered, mouth full. "I gotta eat somethin'."

"Oh, good, you're off the phone," her mother said. "Trisha Burns called—you know, the woman I introduced you to at church who helps run the Christian cheer camp. She said her staff is willing to put together a temporary team for individual girls. Isn't that great?"

Michelle just stared at her mother, and then shook her head. "Mom, you are something else. Are you sure? I don't want to get Tabby's hopes up—and besides, Jared and I were actually glad she might have to wait a year or so before getting into all this cheerleader stuff."

"Now, now, Micky, you listen to me." Her mother practically pushed her into a chair at the kitchen table. "From what I know, this camp is different. They talk a lot about character and good sportsmanship, and they even have morning devotions with the girls. I think it'll be good for Tabitha. She can stay with us and we can take her back and forth. And I've already talked with your father—isn't that right, Martin?—and we want to pay half her tuition. It's only two hundred dollars for the week, so that leaves just one hundred for you and Jared to cover. Can you do that?"

"*Mom*, it's not about the money . . ." Although, yes, in a way, it was about the money. The money it took to provide safe activities for three teenagers in the city all summer long. "But thanks for the offer. That would be very helpful. I do need to talk to Jared first before we sign on the dotted line, though. So—"

"Did she call?" Tabby bounced into the room, eyes alight. "Bibi? Mom?" She looked from one to the other. "She *did* call, didn't she! And she said I can come, didn't she! Oh, Babu!" She ran to her grandfather and gave him a hug around his neck from behind his chair. "This is so exciting! And I can come back and stay with you for a whole week!"

Michelle eyed her mother and sighed. Tabby was already way down the road.

Tabby chatted excitedly about cheerleading camp on the way back to Chicago that afternoon, and Destin pouted. "How come you guys and the grandpeeps are gonna pay *her* way, but I have to pay you guys back for *mine*?"

So much for waiting to talk it over with Jared before the details became common knowledge. But Michelle was going to try. "I haven't even talked with your father about it yet, and besides, how we pay for Tabby's camp isn't really your business." Michelle was trying to keep her voice calm. "And don't call your grandparents the 'grandpeeps.'"

Tavis snorted. "'Grandpeeps'—that's funny."

"Don't you start." Michelle gave her youngest son a warning look in the rearview. Then she glanced at her oldest in the front seat beside her. "Besides, Destin, the Five-Star Basketball Camp costs a lot more—and you're seventeen. You didn't pay for your summer camps when you were thirteen either."

"See?" Tabby swatted her big brother's head from behind.

"Stop it, squirt," he yelled, lunging back at her as far as his seatbelt allowed.

"Stop it, both of you!" Michelle snapped. "Or I'll pull off the highway and we won't move until you do." Now she had a headache, and they still had two hours to go. Or more. Traffic was getting heavier the closer they got to the city, and it had started to rain.

But after coming over the Skyway into the city and inching the car along Lake Shore Drive, Michelle finally turned the minivan into Beecham Street at five o'clock. The rain had stopped and the extra traffic had only added another half hour—well, maybe forty minutes—to the drive. Not too bad. But she was tired. Really tired.

"Everybody take something in," she said wearily, popping open the back of the minivan so they could unload their suitcases, food cooler, and the box of loose snapshots her mother had insisted she take home with them. They trooped into the house, and the kids immediately scattered. Michelle flopped on the couch. Jared was already at work, of course. And by the time he got home, he would've put in a twelve-hour day.

Which would make both of them too tired to talk. Or anything else.

Tavis popped back into the living room. "What's for supper? I'm starving!"

"Me too!" Destin yelled from somewhere.

Starving? They'd had a huge brunch at eleven, and Bibi had sent along a whole bag of munchies for the trip home. Michelle didn't want to think about cooking. Or unpacking. Or doing laundry. Or anything that took work. Vegging out downstairs in the family room watching a movie sounded about right. Let the kids forage for themselves—

The doorbell rang. *Uhh.* She was too tired to get up.

"I'll get it!" Tavis yelled. Running to the door he pulled it open. "Oh, hey, DaShawn. Come in."

"Nah, can't. We're cookin' out. Miz Estelle saw you drive up, sent me over to invite you guys to come over for some grilled chicken an' stuff. We got plenty an' she says you just got home, your mom don't need to be cookin'."

"Oh, hey, can we, Mom?"

The commotion had already attracted Tabby and Destin. "Yeah, can we, Mom?"

Michelle felt outnumbered. It was tempting. She wouldn't have to cook. But she'd have to get off the couch. And talk to the Bentleys. Wasn't sure she had the energy for either.

The kids were halfway out the door. "All right. Thanks, DaShawn." She struggled to sit upright. "You kids can go over if you promise to behave yourselves. Tell Miss Estelle I'll be along a little later. I need a few minutes to get myself together."

After all, it was just the Bentleys.

# Chapter 18

E XCEPT IT WASN'T.

By the time Michelle crossed the street and walked down to the Bentleys twenty minutes later, she not only heard the *thump, thump, thump* of kids shooting baskets behind the Bentleys' garage—no surprise there—but voices she didn't immediately recognize and the giggles of younger children. *Oh no.* She definitely wasn't up for a full-fledged backyard party.

But she couldn't back out now. She'd already sent her kids over. Coming around the side of the two-flat to the backyard, she saw Harry Bentley hovering over a charcoal grill wearing a big white apron, his shaved head glistening with sweat, waving a pair of tongs as he talked with Greg Singer and an older white man . . . oh yes, the husband of the retired couple who lived on the other side of the Bentleys. *Uh-oh.* She totally blanked on their names, if she ever knew them at all.

Estelle Bentley, setting out food on a couple of card tables covered with blue plastic tablecloths, was chatting with some women sitting in the shade of a round umbrella table, but caught sight of her and immediately waved her over. "Sister Michelle! So glad you could come. You know Nicole Singer, don't you? And Miss Mattie, of course. And this is our next-door neighbor, Eva Molander."

Molander . . . that was the name. Michelle smiled and held out her hand. "Of course. Nice to see you, Mrs. Molander. And Mrs. Krakowski." After shaking hands with the two older ladies, she nodded at Nicole Singer. "Hi, Nicole. Good to see you again too. You look really nice." Nicole had on white jeans, white sandals, a loose, flower-print blouse, and her blonde hair had been twisted into a fat braid that hung over her shoulder.

Nicole flushed, seemed shy. "Thanks."

Michelle looked around. "I thought I heard your kids—"

"Boo!" A childish giggle was immediately followed by the Singers' little boy poking his towhead out from beneath the plastic-covered card tables. "Ha, ha. Scared you. Bet you can't find Becky. She's hiding."

"Nathan!" His mother frowned. "That wasn't polite. Come on out of there and say hello to Mrs. Jasper properly . . . Becky?" she called. "You too."

Becky Singer, wearing a pretty pink sundress, appeared tentatively from the other side of the house. "We were just playing, Mommy."

Michelle smiled warmly at the children. "Hi, Becky. Hi, Nathan."

"Hello, Mrs. Jasper," they chimed in unison, eyes down, sounding like penitents at a confessional.

Good grief, they were just kids. She winked at Nathan. "You didn't scare me, but you did surprise me." Spying a drink cooler under the card tables she thought fast. "Do you think one of you could surprise me with something cold to drink?"

"I will!" Nathan dived back under the card tables and came up with a can of lime-flavored LaCroix. "This okay?"

"Perfect."

She popped the tab of the sparkling water just as Estelle pulled over two more plastic lawn chairs. "Sit, sit! Those ribs should be done quicker'n Uncle Ben's rice." Their hostess sank down into one of the empty chairs and fanned herself. "Harry's been nursin' 'em all day."

Michelle sipped her lime-water, eyeing the men around the grill. It was an odd mix of folks. The Molanders had always kept to themselves pretty much. She was surprised they even came. And the Singers? Estelle was the type who'd probably invited them because of what she'd let slip about him not having a job right now. *O Lord, I hope she didn't say anything!* But the Bentleys *were* pretty tight with Grace Meredith across the street . . . Why wasn't she invited?

She wished Jared were here. He was better at small-talk than she was.

Almost as if reading her mind, Estelle said, "So glad y'all could come." She beamed at them around the table. "Just wouldn't be

Memorial Day weekend without a backyard barbecue. We invited Farid and Lily too"—she waved at the bungalow on the other side of them—"but they had somethin' else goin' on. And Grace is out of town, has a couple concerts this weekend. But Rodney should be here any time—that's Harry's son." She added, "DaShawn's daddy," almost as an afterthought.

*Grace out of town . . . of course.* She'd wanted all those brochures for her concerts this weekend. What was wrong with her brain, anyway?

"Yah, it's nice, ver-ry nice." Eva Molander smiled nervously. "We don't get out much. Mostly just church and the grocery store. Karl's health, ya know."

Michelle didn't know, wasn't sure any of them did. Eva Molander had a slight Swedish accent, white hair, pale blue eyes. Pleasant face, really. Did they have family in the city? Grandchildren? She guessed the woman's age to be late seventies, her husband too. Which wasn't *that* old. Her mother was about the same age but seemed a lot more vigorous.

"We gonna eat soon? Don't wanna miss my TV program," Mattie Krakowski mumbled. "*Dancing with the Stars* comes on at seven."

Estelle chuckled. "Don't you worry, Miss Mattie. It's not even six yet. But we can bring out the appetizers and get started. Sister Michelle, want to help me?"

Michelle hopped up and followed their hostess up the outside back stairs to the second floor apartment, glad to have something to do. "Don't these stairs get a little tiring?" she asked, panting a little as they reached the kitchen. "Oh—!" She was startled when a black Lab raised its head from where it was lying near the back door and gave a little *woof*.

"Oh, don't mind Corky. That's Harry's dog. Specially trained—Harry does security with Amtrak, you know. But sweet as a lamb . . . Here, why don't you take this down?" Estelle handed Michelle a long cake pan of deviled eggs. "And just to assure you"—she winked—"we didn't say anything to the Singers about knowing Greg quit his job. But thought maybe they could use a bit of fellowship."

126

Michelle grinned. "Thought as much. But thanks for not telling on me."

Estelle pulled a pan of hot pizza rolls out of the oven. "You still good goin' to Manna House next Saturday to talk to the young ladies?"

Was that coming up already? "Sure—oh, wait. What time are you thinking?"

"Mm, morning would be best. By afternoon, everyone's out an' about."

*Morning.* "Oh, Estelle. I . . . that's when I volunteer at Lifeline. And I wasn't there this past Saturday. I really don't think I should cancel two weekends in a row."

Estelle's brow furrowed as she covered the pizza rolls with aluminum foil. "All right. Let's see . . . maybe I could arrange for either Friday evening or Sunday afternoon. Would either of those work for you?"

"Sunday might be best, but I could probably do either. What about Grace? You wanted her to go too."

"I'll check with her and get back to you soon as I know. Sound good?"

The two women made their way back down the stairs, Michelle with the deviled eggs and Estelle with a platter of pizza rolls straight out of the oven. The kids would be in food heaven.

Michelle was surprised that she lasted as long as she did. In spite of her family being added last-minute, there was plenty of food—marvelous messy ribs, homemade potato salad, collard greens with ham hocks, a Jell-O salad full of whipped cream and fruit, potato chips, a few other bags of salty munchies, chocolate cake, and enough sweet tea to float a battleship.

The Singer kids had latched onto Tabby, who was playing hopscotch with them out on the front sidewalk. Rodney Bentley showed up just about the time Estelle was helping Miss Mattie back into the house so she could see her TV show. Harry looked annoyed, but DaShawn nearly knocked his father over with a big

127

hug. "Hey, Dad! Wanna play a little two-on-two? We got Destin and Tavis, but we need a fourth."

Rodney untangled himself. "Hold on, buddy. A man needs some of those ribs, ya know. You kids didn't eat 'em all, didya?"

"And, uh, we need to be going soon ourselves," Michelle put in. "School day tomorrow. Workday too."

"Aw, Mom. Can't we stay just till eight thirty? Please?" Tavis put on a good puppy-dog face.

Michelle wavered. "You got any homework?" A little late to be asking, she realized, but better late than never.

"Just a little math. Gonna take me half an hour max."

Destin nodded, devouring a second piece of chocolate cake. "Yeah, me too."

Rejoining the group, Estelle gave a *fine-with-me* shrug. "Don't worry, these wannabe basketball stars are gonna get a workout helpin' me take all this food back upstairs . . . right, Rodney?" She chuckled as she handed a plate to her stepson.

The Molanders excused themselves and headed next door via the alley. "We need to be going too," Nicole said. "Thanks for everything, Estelle. Next time let us bring some food, okay? . . . Coming, Greg? I'll collect the kids."

"Give me a minute," her husband said, still talking to Harry.

Michelle and Nicole walked together alongside the house to the front, where Tabby was drawing on the sidewalks with Nathan and Becky using big colored chalk. "Look, Mommy!" Nathan proudly pointed to something that looked vaguely like a snake—or maybe a dragon—covering the entire length of the Bentleys' front walk from the porch to the sidewalk.

Michelle laughed. "Looks like Tabby found a good use for all that sidewalk chalk she's been hoarding ever since she was Nathan's age. Every time I wanted to send it to the Salvation Army along with her old toys, she wouldn't let me touch any of it."

Tabby flashed her mother an embarrassed look and kept drawing with Becky out on the main sidewalk.

Nicole smiled. "Smart girl. Always be prepared." The homeschool mom was quiet a few more minutes as they watched the sidewalk artists, then she murmured, "Does Tabby do any babysitting?"

Michelle was surprised at the question. "Well . . . not really. Though she often helps entertain kids at church, like at the workday they had recently. I did quite a bit of babysitting at her age—though it was called 'looking after your brothers.'" Michelle snickered. "But Tabby and Tavis are our youngest, so she missed out on that."

Nicole nodded. "I was just wondering. She seems like a natural. Do you think she'd be interested in babysitting some time? Our kids seem to like her."

"Oh . . . I'm sure that would be fine. You'd have to ask her though."

"It's just a thought. I don't have any particular time in mind at the moment. But I might need someone this summer. Things are . . . well, kind of up in the air at the moment, as you can probably guess."

Michelle wasn't sure what to say. She could certainly understand how things could be "up in the air" at the Singer household if Greg was between jobs, but she wasn't sure how that had anything to do with Tabby and babysitting. So all she did was nod sympathetically and say, "I'm sure things will work out."

Greg Singer came around the side of the two-flat just then. "There they are! Thought you three would be all the way home by now . . . What's this?" He crouched down to admire Nathan's snake-dragon, and then wandered out to the sidewalk to see what Becky and Tabby were doing.

Nicole touched Michelle on the arm, her voice low and soft. "Would you mind asking Tabby if she'd like to babysit? That way she'd be free to say yes or no without me putting her on the spot."

"Well, sure. If you'd like." Michelle watched as the father took both kids by the hand and started for home. Nicole hurried to catch up. Both Nathan and Becky turned back and waved good-bye to Tabby.

"Cute kids," Tabby said as she and Michelle headed for their own house at the north end of Beecham.

"Their mom wants to know if you'd be interested in babysitting some time."

Tabby stopped midstreet. "For real?" Her dark eyes danced as her face broke into a wide smile. "Yeah! Like, would they pay me money?"

"Shh." Michelle glanced back to be sure the Singers were far enough away not to hear. "I'm sure they would. Mrs. Singer doesn't have any specific time in mind. She was just wondering."

"Cool." Tabby bounced on into the house, but Michelle sank into one of the lawn chairs on their small front porch. The momentary bump in her energy while at the Bentleys now seemed to drain right out the soles of her feet . . . and the delicious ribs with their rich, spicy sauce weren't digesting that well either. It was too early to go to bed—still light out, and the boys wouldn't be home for another half hour. But the earlier high of eighty-plus degrees was now in the comfortable low seventies. Maybe she'd just sit out here for a while till the boys came home.

Would be even nicer if they had that porch swing.

But could they afford it? She should at least go online and check out what porch swings cost. It looked as if the cheerleading camp would work out for Tabby after all, but that meant another camp fee—except her parents were offering to pay half. Jared wouldn't want to take it, but they still needed to find some kind of camp for Tavis. And the cheerleading camp was only one week. They still had all of July and August to cover for the twins, a patchwork of other programs and activities. Most of which would cost money.

She sighed. All of which she and Jared needed to talk about . . . soon. School would be out in three weeks. Michelle felt a flutter of anxiety. It was hard enough making plans for the kids each summer, but finding time to talk about it was the real sticking point. Given Jared's schedule, Wednesday would be the soonest—he got home at two that afternoon, though she didn't get home till six and then there was prayer meeting at church. So maybe Thursday evening, before he had to leave again at ten . . .

She groaned. Why did life have to be so complicated?

*"Do not be anxious about anything . . ."*

The familiar phrase from the New Testament flitted through her mind just as a warm breeze kissed her face and ruffled the leaves of the trees all up and down Beecham Street. *"Do not be anxious . . ."* She should read that whole passage before going to bed. But even without looking it up, she knew it talked about *"praying with thanksgiving"* about everything instead of worrying, and promised a peace greater than her own understanding.

Michelle stood up and looked at her watch. Eight thirty. Maybe she'd go back to the Bentleys and chase the boys home so she could go to bed.

As for thanksgiving . . . at least she and Jared *had* jobs, unlike the Singers right now.

# Chapter 19

MICHELLE WAS ASLEEP BY THE TIME Jared got home that night, but woke long enough to feel relief as his familiar bulk climbed into bed next to her. "Missed you," he whispered in her ear, pulling her close.

"Missed you too," she murmured, pressing her back against his bare chest, stroking the strong arms he wrapped around her. "Let's not do separate weekends again."

"Mmm, good idea. 'Night, Gumdrop."

All the things she wanted to talk about with him started to flood into her consciousness—but she stuffed each one back into its mental cubbyhole. He'd just come off a twelve-hour shift. And she needed sleep too. *Patience, Michelle. All in good time—*

Wait. She had to know. "Jared? Did Bucky's baby arrive? Boy or girl? Is his wife okay?"

No answer. His breathing was already slow and deep . . .

*Oh, brother.*

Michelle awoke two minutes before her alarm rang the next morning and she shut it off so as not to waken Jared. He was still asleep when she tiptoed in later to say she was leaving for work. She stood for a few extra moments at the side of the bed just looking at him . . . his smooth dark skin, mouth slightly parted, eyes closed, perfect ears, a bit stubbly around the chin line. How'd she snag this guy? Still a head-turner, even at forty-two. She leaned down and kissed him gently on the cheek.

"Mmm." He shifted but didn't awaken.

She called later in the morning, but he said the baby hadn't arrived by the time he'd left the tower last night. However, once he got to work for his two-to-ten shift he sent her a text: *Mother and baby girl doing fine. Father a wreck.*

That made her laugh . . . but the next text wasn't so funny. *Sorry, sweetheart, but I might as well sleep over tonight since my shift change starts at six tomorrow morning.*

At the supper table she could tell the kids were feeling his absence too. They'd all been in bed when he got home last night and had left for school before he got up. Which meant they hadn't seen their father since Saturday morning when he'd waved good-bye, and now it was going to be another twenty-four hours.

*O God, this is crazy.*

Scooting her chair back, she started carrying the leftover rice and lonely pork chop back to the kitchen. "Destin, your turn to load the dishwasher."

Destin came into the kitchen carrying his empty plate in one hand and some papers in the other. "Hey, Mom, forgot to give this to you last week."

She took a quick glance. A crumpled copy of Lane Tech's newsletter. "Oh, thanks. Put it on the counter. I'll look at it later."

"No, Mom. Thought you'd be interested in this . . ." Destin turned to one of the inside pages and handed it to her.

*Lane Tech Boys Basketball Summer Camp,* the page title said. *Week One—June 28–July 2 . . . Week Two—July 12–16 . . . Time: 9th grade 8:00—10:00 am . . . Cost: $40.*

"Forty dollars!" Her eyes widened. "You mean you could've done *this* basketball camp for *forty dollars?* Wait . . . it says ninth grade. Don't they have one for incoming seniors like you?"

"Mom." Destin had that *be-patient-she's-just-a-mother* tone. "You're missing the point. Look . . ." He pointed beneath the initial headline. *Grades 4–9.* And then to where it said, *4th–8th graders 10:30—12:30.*

She looked at him. "Tavis."

Destin patted her on the shoulder and grinned. "Thatta girl."

"Oh you." She swatted him with the newsletter. "You knew about this? And you're only just now telling me?"

Destin shrugged. "Sorry. They only do these summer camps for middle school and incoming freshmen. It didn't apply to me, so I didn't really think about it. Till one of my buddies at school said his little brother was going to sign up."

"Okay, okay, you're forgiven . . . Finish up, will you?" Michelle walked out of the kitchen with the newsletter. "Tavis? Come here a minute!"

Tavis no sooner heard about the basketball camp than he ran the newsletter across the street to see if DaShawn wanted to go too. When he came back, he handed his mother a note. "Miz Estelle said give this to you."

She unfolded the note, smiling at the lovely, large handwriting. So like Estelle's personality. *Talked to Grace. She says Sunday afternoon or evening would work best for her. Is that okay for you? In fact, this might be the best after all! Manna House has a worship service for the ladies Sunday evenings, different people come in to lead it. We could just turn that hour over to you and Grace. What do you think? Estelle.*

Michelle hardly knew what to think. Sounded like a bigger deal than it had at first. A worship service? How did what she had to offer fit in with that? But she couldn't back out now. Hopefully she could talk to Grace and at least get an idea of what she'd be doing.

At least by the time she and Jared got a chance to sit down together Thursday evening for a real talk before he left for work at nine for his weekly night shift—ten to six—she had the three summer camps marked in pencil on the big kitchen calendar.

Jared snorted when he heard about the forty-dollar basketball camp. "Well, that's a no-brainer. Okay, let's see how this is gonna work . . ." He studied the calendar. "School's out on the third Friday of June—man! No wonder the natives are restless. That feels so late! How are kids like Destin supposed to get any summer jobs starting so late?"

"I know, hon. But let's talk about that later. Right now we have to finish making a decision about Tabby and Tavis."

"Okay, okay." Back to the calendar. "This cheerleading camp business starts the Tuesday after school's out, so guess we'd have to drive Tabby to your folks' that weekend—"

Michelle noticed that Sunday said "Father's Day" on the calendar. *Too bad.* Driving to Indiana wouldn't be Jared's idea of a great Father's Day. But the upside was, it'd give her a chance to celebrate Father's Day with *her* dad.

"—and pick her up the following weekend. Man . . ."

Michelle could guess what he was thinking. That was a lot of driving two weekends in a row. "Yeah," she acknowledged. "And then Destin's Five-Star Basketball Camp starts midweek the next week. So we have to get him to the South Side on Wednesday and pick him up on Saturday."

Jared leaned back in his chair and rubbed a hand over his hair. "Gonna take some coordination, but it's a start. Guess we should say okay to the camp for Tabby—though that's a lot of driving to Indiana two weekends in a row. Picking Destin up on Saturday is no problem . . . Not sure how we'll get him there in the middle of the week though. Romeoville's way on the South Side, a good hour, maybe more if there's traffic."

"I'm sure we can work something out." Michelle laid her hand on top of Jared's. "At least Tavis' basketball camp the *next* week is at Lane Tech—I could take him on the way to work, or he could ride the city bus like Destin does. That's right after the Fourth of July holiday, see? At least each of the kids can start the summer with a sports camp. After that . . ." She shrugged, and then sighed. "Wish I could take the summer off and just be here for the kids." She started to add, *Could really use a break from work.* But it sounded so whiny. Jared's work schedule was even more demanding than hers.

"Huh. Not sure you'd want three teenagers underfoot all day even if you could." Jared tossed her a pen. "Might as well write those dates on there in ink. And tell your folks we'll take them up on their offer. Frankly, it's the least they can do after your mother overrode all the usual camp rules and regulations, but don't tell her I said that."

Michelle couldn't help but laugh—and then remembered Estelle's note a couple of days ago. "Oh, something else I need to ask you about. Estelle Bentley asked me to come to the women's shelter where she works and talk to some of the women there about the resources that Lifeline Care Center offers. Grace Meredith is going too, and it looks like Sunday evening would be the best time for her. What's your weekend look like? Any conflict you can see?"

He shrugged. "Sounds like a great ministry opportunity. The men's prayer breakfast meets this Saturday—first Saturday in June. Not sure about Sunday yet. Pastor Q phoned, said he wants to meet with the deacons this weekend—probably to catch up on what happened while he was gone. Didn't say when. Hope it's not on Saturday, though, because after the men's breakfast, I'm going to ride Destin's tail the rest of the day to get out there hustling about that summer job, even if I have to drive him around to do it." Jared stood up and stretched. "We done here? I'd like to relax a little before I have to leave for work."

Her husband headed downstairs to the family room and a moment later she heard the TV go on. She'd like to relax too, but . . . She sighed. Probably should make a few calls to her women's ministry committee about what needed to be done to be sure things were moving along for their monthly women's event the second weekend in June.

Jared sat Destin down Friday evening at the computer and they searched for summer jobs in the Chicago area open to teenagers. Some had applications he could fill out online, but Michelle overheard her husband lecture their oldest that going in face-to-face was always the best policy.

Hauling a basket of dirty clothes to the basement to get a head start on the laundry, Michelle felt grateful that Jared was the one on Destin's case. She had enough nagging opportunities without adding another one.

Like these school pants of Tavis's! She held up a pair of dark blue pants to examine a new rip in the knee. And so dirty! Honestly! Didn't the boys wear sweatpants or shorts for outdoor P.E.? What had he been doing—sliding into home base in his good school pants?

Michelle took the pants back upstairs to find Tavis, then remembered he was outside riding his skateboard in the street with DaShawn. She didn't really like them playing in the street, though with Beecham being a dead-end because of the cemetery, it was relatively safe. Opening the front door, she saw the boys sitting on the curb with a screwdriver, fixing something on the bottom of a skateboard. Tabby was on her bike, watching the operation.

"Tavis? Come here a minute."

Tavis looked up, sighed, and got to his feet. "Whassup, Mom?"

She waited until he came up onto the small porch, then held out the pants. "Don't 'whassup' me. What happened here? These are your good school pants."

Tavis shrugged. "Uh, just tripped and fell down on the way home from school yesterday. Sorry about the pants. Forgot to tell you."

Michelle looked at the rip. The material below the damage was stiff. Her tone changed to concern. "This looks like blood. Did you hurt yourself?" She glanced at his knees but he had on a pair of jeans—some protection for skateboarding at least.

Tavis shrugged again. "Scraped my knee a little. It's okay."

"Well, the pants are *not* okay, but I'm not going to buy you a new pair until next fall—you'll be needing a new size then anyway. So I'm going to iron on a patch for now, and I don't want to hear any complaining about it."

"Didn't either fall down." Tabby had leaned her bike against the steps and stood on the porch, arms crossed. "He got pushed."

"You shut up, Tabby." Tavis glared at his sister, then said defensively, "It's no big deal, Mom. We were just foolin' around and I fell down."

Tabby rolled her eyes and disappeared into the house. Michelle looked after her tattletale, then turned back to see Tavis already back at the curb with DaShawn tinkering with the skateboard.

Michelle opened her mouth to call him back, then shut it again. Was that bully messing with Tavis again? She ought to get him alone and get to the bottom of it before he really got hurt. Or . . . would she be making a mountain out of a molehill? He didn't seem to want to talk about it, acted like it was no big deal. Maybe she'd better just leave it alone. Jared would probably tell her boys would be boys.

Still, if something like this happened one more time . . .

Michelle sighed and went back inside to finish the laundry. Right now she had more important things to worry about than ripped pants—like Hannah West, the new client at Lifeline she'd met two weeks ago. Hopefully she'd come back again tomorrow and Michelle could tell her about the next Hope and Healing group that would be starting soon.

# Chapter 20

W HERE CAN I PUT THIS so Destin will be sure to see it?" Jared held up a note he'd written on a sheet of notebook paper as Michelle poured coffee into a travel cup for him the next morning. "In case you're gone by the time he gets up." The note said: *Destin—Gone to men's prayer breakfast. Don't go anywhere! I'll be back at 10:00. Dad.*

She opened a kitchen drawer and pulled out a roll of tape. "Stick it on the bathroom mirror." She grinned as Jared headed down the hall with the note and tape. Destin was seventeen and body conscious. He'd see it.

A few minutes and a quick kiss on her cheek later, Jared headed out the front door with his coffee. The men from Northside met on the first Saturday of each month from eight o'clock till nine thirty at Sanders Restaurant—their version of "men's ministry." A core of eight to ten men usually came, others showed up from time to time. But Jared had mentioned again just today that the prayer breakfast was a good spiritual anchor for the guys, even for him. "Nothing as powerful as a group of brothers praying together," he said. "Okay, praying and eating." Then he laughed.

But it made her think of the couple of times she'd prayed with Estelle and Grace. There was something compelling about praying with a group of "sisters"—something she wished she could do more often. "Yeah, like I need something else to shoehorn into my schedule," she reminded herself as she shut off the coffeemaker and put on water for tea. Coffee just didn't sound good this morning for some reason.

An hour and two laundry loads later, she left another note on the bathroom mirror, since all three kids were still asleep, and headed for the Humbolt Park neighborhood in the minivan. As usual, Bernice was already at the reception desk when Michelle got to the Lifeline Care Center at nine, and a new crew of volunteers was sorting and folding contributions to the Wee Welcome Shop. As she passed the supply cabinets, Michelle suddenly stopped. *Brochures.* She should take a bunch of brochures to leave with the women at the Manna House shelter tomorrow. But now they'd definitely need to order more.

Michelle was glad she'd arrived early. Her Hope and Healing group didn't start till ten. Shutting the door of the meeting room, she sank into a comfy chair, poured more hot peppermint tea from the thermos she'd brought with her into her travel cup, and pulled her Bible out of her briefcase. Probably should've taken time for devotions at home, but somehow she got busy with laundry and making up the grocery list. *Huh.* The tyranny of the urgent crowding out the important.

Well, she had a few minutes now. Turning to Paul's letter to the Philippians, she reread the passage about "do not be anxious about anything," then she flipped back to the Psalms, searching for something to share with the young women in the post-abortion group. A verse she'd underlined at some point in Psalm 27 stood out: "The Lord is my light and my salvation—whom shall I fear? The Lord is the stronghold of my life—of whom shall I be afraid?"

*Fear.* That had been a constant refrain in the stories these young women had shared in the group. Fear of an unplanned pregnancy . . . of becoming a single mom. Afraid to have an abortion . . . afraid not to. Fear that parents would find out. Worry about what people would say. Anxiety about the future. Fear that God wouldn't forgive them . . .

Why had she underlined this verse? Michelle couldn't remember. But it'd be a good one to share with the group today as a reminder that they didn't have to live in fear.

Funny thing, though. Even as LaVeta and Ellie and Maria filed in a while later, followed by Denise and Linda, giving each other hugs, showing off the "creative expressions" they were each working on to share at the memorial service next week, Michelle couldn't shake the feeling that God had led her to that scripture today, not just for these women, but for herself.

* * *

They planned the memorial service for two o'clock next Saturday since Michelle had her monthly women's ministry event at Northside that morning. But the later time seemed to suit the group, who wanted to invite a few family members and friends. That would be the last meeting for this particular group, which was probably a good thing, since Michelle could tell Hannah West a new group would be starting soon.

Maybe she'd take a couple of Saturdays off and start the new group in July. Each group usually met for nine sessions, which would take them through the rest of the summer. Perfect.

By the time Michelle did her Saturday errands, it was almost three o'clock when she got home, and she was almost shaking with hunger. She'd only had a piece of toast with her tea early that morning, but had decided to save time by doing her grocery shopping on the way home from Lifeline . . . though she knew it wasn't smart to shop on an empty stomach. She'd probably thrown a few too many "impulse buys" into her grocery cart today.

Jared and Destin had gone out job hunting, but she'd been in touch with the twins by phone . . . Tavis was over at the Bentleys, and Tabby had actually gotten a call from Nicole Singer asking if she'd come down to the house to entertain the kids as a "mother's helper" for a few hours that afternoon—prelude to babysitting, no doubt. Scrambling a couple of eggs for her late lunch, Michelle was just about to go downstairs to move the laundry when she decided to lie down instead, *just for a few minutes,* get off her feet . . .

"Michelle? Honey? You okay?"

She felt someone shaking her shoulder . . . Jared's voice . . . felt herself swimming up, up, through a deep darkness, up toward the light . . .

Michelle opened her eyes. "What? . . . Oh . . ." She struggled to sit up. "Goodness, what time is it?" She squinted at the bedside clock. "Six fifteen? Can't believe it. I just laid down for a few minutes . . ."

Hadn't realized she was *that* tired.

"Didn't mean to take such a long nap." She swung her legs off the bed and slipped her feet into her sandals. *Uh-oh, the twins.* "Are Tavis and Tabby home?"

Jared nodded. "Yeah. Begging for food. Uh, got any supper plans?"

She followed him out of the bedroom, still shaking sleep from her brain. "Just went shopping—I'll come up with something." Okay . . . baked potatoes in the microwave, canned chili and grated cheese on top. Couldn't get easier than that. But the kids liked it. Opening the refrigerator, Michelle pulled out some cheddar cheese and green onions. "How did the job hunting go?"

Jared shrugged. "We stopped at Starbucks, Mickey-Ds, several other fast-food places, talked to the managers, he filled out applications . . . got the usual 'we'll call you if something comes up.'" Her husband shook his head as she handed him some large potatoes to scrub. "I dunno, Michelle. Don't think the job market's very good for teenagers right now. But it was a good experience for Destin, I think. He's going to need to do most of this on his own from now on, but at least he got the idea."

"Speaking of Destin, where is he?"

Jared handed back the five baking potatoes, scrubbed clean. "Back on the laptop. I told him he needs to show up and apply to at least one place each day after school next week, but he has to get himself there—bus or 'L' or even his bike if it's close."

"You're a hard taskmaster," she teased. But it was good. Destin was a good kid, but he had a lazy streak if it didn't involve basketball or sports.

Supper was on the table in twenty minutes. She'd added chopped green onions and sour cream to top the hot chili and cheese, and wasn't surprised when she had to microwave a few more potatoes for her hungry crew.

"How'd babysitting at the Singers go?" she asked Tabby.

Tabby shrugged. "Okay. Wasn't really babysitting, because both their parents were there, which felt a little weird. Mr. Singer was busy on the phone in the living room and Mrs. Singer was doing

. . . something. But I had fun with the kids. They showed me their 'school' in the basement—man, do they have a lot of books! We played board games down there for a while, then went out in the backyard, played 'Mother May I?' an' stuff like that." Then she grinned. "They paid me too."

Jared nodded his approval. "That's good. Maybe it'll turn into a real job."

"Yeah," Destin muttered, "then *you* can pay for your stupid cheerleading camp, like I have to."

"Da-ad!" Tabby wailed.

"Destin, that's enough," Jared barked. "We're not going to go over that again."

The phone rang. Tavis and Tabby both jumped up to get it . . . but it was Shareese Watson for Michelle, wanting to check on whether the video series for the summer women's events was going to be announced in church tomorrow. "I went ahead and made some flyers to hand out, Sister Michelle, hope that's okay . . ."

Sunday morning . . . finally in the car and off to church. At the last minute, Jared handed the keys to Destin in spite of groans from the twins. "Dad! Don't let him practice on us!" Tabby wailed. "I haven't lived long enough yet!"

"No comments from the peanut gallery," Jared ordered as he climbed into the front passenger seat. "Everybody buckled up?"

Michelle climbed into the third seat and tuned out. At least she didn't have to be the "responsible adult" in the front seat. She was too distracted this morning. She'd spent half the evening last night on the phone, making sure everyone on the committee had followed through on their assignments. So far so good . . . Sister Norma had given an enthusiastic thumbs-up on the *Discerning the Voice of God* video series. Sister Mavis had gotten approval from the church treasurer to purchase the leader kit and had put a rush order on it. It was supposed to arrive by Wednesday of this week. And Sister Gleniece had put an announcement in that week's bulletin. With Shareese's flyer—which no one had asked her to do, but would probably be helpful—they should be good to go by next weekend. All she had to do was arrange for a DVD player and projector. *Huh.* Did the church even have one?

The other half of the evening had been spent washing and braiding Tabby's hair, which was really getting unmanageable. Taking longer and longer to care for. And it was time to get her own hair permed again too. Next weekend? Mmm, no, the women's event at Northside was in the morning, and she had the memorial service for the Hope and Healing group in the afternoon. She'd better make appointments *tomorrow* for both of them for the Saturday after that.

In spite of some jerky starts and stops—and Tabby squealing, "We're all gonna die!" when her brother bumped over a curb— Destin pulled into the church parking lot with the minivan still in one piece and a triumphant grin on his face. But by the time he also drove the family home after church—stopping by Eng's to pick up the Chinese takeout she'd called in while they all waited for Jared to get out of his meeting with Pastor Q and the deacons—Michelle felt ready for a nap. Riding with a teenage driver took more emotional energy than she had at the moment. She needed to recharge her batteries before Estelle Bentley picked her up at five o'clock for the visit to the Manna House shelter that evening.

She never did get a chance to talk to Grace Meredith about what she planned to do and how her sharing would fit, but Estelle had said not to worry, these Sunday night meetings were very informal and she knew God would fit everything together just right. Well, hopefully Estelle Bentley had an inside track on what the Almighty planned to do, because Michelle didn't feel all that confident.

She'd just kicked off her shoes and stretched out on the bed when Jared came into the room and flopped down in the bedroom chair, a thoughtful frown on his face. "You okay?" she asked. "Is something wrong?" *O Lord, don't let him get fired from his job or anything . . .*

He shook his head. "Nothing's wrong. But I uh, wanted to tell you what Pastor Q said to me after the other deacons left the meeting after service. Would like to know what you think." He scratched his chin absently, as if mulling over what he wanted to say.

She plumped the pillows and sat up against them. Whatever it was didn't seem like lying-down news. "Okay . . ."

"Well, he said he'd heard a lot of good things about my sermon last week, and told me I should consider going to seminary, get my MDiv, maybe take over the pulpit when he retires down the road."

Michelle blinked. "Wait . . . take over the pulpit? Do you mean . . . like, quit your job? Go into the ministry?" The idea made her head swim.

Jared threw up his hands. "Back up . . . waaay back. Mainly he was suggesting I consider going to seminary. Forget about the rest."

"Still . . ." She blew out a breath. "How would you manage that? Not just the money, but even the *time*. You hardly have time now for"—she almost said, *for me, for your kids*. But she just finished with—"for *life* beyond work and church responsibilities."

He shrugged. "I know. The whole idea sounds crazy to me too. Except that . . . I felt really energized giving that sermon last week. You know I've always enjoyed doing ministry. Never really thought about going *into* the ministry, but . . ." He lapsed again into a thoughtful silence.

Michelle's thoughts tumbled. Jared go back to school at this stage of their life? Why, Destin would be going to college in a year . . . how were they going to pay for *that*, much less seminary for Jared? "I hardly know what to say." They sat in silence for several long minutes. Then she leaned forward. "Except for one thing. It's really a compliment to you, coming from Pastor Q. I . . . I really wish I'd been here to hear your sermon."

The doorbell rang. Michelle glanced at the bedside clock. It was only four. She hoped it wasn't Estelle, wanting to leave earlier.

"I'll get it." Jared stood up. "But yeah, Pastor's affirmation really meant something to me, even if the seminary thing is just a wild idea. I'd like us to at least pray about it, see if God gives us any leading." The doorbell rang again. "Better see who that is."

She let him go, hoping it wasn't for her. She heard him open the door and then say, "Singer! Uh . . . come in."

Their neighbor from down the street? Was it just Greg or Nicole too? She hopped off the bed and listened at the half-open door and heard Greg say, "Hope I'm not bothering you folks. But I, uh, wanted to share something with you. You got a minute?"

# Chapter 21

Jared didn't call her, so Michelle assumed it was just Greg Singer, come to talk to her husband about something. *Good.* She really should start to get ready for the visit to Manna House this evening. She only had an hour—enough time to change clothes and hopefully a little more time to think and pray about her sharing this evening.

Now . . . what to wear to the women's shelter? The women at the shelter certainly wouldn't be dressed up, but it *was* kind of a worship service, Estelle had said. Michelle still had on the good white pants and purple blouse she'd worn to church, though she'd long since shed the matching white jacket. Pastor Q asked women who took part in the service, even the choir, to wear dresses, but he and First Lady Donna were tolerant of modest slacks and pantsuits in the pews. She finally decided on a pair of tan slacks, black fitted T-shirt, tan jacket, and brown ankle boots—business casual—as the day was fairly cool for June, low seventies, even a sprinkle now and then.

As she came out of their bedroom to slip across the hall to the bathroom, Michelle could hear the men talking in the living room . . . something about a new business opportunity. She listened a moment. Singer sounded quite enthusiastic about selling a new sports drink. Well, good. She wished him the best. But she was glad Jared hadn't asked her to join them.

Locking herself in the bathroom, she freshened her makeup to bring out her coppery skin tone and used a pick to lift her straightened cap of black hair. *Hmm.* She really did need to get to the beauty shop. How long had it been? Four, maybe even six, weeks? Could she squeeze a hair appointment into next weekend, along with the Northside women's event *and* the last session of her post-abortion group? Probably not. She sighed. She'd just have to make do a while longer.

Coming out of the bathroom ten minutes later, she noticed Destin leaning idly in the archway between dining room and living room, listening to Mr. Singer's animated spiel. Should she let him eavesdrop like that? Not that it was a private conversation. In fact, Greg Singer's enthusiastic voice could probably be heard anywhere in the house. She'd let Jared handle it if it was a problem.

At five minutes to five, Michelle walked into the living room. Singer had been there for almost an hour. Did Jared need rescuing? "Hi, Greg! I hope you'll excuse me for not coming out earlier." She held out her hand to him. "I have an appointment downtown this evening. Someone is picking me up at five and I needed to get ready. How are Nicole and the kids?"

Greg jumped up apologetically and shook her hand. "They're fine, fine. Didn't mean to keep you folks. It's just such a wonderful opportunity, I wanted to let Jared, here, know about it on the ground floor."

Jared stood up too. "I appreciate it. But I'm really not in a position to take on anything like that."

Michelle slipped out the front door. She'd let her husband take care of saying good-bye. Had to hand it to him . . . Jared was being extraordinarily polite and patient, even though she knew he had absolutely no interest in getting involved in any kind of "business" selling whatever-that-was, that sports drink Greg was so excited about.

Estelle Bentley came out of their two-flat, *yoo-hooed* at her, and waved her over to the small black SUV parked in front. Estelle was wearing one of her classy African tunics with a head wrap, and Michelle worried that she should've dressed up a bit more. But when Grace Meredith came out the front door of her bungalow and headed across the street too, Michelle was relieved to see her next-door neighbor was also wearing slacks—black, slightly flared over boots, a long black blouse worn casually over a white tank top, leather hobo bag slung over her shoulder, and no jewelry except simple hoop earrings. Very understated—but, Michelle had to admit, the professional singer was so attractive, she'd probably look pretty just out of bed with no makeup and bedhead.

"Oh, Estelle!" Grace called, even before she got to the car. "Can we wait just a few minutes? Sam isn't here yet, but I just got a call. She should be here anytime. She really wants to go with us—oh, wait. That's her car turning the corner."

Samantha Curtis's gray Honda Civic pulled up to the curb in front of Grace's house, and a moment later the vivacious young woman with the wild sassy twists and yummy caramel skin bounced across the street to join them. "So sorry! Hope I didn't keep you waiting long! For some reason traffic was all snarled up on the Drive. On a Sunday afternoon too!"

Estelle Bentley chuckled. "We waited all of two seconds. It's only just five now. Glad you could join us, young lady. Well . . . climb in, everyone. DaShawn supposedly cleaned the car yesterday, but let's just say his standard of 'clean' needs an upgrade."

Grace and her young assistant climbed into the backseat of the RAV4, so Michelle got into the front passenger seat and fastened her seatbelt. "Thanks for letting me tag along again," Sam said from behind them. She was one of those people who had a perpetually cheery voice. "Since Grace is singing this time, I used that as an excuse to invite myself . . . I hope you don't mind, Michelle. I think it's great that you're going to share about the crisis pregnancy center."

The young woman was nothing if not friendly. Michelle twisted slightly in her seat to address her as Estelle started the car and drove down Beecham. "Did you say 'again'? You've been to Manna House before?"

Estelle chuckled at the wheel. "Now you walkin' where angels have trod."

*Huh?* Michelle had no idea what *that* meant. But Grace spoke up and quietly said Estelle had invited them a few months ago to visit Manna House, and a young Latina had given a wonderful Bible study on God's gift of grace, which had been a turning point in her own life. "Somehow that was the day I started to understand, maybe for the first time, what my name—Grace—means. After years of trying to earn God's favor by my good works."

Sam piped up. "And that led to a whole new theme for Grace's concerts . . . 'Just Grace.'"

The way she said it almost took Michelle's breath away. *Just grace.* She almost wished they'd say more, but then the talk turned to a girl Grace and Sam were hoping to see tonight.

"For some reason I feel nervous about seeing Ramona again," Grace confessed. "Our last meeting was so . . . so . . ."

"Weird," Sam finished. "To put it mildly."

"Poor Sister Michelle has no idea what you're talking about," Estelle chuckled. "Better fill her in."

Between the two of them, Grace and Sam told how they'd met this young Hispanic girl on the train coming back from Grace's West Coast tour, in the company of a guy at least ten years her senior. But something hadn't seemed right, he'd been too controlling, and the girl seemed afraid of him. While trying to befriend her, Grace had accidentally spilled coffee on the girl's suede jacket—

"Oh, no, you didn't." Michelle twisted in the front seat again to catch Grace's eye.

Grace flushed. "I did. Offered to get it dry-cleaned and back to her when we got to Chicago, but I was actually able to get it cleaned when we stopped over in Denver, taking a later train—"

"Which is *another* story," Sam giggled.

But Grace ignored her and went on, about how Ramona had met them at Union Station, wanting her jacket back . . . "And then she fainted, right there at our feet! Unfortunately, while we were trying to take care of Ramona, I left my suitcase unattended and someone made off with it—"

Estelle Bentley made a funny snorting sound at the wheel, and Sam snickered. "Told you it was weird."

"—but in the confusion, Ramona disappeared. I was really worried about her, and afraid I'd never see her again."

"But, ta-da," Sam chimed in, "Mister Harry was on duty at the station and caught the thief, got Grace's suitcase back, and later found Ramona. Told Grace he took her to the Manna House shelter."

"Mm-hmm," Estelle sing-songed, almost humming.

"Strange that she's still there," Grace mused. "I would've thought she'd try to get back to her family in LA or Mexico—

wherever she's from. She told me on the train she'd never been to Chicago before, just coming along with Max. But at least if she's there, she's not still with that jerk. He was bad news."

Michelle had no idea how to respond. It really was a strange story. They all fell silent as Estelle got off Lake Shore Drive and navigated a series of side streets. Finally Michelle said, "Well, I'm glad you'll get to see her again, since your meeting at the train station ended so, well, abruptly. I bet she'll be glad to see you again too—oh. Are we here already?"

Estelle had pulled up in front of a churchy-looking two-story building squeezed between an apartment building on one side and a row of storefronts on the other. Michelle felt slightly panicked. She still didn't know exactly what was going to happen tonight. Almost as if reading her mind, Estelle shut off the ignition and then turned to her passengers. "Don't worry about tonight. We'll gather the women, I'll introduce you to folks, and then Grace, why don't you sing a few songs—you said you'd chosen some from your last tour? And then Michelle, just share some of your experience at Lifeline, tell some stories if you want, but also let the girls know what kinds of resources the crisis pregnancy center has to offer. Then, Grace, you could sing another song or two at the end—let the Holy Spirit lead."

"I brought some brochures to leave at the shelter." Michelle patted her tote bag.

"Good idea. Now, let's pray a minute before we go in."

As the older woman prayed in the car, Michelle felt herself relax. *"Let the Holy Spirit lead."* That's right. Jesus had promised his disciples that the Holy Spirit would give them words to say when they had to speak before kings and princes . . . or homeless women in this case.

The day had been fairly cool for June—low sixties and cloudy— but several women sat out on the wide concrete steps leading up to the two oak doors, smoking. "How' ya doin', Miz Estelle," said one woman—darker than white, lighter than black, blackish-brown hair pulled back in a ponytail at the nape of her neck. Michelle had no idea what her nationality was. "Ya here for the meetin'?"

"That's right, Lottie. You comin' in? Somethin' special tonight."

"I'll think about it." Lottie chuckled and a few of the other women snickered.

Estelle pushed a button beside the doors and someone let them in. Once inside the foyer she murmured, "Don't worry, they'll come in. They just don't want to seem too excited about it . . . Oh! There's Edesa and Josh—and my babies!"

There was a flurry of introductions. Sam leaned close to Michelle's ear and whispered, "Edesa is the woman who led the Bible study last time we were here."

*Interesting couple,* Michelle thought. Edesa Baxter might be mistaken for African American—coffee-colored complexion, hair worn in a plethora of small, tight ringlets pulled back from her face with a wide, bright yellow cloth headband—but she spoke with a rich Spanish accent. Might be African Honduran or from some other Central American country. Bridges Family Services had worked with an Afro-Honduran organization in Chicago. Edesa's husband Josh, on the other hand, looked like a typical white college boy—tall, slender, brownish-blond hair, boyish grin, midtwenties.

The "babies" Estelle was fussing over fell somewhere in the middle. A little girl about five years old clung to her mommy's hand, her skin creamy tan and her straight dark brown hair had been gathered into two side ponytails . . . like many of the Hispanic children Michelle worked with at Bridges. Daddy Josh was wearing a baby in a backpack peering wide-eyed over his shoulder. The little boy looked about one and a half, and definitely mixed.

"I am so happy to see you again, Grace!" Edesa gave both Grace and Sam a hug. "I was excited to hear you were coming back to Manna House to sing, so I brought *mi familia* to meet you." She bent down to the little girl. "Gracie, this is the *señorita* I told you about who has the same name you do. Can you say, 'Hola, Miss Grace, *como esta?*'"

"Hi," said little Gracie with just a touch of spitfire, looking Grace Meredith up and down. "Do you know Miss *Gato?* She's white like you."

Grace looked puzzled. Josh rolled his eyes as if embarrassed and Edesa hastened to explain. "She's a young woman at our church Gracie has taken a shine to—recently married our assistant pastor. Her name's Katherine, but everyone calls her Kat . . . so to Gracie she's 'Miss Cat.'"

Michelle was feeling a little left out of all this "reunion" and who-knows-whom, but Estelle, ever sensitive, took her arm and ushered her through the double doors of the foyer into a large common room. A couple of women were setting up a semicircle of folding chairs facing a large mural painted on one wall—a rendition of the Good Shepherd with a herd of rather tattered sheep. *Nice*, Michelle thought. Somehow appropriate.

Sam busied herself plugging in a boom box for the instrumental track Grace was going to use for her songs. Between introductions, Michelle found a chair in the half circle and tried to jot a few more notes in her notebook about what she was going to share tonight. But Grace seemed distracted, glancing about as if looking for someone—the girl Ramona probably.

And then Michelle saw Grace's eyes lock on a slender teenager walking hesitantly into the room, long dark hair falling over one side of her face, large dark eyes and lashes, arms crossed, hugging herself. Had to be Ramona the way she and Grace stood for a few moments just staring at each other. But so young! When Grace had said "young woman," Michelle hadn't expected someone who couldn't be more than . . . What? Sixteen or seventeen? *This* was the girl who'd been traveling cross-country with a guy a decade older?

Michelle's mama antennas went up. Whoever that guy was— Max they'd called him—had no business taking a girl that young out of state! He should be prosecuted for kidnapping.

But before Grace even had a chance to say hello, the girl's shoulders started to shake and she burst into tears. "Ramona!" Grace gasped, taking a step toward her. "What's wrong?"

# Chapter 22

RAMONA BACKED AWAY A STEP OR TWO, wiped her face with her hand, and glanced around the room until she found Estelle Bentley, who had stayed discreetly in the background. "Miss Estelle?" she sniffed. "Didn't . . . didn't the detective man who got me out of jail and brought me here—that's your husband, right?—didn't he tell Miss Grace *anything?*"

Grace looked startled. "No, he did not. Mr. Bentley just told me Amtrak security caught the thief and got my suitcase back. But . . . they put you in *jail?*"

Estelle joined the group with a big sigh. "Baby," she said to Ramona, "my Harry figured if you ever wanted to tell Miss Grace what all happened, that was your business."

"But why—?" Grace started, but now it was Estelle who put up her hand.

"Maybe you two need to go into the office and talk a bit, private-like. We'll get started here, give you two time to pull yourselves together . . . five minutes, okay? But then maybe the rest of your catchin' up can wait until after our praise service tonight. Let it rest in God's hands for right now—which is where this situation has been all along." The older woman gave Ramona a squeeze and then gave the two of them a little push toward the main office off the foyer. "It was no accident God brought the two of you together on that train several weeks ago, you know."

As Grace and Ramona disappeared through the double doors leading into the foyer, Michelle realized she'd practically been holding her breath the past few minutes, and she blew it out slowly. The evening hadn't even started yet and already she felt as if she'd been riding a roller coaster. *Lord, how you're going to pull all this together tonight, I have no idea . . .*

For the next few minutes, Samantha Curtis fiddled with the boom box and CDs again while Estelle and Edesa Baxter huddled together at the front. Edesa's husband had retreated with both kids into a corner of the large room to entertain them.

"*Amigas*?" Edesa Baxter raised her voice to the people still scattered around the room and waved them into the semicircle of chairs. "I think we're ready to begin." Michelle figured Estelle had asked the younger woman to be the emcee for the evening. Edesa waited as the shelter guests and staff found their seats, though a few women just stayed where they were in the seating clusters around the room, flipping through magazines or snoozing. And then Grace and Ramona returned, both looking a little red-eyed and sober.

As Grace took her seat in the front row, Michelle heard her say, "Please stay, Ramona, okay? I want to talk to you some more after the service." The teenager nodded and slipped into the row behind them.

"We have a special treat tonight," Edesa said, her face alight with a wide smile. "First, Grace Meredith, who is not only a concert artist but a neighbor of our own Miss Estelle, is going to sing for us—"

Several women started clapping—whether for Grace or Estelle, Michelle wasn't sure—and the woman they'd met outside, Lottie, gave a couple of hoots.

"—and then Michelle Jasper, also one of Miss Estelle's neighbors, is going to share about the resources offered by Lifeline Care Center here in the city. But first, let's ask our Father God to bless our time together. *Oh, Señor Dios, gracias* for these special sisters who have come to share their gifts with us . . ." And Edesa moved right into a heartfelt prayer, mentioning not only Grace and Michelle by name, but Samantha too, translating part of her own prayer into Spanish for the Spanish-speakers in the room.

Michelle felt very moved by the prayer. Sharing her gift? She hadn't thought of tonight that way. She'd often given presentations to various agencies and churches, both about Bridges Family Services and Lifeline Care Center. But nothing like this setting. The women around her seemed restless—whispers, rustling, chairs scraping, laughter going on in a corner of the room. She was glad that the plan was for Grace to sing first.

After the prayer, Edesa beckoned to Grace, then slipped away as Grace came to the front and stood beneath the mural on the wall. She didn't say anything by way of introduction—probably still a little shaken by Ramona's revelations—just nodded at Sam to start the CD player. Michelle closed her eyes to shut out the rustling and listened as Grace began to sing.

*"He giveth more grace as the burdens grow greater . . . He sendeth more strength as the labors increase . . ."* It was an old hymn. Not sung much anymore, though Michelle recognized the tune. *". . . To added afflictions he addeth his mercy . . ."*

The murmurs around Michelle gradually quieted as Grace's clear soprano voice, needing no microphone in this setting, filled the room with a couple of stanzas of the beautiful hymn, ending with the last line of the chorus: *"For out of His infinite riches in Jesus . . . He giveth, and giveth, and giveth again."*

The notes faded away and Sam stopped the CD player. Grace took a sip from a water bottle and then smiled at her audience. "I chose that song because it tells my testimony. Edesa told you I was a concert singer. What she didn't tell you is that my life was falling apart a few months ago—my career, my voice, even the man I thought I was going to marry—*kaput*."

Michelle was startled. Grace? Her life falling apart? Did she say just a few months ago? Why hadn't Grace said anything about that when they'd prayed together at her house with Estelle? One or two women in the semicircle snickered nervously. A raspy voice called out, "That's all right, you go on now, girl. Know whatchu talkin' about."

Grace took a deep breath. "I'd been running from secrets in my past . . . but God had to bring me to a low place to discover what had been true all along—he wanted to offer me forgiveness and mercy and grace, none of which I deserved. It wasn't my performance that mattered, all those things I was doing trying to earn God's favor . . . just simply that I'm his child and he loves me—just as God loves you."

Grace nodded at Sam again, and the instrumental CD began the strains of a contemporary gospel song Michelle recognized. *"Your grace and mercy brought me through . . . I'm living this moment because of You . . ."*

"Yes, yes," several voices murmured behind Michelle. And by the end of the song, some of the women in the circle were humming or singing along.

"Praise Jesus!" someone called out. Michelle noticed that most of the stragglers around the room had joined the circle now.

Grace sang one more song, another old hymn, similar in theme to the others. *"Marvelous grace of our loving Lord . . . grace that exceeds our sin and our guilt . . ."* By the end of this song, everyone was singing along on the chorus: *"Grace, grace, God's grace, grace that is greater than all our sin."* A few women were dabbing at tears as the last words faded away.

From her work at Bridges every day, Michelle could well imagine the difficulties many of these women had experienced that left them homeless. Dysfunctional families. Abusive childhoods. Doing anything to survive. Drugs to kill the pain. Acting out of anger, hopelessness, despair. And some just had a run of bad luck, circumstances beyond their control.

Several people clapped as Grace sat down. Michelle felt a momentary panic. She was supposed to follow those deeply moving songs? But Edesa was beckoning to her. *Okay, Lord, you lead the way.* As she stood and faced the women in the circle, Michelle's heart felt as if it was breaking. There sat Ramona, a mere teenager, far from home, vulnerable, taken advantage of, used and abused. But Ramona wasn't the only one. Each face in the circle held a story—stories she might never hear. But God knew.

"Thank you, Grace," she began. "The songs you sang tonight . . . that's what Lifeline Care Center is all about. Extending the love of God and God's grace to women who find themselves in crisis. LCC is a crisis pregnancy center, offering a lifeline to girls and women who think they don't have choices. At Lifeline we believe each life—even the ones we didn't plan for—is precious to God. But many women, especially those who are single, without support, feel so overwhelmed they think their only option is to end the pregnancy. But Lifeline exists to come alongside women in crisis . . ."

Michelle described the various resources Lifeline offered—free pregnancy tests and ultrasounds, information about fetal development, counseling and emotional support, baby clothes and furniture, as well as referrals to other supportive agencies for women wanting to get their GED, or job training, or information about adoption.

'Yeah, but in th' end, ya still got a kid—or two or three or six," scoffed the woman named Lottie. "Abortion's legal an' it's quick. Seems like th' easy way out ta me. I done it. Why not?"

A couple of other women in the room nodded.

*O Lord,* breathed Michelle. *I need your words—*

"But it's not the *easy* way out," Grace Meredith spoke up from the front row. Startled, Michelle saw the concert singer stand up and come to join her at the front. *Okaay. What is she doing?* As if sensing what was happening, Estelle followed Grace to the front.

Gripping their hands for support as they stood on either side of her, Grace cleared her throat. "Excuse me, Michelle, for interrupting, but . . . I had an abortion as a teenager—and it's haunted me ever since. Carried the guilt around like a monkey on my back. Spent years trying to make myself acceptable to God by traveling around the country telling kids, 'You're worth the wait.' Letting people think I'm this wonderful role model for Christian kids."

The room had gone so quiet, the proverbial pin drop would've sounded like a thunderclap.

"But my secret came back to haunt me. I was living a lie. Even though I was a victim of date rape, I had been sneaking around behind my parents' back. I couldn't bear the shame of it, so I hid my pregnancy from them and everyone else and took the 'easy way out.' But when my career and my personal life started to fall apart, I thought God was punishing me for my mistakes. Then Estelle, my new neighbor"—she held up Estelle's hand, still gripping her own—"helped me understand the meaning of my name—*Grace*— for the first time. Helped me understand that even when we mess up, God offers healing and forgiveness."

Now Grace held up Michelle's hand. "Michelle is my next-door neighbor and I'm just getting to know her. But as I understand it, she volunteers at Lifeline as a post-abortion counselor, helping people like me. Michelle, can you tell us about that?" Letting go of

Michelle's hand and giving Estelle a quick hug, she slipped back to her own seat.

Michelle shook her head in wonderment. She'd barely breathed a prayer, asking God to give her the words, when Grace had gotten up and opened the door to what should happen next. Forgetting that the three of them had probably looked like an ad for Oreo cookies, Michelle briefly described the Hope and Healing group that had been meeting together for the past nine weeks, had shared their stories with each other—some for the first time—supported one another, cared for one another, identified anger they harbored toward others, permitted themselves to grieve the babies they'd aborted, and most importantly had received God's healing grace and forgiveness from the Word of God. "Next week we're planning a memorial service to which family and friends are invited."

Glancing around the circle, she couldn't read some of the faces. Maybe she needed to make it more personal. "Before I close, let me tell you a story . . ." Without using Hannah's name, she told about the young girl who'd been abused for years by a family member, had gotten pregnant, and felt an abortion was her only option to hide the abuse and keep from tearing her family apart. But all the secrets were tearing *her* life apart . . . and now, several years later, she was seeking healing from this traumatic experience. "Shannon"—the fictional name Michelle used—"will be joining our next Hope and Healing group, which starts in July. If anyone here wants to join us, I'd be happy to talk with you. I will also be leaving some brochures about Lifeline, which has a number to call if you want more information or make an appointment."

Michelle sat down, praying silently that what she'd shared would be helpful to someone as Grace got up to sing her final song—which turned out to be "Amazing Grace," with Sam joining her for a surprise duet. Michelle's mouth practically dropped as the two voices blended . . . Sam could *sing*! Actually brought some "soul" to the song. Michelle smiled—what a beautiful statement the two women made, one white, one black, friends and sisters in Christ, transcending their roles as concert star and assistant, singing together about God's amazing grace.

The shelter guests and staff loved it.

Edesa offered a final prayer in both English and Spanish, and the group began to disperse. Michelle put the Lifeline brochures on the coffee cart, which several women casually picked up along with their cup of joe. But no one came up to talk to her about Lifeline or the Hope and Healing group, even though she and Sam and Estelle waited around for an extra thirty minutes while Grace and Ramona huddled together in a corner, talking seriously together.

Until they were back in the car and on their way home, that is.

They'd been driving for ten minutes or so along Lake Shore Drive without saying much, each one seemingly deep in her own thoughts about the evening. Michelle had her face turned toward the open side window, drinking in the deepening dusk over Lake Michigan, wondering about the revelations that had spilled into the evening—Grace's life "falling apart" a few months ago, the admission of her teenage abortion, and that startling story Ramona had blurted out about hiding drugs in Grace's suitcase—when she felt a tap on her shoulder.

"Michelle?" Grace said behind her. "I . . . I think I'd like to sign up for the post-abortion support group next time. Do you have room for one more?"

# Chapter 23

FOR A BRIEF SECOND FOLLOWING THE TAP on her shoulder, Michelle had thought Grace was going to share about her talk with Ramona after the meeting. Michelle was certainly curious! But she quickly assured Grace she'd be more than welcome to participate in the Hope and Healing group . . . Though later, sharing about the evening with Jared as they got ready for bed, he wondered about Michelle being able to keep professional distance with Grace being their next-door neighbor.

Good question. Would Grace feel comfortable sharing so intimately in that setting? The group process could sometimes be very intense.

And yet . . . they *were* more than neighbors. She and Grace shared a common faith, had prayed together, and tonight had even ministered together in a surprisingly compatible way. *Huh.* Mostly Estelle's doing. Before the Bentleys moved into the neighborhood, she and Grace had barely done more than say "hello" and "nice day" pleasantly as they were going in and out of their houses. But it was as if the Bentleys had fanned the wind of the Holy Spirit up and down the street.

Jared was incredulous when he heard about Grace talking with the girl she'd met on the train coming back from her West Coast tour. "And Bentley was riding that same train in his job with Amtrak police?" He wagged his head. "Unbelievable."

Michelle pulled down the comforter on the bed and slipped between the sheets. "Mm-hm. Estelle didn't say much. We were just waiting for Grace and Ramona to finish talking after the meeting, but she did say Harry had figured out this Max person was the so-called mule Amtrak police were on the watch for, who was transporting drugs from LA to Chicago. Using Ramona so they'd just seem like an ordinary couple, I suppose." She shuddered. "Makes my blood boil, thinking about it. Who knows what would've happened to her if Harry hadn't foiled the scheme?"

Though who knew what would happen to the girl now, still so far from home and living in a homeless shelter!

Michelle tried to shake it off. She couldn't take people's problems to bed with her or she'd never get to sleep. Probably one reason she hadn't felt all that great lately, bringing home all the stress and concerns from work. "So how long did Greg Singer stay after I left?" She stifled a yawn as Jared got into bed.

"Oh, maybe another ten minutes. Became clear that he wanted to recruit me, said I could do it on the side, make some extra money for the family. Maybe it's a legit business—hope so for his sake— but even if it is, I'd be a terrible salesman."

"Mm, you sold *me* on spending the rest of my life with you," she murmured.

"Ha!" Jared pulled her closer and nibbled on her ear. "Didn't have to sell you. You were a pushover."

"Mm-hm, but the product was good." Michelle giggled, then stifled another yawn as his hands slid beneath her nightgown. Fighting to stay awake, she tried to respond to his caresses. After all, weekends were the only time they had for intimacy, before the workweek swallowed up their nights and evenings *and* their energy. And Jared was a good lover, kind and gentle . . .

But even though they made love, she wasn't able to climax this time and knew that was a disappointment to Jared. A disappointment for her too.

Spent, they rolled apart. Jared's breathing slowed. Her own eyes felt heavy. She really should get a physical soon, get her blood pressure checked. Or quit her job. *Huh.* Not an option. She'd schedule an appointment with her doc. Soon . . .

Michelle's supervisor tossed a folder onto her desk the next morning. "DCFS says they got another complaint from a neighbor about the Blackwell family, passing it on to us . . . again." Charlotte Bergman rolled her eyes. "Not sure there's enough *mishegas*—you know, craziness—to warrant a charge of neglect, but wouldn't hurt to drop by, see if you can *schmooze* with the mother a bit. Best scenario would be if she came in on her own." And she was gone with a wave.

Charlotte was Jewish, though Michelle doubted she was very religious. The only time she ever mentioned Jewish services was around Hanukkah and Passover—and then it was mostly about food or traditions her family still kept. But she was a good boss, even if she did like to throw around Yiddish expressions.

Michelle sighed and picked up the folder. *Blackwell . . .* Mental pictures flashed through her mind of her last visit. Her first, last, and only. Not a pleasant experience. Not with drunk Otto passed out on the kitchen table and baby Pookey left squalling in a playpen with a loaded diaper and a rash as raw as sandpaper. And getting chased out the door by a livid woman screaming at her. But then there was the little girl, Candy . . .

She'd suck up the courage to try again for Candy.

But she wasn't able to squeeze a visit to the Blackwells' apartment building into her schedule until Tuesday, and no one answered when she buzzed the intercom. No one else happened to come out the door at the bottom of the stairwell this time either, allowing her to slip through the open door like she had last time.

No such luck.

Well, hopefully Candy was at school and mama was at work and Pookey was . . . in decent childcare somewhere.

Yeah. In her dreams.

She'd try during the day again later in the week, but she'd probably have to drop by in the evening or on the weekend.

*Tuesday . . .* This would be Jared's second night on swing shift, not getting home till around eleven. *If* he came home. It was becoming more common for him to sleep at the airport Tuesday nights since his day shifts started at six the next day.

Only the twins were home when she walked in the door. Tavis was holed up in his room, doing homework while plugged into his iPod. Michelle leaned over Tabby's shoulder at the dining table to see what she was working on. *Spanish vocabulary.* "Test coming up?" she asked, giving her daughter a peck on the cheek.

"Mom. *Finals* are next week." Eyes rolled. "But two weeks from today I go to cheerleading camp! Woo-hoo!" Tabby raised her arms and danced her bottom around in the chair. "Fort Wayne, here I come!"

Michelle tickled her daughter under one raised arm, making Tabby squeal. "How could I forget?" She walked into the kitchen and opened the refrigerator door to ponder supper. "Where's Destin?" she called over the counter dividing the kitchen from the dining area.

"I dunno. Out job hunting, I think. But don't bother me anymore, Mom. I gotta finish this."

Michelle pulled out some frozen fish. Quick to thaw. Quick to cook. *Right.* Destin had been given strict orders from Jared to hustle to a few more places after school this week, handing in more applications. But . . . hadn't she seen his bike chained up on the front porch when she came home? To make sure, she peeked through the small window in the kitchen that looked directly out onto the porch. Destin's bike was chained to the far side where, she hoped, they'd hang that porch swing one day. *Huh.* He must've taken the bus or walked. But she didn't like bikes left on the porch. If he wasn't going to ride his bike, he should've locked it in the garage.

The rice had only five more minutes to go and the fish was almost done when she heard Destin come in and head straight for his room. "Destin?"

"Be there in a minute!" he called back.

"Well, tell your brother supper's ready in five minutes! And wash your hands!" Michelle chased Tabby and her homework off the dining table, gave her the plates and silverware to set out, and was setting the food on the table when the boys appeared.

She was curious about Destin's job search but waited till they'd said grace and dished up the food. "So did you make some job contacts today?"

"Uh-huh." Destin speared another bite of fish into his mouth, followed by some buttered potato.

Michelle felt like rolling *her* eyes. Was she going to have to drag the details out of him? She'd forgotten the number one rule for talking with teenagers: don't ask yes or no questions. She tried again. "So where did you go?"

"I stopped in at Kenny the Kleener—no wait, that was yesterday. Today I went down to that car wash over on Clark Street, filled out an application there. Got the usual. 'We'll call you if anything opens up.'" Destin snorted. "You know the drill."

"The car wash? That's too far to walk."

"Rode my bike. Wasn't too bad."

"But I've been home almost an hour and your bike was here the whole time."

"Mom, chill. I rode up there right after school. A lot of places close at five, ya know. So when I got home I went over to the Bentleys and shot some baskets. An' then I saw Mr. Singer, you know, mowing his lawn down the street, so I stopped and talked to him a bit."

"Oh." Greg Singer would be around home more these days since he was between jobs. "Well, that was nice."

Destin shrugged. "Yeah, he's okay."

"Maybe you should ask him if you could get a job mowing his lawn," Tavis goaded. "In fact, all the lawns up and down Beecham need mowing."

Destin glared. "Shut up, shrimp. *You* go mow some lawns. It'd keep you out of trouble."

"Whatchu talkin' about? I ain't in any trouble."

"Uh-*huh*," Tabby chimed in. "You always fightin' with that kid at school. Teacher's gonna put you on probation one of these days."

"Is not! Besides, what's it to you, big mouth?"

"Tabby! Boys!" Michelle spoke sharply. "That's enough." She was tired of playing referee at the table. Jared should be here at suppertimes. But she frowned at Tavis. *Was* he in trouble at school again? She almost said, "Fighting with what kid?" but clamped her mouth shut. Tavis and Tabby would just start arguing again. But if there was bullying going on, why hadn't the school called her?

She really needed to talk to Jared about this—if he just wasn't gone so many nights! Maybe she should call Tavis's homeroom teacher or the principal—

The phone rang and the kids scattered as she got up to answer. She sighed. *Probably Jared saying he's sleeping at the tower tonight.*

But it was Estelle Bentley. "Sister Michelle! I know this is last-minute. But Harry came home tonight with some disturbing news that might affect Ramona, and Grace is very upset. I'm wondering if we could pray together tonight—the three of us. I know you said Wednesdays aren't good, but would you have half an hour or so tonight?"

"Well . . . sure. I could do that." She was tired, but what else was new? The kids would be fine for half an hour. And after all, Grace lived right next door.

At eight o'clock, with the kids settled in different parts of the house and "Destin in charge," Michelle locked the front door behind her and took a shortcut across the front lawns to Grace's house. Estelle was already there.

"Thanks so much for coming, Michelle," Grace said. The young woman's usually clear, peachy skin looked red and blotchy from crying. "Tell her what you told me, Estelle."

Estelle Bentley sighed. "Harry was doin' some work on the computer at work today, tryin' to bring closure to some of the cases he's handled for Amtrak, and he found out that Max, the guy who was travelin' with Ramona and totin' cocaine for that big drug cartel . . . found out he made bail and he's out."

"He's out!"

Grace hugged herself, her shoulders hunched. "I'm so worried about Ramona. I'm sure Max doesn't want her testifying against him—but that was one reason the judge gave her probation and let Harry take her to Manna House, in exchange for her testimony. What if he finds her, tries to make her keep quiet?" Grace's lips trembled.

"Well, now, supposedly he made bail a few weeks ago and he hasn't found Ramona yet." Estelle's soothing voice took charge. "And that's what we're here for, to pray for Ramona's protection. Though I do think she probably should know he's out on bail. I plan to tell her tomorrow when I go to work."

Grace sniffed and dabbed at her eyes with a tissue. "Maybe we could just send her home—you know, buy her a plane ticket back to LA. I'd be glad to do that."

Estelle shook her head. "Maybe. It might not be that simple. She was an accessory to transporting drugs, you know. She might have to stay here . . . but I don't know. But God knows. So come on now, let's pray for protection, for wisdom, for Ramona, for Grace's peace of mind . . . all of the above."

The three women held hands and prayed, one after the other. For some reason Michelle found it easier to pray aloud with Estelle and Grace than she did at the Wednesday night prayer meeting, even though they'd been at Northside Baptist for years. Finally, after ten minutes or so of intense prayer, Estelle murmured, "Is there anything else we should pray for as long as we're here?"

Grace blew her nose and nodded. "Well, this is a little embarrassing, but . . . you both met my agent, Jeff Newman, at Mrs. Krakowski's homecoming."

"I remember." Michelle smiled. She had an idea of what was coming.

"Well"—Grace's cheeks turned pink—"our relationship has become, um, a bit more than agent and client, as I supposed you've guessed . . ."

"Mm-hm," Estelle said.

"He's really wonderful. But it's also awkward. I . . . we . . . well, we need some wisdom on how to work on our relationship. He lives in Denver, I live in Chicago . . . and we're finding that a long-distance relationship isn't very easy. Not to mention that he's also my agent. Darn good one too!" Grace laughed self-consciously.

Estelle chuckled. "Definitely something to pray about. How about you, Sister Michelle?"

*Good grief. Where to start?* "Well, I'm kind of worried about Tavis. I think he's getting into fights at school, or after school, I don't know. He just shrugs it off, doesn't want me to make a big deal of it. And Destin needs a summer job, but there's not much out there. Still, his father and I think he should pay for this expensive basketball camp he's signed up for, and paying us back is part of the deal. We really can't afford it otherwise."

Estelle nodded. "Good for you! Kids shouldn't have everything just handed to them. Grace, would you pray for Michelle's boys? I'll pray for Grace and Jeff. And Michelle, maybe you could pray for my son, Leroy. He wasn't doin' so well when I visited him on Saturday, he'd gotten abusive with the staff at the home he's in . . ."

The three women held hands again and prayed for the various requests. But something nagged at the back of Michelle's mind as Grace prayed that Destin would find a summer job. Something wasn't adding up . . .

"What do you think, sisters?" Estelle asked as they got ready to leave. "Could we maybe pray together for a half hour or so on Tuesday evenings on a regular basis? Seems like there're so many things to pray about—and the Bible says that where two or three are gathered together, Jesus shows up!"

Both Grace and Michelle said they were willing to give it a try as they said their good-byes. *Tuesdays might be good,* Michelle thought, hurrying back home. She didn't have anything regularly scheduled on Tuesday evenings and Jared was at work. And the prayer times so far had been comforting and meaningful.

Except for that nagging feeling in her gut about Destin looking for work. After calling out, "I'm home!" and peeking in on her offspring, Michelle stood in front of the kitchen calendar. School would be out a week from Friday. Tabby's camp was the next week . . . and then Destin's basketball camp started the following Wednesday.

She stared at the dates. *June 30–July 3.*

What employer would hire a kid who was going to take time off a week and a half later? And if Destin waited to start work till he got home from camp, he couldn't start until after the Fourth of July weekend.

Had she and Jared even talked about this Catch-22? No, they'd just been ignoring the elephant in the middle of the room, putting the problem in Destin's lap.

# Chapter 24

J ARED CAME HOME THAT NIGHT even later than usual. Michelle woke up and peered blearily at the orange numbers on the digital clock . . . *12:10*. "Honey? Is everything okay?"

"Hey, Gumdrop," he murmured, sitting on the bed to take off his shoes. "Sorry I'm late. One of the new guys finished his training tonight, and he was all hyped. His wife brought in a big cake, so I hung around the break room for a while. Didn't call, was afraid you'd already be asleep." He crawled into bed, sighing wearily. "Spitball can be a real goof-off—definitely earned his nickname. Acts like a sophomore sometimes." Jared yawned. "Some of the guys were going out to party, but they usually drink themselves silly. Besides, I gotta start day shift tomorrow . . ."

He was asleep in two minutes.

And already gone back to work when she woke up the next morning.

Norma called her cell while she was driving to do a foster care home check, so Michelle sent it to voicemail and called back on her lunch break. "You going to be at prayer meeting tonight, Michelle?" her friend asked. "I finally got the leader kit for the women's event this Saturday—has DVDs and study materials, all kinds of stuff. Thought I could hand it off to you tonight. I know it doesn't give you much time to prepare for Saturday, but it just arrived yesterday. Duh, should've just had the stuff sent directly to your house."

"Uh . . ." With everything that had been happening lately, she really hadn't been thinking about having to prepare for the women's event on Saturday. Michelle was tempted to ask Norma if *she* would take charge of introducing the video series and guiding the first discussion. But . . . what was wrong with her? *She* was head of the women's ministry at Northside Baptist, for goodness' sake! The rest of the committee had stepped up and done their part. She needed to do hers. "Sure. I'll be there. Thanks, Norma."

Filling out her reports for the past three days made Michelle late getting out the door after work, so she swung by Boston Market on the way home and picked up their Family Meal, which included a rotisserie chicken, cornbread, and several sides. Lukewarm by the time she got home at six, but no one complained, and at least she had time to sit down for half an hour with her husband and the kids before she and Jared drove to the church for the seven o'clock prayer meeting.

Seemed like there was something she'd wanted to talk to Jared about, but for the life of her she couldn't remember what. He seemed pensive too, as if his mind was elsewhere. "You're awfully quiet," she told him, after riding in silence most of the way. "You sure everything's okay?"

"Huh? . . . Oh, sorry, hon. Yeah, yeah, everything's fine. Just thinking about this seminary thing. I went online today after work to see what was available. There might be several possibilities . . . North Park Seminary, for one. Not too far. And of course there's Moody downtown. They've got night classes, also an online course."

*Seminary!* "So you're really thinking about it?"

"Well, yeah. Thinking about it. Figured we wouldn't know how to make a decision unless we put the facts on the table."

Michelle was quiet. She didn't want to be a wet blanket, but . . . *seminary?* It boggled her mind.

Jared glanced at her. "So what are you thinking? Think it's a dumb idea?"

"No, no . . . not dumb!" Her heart suddenly went out to her husband. He'd given a great sermon on Memorial Day weekend, which she hadn't even been there to hear, and now the pastor wanted to encourage his gift. "Not dumb at all. I . . . I just don't know how to think about it. Given, you know, everything else."

"I know."

Michelle laid a hand on his arm. "Well, we haven't really prayed about it yet. At least not together. God will make it clear." She said it with more confidence than she felt.

"Yeah, I'd like that."

As they came into the church, Norma was waiting for her in the foyer with a box labeled *Discerning the Voice of God — Leader Kit*. "Here you go. Want to check it out, see if everything's there and what else we might need?"

Telling Jared she'd be back in a few minutes, Michelle headed downstairs with Norma to the fellowship hall, and together they looked through the materials, reading the summaries of the DVDs, and going over the discussion questions. "Looks good," Michelle murmured. *Really good.* She could use some fresh encouragement in discerning God's voice from all the other competing voices in her head. "But did we ask anyone yet to set up the DVD player down here?" She started to jot notes. They needed chairs set up Saturday morning . . . extra paper and pencils . . . and coffee, tea, and snacks, of course.

By the time she and Norma returned to the sanctuary, the prayer time had already started with groups of four or five meeting here and there in the pews. Michelle slipped into a pew at the back joining a group of four, making it five. Deacon Martin, a rather verbose man with nubby gray hair and large black-framed glasses, was praying for all the requests in a deep "prayer voice" full of thees and thous—Mother Willa's arthritis, peace in the city as schools let out next week, jobs for those in the church who were unemployed, somebody's grandson (unnamed) who was "far away from God" . . .

"Are there any other requests?" he asked after a rather long silence.

No one spoke. Michelle definitely had things on her heart that needed prayer—the sticky question about whether Jared should go to seminary . . . Ramona's safety at the shelter now that her drug-dealer "boyfriend" was out on bail . . . a summer job for Destin that would let him take off for basketball camp after a week . . . Tavis and whoever he was fighting with at school . . . the general exhaustion she felt, which wasn't as exciting and specific as cancer or a broken leg—but she couldn't imagine blurting out any of those concerns in this setting. What Estelle had said once was true—all too often prayer requests seemed to become "holy gossip" at church. She didn't know these people that well, in spite of sitting in Sunday services together for years and giving "Sunday hugs" and greetings. And right now her concerns felt too personal, too intimate, and perhaps too trivial to other people.

But feeling a bit guilty at the long silence, she spoke up. "Um, the women's ministry could use prayer. We're beginning a new series this weekend . . ." As Deacon Martin asked a woman whose name Michelle had forgotten to pray for God's blessing on the women's ministry, she felt a surge of gratefulness for Estelle's invitation to join her and Grace to pray on Tuesdays.

She needed praying sisters she could trust. She needed more prayer, period.

Michelle dropped by the Blackwells' apartment building again on Thursday. Again no answer to the buzzer. Drat it all. Should she go back this evening? No . . . this was the first evening all week Jared didn't have to rush off to something—at least not until nine, when he had to leave for his night shift at the tower. And she really needed to wrap up last-minute details for the first session of the video series they were going to begin on Saturday—not to mention getting herself emotionally prepared for the Hope and Healing group memorial service Saturday afternoon. And she usually gave a small gift to each participant afterward, a small memento of their time together.

Thinking of the memorial service, should she invite Grace to attend? It would give her an idea of what the group was about . . . No, no, what was she thinking! Even though family and friends of the group members were invited, the memorial service wasn't open to the public. It wouldn't be fair to the women in the current group. She could talk to Grace a bit more when they got together next Tuesday evening, give her an idea what to expect. But the upcoming memorial service was another thing she could use prayer for. She'd call Estelle Bentley this evening.

When Michelle got off the phone with Estelle that evening, she heard raised voices from the basement family room. "Dad, I'm on it! I'm doin' the best I can!"

"Have you called back? You gotta keep your name in front of the employers, let 'em know you're serious."

"Well, no, didn't know I was s'posed ta—"

"Are you keeping a list of the places where you submitted applications?"

"Uh, not really, but—"

"Destin! This isn't a game! You owe us four-fifty for this Five-Star Basketball Camp—and college is just around the corner. We started that college fund for you at the bank, and *you're* supposed to be adding to it too."

"Okay, *okay*! I'll make a list and call people back this weekend. Are we done now? I'm right in the middle of this video ga—"

"You're done *now*, buster! Shut that thing off. *Now*. Get started on that list." Two heartbeats later Jared came huffing up the stairs, his face a storm cloud. "Kid doesn't have the vaguest idea what it takes to get a job these days," he muttered at Michelle, as he passed through the dining area. "*Hmph*. Video game . . ."

Michelle watched as her husband disappeared into the living room. *That* was the trouble with Thursday nights. Jared was short on sleep, had probably only snatched a two-hour nap between getting home at three and getting up for supper. She glanced at the clock. Eight already. He'd be leaving in an hour for his night shift. She sighed. Had she even told him her schedule for this Saturday?

Maybe she should start the laundry since the weekend would be so full.

She was downstairs stuffing dirty clothes into the washing machine when the phone rang. A moment later Tabby ran down to the landing and yelled into the basement. "Mom! Mrs. Singer wants to know if I can babysit tomorrow after school. She wants to run some errands or something."

Michelle came to the bottom of the stairs. "Well, sure." She smiled up at her daughter. "Guess they like you. Just get her cell phone number or something so you can call her if you need to."

Tabby dashed away. Michelle shook her head and went back to the laundry. If only getting a job was that easy for Destin.

Michelle only had time to say hi and good-bye to Jared when he got home from his night shift the next morning. Waiting until she was pretty sure he'd caught up on his sleep during the day, she finally called him about four o'clock that afternoon. He sounded awake when he answered.

"Jared. I think we ought to take the kids to a movie tonight. Or go bowling. Do something together, the whole family."

"Ugh, not bowling. Maybe tomorrow night. I'm still too tired from my night shift."

"Well, a movie then. All you have to do is sit down."

"And pay for the popcorn." She heard him chuckle a bit.

"That's what dads are for, right?" She laughed. "So we're good? You and the kids want to pick a movie?"

"Nobody's around. Tabby went babysitting down at the Singers, Destin is supposedly out job hunting, and Tavis . . . hm, where *is* Tavis? Oh yeah. I think he's over at the Bentleys playing with DaShawn."

"Okay. Well, would you order some pizza? I'll try to be home by five thirty so we can eat and see the early show."

Only Tavis and Jared were in the house when Michelle walked in the door, but Destin came in from the garage shortly after six, and Tabby ran in the front door at six fifteen. But by then supper was hurry-scurry because they had to leave by six thirty to get to the seven o'clock showing of *The Karate Kid*, which had just come out that week. Wouldn't have been Michelle's top pick, but the kids were definitely outgrowing most of the animated family movies they used to watch.

"Can I drive?" Destin made a beeline for the minivan as Michelle herded them out the door.

"Dad, nooo! He'll make us late!" Tabby protested.

"Will not. I'll drive fast, twerp."

"Then we'll get in a wreck! Dad, pleeease, you drive."

"*I'll* drive." Michelle rolled her eyes. This was supposed to be a stress-free evening. "You and Dad can practice driving another time."

"Huh. Good luck with that," Destin muttered, climbing into the back seat.

If Jared heard, he pretended not to notice.

"Thanks," Michelle murmured to Jared as they walked into the house after the movie. "We needed that. Especially since I've got a full day tomorrow . . ." She ran down her list, including trying to contact the Blackwell family after the memorial service in the afternoon. "You?"

He shrugged. "Hoping to sleep in a bit tomorrow. It's been a rough week at work. Summer flight schedules are stacking one on top of the other, so everyone's a bit on edge. But can't sleep too late, 'cause I gotta take the Nissan in for an oil change. Mostly trying to catch up on stuff at home."

"Okay—though if you can squeeze it in, maybe you could give Destin some driving time?" She gave him a kiss on the cheek before he could protest. "Go on, go to bed. I'll say goodnight to the kids."

By the time Michelle switched laundry loads, turned on the dishwasher, and locked the doors front and back, Tabby was in bed, writing in her diary. Michelle sat on the corner of the bed and started rubbing her back. "How'd babysitting go this afternoon?"

Tabby put her diary down and turned full on her stomach to enjoy the back rub. "Good, I think. Mrs. Singer left in the car, but Mr. Singer was at home, which was kinda awkward—you know, babysitting with one of the parents around. But it was okay. He was busy in the living room—using it as his office, I think. But, Mom, I saw something kinda weird . . ." Tabby rolled over and half sat up. "Just before Mrs. Singer came home, I was out front playing hopscotch with the kids, and I think I saw Destin and Mr. Singer out by their garage. I mean, I only had a glimpse alongside the house, but it sure looked like Destin."

Michelle frowned. Destin had come in just a few minutes after Tabby—had come in the back door, if she remembered right. Probably just putting his bike away. Even if Destin had stopped at the Singers', it couldn't have been long. "Don't worry about it, honey. I'm sure it's fine."

She gave Tabby a kiss, turned out the light, and closed the door softly. Might not even have been her brother Tabby had seen. Even if it was, maybe Destin just wanted to borrow something. Or maybe Mr. Singer saw him coming home on his bike and needed his help for a minute. After all, his own kids were a lot younger.

Well, she'd ask Destin about it just to be sure.

# Chapter 25

EVERYBODY SLEPT IN SATURDAY MORNING except Michelle. But the quiet house was a blessing as far as she was concerned. Time to go over the discussion guide once more for the first session of *Discerning the Voice of God*, as well as review the simple service she'd planned for the memorial service at Lifeline.

Just toast and tea again for breakfast . . . Was she that nervous about leading this first session for the Northside women? She didn't think so, just didn't feel like eating. Her morning appetite had been on the wane lately. But maybe she should take some yogurt and a granola bar along, just in case.

It wasn't a Sunday morning service, but Michelle wore a summer dress today since she'd be up front leading the monthly women's meeting. But, *ugh!* Her hair. She really needed to get herself to the beauty shop and get a cut and perm. Tabby too. Her daughter's bushy hair was looking more Afro every day. At the very least it needed shaping. Maybe it was time for some twists or braids.

The sky looked ominous by the time Michelle arrived at the church. And she'd forgotten her umbrella again! Still, the frequent June rains had been keeping the city green. Lawns, parks, trees, and flowering bushes were lush, softening the harsh concrete lines of city streets and buildings.

The meeting didn't start till ten, but Michelle arrived at nine fifteen just to make sure everything was set up. Sister Mavis was perking coffee and slicing bagels, and Norma was setting up a laptop and projector she'd borrowed that could play the DVD. The church didn't have a screen, but a blank wall in the fellowship hall would have to do. Shareese, her substantial bosom quite evident in her low-cut yellow blouse, was rearranging the straight rows of chairs the janitor had set up into a semicircle. "Much more friendly, don't you think, Sister Michelle?" the young woman gushed.

Michelle just nodded and smiled. She really did need to speak to Shareese about the way she dressed. If the "church mothers" hadn't already given her what-for, Michelle had a responsibility as head of women's ministry.

As women started to arrive, Michelle noticed several had brought guests—family members and friends—and she made a special effort during the coffee-and-bagel time to welcome them before starting the meeting. The turnout was good, though as usual several Northside women came in late as Sister Paulette led the group in singing, *"Oh, how I love Jesus . . ."* They didn't slip in quietly either, but headed for the coffee table, greeting people who were already singing.

Once the DVD started, everyone settled down and seemed attentive as the popular daughter of Tony Evans spoke about "anticipating the voice of God." The scripture she used in the first session focused on Jesus' words in John's gospel, chapter 10: "My sheep *hear* My voice, and I *know* them, and they *follow* Me." All about listening for the voice of a beloved person—in this case Jesus—and responding to that voice.

When the DVD was finished Michelle passed out worksheets listing other scriptures, which she asked various women to read aloud from their Bibles, to help them focus on the intimate relationship Jesus has with his "sheep." "Keep in mind, Jesus is talking about us, sisters," Michelle encouraged as they worked through the discussion questions. *About me,* she thought. Did she really expect to hear God speaking to her? Or were her own prayers mostly a one-way street?

The discussion was lively, and as the meeting broke up, Michelle breathed a prayer of thanks. *Lord, thank you for bringing this together in spite of how scattered I've been lately.* She really should thank Shareese too . . .

Michelle waited until most of the women had left and the committee was doing cleanup before taking the young woman aside. "Sister Shareese, I want to thank you for your idea of doing this video series with Priscilla Shirer. I think it's going to be really good."

"Oh, thank you, Sister Michelle! I wasn't sure, you know, you seemed so hesitant at first." The young woman tossed her long weave. "Do you think we can do the whole series? Or just do it for the summer? If we need to do something else in the fall, I thought of another good idea. Maybe we could—"

Michelle held up her hand with a half laugh. "One thing at a time, Shareese. But I did want to mention something else to you." Could she do this without offending her? She lowered her voice a bit. "It's important, um, for us on the women's ministry committee to be good role models to the other women in the church. You're a very attractive woman, Sister Shareese, and I'm sure you don't mean to be immodest, but—"

"Oh!" Shareese's eyes widened and her hand went instinctively to her chest, covering her cleavage. "My blouse! It's too low-cut, isn't it! Oh, Sister Michelle, thank you so much for pointing this out to me. It's just, oh dear, yellow is one of my favorite colors, and I just didn't think . . ."

Michelle laid a hand on her arm. "I know. It's all right. You do look wonderful in yellow. But let me assure you, Shareese, you'll still turn heads even if you wear turtlenecks clear up to your chin—which I'm not suggesting, by the way! Just . . . no cleavage showing at church, okay? And go easy on the tight pants and short skirts too. You don't want to call the wrong kind of attention to yourself."

Shareese nodded, her eyes downcast and blinking rapidly, but she let Michelle give her a hug before she scurried away.

Michelle watched her go. She had to give the girl credit. She took that correction amazingly well. Would she have responded like that in her twenties if an older woman in the church had taken *her* aside?

Probably not.

By the time Michelle left Northside, it was already past noon, and the rain had come and gone—but she still needed to pick up some little token to give to each of the women in the Hope and Healing group. The Ten Thousand Villages Store in Evanston . . . they had nice gifts. It was a fair-trade store too, giving artisans from different countries a fair price for their handiwork. A bit out of her way, but she should have time to get there and back before the two o'clock memorial service.

She didn't even want to think about visiting the Blackwells afterward. Or doing the grocery shopping. She should've asked Jared to do it . . . maybe she still should. Although, it *was* a bit unfair to spring that on him so last-minute. But still.

Sitting at a red light, she called home but only got the answering machine. She tapped the speed dial number for Jared's cell and got his voicemail. He was probably out getting the oil changed in his car. She tossed the cell phone into the seat beside her. Just as well. Chicago had a law against using cell phones while driving. Besides, maybe the Blackwells wouldn't be home and she could do the grocery shopping instead. Or even do it Sunday afternoon. She didn't like to leave stuff like that for their "day of rest," but God would surely understand.

Uh-oh, the light must've turned green while she was using the phone, because it was turning red again. She waited, drumming her fingers on the steering wheel. The light turned green . . . why were the two cars in front of her just sitting there? She honked. They didn't move. *Oh brother.* The last thing she needed was a traffic tie-up. She honked again, longer. The light turned red. Okay, okay, maybe they'd had a fender bender.

She glanced in the rearview mirror. No cars behind her. She backed up half a car length, waited till the light turned green again and the cars in the left lane were moving, finally saw her chance, and quickly cut into the lane—but not before getting stopped by the red light again. *Argh.* Casting a frustrated glance at the cars in the right lane that were tying everything up, she suddenly had a startling realization.

No drivers in either car.

She'd waited through four red lights behind two parked cars.

Michelle didn't know whether to laugh or cry. How dumb was that! Was she losing her mind?

At least she found the perfect gifts at the fair trade store. Small rock paperweights about the size of an apricot, polished to smooth perfection, and each one had one of the fruits of the Spirit carved into it. *Love . . . Joy . . . Peace . . . Patience . . . Kindness . . .* The store had rock paperweights with the other "fruits" from the Scripture passage in Galatians too, but she only needed five.

Michelle wanted to wait until the end of the memorial service to give the gifts. The meeting room at Lifeline was fairly full. Each group participant had invited several family members or friends to be there—all except Linda Chen. Michelle didn't question her about it. Each woman had to do what she felt comfortable doing. But Bernice the receptionist and Margie Sutton, the LCC director, also attended.

The service was simple, using the same format she'd used for previous memorial services: She played the hymn "Children of the Heavenly Father" on a CD, but she also passed out lyrics she'd photocopied so everyone could sing along. A few Scripture verses, including Jeremiah 1:5: "Before I formed you in the womb, I knew you." And a brief description of the process the group had gone through.

What was different each memorial service was the sharing from each of the participants. Ellie Baker read her letter to her baby. Maria Gonzales modestly showed the little heart she'd had tattooed above her left breast, "So I won't ever forget." Denise Martin shared a poem she'd written titled, "Forgiven." LaVeta Gates thanked the Lifeline staff, and Michelle in particular, for being there for her, for not just reaching out to girls who had a "crisis pregnancy," but caring for women like her who *didn't* "choose life."

Michelle wondered what Linda Chen would do. To her surprise, the young Asian woman simply said, "I dedicate this song to *wo de jia ting*—my family." Closing her eyes, she sang a plaintive song in

Mandarin Chinese without translating the words, or even the title, into English.

But there wasn't a dry eye in the room.

Afterward, as Michelle hugged each of the five women in the group, she gave them the little gift bags from Ten Thousand Villages. "Just open them when you get home. A remembrance from me. And if you ever want to talk more, or have something you'd like to pray about, please call. I'm here every Saturday morning."

The room slowly emptied. More tears. More hugs. A lot of tissues.

Once everyone was gone, Michelle sank down in a padded chair. The service had gone well, thank God. But she was ready to go home. Forget the Blackwells. Forget the groceries. She was exhausted.

"You okay, honey?" Bernice eyed her critically with a practiced grandmotherly eye. "Want some water? No, I know what you need. Some of my herbal peppermint tea I keep stashed in my drawer. You wait right there."

Bernice was right. The hot peppermint tea and an extra fifteen minutes just sitting revived her somewhat, along with the yogurt and granola bar she'd almost forgotten about. Maybe she could swing by the Blackwells' apartment after all.

# Chapter 26

Only when Michelle was halfway to the Albany Park neighborhood where the Blackwells lived did she realize she'd forgotten the folder with their actual address and the Google map she'd made to help her find it. But she'd been there twice already that week, so maybe she could find it again without the map.

After turning onto a one-way street that sent her several blocks out of her way before she could get turned around again, she finally recognized the three-story apartment building and pulled into a parking space, double-checking that there wasn't a fire hydrant, yellow stripe along the curb, or No Parking sign anywhere nearby. A number of kids were out and about, playing in the street and on the sidewalk. Michelle walked slowly up to the apartment building, searching faces, hoping to see Candy among the others, but she didn't recognize any of the children.

A girl about ten hollered, "You lookin' for somebody, lady?" The girl looked Michelle up and down, almost like a challenge.

"Yes. I'm looking for Candy Blackwell. Have you seen her?"

The girl shrugged. "Candy? Ain't seen her. She ain't out here."

Michelle nodded. "Okay. Thanks. I'll try their apartment." She pushed open the outer door into the small foyer, found the Blackwell buzzer and pushed. Not really expecting anyone to answer, she idly pushed it again—and was startled when the buzzer that opened the door into the stairwell blared back.

She grabbed for the door handle and pulled. You had to get the door open while the buzzer was buzzing or it stayed locked. *Success!* Mounting the stairs to the third floor, Michelle's feet dragged slower and slower, not knowing what to expect when she got to 3B. But finally she stood in front of the door and knocked. A moment later a lock turned and the door opened a few inches, stopped by a door chain. Michelle looked down at the big eyes peering at her.

"Hi, Candy." She smiled. "Do you remember me? Mrs. Jasper from Bridges Family Services."

The small brown face nodded, then broke into a shy smile. "I still gots your card."

"Is your mommy home?" She hoped she was, hoped she wasn't . . .

Candy shook her head. "She out."

"Oh." Michelle felt her gut relax. Couldn't say she was disappointed. But her tension was replaced by concern. "Is Pookey here with you?" *That* would be a problem. A baby left in the care of a seven-year-old?

Again the little braids shook sideways. "Mama took Pookey to the Walgreens. He gotsa fever. Tol' me to stay inna house."

Took Pookey to Walgreens with a fever? Oh . . . right. The drugstore chain had recently opened small walk-in clinics in their stores to treat minor ailments. Michelle heard the chain rattling and realized Candy was unfastening it. The door swung wider. "You wanna come in?"

"No, sweetie, I don't think so." No way did Michelle want to be inside the apartment when Mama Bear came home. She crouched down to Candy's eye level. "How are you? How's school?"

"It's okay. Only gots to go one more week. Then I be in second grade."

"That's great! And then what are you going to do this summer?"

Candy shrugged. "I dunno. Nothin'. Just help take care of Pookey."

"Do you play with the kids outside?"

Another shrug. "Sometimes. Mama doesn't like me playin' outside too much. Too many crazy gangbangers with guns, she says."

Michelle shuddered. At least the woman cared about Candy's safety. Maybe she'd misjudged her. But . . . keeping a kid inside all summer? Surely one of the nearby parks had a summer day camp that would get Candy out of the house in a supervised program. She was going to look into that.

Michelle stood up. "Tell your mama that I came by again, will you?" She dug into her purse. "Here's another of my cards. Now you have one and your mom can have one. Remember, you can call me if there's anything you need, okay, sweetheart?"

Candy nodded, her smile fading. The little girl waggled her fingers good-bye as Michelle waved and started back down the stairs. The door clicked shut behind her.

Michelle hustled down the stairs, not wanting to run into Candy's mother. But she felt torn by ambivalence, hating to leave. Hated to leave Candy alone in the house, though the child was probably safe enough.

Maybe she could bring the child some books and games. Tabby had long outgrown her early readers and pictures books. She'd probably get a kick out of choosing some to give to Candy. Maybe give her the whole lot!

Trying to give away Tabby's old toys and books to the Salvation Army or Goodwill had always been like trying to get gum out of her hair—but Tabby seemed really interested when Michelle told her about Candy, a specific little girl who needed some toys and games. "Yeah, sure. I've got lots of stuff she might like." By evening's end, Tabby had a box of picture books, a couple of stuffed animals, several board games—*Candy Land, Sorry,* and *Mouse Trap*—two black Barbie dolls with clothes, and some plastic play dishes.

Michelle pulled out one of the books. *Look-Alikes Jr.* An adorable large picture book of ordinary scenes—a farm, a house, a kitchen—created out of ordinary objects: paperclips and clothespins, toothpicks and buttons. Memories of looking at it together and identifying all the objects tugged at her. "Are you sure you want to give this one away?"

Tabby gave her The Look. "Mom! You *asked* me to find some things to give this little girl. She'll love it, just like I did.

Michelle put the book back in the box. "You're right. She'll love it." But would Candy's mother look at the book with her and enjoy it together? Michelle doubted it.

She sighed. *I'm getting too cynical.*

"And here. Put this in too." Tabby held out a music box with a figure of Jesus holding a lamb on top that went around and around when it was wound up.

"Tabby . . . Grammy Jasper gave this to you! It's a keepsake."

Tabby nodded. "I know. But I was remembering how I used to wind it up and play it at night when I was all alone in bed—especially if there was a thunderstorm or I felt scared. Here, listen . . ." Tabby turned the music box upside down and wound the brass key, then turned the box upright again. The tinny notes of "The Lord Is My Shepherd" plinked their way through the tune as the shepherd slowly turned around and around.

The song ended. Tabby shrugged and held the music box out again. "Thought maybe that little girl could use something to comfort her when she gets scared."

A lump caught in Michelle's throat as she put the treasure in the box for Candy. Even though it had sentimental value, she certainly didn't want to "quench the Spirit" in her thirteen-year-old.

"Thanks, honey. That's very thoughtful. Goodnight." She kissed Tabby and started to leave the room.

"Besides," Tabby called after her, "the best thing Grammy ever gave me was herself. You know, when she lived with us here in this house. She always had time to talk to me, gave me all those back rubs . . . that's what I remember best."

*"The best thing Grammy ever gave me was herself . . ."*

For some reason Tabby's comment niggled at the back of Michelle's mind even during Pastor Q's sermon at church the next morning. She'd been touched by her daughter's remembrance of the relationship with Jared's mother. But for some reason Michelle squirmed inside at those words. Would her daughter characterize her that way when she looked back on their relationship? What was she giving her daughter these days?

Mostly an empty house when she got home from school, that's what.

She shook the accusing thought out of her mind and tried to concentrate on Pastor Q's sermon. But "bad mother" and "too-busy mother" kept sticking their barbs into her concentration. Her friend Norma would sniff and say, "That's just the devil trying to bring you down, girl! You know he's a liar!" But what if it was the Holy Spirit pricking her conscience, whispering in that still, small voice?

And just yesterday she'd led a session on "discerning the voice of God." *Huh.* Some leader she was. Had no idea if she was hearing lies from the devil or the voice of God.

For some reason, tears sprang to her eyes and she had to quickly search for a tissue in her purse. *O God, I need help sorting out my life!* Which, on second thought after blowing her nose and dabbing at her eyes, felt like an odd prayer. Compared to a hard-nosed woman like Candy's mother, or most of the clients she worked with at Bridges, she had a wonderful life! Good husband, a decent job, three healthy children, a good church, a comfortable home . . .

So why did she feel off balance, like something wasn't quite right?

Her roaming thoughts hushed themselves after the service as she was giving her usual "church hugs," especially when several women told her how much they'd liked the women's ministry event yesterday. "What a great idea to use those DVDs and get such great teaching!" . . . "Almost like going to one of those big women's conferences, don't you think?" . . . "Do we really have to wait a whole month to get the next session?" . . . "Good job, Sister Michelle. Pastor knew what he was doin' puttin' you in charge."

Well, praise the Lord. If interest remained high, maybe they'd just continue on through the fall and use the whole series. The committee would probably say yes. She wasn't the only one who felt the challenge of coming up with a new event each month for women's ministry meetings.

As much as she would've liked to just kick off her shoes and vegetate that afternoon after her busy day yesterday, there was still . . . grocery shopping. Better just do it and get it over with. She usually shopped the big Dominick's grocery store east of them on Howard Street, but the Jewel store had some nice sales this weekend and wasn't much further in the other direction.

Pushing her cart through the produce section, Michelle felt frustrated at how crowded it was . . . then realized she'd forgotten that this Jewel catered to a large Jewish clientele. Women in long skirts and gym shoes, hair bundled in caps or scarves, many with a toddler in the cart and one or two more children tagging along, filled the aisles. Men in black hats or yarmulkes, some with the fringe of their prayer shawls showing beneath the hem of their black coats, chatted with great animation in front of the "kosher fish" display case, others trailed along behind their families.

Of course they shopped on Sunday. Saturday was the day Jews attended their religious services.

Well, another good reason for her to *not* shop on Sunday and avoid the crowd.

She hadn't had time to make a shopping list before heading out to the store, and was already in line at the checkout when she remembered they were out of Dr. Pepper. Three people were still ahead of her, and at least three more behind her in line . . . should she forget it? No, Jared really counted on that pick-me-up at work. But getting out of line might turn into another half hour of waiting.

The woman behind her, hair bundled in a knitted snood, was sing-songing to a baby in the child seat and shushing a restless little boy and girl hanging onto opposite sides of her full cart. "Excuse me," Michelle said. "Would you mind if I just ran back to the soft drink aisle and got some pop for my husband? I'll only take a minute."

The young woman looked at her strangely. "Michelle?"

Startled, Michelle really looked at the woman's face for the first time. Of course! Her neighbor at the end of the block on the other side of the street, the one who'd decorated their front porch for one of the Jewish holidays. "Oh my goodness. Rebecca, right?" She gave an embarrassed laugh. "I'm so sorry I didn't recognize you at first. I don't usually shop here on Sunday . . ." Michelle stopped. She had no idea what to say next.

Rebecca gave a pleasant laugh. "To tell you the truth, I don't usually either. I usually go midweek when Ruthie and Jacob are in Hebrew preschool. But Benjy was sick this week—teething I think—so . . . here I am." The young mother cast a sideways glance at the whining duo hanging onto the cart. "I always give in to too many treats when the you-know-whos are with me."

Michelle had a strange sensation. In three sentences, Rebecca Horowitz had told her more about herself than Michelle had known the entire time the Horowitzes had lived in the neighborhood, which was two or three years at least. And she seemed so . . . *normal*. Her baby teething. Trying to do her shopping when the kids were in school. Giving in to the begging of preschoolers.

"I know what you mean." Michelle made a face. "I don't like to take my teenagers grocery shopping for the same reason—*or* my husband."

At that Rebecca laughed right out loud. "Now you're talking! . . . Oh, look. The line is moving. Go on, go get whatever you need to get. I'll push your cart forward."

Giving her a grateful nod, Michelle scurried to the soft drink aisle, hefted a twelve-pack of Dr. Pepper into her arms, and hurried back to the line. "Thanks so much, Rebecca."

They chatted back and forth until it was Michelle's turn to check out, then she waved good-bye as she pushed her loaded cart out of the store. As someone who worked with all kinds of people day in and day out, why had she let the Horowitz's odd dress—okay, *distinctive* dress, identifying their strict religious beliefs—make her think of them as so "other" that they wouldn't have much in common?

Probably the same reason she'd never gotten to know Farid-the-lawn-service-guy's wife. Couldn't even remember the woman's name, though she knew she'd heard it mentioned. The headscarf. The long skirt. The Middle Eastern accent. So . . . "other."

Pulling the minivan to the curb in front of their house on Beecham, Michelle got out and stood looking up and down the street, trying to see if she knew who lived in each house. She prided herself on working well with a wide diversity of people at Bridges Family Services. At Lifeline Care Center too. Treating everyone with respect. No discrimination, no prejudice—she made sure of that. But that was at *work*. Her own neighborhood, even just this block on Beecham Street, had people of all different ethnicities and religious backgrounds too. But to be honest, she made very little personal effort to get to know any of them. Even if she wanted to, she always felt too busy.

What kind of Christian *was* she?

# Chapter 27

MONDAY . . . THE LAST WEEK OF SCHOOL—and already the third week of June. Michelle didn't remember having to go to school so long into the summer when she was a kid. Once Memorial Day came and went, kids were so restless teachers considered each day of school a lame duck except for final exams and end-of-year parties.

"Don't you listen to the news, Mom?" Destin said when she brought it up at breakfast—well, what passed for breakfast as each kid grabbed a toasted bagel and glass of juice between stuffing books and school papers into their backpacks. "Hot summer, more shootings. School officials think they're keeping kids safe by keeping us in school longer. But if you ask me, feels like they're punishing thousands of us ordinary kids just 'cause the gangbangers and wannabes ain't got nothin' better to do than carry on their stupid feuds." He headed out of the kitchen munching on his bagel.

"I'm goin', Mom!" Tavis yelled from the front door.

"Wait for me!" Tabby was right on her brother's heels. "'Bye, Mom! Tell Dad good-bye, 'K?" Then Michelle heard, "Only one more week till cheer camp! Woo-hoo!" . . . just before the front door slammed.

Where had Destin gone off to? "Destin? Aren't you going to the bus with the twins?"

"Gonna ride my bike today!" His yell came from the basement. Michelle stepped to the top of the basement stairs to say good-bye just as her eldest came running up the steps to the landing halfway and started out the side door. "'Bye, Mom!"

"Wait a minute." Destin's backpack bulged, its seams straining. "What in the world are you taking to school? The entire works of Shakespeare?"

189

"Ha ha, funny. See ya!" And he was out the side door, heading for the garage where he kept his bike.

Michelle went down the few steps to the landing and poked her head out the side door in time to see Destin come out of the garage with his bike and head off down the alley, slightly wobbling because of the load he was carrying on his back. What in the world was *that* about?

But it was time for her to leave for work too. Jared was just getting ready to get in the shower as she headed for the bedroom to get her purse and briefcase. "I'm going, hon!" she called out. "See you later tonight. Have a good day!"

"You too!"

She heard his electric shaver go on. Except for his trim mustache, which wasn't all that visible since it blended in with his dark skin, Jared had always been clean shaven. Michelle was tempted to wait till he was done to give him a good-bye kiss, just to get a whiff of that great aftershave he wore . . . but nope, she didn't want to be late first thing Monday morning. And besides, she was hoping to get to the office early so she could do some research on summer day camps in the Albany Park neighborhood.

But what she found when she actually got on her computer at work were just a lot of sports camps: T-ball, soccer, basketball . . . nothing much for kids Candy's age. That was disappointing.

Well, she'd figure out a time to drop by this week with Tabby's box of books and games. Maybe toward the end of the week, sort of a "school's out" gift.

Jared was still at work when Michelle got home—his Monday swing shift as usual—and only Tabby was home, fixing herself a box of macaroni and cheese.

"Hi, honey. Where're the boys?"

Tabby shrugged. "Dunno where Destin is. Tavis got detention, had to stay after school."

"Detention! What for?" The school was supposed to phone her if a child misbehaved and disciplinary action was needed.

Michelle dug in her purse for her cell phone. *Uh-oh.* She'd missed a call from the school around 1:15. The message on the voicemail said Tavis Jasper had been disruptive in the lunchroom and was being assigned same-day afterschool detention. If she had any questions, *blah, blah, blah . . .*

Michelle tossed her phone on the kitchen counter. "What happened?"

"It's just that jerk in eighth grade who's always bugging Tavis. I think he was bothering Tavis in the lunchroom and Tavis tripped him or something. I didn't see it, I was eating lunch with Nina an' LaToya. But it wasn't Tavis's fault, Mom. The lunchroom monitor was so unfair to give him detention."

Michelle sighed. "All right. You got your homework done?"

"Don't have any homework this week. Just gotta study for tests." Tabby sailed out of the kitchen with her gooey bowl of hot mac 'n cheese . . . just as Michelle heard the front door open and close quietly.

"Tavis? Come in here."

Five long seconds went by before Tavis poked his head around the archway that led from the living room into the dining area and kitchen. "Mom, I can explain . . ."

His story was pretty much the same as Tabby's. Spitballs blown from a straw at his head from the table behind him. Boys laughing. One of the big boys sauntered behind him on the way to the trash can, making snide remarks and calling him nasty names—

"Like what?" Michelle interrupted.

Tavis looked horrified. "Mom! You don't wanna know!"

"Okay, okay." She sighed again. "What happened?"

"I just . . . didn't really think about it, just stuck out my foot and tripped him. Oh man, he went down flat on his face." Tavis started to laugh. "It was so funny."

Michelle struggled to keep the smile off her face. She was so tempted to say, *Good for you!* . . . but instead she said, "Tavis. I know it hurts to be laughed at and called names. But you can't retaliate. It doesn't solve anything. And, as you know, then *you're* the one who gets in trouble."

"I know." Tavis was still grinning. "But, Mom, it was really worth it to see him go down—"

"Tavis. You think that'll end it?"

The grin disappeared. "Okay, okay. I'll try. Uh . . . are you gonna tell Dad?"

Was she? As far as she was concerned, the detention was punishment enough. Would Jared think so? But Jared wasn't home. She was the parent in charge. "Just . . . go on now. Supper will be ready in an hour."

She almost had supper on the table when she heard the side door open. "Destin? That you?"

"Yeah, Mom. Be up in a minute." He headed down toward the basement—but not before she got a glimpse of his backpack. Half the size it was when he went out this morning.

Destin came back up the stairs two at a time. "Supper almost ready? I'm starvin'!" He reached for a piece of cornbread from the basket she'd already put on the dining table.

"Where've you been? And put down that muffin. You haven't washed up yet."

Too late. Half the muffin was already in his mouth. "You know . . . job stuff," he mumbled, his mouth full. Destin chewed and swallowed. "Dad's on my case about getting a job, so that's what I'm doin' after school."

Made sense. "But don't forget you're supposed to call me if you don't come right home after school and let me know where you are."

"Oh. Right. Sorry." The other half of the muffin disappeared. "I'll go wash up."

"Wait." Michelle brought the steaming hot hamburger-noodle casserole to the table, then took off the hot mitts and put one hand on her hip. "I want to know what was in your backpack this morning—and not there when you came home just now."

Destin kept edging toward the hallway. "Nothin' much. Just, uh, some cans of that energy drink Mr. Singer is sellin' now. We were talkin' the other day, and I told him I'd take some to school, thought maybe the guys on the track team an' baseball team might try it out. You know, make some sales for him." His mouth curved in a half grin. "It worked too. The guys liked it."

"Oh." Michelle blinked. That would explain the bulging backpack. And Destin didn't usually lie if asked a direct question. "Well, that was nice of you . . . I guess. But, what does the school think of you selling stuff to the team on school property? I mean, seems like they'd have a policy against something like that."

Destin shrugged, still edging out of the room. "I dunno. Actually, I didn't sell it. I just gave out samples, you know, to see if they liked it. That's what Mr. Singer says he does. I was just kinda helpin' him out. 'Cause he said athletes would probably be good customers, an' Lane Tech is crawlin' with athletes. Uh . . . can I go now? Looks like supper's ready an' I still gotta wash up." He disappeared toward the bathroom.

"Don't think you should feel obligated to help Mr. Singer with his business!" she called after him. "After all, it's *his* business!"

To her surprise, Destin stuck his head back around the archway. "Oh, well, that's the thing . . ." He followed her back into the kitchen and lowered his voice. "This was kind of a test to see if I could sell the stuff. 'Cause, you know, I haven't had any callbacks on all the job applications I've filled out. Thought I could do something like this in the meantime, at least make a little money. But . . ." Now his voice had fallen to a whisper. "Don't tell Dad yet, okay? I kinda want to see if it's something I could do, let it be a surprise if it works."

"Honey, you know I don't like to keep secrets from your dad."

"I know, I know! Just don't tell him yet, okay? And I promise, I'll keep lookin' for a regular job, but it's not easy with me goin' away to camp so soon. At least with SlowBurn, I can do some selling now, and some more when I get back. To, like, fill in the gap. Good idea, don't you think?"

"I . . ." Michelle didn't know if it was a good idea or not.

Destin grinned big and gave her a big kiss on the cheek. "Thanks, Mom. You're the best. Hey, want me to tell the twins supper's ready?"

# Chapter 28

A CRACK OF THUNDER SAT MICHELLE UPRIGHT in bed, awakened out of a sound sleep. Jared was snoring softly beside her—she hadn't even heard him come in. A lightning flash lit up the bedroom window, followed by another crack of thunder, but this time farther away.

She slid back down under the sheet and snuggled up against her husband's broad back as she listened to the *pitty-pat-tap* of rain against the window. At least he was home, not at work having to deal with planes trying to land in a storm. Pity the poor guys on night shift tonight.

The storm had passed by the time she got up Tuesday morning. The early morning temp was a cool sixty degrees under cloudy skies. She let Jared sleep. Tonight would be a short night switching from swing shift to day shift. He might as well get a few extra z's.

Destin went off to school with his backpack bulging again, but she said nothing. Let him try. If he sold some energy drink for Greg Singer, fine. If he didn't, well, nothing was lost. But if he did start selling, she was going to remind Destin every penny had to go toward paying back his basketball camp tuition.

Michelle's cell phone reminder dinged at ten while she was still at the office: *Prayer tonight w Estelle & Grace.* Yikes. Good thing she'd put the reminder into her phone. She'd forgotten they'd decided to get together Tuesday nights to pray. But Michelle looked forward to it. She was going to add Candy and her family to their prayer list.

She'd put another reminder into her phone recently . . . what was it? Michelle scrolled through her reminders. Oh, there it was. *Call doc on Monday, make appt for physical.* Why hadn't she gotten the reminder yesterday? She looked at the time she'd set for Monday:

1:00. Right around the same time she'd missed the call from the school . . . Oh, no wonder. Her supervisor had called a staff meeting right after lunch, and she'd left her purse and phone locked in a bottom drawer of her desk.

Well, she'd just call for an appointment now.

The medical receptionist was all business. "Let's see . . . Dr. Craven's first opening is July twenty-first at two thirty."

"July twenty-first! That's five weeks away! There's nothing sooner?"

"Not unless you're sick. Dr. Craven likes to allow a good hour to ninety minutes for a yearly physical and the last one you had was"—the phone went silent for several long moments—"hmm, two years ago. So he's going to want to allow the full time."

Michelle sighed. "All right. Put me down. But if someone cancels earlier and you need someone to fill the slot, will you call me?"

"Of course. Thank you, Mrs. Jasper. See you in five weeks."

A call from the doctor's office came as Michelle was driving to a foster home inspection that afternoon. When she saw the caller ID, she pulled to the side of the road and answered the phone.

"Mrs. Jasper, we did get a cancellation just this afternoon. We can take you Friday July second at ten a.m. Will that work for you?"

*Friday the second* . . . Her mind raced. Destin would still be at basketball camp, didn't need to be picked up till Saturday. "Great. I'll take it. Thank you!"

She'd put *that* on the praise list tonight.

But by the time she completed the foster home inspection, the sky had darkened and the weatherman on the car radio said a major storm was moving into the city. Cars were already driving with lights on and it felt like nine o'clock already. Pulling into a gas station, she phoned Bridges and told Mercedes she was going to head home rather than come back to the office if anyone asked.

Sheets of rain blurred the windshield as traffic crept north on Western Avenue toward Rogers Park and home. The sky lit up with frequent lightning flashes, and thunder cracked and rolled. She wanted to call home and check on the kids, but kept going. Hopefully Destin had sense enough to come home on the bus and not ride his bike! All CTA buses had bike racks on the front of the buses now.

The wind made it even worse. The minivan seemed to shake every time she came to a stoplight, and when she finally turned into Beecham Street, the treetops were whipping back and forth in a frenzied dance, and several good-sized branches had fallen into the street.

*O Lord, the airport must be a mess! Help Jared and the other ATCs stay alert and focused.* She couldn't even imagine what the stress in the control tower must be like on a night like this.

She didn't even bother with her umbrella but ran for the porch. The front door opened before she even got out her key. "Mom!" Tabby threw her arms around her. "I was so worried about you, but Destin said not to call 'cause you were probably driving."

Michelle gratefully returned the hug before pushing the door shut against the wind. "So Destin's home? And Tavis?"

Tabby nodded. "Yeah. We all came straight home and got here before it really started. They're downstairs."

"Good girl. You did the right thing." Relief eased the knots in her stomach as she took off her wet shoes and went for her slippers. But what if the storm had hit yesterday when Tavis had afterschool detention? Or Destin had been out on his bike? She shuddered, thinking of her kids out in this mess. Destin had a cell phone, but maybe the twins needed one too—though that was something she and Jared hadn't wanted to do for a couple of years yet. Still, if she could've called them, she could've picked them up in a pinch.

And Jared . . . how was he doing? Would the storm be over when he got off at ten? She didn't dare call him. He usually turned off his cell phone anyway during bad weather or high-traffic hours in the tower.

The rain was still pretty heavy after supper, and Michelle was tempted to call Estelle and cancel going to the prayer time at Grace Meredith's house . . . until her cell phone beeped that she had a text message. Jared's ID . . . *Won't be home 2night. Couple night crew can't make it bcuz of flooding. Airport's a mess. Delays going & coming. Need prayer! Tower is tense. Had a near miss 2night.*

A near miss! That was one of Jared's greatest fears—a crash on his watch. She breathed a prayer of thanks that it was a "near miss," not a crash, but still.

He asked for prayer. Well, prayer was what he was going to get.

Telling the kids they could make popcorn and watch the original *Pirates of the Caribbean* video they owned—all three swore they'd studied for the next day's tests before supper—she made a run for the house next door with a raincoat over her head.

Grace answered the doorbell holding tight to the cat in her arms. "Oreo tries to sneak out every time the doorbell rings—but no way do I want to chase after him in weather like this." She peeked out. "It's still coming down. Hope my basement doesn't flood."

Estelle was already sipping tea on Grace's velvety sectional couch. "Mmm, so glad you braved the rain, Michelle. We better pray that *all* the neighbors' basements don't flood on a night like this. How's your husband? Is he workin' the airport tonight?"

Michelle nodded and read the text message from Jared. "This is what got me here tonight. I'm really worried about Jared. I don't know how he can work the night shift too—and he's supposed to start day shifts tomorrow!" It hit her like a slap upside the head. Three shifts in a row? Impossible! Surely they'd have to make some adjustments.

Estelle put down her teacup. "Then we better get started. There are planes in the air full of people wonderin' if they're goin' to land safely tonight—and people like Jared under a lot of pressure to bring 'em down in one piece."

Even though Estelle usually started all her prayer times with "praise and worship" prayers, she took their hands and started praying for all the people affected by the storm in the air and on the roads, praying especially for Jared and others in the tower under so much stress. She even prayed for Michelle, " . . . that she will be able to entrust her husband into God's care and experience a peace that passes understanding—so she'll give up this death grip that's killin' my fingers."

*What?* Startled, Michelle realized she'd been holding Estelle's and Grace's hands so tightly her own fingers ached. "Oh! I'm so sorry!"—but Grace and Estelle burst out laughing as she let go.

Grace poured more tea and they just talked for a while. Michelle mentioned the beautiful memorial service at Lifeline last weekend and, feeling a bit silly for mentioning something so trivial, said she was even grateful she was able to get a doctor's appointment sooner than she'd thought. Noticing the concerned looks on Estelle's and Grace's faces, she hurriedly added, "No, no, it's nothing important. I skipped my physical last year and it's high time. Been feeling a bit worn out lately."

"Well, then, praise the Lord," Estelle said. "Better sooner than later. Grace?"

Their hostess, her cheeks getting pink, said Jeff Newman had to fly to DC next week for his job with Bongo Booking Agency and managed to get a flight with a stopover in Chicago—which he was going to stretch into twenty-four hours. "I'm so grateful. We really need some face time. This long-distance relationship is harder than I thought."

"Sounds like a thank-you *and* a prayer request." Estelle patted Grace's knee. "I'm thinkin' you two need more than just twenty-four hours from time to time. Let's pray for something to shake loose in your schedules to give you more time together—either here or there. Now . . ." She looked from one to the other. "What else is heavy on our hearts tonight? Michelle?"

Michelle shared the situation with the Blackwell family, especially her concern for young Candy. "All the families I work with at Bridges need prayer, but for some reason this little girl has wormed her way into my heart."

"I know what you mean." Grace shook her head. "I worry all the time about Ramona, especially since I heard that Max was out of jail. I'm so worried he'll find her and spirit her away somehow."

"Well, uh, you're right to be concerned." Estelle cleared her throat, as if reluctant to say what she had to say. "A guy showed up at the shelter today asking if someone named Ramona was stayin' there—white guy, late twenties, tallish, spiky blond hair—"

"That's him!" Grace shrieked. "That's Max. Oh, Estelle, what . . . what happened?"

"Calm down, sweetie. Our receptionist knows better than to give out any information about who is and who isn't staying at the shelter, and fortunately, Ramona happened to be out at the time. When no one would tell him if she was staying there or not, this man got a bit hostile—but he left when Angela threatened to call the police."

Grace's face had drained of all color. She stood up and started pacing around her living room, nearly tripping over the black-and-white cat that insisted on being right under her feet. "He'll be back, I just know it. Oh, Estelle, we've got to send her home—right away. I'll . . . I'll buy her a plane ticket."

Estelle shook her head. "Can't. She was party to movin' drugs from LA to Chicago, and accordin' to Harry, the only reason she's not in jail is because she agreed to cooperate and testify against this Max when he comes to trial. That means she can't leave the state. If she does, she's a fugitive."

"But none of this is her fault! He coerced her! I mean, he's . . . what, twenty-nine or thirty? And she's all of sixteen or seventeen? Her safety—maybe even her life—is at stake!" Grace was wringing her hands, her voice high, strained.

"I know, honey," Estelle said patiently. "Come on, sit down. Let's pray about it, ask God to give us some wisdom about what to do. Though it may be out of our hands."

The younger woman sat down, and the three of them held hands again—though this time it was Grace whose grip felt as if she was hanging on for dear life. And no sooner had Estelle said "amen" than Grace did a sharp intake of breath.

"I know what to do." Her large amber eyes looked from one to the other. "Ramona can come stay with me!"

# Chapter 29

MICHELLE HAD TO LEAVE while Estelle and Grace were still talking about the notion of Ramona coming to stay with Grace, but she could appreciate the questions Estelle was raising. What about Grace's travel schedule? What if Max figured out where Grace lived? After all, he'd hidden drugs in her suitcase—did the tag have her name and address on it? And what about the time Ramona called Grace from the train on Max's phone—did he still have her phone number in his call list? "Might be more dangerous for her here than at the shelter," Estelle had told Grace soberly.

It seemed like a crazy idea to Michelle. What did Grace know about being a "safe house" for someone? Kind of like "witness protection." But if this Max was as dangerous as Grace feared, it seemed risky to bring Ramona to a house with only two unprotected women in it. Not to mention that her own family—with kids!—lived right next door.

But she did understand Grace's gut feeling, wanting to personally protect this young girl who'd naively gotten herself mixed up in something bigger and badder than she ever realized, and was now so far from home. Michelle often felt that way about some of the kids she had to place in foster care. Their tears and bewilderment often made her want to wrap her arms around them and just take them home.

Even Candy Blackwell made her feel that way. Tabby would love a little sister . . .

*Michelle Jasper! Stop it!* She scolded herself as she ducked through the rain and let herself into the house. Back to reality—which was the beginning of a headache and three teenagers who set up a protest when she shut off the movie before it was finished.

"Still a school night for two more nights," she told them, herding them upstairs to bed. "Go, go!"

Once the kids were settled, Michelle got ready for bed herself, but wasn't sure she could go to sleep. She still had a nagging headache, and thunder continued to rumble somewhere out in the suburbs. She hated the nights Jared had to stay at the airport. But maybe he'd still call. Heating up some milk and honey, she fished forms out of her briefcase and started to write up the reports on her client visits from the past two days. The house quieted . . . the hands on the wall clock inched past ten, the time Jared's swing shift should be ending . . .

The house phone rang. She snatched it up. "Jared?"

"Hi, hon. Glad you're still up. Just wanted to let you know I'm off now till midnight, so I'm going to try to get a little shut-eye. We're going to do two hours on, two hours off tonight in staggered shifts, not sure what's going to happen tomorrow. It's still a mess out here, though the storm's passing. We've still got planes sitting on the ground that should be going out, and a bunch more incomings circling in Wisconsin."

"We prayed for you—Estelle and Grace and me."

He chuckled. "Much appreciated. Keep those prayers coming. Okay, gotta go. Love you." The line went dead.

"Love you too," she whispered. Now she could go to bed.

The weather the next few days pretended like there never had been a storm. The sun played hide-and-seek with patchy clouds and the temp rose into the eighties, pumping up the humidity. Most people just went about their business—except for the ones who were still stuck at the airport, or whose basements had flooded, or who had to take long detours because of roads that were still impassable.

Jared was so bushed from covering three shifts in the control tower, he called Pastor Q, told him he wouldn't be at prayer meeting Wednesday night, and went to bed by eight. Michelle couldn't remember the last time he'd missed prayer meeting. And Thursday was another day shift (6 a.m. till 2 p.m.) and the switch to night shift (10 p.m. till 6 a.m.)—which meant Michelle had only eyeballed her husband for a few hours the entire week.

But she did manage to sneak in a kiss and a hot breakfast when he got home Friday morning before he hit the sack. "Today's the last day of school," she reminded him. "We should do something to celebrate with the kids tonight, okay?"

Her husband just stared at her, bleary-eyed, over his glass of orange juice. "Okay," he mumbled. "Whatever you want to do . . . I'm too tired to think." Leaving his scrambled eggs and toast half-eaten, he stumbled off toward the bedroom.

Fighting down a tickle of irritation—it'd been a brutal week at the airport, after all—Michelle set the dining table and called the kids. "Scrambles and salsa this morning—special breakfast for three special teens!"

Destin was the first to appear. "Uh, thanks, Mom, but don't really have time to sit." He slung his backpack to the floor and started heaping eggs onto a piece of toast. "Mind if I just make a sandwich out of this I can eat on the way?" And he was out the side door to get his bike, egg sandwich in hand, by the time the twins showed up.

Tavis slid into a chair, but scarfed up his eggs in two-and-a-half minutes and bounced up again. "'Bye, Mom! DaShawn's waitin' for me!" The front door slammed.

"Thanks, Mom," Tabby said, eyeing the table. "Looks good. But I'm not very hungry. Got my . . . you know." She made a face.

"Oh, honey. I'm sorry. On your last day of school too. You going to be all right?"

Tabby shrugged. "Sure. Can't be a big baby every time 'Aunt Flo' comes to visit."

"Ha. Bet you got *that* from your grandma." Michelle wished *her* "Aunt Flo" would hurry up. Hopefully Tabby wouldn't be as irregular as she was.

Tabby giggled. "Yeah. The good thing is, Aunt Flo'll be gone by the time I get to cheer camp." She eyed the scrambled eggs. "Maybe I should eat a little something so I don't feel all faint or something before we get our report cards. We get out early today, y'know."

"Smart girl." Michelle dished up a plate for her. "You get out early? When?"

Tabby reached for the toast. "Eleven, I think."

Michelle's mind did a few gymnastics. "Hey. What if I picked you up at school and took you out for lunch—just us girls? And then you could go with me to deliver the box of toys and games you packed for Candy. She probably gets out of school early today too."

"Go out for lunch? Cool. An', yeah, I'd like to help take the box to Candy."

* * *

Michelle waited in her car across the street from Stone Scholastic as a wave of big and little kids poured out of the front doors at eleven o'clock. Her eyes searched the sea of navy-blue-and-white uniforms for her daughter's bushy Afro . . . and was startled to see Tavis come racing down the steps with DaShawn Bentley and some other boys, stop, pull his shirttail out, loosen his belt, and pull his pants down around his hips.

Michelle gaped. *What does that boy think he's doing?!*

She opened the car door and stepped out. "Tavis!" He didn't seem to hear, but started down the street with the crew of boys similarly "undone," laughing and bumping each other. "Tavis Jasper!" She raised her voice. "Over here!"

This time Tavis's head jerked around. Their eyes met. Muttering something to the other boys, he ran across the street to the car. "Mom! Whatchu doin' here?"

Michelle almost snapped, *"Get in the car!"* . . . but remembered she was there to pick up Tabby for lunch. "The question is, young man, what are *you* doing, pulling your pants down like some hip-hop rapper?"

Tavis squirmed. "Nothin' . . . We're just messin' around." He glanced anxiously over his shoulder, then back at his mom. "Can I still go home with DaShawn? We're on summer vacation now. We wanted to do some skateboardin' or something. I was gonna call you when I got home."

Out of the corner of her eye, Michelle saw Tabby wave good-bye to some girlfriends and wait on the curb for a car to pass before coming across the street. She'd deal with Tavis later. "All right," she hissed. "But you listen up, Tavis Jasper. Pull those pants up, buckle your belt, and you call me as soon as you get home. But be quiet—your dad is probably asleep and he's had a rough couple days at work. Is anyone home at the Bentleys'?"

Tavis shrugged and again looked back at his friends. "Mom, they're gonna go without me if I don't hurry up. I'll call you. Promise." At her nod, he ran off.

*Lord, Lord. Help me here.* Was Tavis going to be her problem child?

She got back in the car as Tabby climbed in the minivan on the other side. "Hey." Michelle put on a smile. "Congratulations. You're an eighth grader now."

Tabby grinned and pumped her fist. "Yeah!" She looked back over her shoulder as Michelle pulled away from the curb. "Was Tavis trying to cut in on our girls-only lunch? *Huh.* Glad you didn't let him." She clicked her seat belt triumphantly.

"Something like that. So . . . where do you want to go for lunch?"

As much as she would've like to spend another hour lingering over the panini sandwiches and fruit smoothies they ordered at the Deluxe Diner on Clark Street, Michelle *was* combining business with pleasure—taking her lunch time and doing another visit to the Blackwell family. So they'd better get on with it.

Her phone rang just as she pulled the minivan to the curb across the street from the Blackwell apartment. *Tavis.* "Hi, Mom. Promised I'd call when I got home. Can DaShawn eat lunch here at our house? His grandpa's at work and Miss Estelle said she'd be home 'round one thirty. Can we eat the leftover beans an' sausage from last night?"

"I guess so. Where's your dad?"

"Sleepin'. Like you said."

"Well, okay. *If* you two can be quiet. Can you eat out on the front porch or something? And stay there till Miss Estelle gets home. Then you can go over to the Bentleys—but call me when you do, okay?"

"Okay."

She shut her phone but sat staring out the front windshield a moment, the reality of what "school's out" really meant sinking in. Three kids with time on their hands. Long hours when both she and Jared were at work. And even when Jared was at home during the day, he was usually sleeping.

"Mom? Are we going to go in?"

"Yes, yes. Sorry. Why don't you carry the box, since it's really from you?"

They threaded their way through a passel of kids running up and down the sidewalk letting off steam. Michelle didn't see Candy anywhere, but she was glad to see a few adults out and about—a mom with a baby on her hip talking to another mom, an older woman sitting in a lawn chair and fanning herself in front of the apartment building next door, a couple men tinkering with a car. But Michelle bet at least half the children were latchkey kids. Like her own. *But my kids are responsible,* she argued with herself. *We keep in touch by phone, Jared is home at least part of the time, and they each have a summer camp . . .*

Inside the foyer, she rang the buzzer beside the name BLACKWELL. To her surprise, the door buzzer buzzed back loudly without anyone asking "Who is it?" on the intercom. She pulled the inside door open before the buzzer stopped, and she and Tabby climbed the musty-smelling, carpeted stairs to the third floor, stopping in front of 3B.

The door was open a few inches. Michelle pushed it open a few more inches and called out a tentative, "Hello? Ms. Blackwell?"

They heard footsteps, *slap, slap, slap.* Then the door was pulled opened and Candy's mother stood in front of them. "You again! I thought you was somebody else I was expectin'." Her eyes narrowed, looking at Tabby. "Who this?"

"Ms. Blackwell, this is my daughter, Tabby. She brought something for Candy—some games and books she's outgrown."

Candy's small brown face peeked around from behind her mother. "For me?" She popped out in front of her mother, grabbed the edge of the open box, and peered in. "Are these for me?"

"Hmph. Whatchu think we are—some charity case?" The words were hostile, but the tone sounded . . . curious. Less gruff anyway. And she didn't slam the door shut.

Michelle decided to press on. "I've been after my daughter to weed out some of her games and books now that she's older, but she wanted to pass them on to someone who'd appreciate them. I thought of Candy . . ."

By now, Tabby had crouched down, lowering the box to the floor, and Candy was pawing through it, lifting out the games, squealing over the books . . . and then her eyes widened as she lifted out the music box. "Is this for me too?"

Tabby grinned. "Uh-huh. Here, let me show you." She turned it over and wound the key, then turned it upright again. The Jesus figure holding the little lamb turned round and round as the sounds of "The Lord Is My Shepherd" tinkled in the musty hallway.

"Mommy, look!" Candy took the music box and bounced up to show her mother. "An' she said it's mine!"

The mother nodded. "Well. That's right nice," she said, trying to hold on to the gruffness in her voice. But her face had softened.

"Oh, thank you!" Candy threw her arms around Tabby's neck.

Tabby, who was still kneeling on the floor, said, "I'll tell you a secret about the music box." And she whispered in the little girl's ear. Candy giggled.

Time to go while things were still on the upswing. "Well, we'll be off. Just wanted to drop by long enough for Tabby to give the box to Candy." Should she shake hands with the mother? No, better not push it. "Come on, Tabby."

They started down the stairs with a wave. Candy disappeared into the apartment with Tabby's box. Michelle heard the door click shut even before they got to the first landing.

"So what 'secret' did you tell Candy?"

Tabby shrugged. "I just told her I especially played the music box when I felt scared or alone, and she could too, to remind her that Jesus was there with her."

Michelle paused on a step as Tabby continued down the stairs, staring at the back of her daughter's bushy hair as it turned on the next landing. Who was this child? Growing up before her very eyes. Letting her light shine in a very dark place. She was so glad Tabby had come with her. *Thank you, Jesus,* she breathed before catching up with Tabby, who had disappeared from sight.

Michelle's cell phone rang as they got back into the minivan. "Mom?" It was Tavis again, his voice high pitched, anxious.

"Tavis? What's wrong?"

"Dad's on the floor outside the bathroom, says he can't get up. Says it's his back or something. Please, can you come home? I don't know what to do!"

# Chapter 30

MICHELLE DROVE HOME AS FAST AS SHE DARED and found Jared on the floor of the hallway, just as Tavis had said. "Don't know what happened," he gasped, his face etched in pain. "I woke up . . . went to the bathroom, then—*bam!* My lower back just . . . all locked up. Managed to . . . get on the floor and roll onto my back . . . but now I can't get up."

Michelle knew what happened. All that stress in the tower the past few days was finally taking its toll. "Don't move. I'll get some ice." She hurried into the kitchen, the twins right on her heels, grabbed a gallon-sized Ziploc bag, and pulled two ice trays out of the freezer.

"Is Dad going to be okay?" Tabby's eyes were frightened.

"Yes, honey, I'm sure he will. He's having a muscle spasm, but eventually it will loosen up. Here, hold that big baggie open so I can put this ice in it."

Once the bag was sealed and she'd pounded the ice cubes into smaller pieces with a wooden kitchen mallet, Michelle took the makeshift ice pack back into the hallway and slid it under Jared's lower back.

"Ai . . . ai . . . ai," he groaned, wincing with every move.

The doorbell rang and Tavis ran to open the door. In a moment, Estelle Bentley stood in the hallway, DaShawn peering around her. "Okay, what happened? Did he fall? We got a broken hip here? Should I be callin' 9-1-1?"

"No, no . . ." Jared gritted his teeth with the pain. "Just a back spasm. Really, just . . . just let me lie here a bit."

Michelle shooed everyone into the living room. "Sorry, Estelle. I wasn't home, the boys were here and Jared was sleeping—then when he got up, this happened."

"Well, God be praised. Didn't know what to think when DaShawn came runnin' in, actin' like the sky was fallin'. Still, these muscle spasms are painful. I know, I've had a few myself." She frowned. "You might need some help gettin' him up off that floor and into the bed."

Tavis suddenly snickered. "Yeah, otherwise we gotta step over him every time we wanna use the john."

Michelle couldn't help her own smile. "Okay, okay, you kids go on now. Go down to the family room or outside or . . . something."

"Can we go shoot baskets at the Bentleys?"

At a nod from Estelle, all three kids were out the door. "Want me to wait, help you get him up when he's ready?" the older woman asked.

Michelle had no doubt Estelle was strong enough, but she shook her head. Jared would no doubt feel too awkward to accept outside help, from a woman at that. "I'll call if we need you." And Destin would hopefully be home before too long.

After half an hour on the ice, Jared finally managed to roll onto his hands and knees with help from Michelle, but he crawled back into the bedroom. In fits and starts, she managed to get him onto the bed, with two pillows under his knees and a fresh ice pack under his back. Kissing his forehead, she slipped out of the bedroom. She'd better call their doctor and get a prescription for a muscle relaxant.

On her way to the drugstore to pick up the prescription, she heaved a sigh. So much for a "school's out" celebration with the kids that evening. Not with Jared feeling so miserable.

Michelle slept on the family room couch that night so as not to bounce the bed, but got up a few times to check on Jared. She stood in the darkened bedroom on one of these nighttime checks and watched him sleep. *Poor baby.* At least he was sleeping. Hopefully the muscle relaxant was working. Maybe he'd be better by Sunday and they could still drive to Fort Wayne together.

She was still tired when she got up in the morning. The couch wasn't that comfortable, and frankly she hadn't been sleeping that well lately anyway. But she'd made hair appointments for her and Tabby and they didn't dare miss. She only had two Saturday mornings before the next Hope and Healing group started, and next Saturday they had to pick up Tabby from the grandparents, so it was now or never. Saturday hair appointments were hard to come by anyway.

"You gonna be okay?" she asked Jared, bringing him some toast and coffee.

He actually inched his legs over the side of the bed and sat up. "Yeah, yeah. The spasm has loosened, just . . . my whole back is sore, feels real tentative."

"Well, if you get up, don't *do* anything, promise?" She gave him another muscle relaxant and a glass of water. "And call me if you need me. I'll be at Dani's salon."

The phone rang just as she and Tabby started out the door to make their ten thirty appointments. "Quick, honey, get the phone. Don't want your dad trying to get up to answer it." And both boys were still zonked. Michelle went on out to start the minivan and Tabby climbed in a few minutes later. "Who was it?"

"Mrs. Singer down the street. She wanted to know if I could babysit this afternoon. I told her sure, just didn't know when we'd be back from the beauty shop."

Michelle glanced at her daughter as she did a turnaround in the cul-de-sac of their dead-end street and headed back down Beecham. "She must really like you to keep asking you to babysit."

"Yeah, I guess. All it's been so far is 'mother's helper' with one of them around. Wish they'd trust me with *real* babysitting."

"They will, honey. Trusting your kids to a babysitter is a big deal for many parents—or should be. Nicole Singer is actually very smart to start you off this way."

Michelle and Tabby walked through the door of Beautiful You—Hair by Dani at 10:29, but ended up having to wait on a young woman who was getting her hair done for her wedding that afternoon. "Can't take any shortcuts on the bride, ya know," Dani said with a wink. No apology. But that was the way it was at Dani's. Each person got her undivided attention. Michelle always marveled that Dani could turn out hairstyles worthy of living sculptures, while the stylist's own hair was close-cropped into a plain nubby cap, set off by huge dangly earrings.

Dani finally handed the bride a mirror. The results were indeed striking—a swept-up combo of French braids and twists and a cascade of loose curls falling from the top of her head, with silver sparkles woven in throughout. The whole shop sent off the nervous bride-to-be with hoots and hollers and much laughter. "Woo-hoo! You look gorgeous, girl!" "Don't have *too* much fun tonight. Save some for tomorrow!" "Come back here and throw your bouquet— I'll catch it!"

Still grinning, Dani finally beckoned for Tabby to get in the chair. "All right now, what's it gonna be, young lady?" Dani ran her hands through Tabby's bushy hair. "Long enough to do some real stylin' now."

Michelle stood nearby. "I thought maybe some cute braids or twists—"

"Uh-uh." Tabby shook her head vigorously. "Want to go natural. Just a wash and a trim is all, so it grows out lookin' good."

"But, honey, it's already—"

"Mom! It's my hair. Afros are comin' back in. I'm proud of my heritage, aren't you?"

Heavens! Where was this coming from? "Of course, honey, but—"

"Hold it down, girls," Dani said. "Let Dani do her thing. How about this, sweetheart?" The stylist flipped through a hair magazine and showed it to Tabby. "That should keep your mom happy and you happy too. What d'ya think?"

A slow smile spread across Tabby's face as she looked at the model in the magazine. "Cool. Yeah, sure."

Dani handed the magazine to Michelle with a smug smile, then whipped a black plastic cape around Tabby. Michelle looked at the picture. Three rows of tiny braids crowned the front of the model's hair ear-to-ear, almost like a headband, while the rest of her hair behind the ears puffed out in a natural 'fro. It did look nice.

"Keisha's ready for you in the third chair," Dani said, waving Michelle away. "Go on—we already know what *you* want. Same ol' perm to relax that bob, right? When you gonna let us give you a new style, girl? Ain't you got an anniversary comin' up—like twenty years or somethin'? Time to put some jazz back in your marriage, girl."

Michelle slid into the chair. "I'll think about it. The usual today, Keisha."

When they got home a few hours later, Tabby headed for the phone to call Mrs. Singer and tell her they were back. Michelle found Jared down in the family room sitting in the recliner watching a White Sox game on TV.

"Hey, look at you. You made it downstairs." Michelle gave her husband a kiss, then stood back and looked him over. "How're you doing? You want something to eat?"

He nodded. "Better. And something to eat would be great." But as she headed back up the stairs to the kitchen he said, "Uh, honey, I don't think I can make the drive to Fort Wayne and back tomorrow. I should go real easy on my back another day. Can you take Tabby to your folks' yourself? I mean, I gotta get over this muscle spasm so I can go back to work on Monday—and I can't be on those muscle relaxants when I'm on duty."

Michelle's jaw tightened. *Great. Just great.* She'd been hoping the whole family would go, then they could celebrate Father's Day with her dad *and* Jared with dinner in a nice restaurant in Fort Wayne before the drive home. But it was still early Saturday afternoon. She wasn't going to give up their plans for Sunday yet.

Tabby had already made herself a quick PB&J and taken off down the street to the Singers. Michelle had to admit her daughter's hair did look really nice—even if the back half still stood out in a 'fro about two-and-a-half inches. But Toni had washed and conditioned Tabby's hair, gave it a trim, and then braided the front and styled it like the magazine picture. But would it stay that way during a week of rambunctious activity at cheer camp? No guarantee.

A note on the kitchen counter from Tavis said he was playing with DaShawn across the street, and another scrawl at the bottom just said, *Out on bike doing job stuff. Back by supper. D.*

*"Doing job stuff"* . . . What did that mean? Looking for work? Or trying to sell that energy drink for Greg Singer? Whatever. At least Destin was trying. Had he told his dad yet what he was doing? He'd asked her to let it be a surprise. But she didn't like being the buffer between father and son.

Michelle perused the refrigerator. Pretty bare. She still needed to go food shopping. She fixed Jared a tuna sandwich, sliced an apple, and added a bag of his favorite chips, salsa, and the last Dr. Pepper. But she settled for a yogurt herself. She felt too tired to eat. And to be honest, her tummy felt unsettled. Not sick, just a bit "off." Good thing she had a physical checkup coming up. Frankly, what she wanted right now was a nap. Jared was set up in front of the TV, the kids were gone, the house was quiet. Michelle kicked off her sandals and flopped on the living room couch . . .

# Chapter 31

MICHELLE STARTED THE MINIVAN the next morning and let it idle as Tabby threw her suitcase into the backseat and then jumped into the front passenger seat. "Can't believe you're skipping church to take me to camp. You never skip church!"

"Yeah, well . . ."

Was she being rebellious? Maybe a little. The whole idea of making a "family day" out of the trip to take Tabby to camp had crashed and burned with Jared's back going out. The boys didn't want to go either and put up a fuss. First one: "Aw, Mom. We just went to Bibi and Babu's on Memorial Day weekend!" Then the other: "It's no fun just riding in the car all day. Can't we stay home?"

She didn't argue. "Fun" had evaporated from her expectations too.

But having to drive the three-and-a-half hours to Fort Wayne and back again herself in the same day had made up her mind: *Skip church.* That way she could spend most of the afternoon with her folks and rest up before heading home alone.

Because she was still tired. Yesterday's nap had felt good, but it meant running out to pick up groceries late in the afternoon and doing laundry in the evening so Tabby could pack for a week. And after spending all of Friday and half of Saturday in bed, Jared had wanted to stay up for a while, watching another ball game on TV in the family room downstairs—and the boys were bored. So when the Bentleys asked Tavis to sleep over, Michelle said yes easily. And when she told Estelle that Jared was still off his feet and she needed to drive Tabby to Indiana the next day, the Bentleys had invited Destin to sleep over as well. Said the boys could go to church with them too.

Bless them.

But it sure shot a hole in Father's Day.

They were driving across the Skyway heading for Indiana when Tabby said, "Did I tell you Mrs. Singer asked if I'd be interested in babysitting for real sometime?"

"Really?" Michelle reached over and playfully punched Tabby on the arm. "See? I told you they liked you. The kids must too." She let her eyes rest affectionately on her daughter for a brief moment before turning back to the road. "I saw how you related to Candy Blackwell. You're good with younger kids, honey. I'm proud of you."

Tabby shrugged. "Yeah, well, I have a hunch she might like to go back to work part-time or something. Told me once she used to be a paralegal—whatever that is."

A paralegal? Nicole Singer? *That* was interesting. Who would've thought?

The time flew by faster than Michelle anticipated, and she pulled up in front of her parents' house just as they were getting home from church. "There's my girl!" boomed her father, holding his arms wide. Michelle grinned . . . then realized he meant Tabby, as her daughter ran into his bear hug.

"Come here, baby, give me some sugar," her mother said, and Tabby complied, bouncing from one grandparent to the next.

"Hey, I want some of that sugar," Michelle complained, then had to giggle as her father swung her around as if she were thirteen too. "Happy Father's Day, Dad."

"Best Father's Day I can think of." Martin Robinson beamed. "Got my three best girls all to myself."

His wife slapped him playfully on the arm. "Oh, you know you wouldn't complain if the boys lived close enough to drop by." Michelle's brothers had both gone to school "back east" and ended up settling on the coast. "Got enough food to feed an army, so hope you're hungry."

Michelle's mother had cooked up a feast, thinking Jared and the boys would be coming too. "Oh, Mom, I didn't mean for you to go to all this trouble. I wanted to take you and Dad out to a restaurant for Father's Day."

"What? And waste all this food? Nonsense." And soon the table was loaded with a roasted turkey breast, mac 'n cheese, green beans with sliced almonds, potato salad, sliced tomatoes and cucumbers, and cherry pie. After lunch they sat out on the front porch and played Monopoly—Michelle's least favorite game, but worth it to see Tabby and her dad gleefully cut each other off at the knees with each round. Had to laugh, though, when her mother quietly won the game.

When it was time to head home a few hours later, Michelle had a lump in her throat as she hugged Tabby good-bye. This would be the longest she'd ever been away from her baby girl. "'Bye, sweetie. Have fun. You call me every day, you hear? I want to hear all about it when you get home. We'll pick you up Saturday, okay?"

"Don't you worry about Tabby, sweetheart," her dad said. "We'll be truckin' her back and forth every day, so you know we got it covered."

"You call us the second you get home," her mother said, tucking a cooler of leftovers into the minivan. "Don't like you driving all that way by yourself. *Hmph.* You tell that husband of yours he's on my bad boy list until he gets himself down here in the flesh." She slammed the side door of the minivan muttering, "Drivin' himself over the edge with that crazy schedule of his, that's what." A moment later Coral Robinson poked her head into the open driver's side window. "You too, baby. You see the doctor yet? Stress gonna kill you, an' no mother wants to bury one of her kids."

"Mom!" Michelle rolled her eyes with a short laugh. "I'm fine. We're all fine. Quit worrying."

But as she pulled away from the curb and glanced in the rearview mirror at the three of them standing on the curb waving good-bye, a tear snuck out of her eye and rolled down her cheek. The mom-and-daughter time she'd spent with Tabby the past few days had been special . . . but didn't happen often enough. Tabby was starting to grow up. Going to camp, babysitting, going off to high school next year . . . more good-byes.

By the time she got home tonight, the weekend would be over . . . and she'd spent zero time with her boys, much less her husband.

Even though the afternoon with her folks had been pleasant, it still felt as if she hadn't once gotten off the roller coaster she was on and it was picking up speed.

Michelle had hours to think on her way home from Fort Wayne, though her assortment of CDs in the car needed serious updating. *WOW Gospel 1998* and *Radical for Christ* from 1995 . . . really? Talk about old.

She felt chagrined that it took her hairdresser to remind her that she and Jared had an anniversary coming up—their twentieth. That was one of the biggies! They really should do something special, but what? Their anniversary fell this week on Wednesday . . . *huh.* Jared would probably feel like he *had* to go to prayer meeting since he missed last week. But they could do something on the weekend.

Oh, wait. They had to go pick up Tabby this coming Saturday. Another trip down and back. Another weekend down the drain.

*Unless . . .*

Michelle could hardly wait to get home and tell Jared her idea. Surely he'd be totally over the back thing by next weekend, and his 2-2-1 work schedule ended by breakfast time Friday morning. Maybe she could weasel a day off from Bridges. Even half a day would be great. She'd talk to Charlotte in the morning.

Only . . . what if her period came next weekend? She'd always been irregular, which was a bummer, because she never could plan adequately. And seemed like once she hit forty, the time between periods had gotten even more erratic. Wasn't even sure when her last period was. That was something she should talk to the doctor about when she got her physical. Was she going through menopause early? *Sheesh.* She wasn't ready to be *that* old.

Traffic through the city was minimal this late on Sunday evening, and she pulled onto Beecham Street right at nine o'clock. "I'm home!" she called out, carrying the cooler of leftovers into the house. "Come see what Bibi sent you guys!"

The TV in the family room went silent and footsteps thundered up the stairs. "Hey, Mom." Destin gave her a smack on the cheek, and then snatched the lid off the cooler. "All *riiiight*! Pie! An' is that turkey?"

Tavis was right behind him peeking into the cooler. "Hi, Mom. Bibi sent food? Great. I'm hungry. We didn't have any supper. Just some potato chips an' stuff."

"No supper? Where's your dad?" Oh dear, was he still having a lot of back pain?

Destin was already unloading the cooler. "At church I think. Pastor Q called, asked Dad if he could come to a meeting of the deacons tonight. Something about the budget and a congregational meeting . . . Hey, Tavis, get some bread. We can make turkey sandwiches."

Michelle stood in the kitchen open-mouthed. Jared stayed home today because he'd needed to recover from his back spasm . . . and now he was at *church*? At nine o'clock at night?

She was going to kill him. Or Pastor Q. Whoever she got to first.

# Chapter 32

SHE WAS WAITING FOR JARED in the kitchen when he let himself in at ten thirty.

"Michelle?" he called out. But she didn't answer. She was too upset. She'd gotten ready for bed but no way was she going to get *in* the bed. Not until she'd given him a piece of her mind.

Jared poked his head around the wide archway leading from the living room into the dining and kitchen area, which were separated only by the kitchen counter with its bar stools. "Hey, Gumdrop. Glad to see you made it home safely." He ventured as far as the counter. "When did you get home? I thought you'd text me, let me know."

She eyed him, arms crossed, daring him to come any closer.

He hesitated, still at the counter. "Uh . . . you okay?"

"Don't 'Gumdrop' me." She spit it out. "I see you made a miraculous recovery."

"Well, yeah, my back's feeling a lot better."

"Uh-huh." She was all but tapping her foot. "Couldn't go with me to Fort Wayne today, but, oh my. Pastor Q calls, and you're suddenly hunky-dory."

Jared threw up his hands. "Oh, come on, Michelle. That's not fair. I rested all day, didn't go to church . . . when was the last time I missed church? But when Pastor Q called this afternoon, I *was* feeling a lot better. These back spasms *do* go away eventually, you know."

"Right." Her eyes narrowed. "How convenient. Not 'better' enough to fix supper for the boys tonight, but 'better' enough to jump through hoops when the Almighty Quentin calls."

He gaped at her. "What? You're mad because I didn't fix supper for the boys tonight?" He jerked a thumb over his shoulder. "Look, those two went to church with the Bentleys this morning, and they were well fed by Estelle Bentley before she sent them home this afternoon. I should know, because they brought over a plate for me. Beef-something-or-other over fat egg noodles. A heap of green beans. Cole slaw. Even chocolate cake. Don't know what those two ingrates told you, but they *weren't* starving."

"Well . . . still." Michelle didn't want excuses. "You made a big deal about taking it easy today, not taking any risks—like riding in the *car*—so you could get completely over this back thing, to make sure you're able to go to work tomorrow. And then you *drive* to the church, sit through some dumb meeting, who knows how long, and don't get home till ten thirty—"

Jared rolled his eyes. "Oh, come on, Michelle. I was feeling better by this afternoon! I'd missed prayer meeting this week, missed church . . . So when Pastor Q called, I didn't have an excuse *not* to go."

Michelle pressed her lips together, her arms still crossed. She felt dangerously on the verge of either yelling at him or bursting into tears. She squashed both impulses, and instead just marched past him, down the hall, and into the bathroom, locking the door behind her.

Turning the water on in the sink full force, she gave in to the tears. If he was that close to "feeling better," couldn't he have gone with her today? Even if she had to drive the whole way, she'd at least have had his company. And she'd been so excited to tell him about her idea for their anniversary . . . and instead, they were fighting.

But she wasn't ready to forgive him. Or be understanding.

She half expected him to tap on the bathroom door and say her name, but he didn't. She waited a good five minutes, held a hot washcloth to her face, then unlocked the door and slipped out of the bathroom into their bedroom. No Jared. The light was still on in the living room and kitchen.

She closed the door, turned out the light, and crawled between the sheets, her back toward Jared's side of the bed.

Michelle quietly slid out of bed the next morning, trying not to wake Jared. She didn't feel like talking yet. If she could get out of the house before he got up, he'd be gone when she got back and wouldn't be home till eleven or so.

Maybe she could pull herself together by then.

To her surprise, Destin dragged himself into the kitchen just as she was gathering her lunch, purse, and keys to get out the door. "Hey, you." She gave him a peck on the cheek. "What are you doing up so early? School's out. You get to sleep in."

"Yeah, you'd think." An ugly frown distorted her son's normally placid face. "But Dad told me last night I'm supposed to see *getting* a summer job as my *job* right now, which means he wants me up and outta the house by eight, or else."

Michelle blinked. "Or else what?"

"*I* dunno!" Destin stalked to the cupboard, snatched a clean cereal bowl, then opened another cupboard and pulled out a box of Raisin Bran. "He didn't exactly say 'or else,' but he was acting like, I dunno, if I can't pay it off, maybe I shouldn't go to camp after all."

Michelle tried to ignore the cereal and milk that slopped onto the counter from Destin's disgruntled efforts to make his breakfast. "Uh, well, honey, I'm sure he doesn't mean you have to pay us back *before* camp starts. Camp is next week."

"Don'tcha think I know that?" Destin perched on a bar stool and shoveled cereal into his mouth. "He just expects me to *have* a job before I go, which means I gotta find something *this* week. But it's not fair, Mom! I've applied for a whole mess of jobs but nobody's called me back. That's not my fault. So what am I s'posed to do?"

Michelle sighed. "I don't know either, honey. What about this SlowBurn thing you're doing for Mr. Singer? Why don't you tell your dad about that? That's a job . . . of sorts . . . I guess. Are you having any luck selling this energy drink?"

Destin glanced nervously over his shoulder, as if afraid his father would walk in and overhear. "Some. But I haven't had that much time 'cause school just let out on Friday. And . . . I wanna have a bit more success doin' it before I tell him. Or he'll think I'm just foolin' around and tell me to stop."

Michelle glanced at the clock. Oh, no, she was going to be late if she didn't leave *now*. "I'm sorry, honey. I gotta get to work. Maybe we can talk later. Just . . . do your best today." She gave him a quick hug and hurried out to the minivan. One more thing she and Jared should probably talk about—once they were speaking again.

She felt frustrated too. The whole plan for Destin's basketball camp wasn't very realistic—agreeing he could go to camp early in the summer, but saying he had to pay for it after the fact. Couldn't use it as leverage that way. And it was going to come back and bite them if he couldn't find a summer job. They'd be out five hundred dollars, Jared would be upset with Destin . . .

Michelle groaned as she threaded the car through morning traffic. "But to be honest, God, I don't know what else we should've done!" she blurted aloud. "Sending Destin to that Five-Star Basketball Camp is a good thing! He needs a good summer activity, and he'll have good mentors and coaches . . . And the fact that college scouts will be there might lead to some scholarships. Right?"

She sighed. No answer from on high. Maybe they'd just have to eat the five hundred dollars, though God knew it wasn't in their budget, stretched thin as it was. How long had it been since she'd had a raise? Too long. Though in this economy, she should be glad she still had a job.

After the weekend, Michelle had to hit the ground running at Bridges Family Services, dealing with the usual Monday onslaught: answering a pile of phone messages, scheduling her case management visits throughout the week, attending a staff meeting, turning in her expenses for mileage so she could get reimbursed before the end of the month, and squeezing in afternoon visits to two of her regular foster care homes plus an interview and assessment of a new foster home application. But she was glad to keep busy. No time to think about the unfinished business at home.

Her cell rang shortly before noon. Didn't recognize the number but she answered. To her surprise it was Nicole Singer, her neighbor down the street. "Thanks for taking my call, Michelle. Sorry to bother you at work, but I was wondering whether Tabby would be available to babysit for the next few days, starting tomorrow. I figured I should ask you first before I talked to her."

Michelle smiled, remembering Tabby's hunch. "Oh, I'm sure she'd love to, Nicole, but Tabby's down in Indiana at cheerleading camp this week. Won't be home till Saturday evening. Maybe next week, though. She's said how much she enjoys watching your young ones."

"Thanks, Michelle." Her neighbor seemed disappointed. "Yes, next week might work. I'll get back to you."

Well, that would be great for Tabby if it did work out. Michelle hung up, but as long as she had her cell out, she tried calling her parents' house, knowing that Tabby's camp didn't start until Tuesday. But there was no answer. They were probably out—shopping or getting nails done or having lunch somewhere awesome. Or all of the above. Oh well, that's what grandparents were for, right?

By the time she got home, her anger at Jared had dissipated. What was the point of holding on to it? Deep down she knew Jared hadn't blown her off intentionally. But the disappointment was still there. She'd wanted to surprise him with her idea for their upcoming anniversary, but it got derailed. Now when could they talk about it? They were on the O'Hare Control Tower weekly schedule roller coaster, with only a slight hiccup of overlapping time on Wednesday evening.

Their actual anniversary.

Also prayer meeting night. *Argh.*

But her idea wouldn't kick in until Friday anyway, so maybe . . .

Destin was monosyllabic at the supper table. Tavis bounced up after ten minutes of scarfing down two helpings of the frozen lasagna she'd heated up, wanting to skateboard in the street with DaShawn while it was still light. Good thing they lived on a dead-end street. Destin said he was going out to sell you-know-what and she let him go with the promise he'd be back before dark, so for the moment at least, she had the house to herself.

After calling Tabby to wish her well at camp the next day and booting up the family laptop, Michelle surfed the net and felt a tickle of glee when she found just what she wanted. Should she go ahead and make a reservation? Why not? If it all fell through, she could always cancel. On the other hand, if she already had a paid reservation, it was more likely that Jared would accept it as a gift.

The boys came in at nine. Destin surprised her by going to bed by ten, same time as Tavis. Was he trying to avoid his father? She, on the other hand, wanted to stay awake until Jared got home and mend the barbed-wire fence between them. That had to happen before anything else. But it'd been a long day and she was so tired . . .

Jared was shaking her gently. "Hon? You're still in your clothes. Don't you want to get ready for bed? Are the boys asleep already?"

Michelle sat up groggily. She'd fallen asleep on the couch. "Oh. I . . . I was trying to wait up for you, see if your back survived work today."

"Really?" He stood looking at her a long moment, then held out a hand and helped her up. "You didn't need to wait up. It's late. My back's okay."

His touch melted the last of her anger. "Actually, I didn't want us to go to bed another night mad at each other." She followed him into the bedroom.

"I'm not mad at you." Jared sat down on the bed and began taking off his shoes.

"Yeah, well, I was mad at you."

A shoe thumped on the floor. "Mmm. I know."

"I'm sorry I got so angry. It's just—"

He stood up and put a finger on her lips. "You don't have to say any more. I think I understand why you got upset. I'm sorry the weekend worked out the way it did. I know it was hard on you, me laid up and you having to take Tabby all the way to Indiana and back by yourself. Not sure what we could've done different but . . . I'm sorry."

She nodded and leaned against his chest as he put his arms around her. She was so tired. Too tired to talk. They had things to talk about but . . . not now.

# Chapter 33

Estelle Bentley called her cell the next day, said she was sorry to bother Michelle at work, but did she want to get together to pray at Grace's house again tonight?

*Tuesday.* Right. Seemed like a month had gone by since the last prayer time during that big storm. Jared's triple shifts . . . last day of school . . . taking Tabby's box of toys to Candy Blackwell . . . Jared's back spasm . . . driving to Indiana and back on Father's Day . . . the fight with Jared . . .

"I think so. Tabby's gone for the week and Jared will be at work, so it's just the boys and me tonight." And she really could use some extra prayer. Jared had gotten up before eight that morning to check on Destin and his job hunt, and she'd left the house with both of them arguing.

"Just one thing," Estelle said, "hope you don't mind, but there'll be someone else there—Ramona."

"Ramona!" Michelle could hardly believe her ears. "She's staying with Grace now?"

"For now. Still not sure it's the best thing, but . . . I know you're at work, so we can fill you in later."

Sure enough, when Grace opened the door for Michelle at seven that evening, Ramona was curled up on the couch holding Grace's black-and-white cat on her lap. "Ramona." Michelle smiled at the girl. "I'm glad to see you again."

"*Buenas noches,* Miss Michelle," Ramona said shyly. "So you live next door to Miss Grace? And Miss Estelle lives across the street?" Her voice turned wistful. "Wish I lived here. Almost like my grandparents' village in Mexico."

Michelle exchanged a glance with Estelle and Grace. She couldn't imagine that *any* neighborhood in Chicago was like a small village in Mexico where families had lived for generations. Though, getting to know some of her neighbors in recent months had certainly changed how she felt about Beecham Street. More like a small town.

She was curious about the decision to bring Ramona to Grace's house instead of staying at the shelter, but she didn't want to ask in front of the girl. But the story came out anyway. The guy—Max—had shown up at the shelter again, this time at breakfast time when most of the women were still on site, and had bullied his way in, looking for Ramona. Fortunately, the dining area was on the lower level, and some of the other women had time to hide Ramona in a tiny office before he thundered downstairs. He'd left when the person on security called 911.

Ramona giggled. "Never thought I'd see a woman stand up to Max, but Sarge—"

"Sarge?" Michelle raised an eyebrow.

Estelle grinned. "She used to be a sergeant in the army. Knows how to throw her weight around. She's our nighttime security."

"But what about this Max having Grace's phone number on his cell?" That had been one of the concerns Estelle raised last week when Grace brought up this idea, because Ramona had used his cell to call the number Grace had given to her. Michelle was concerned about Ramona's safety, of course—but she didn't like the idea of bringing that kind of danger to Beecham Street, either. "I mean, what if—"

Estelle shook her head. "Don't worry, honey. Harry found out the CPD is holding Max's cell phone as evidence until the trial. Detectives are following up on a lot of his phone contacts, trying to bust the whole drug ring wide open. But bottom line, he doesn't have that cell phone, so doesn't have the number Ramona used to call Grace from the train."

"Doesn't matter," Grace said stubbornly. "I canceled that number today and got a new one. Should've done it weeks ago." She leaned over and laid a hand on Ramona's knee. "I'm glad you're here, sweetie. So is Oreo, I can tell."

Ramona lifted the cat and nuzzled its fur. "I like cats. Never had one of my own." Then she eyed Grace. "But what happens when you get married? I mean, that Jeff guy calls here twice a day!"

"Oooo," Michelle and Estelle said together, then laughed.

Grace reddened. "Hey! I meant to tell you, young lady, what happens in this house stays in this house." But a grin tipped her mouth. "Besides, he's my agent too, we have business to discuss . . . and we're not even engaged."

"Yet!" Michelle and Estelle chorused again. By now all four of them were laughing.

"All right, all right," Estelle finally said, still chuckling. "We've got a lot of things to pray for—like Eva and Karl Molander next door to us, who are still trying to get things back to normal after their basement flooded last week during that storm."

"The Molanders' basement flooded last Tuesday?" Michelle was surprised. "I didn't know."

Estelle nodded. "I didn't either, not till I got home after our prayer time and saw Harry and some of the guys from his Bible study over there tryin' to salvage their stuff. It was too much for Karl to handle. He has some heart issues, you know. And Eva's upset. Some of the things they had stored in the basement were ruined."

"Oh, I'm so sorry." Michelle felt a tad guilty. The Molanders were the oldest couple on the block—except for Mattie Krakowski, of course—but it'd never crossed her mind to check on them during that awful storm last week. Just like it had never crossed her mind to check on Mattie last winter after the snowstorm—and look what happened.

*O God.* Whatever happened to "love your neighbor"? But her own plate was so full! Work, church, three teenagers, Jared's crazy schedule, the crisis pregnancy center, her post-abortion group, the women's ministry at Northside . . . She couldn't do everything, couldn't be everywhere at once, could she?

"Any other neighborhood concerns?" Estelle was asking.

Well, she could mention the Singers . . . "Nicole Singer was disappointed that Tabby couldn't babysit this week, because she's trying to get some part-time work and her husband is away at a conference. I know job transitions can be hard. I'm sure they could use our prayers."

"Really?" Estelle looked thoughtful. "I thought I saw . . . never mind. Yes, of course, we should keep the Singer family covered in prayer. Greg went with Harry once to his men's Bible study—that would be good support for him if he'd make it regular. I'll encourage Harry to ask him again. And maybe we should ask Nicole if she'd like to join us. Would that be all right with the rest of you?"

Grace nodded and Ramona shrugged. "Whatever. Not my show."

Michelle wasn't sure how to respond. "Well," she hedged, "if you think it's a good idea." She hadn't been praying with Grace and Estelle that long herself and was just beginning to feel comfortable. Now Ramona was here. Add Nicole Singer and it would take a while to feel safe enough to share openly—though she wasn't sure why.

Estelle had moved on. "Grace, don't you have some concerts coming up soon?"

Grace nodded and mentioned the dates. Estelle must have seen the worried glance Grace sent in Ramona's direction, because Estelle jumped in with, "Don't you worry about Ramona. She can stay with us while you're gone. Might have to sleep on the couch, but you won't mind for just a couple nights, will you, honey?" Ramona shook her head and Grace looked relieved.

"Michelle? How is Jared's back spasm?" Estelle's question turned all eyes her way.

"Better so far. But it ruined our weekend plans . . ." Michelle found herself spilling her pent-up frustrations from the past week. "We even had a huge fight when I got home from Indiana." She made a face. "And it's our anniversary tomorrow—our twentieth, believe it or not, and—"

"Twentieth!" Estelle clapped her hands. "You go, girl!"

Grace and Ramona joined in with congratulations. "Oh, you have to do something special!" Grace said.

"Well, that's something you can pray about too. Jared hasn't even mentioned our anniversary, but I'm hoping to talk to him about it tomorrow. Really, it'll be the first chance we've had to talk since . . . I don't know when!" She couldn't help adding, "Although it's prayer meeting night at church, and Jared never misses. Except he did miss last week, when he came home exhausted from triple shifts at the control tower. So he's probably going to feel duty-bound. He's a deacon at our church. You know how it is."

Estelle nodded her head knowingly. "Sister, *some* things are more important than church prayer meetings. But not more important than prayer . . . so let's pray. Come on, honey"—Estelle held out a hand to Ramona—"we're gonna pray for you too."

Before she left, Michelle worked up the courage to ask Estelle if she'd be willing to let both boys sleep over again Friday night so she could spirit her husband away for their anniversary. "Of course, honey," the older woman said. "You just made DaShawn's day. I think Harry's on an overnight run for Amtrak that night, so I'll be glad for the company."

Jared came home by eleven that evening, even though he had to be back at work at six the next morning. "Figured a few hours in my own bed would be easier on my back than those awful bunks at the airport," he murmured, turning out the light Michelle had left on for him and crawling into bed beside her.

"Mmm." She snuggled close. "Just in case you sneak off in the morning without waking me . . . happy anniversary."

"What? Tomorrow?" Jared raised up on one elbow to face her in the darkness. "What's tomorrow . . . the twenty-third? Oh, man, can't believe I forgot. And it's our twentieth too, right?" He groaned as he flopped down again. "Oh, man, don't tell the guys in the tower I forgot, or I will never live it down."

She almost retorted, *Don't worry about the guys in the tower, worry about me not letting you live it down* . . . but she didn't want to get off on the wrong foot. "Don't worry," she cooed, "I've got it covered. Tell you tomorrow." And she rolled over on purpose, back to him.

"Can't tell me now?"

She yawned. "Nope. Too tired. Tomorrow."

By his heavy breathing a few minutes later, Jared obviously wasn't going to lose any sleep over forgetting. Well, so what. She'd almost forgotten herself. But that didn't mean they couldn't celebrate this weekend, if all went according to plan . . .

And he was gone in the morning when her alarm went off at six. But there was a sticky note stuck to the bathroom mirror in the basement when she stumbled downstairs for her shower. *Happy 20th, Gumdrop!* And another on the coffeepot. *Let's sign up for another 20!*

She smiled as she gathered her things together for work. Okay, so it wasn't exactly poetry, but he was trying. Good thing they weren't trying to celebrate today anyway, because the weather report said periodic thunderstorms all day.

A loud crack from the heavens underscored the weatherman.

The house was still quiet . . . no Destin up early today. Had Jared given him a break? Or was it just too early when he left for the airport to drag the kid out of bed? Just as well. Michelle wouldn't like Destin to be out and about on his bike during a thunderstorm.

It rained on and off all day, making Michelle's case visits a bit challenging, but at least it wasn't drenching rains like last week. Still, she thought of the Molanders as she drove up Beecham Street at five thirty. Had their basement dried out? Hopefully they'd gotten their sump pump to work again.

Jared was on the kitchen phone when she came in and he motioned her over. "It's Tabby," he stage-whispered and handed the phone to her, at the same time pointing proudly to a bright-colored bouquet of mums and daisies on the dining room table. "Happy anniversary, sweetheart. And I ordered in so you wouldn't have to cook. Should be here in a few minutes."

Michelle gave him a smile and took the phone. He was definitely trying.

"Mom?" Her daughter's voice was breathless. "I was just telling Dad that this camp is *so* cool. The lady that Bibi knows from their church? She's really good. You should see the stunts she taught us, and she even gave me a thumbs-up today . . ." Tabby rattled on for five minutes with hardly a pause for breath before saying, "Oh, yeah, Bibi wants to say something . . ."

The phone must've been handed off, because the next thing Michelle heard was her father and mother warbling, "Happy anniversary to youuu . . ." in her ear. She motioned to Jared to listen too, but the doorbell rang and he had to hustle off to pay the delivery guy.

The delivery was Crab & Shrimp Cannelloni from Maggiano's and a large Italian salad. "Boys! Come and get it!" Jared yelled, hustling around to put plates and silverware on the table as the boys slid into their chairs. He seated Michelle and gave her a lop-sided grin as he dished up the pasta. "Best I could do on short notice, with prayer meeting tonight and everything."

Okay. Prayer meeting tonight. Not that she was surprised. "Yep. Not the best night to celebrate an anniversary. Which is why we're doing this instead." She fished out the anniversary card she'd bought with the folded sheet of paper inside.

Jared read the card, leaned over, gave her a kiss, and then un-folded the paper. "What's this?" He read the computer printout. "A reservation for a bed-and-breakfast in South Bend?" He looked up. "I thought we had to go pick up Tabby this weekend from your folks'."

"We do. Which is why I picked a bed and breakfast kinda on the way to Fort Wayne." She smiled smugly. "See? It's for Friday night. You and I can drive to Indiana Friday evening to the B&B, go out for dinner, sleep in, have a leisurely morning—the web-site says they make a big, scrumptious breakfast—and then drive down to Fort Wayne to pick up Tabby and come home later that afternoon. What do you think?" She was grinning at her perfect plan.

"Gee, honey, it's really a great idea . . ." He peered at the print-out again. "Uh, is that *really* the price for just one night?" He looked a little bug-eyed.

She backhanded him on the arm. "Jared Jasper. It's our *twentieth* anniversary. Some people take cruises, or . . . or trips to Europe. We can certainly do one night at a bed-and-breakfast." Besides, she'd already put it on the credit card.

"Uh, happy anniversary an' all that," Tavis broke in, "but can somebody say a blessing for the food so we can eat?"

# Chapter 34

MICHELLE DIDN'T PARTICULARLY WANT TO GO to prayer meeting, but she'd missed church on Sunday, so it'd probably be good to show up. Besides, it was one way to spend time with Jared. Sorta.

It was also a good chance to see her friend Norma and some of the other sisters who faithfully attended the women's ministry events each month—though she didn't appreciate Sister Betty's guilt trip when the heavyset woman asked, "Where're the twins and that big boy of yours? They're old enough to come to prayer meeting." Sister Betty always brought *her* kids to prayer meeting, even though the youngest was only four and the oldest eleven.

"Uh, they usually have homework on weeknights."

"Well, school's out now, you know!" the woman said before herding her four kids into the second pew.

*Arrgh.* What Northside really needed was to start up the middle school and high school youth groups again, both of which had been abandoned after their youth minister left last year. Schedule youth groups on Wednesday nights, and she'd bring the twins *and* Destin . . . at least during the summer. Though she was *not* going to suggest it to Jared. He'd mention it to the pastor and Pastor Q would toss it back to him. *"Great idea. Make it happen, Brother Jared."*

"Girl," Norma leaned forward and stage-whispered from the pew behind her, "it's been too long since we've had any girl time. What're you doin' this Saturday?"

Michelle shook her head. "Out of town. Our anniversary. And picking up Tabby from camp."

"Ohmigosh, that's right! Twentieth, right? How 'bout next Saturday?"

Again Michelle shook her head. "Starting up a new PA group at Lifeline next week. And, you know, grocery shopping, laundry, cleaning the house. Maybe we could try a Sunday afternoon?"

Big sigh from behind her. "Not good. You know my mother-in-law—we all supposed to show up every week for Sunday dinner. Mama calls, Gentry and his siblings say, 'Yes, ma'am.' A few other strange relations usually show up too. We don't get out of there until maybe four or five." A moment later Norma leaned forward again. "Did I say 'strange'? I meant 'stray'." Her friend snickered loudly.

Michelle caught Jared's slight frown from the front where he and the other deacons were sitting, and focused her attention on Pastor Q's devotional, but she had to fight to stay awake. Still, the prayer meeting got over by eight thirty. They'd be home by nine—

"Brother Jared, hold on a minute." Pastor Q hustled toward them as Jared and Michelle gradually shook-hands-and-hugged their way toward the foyer. "Came in the mail this morning. Pretty fast if you ask me." He handed a bulky white envelope to Jared.

"What's this?" Jared peered at the return address. Michelle looked too. *Moody Theological Seminary.*

"Materials for your seminary application. I told you I'd ordered them at the deacons' meeting last Sunday. Look them over, tell me what you think." Pastor Q beamed. "And by the way, church calendar says congratulations are in order. Twenty years married! Hope you two have big plans to celebrate."

Michelle found herself wrapped in a bear hug from the pastor before he broke away and cheerfully hailed someone else. She eyed Jared. But he just took her elbow and steered her outside, dodging rain puddles until they climbed into the Altima.

"When—" she started.

"Honey, he just mentioned this to me Sunday night at the deacons' meeting. Was going to tell you when I got home, but, you know, you were upset, we had to work all that through, then the week started and . . . I just forgot." He handed the packet to her. "It's just information. Nothing's been decided."

Michelle tossed the big envelope into the back seat and stared out the side window. One *more* thing they needed to talk about. The list was growing. Not exactly what she had in mind for their anniversary getaway.

Thursday was another crazy day—Jared's second day shift, which got him home by three, then back to work for his night shift, which got him home Friday morning just as she was leaving for work. But her boss told her she could leave at noon on Friday—"Consider it your anniversary gift," Charlotte deadpanned gruffly—and Michelle flew out of the office without even taking her report forms to fill out. She'd make it up somehow.

She did a quick grocery shop on the way home and wasn't surprised that Jared was still sleeping when she let herself into the house. Nobody else seemed to be home until she heard some loud thumps coming from the back of the house. Michelle wandered out to the garage. Destin was gathering miscellaneous pieces of lumber from around the garage and piling them in a corner, dropping them with a little more force than necessary.

"Hey, what's up?" she asked.

Destin glowered. "Cleaning the garage. Dad said if I wasn't workin' a job, I could just do some work here at home." He yanked another board from under his dad's workbench. "But I should be out sellin' you-know-what."

"Destin! Just tell your dad what you're doing. He'll understand. If you won't, I will."

"No, Mom, please. I . . . I'm gonna spend tomorrow workin' for Mr. Singer while you're gone. If I have a good day, I'll tell Dad about it when you guys get home."

"Well, okay. Not sure I understand though. Where's Tavis?"

"Huh. Over at the Bentleys already. Don't see why Dad didn't make *him* help me. He's not a baby anymore."

*Good point*, she thought. On the other hand, those two working together would've needed an adult referee. Or better still, father and sons working together.

But . . . she couldn't go there. Jared's schedule was what it was. She didn't begrudge him his sleeping during the day when he'd just pulled an all-nighter.

Michelle went back inside, did a load of laundry to tide them over till Sunday, and then tiptoed into the bedroom to pack an overnight bag for both of them. She stuck in her best lingerie. Waking her husband at two thirty and giving Destin last-minute instructions about locking the house before going over to the Bentleys, they were in Jared's Altima heading for the Loop by three o'clock. Hopefully they'd miss the worst of the afternoon rush hour this way.

After cloudy skies and intermittent thunderstorms all week, the afternoon sun shone unhindered in a brilliant blue sky. To the east Lake Michigan shimmered like a living thing, dotted with sailboats and cruisers, and on their right the Chicago skyline rose in majestic glass and steel as they drove south on Lake Shore Drive. Michelle tilted her seat back to enjoy the ride. The good weather was like icing on the cake to her little plan.

Jared seemed restless, however. He turned the car radio to 1390, the gospel music station, and drove without speaking as he navigated a few traffic clogs that slowed them down on the way toward the Skyway that would take them into Indiana. She tried to ignore the little frown on his face. He just needed some time to unwind and relax.

Then he suddenly punched the Off button and said, "I don't know, Michelle . . ."

She moved her seat upright again. "You don't know what?"

"This weekend . . . Destin . . . I should really be at home staying on his case about finding a job." He slapped the steering wheel in frustration. "School's been out for a week and he still doesn't have a summer job. What's wrong with this kid? We had a deal!"

Michelle clenched her teeth. If he was second-guessing their anniversary trip, she was going to scream. But she took several deep breaths to calm herself. *Focus on his concern about Destin.* After all, she'd wanted to talk to Jared about their son too.

"Honey, there's nothing wrong with Destin. I think he's been really trying. Filled out a dozen applications. It's not his fault those places haven't called him back."

"So we're just stuck with shelling out five hundred bucks for this Five-Star Basketball Camp? No way. Maybe we should cancel his registration. No job, no camp."

"Jared, I don't think that's fair! The camp is a good thing with possible long-term benefits. Sure, ideally a kid works for something, earns the money first, *then* gets to go to camp or whatever. But this camp happened to be scheduled early in the summer. He hasn't had time to earn the money."

"Yeah, well . . . maybe I'd feel differently if he at least had a job to come back to after camp next week."

"Well, he does." Uh-oh. That slipped out without her intending it to.

Jared gave her a sharp look. "What do you mean?"

Michelle sighed. "He wanted to surprise you . . . in fact, I really shouldn't be telling you this. But he's been working for Mr. Singer, helping to sell that SlowBurn energy drink."

"He what?!" The Altima swerved and a car somewhere behind them honked. Jared glued his eyes back onto the highway. "You're kidding me, right?"

"No-o." She laid a hand on his arm. "Calm down, honey. I know you don't think much of those kinds of selling jobs, but at least he's trying."

"Trying? Is *that* what he's been doing instead of looking for a real job?"

"No, no, I didn't mean that. He says he's been following up on the applications he filled out and applying at new places, all the things you've told him to do. But at the same time, he's been trying to sell this energy drink. At least it's something. I mean, what can it hurt? Let's give him credit for trying."

Jared snorted and wagged his head. "Can't believe it . . . why on earth didn't he tell me?"

She let that one pass.

Michelle gasped in delight as they pulled up in front of the Oliver Inn—a large, rambling Victorian house in mint condition surrounded by huge trees. As they checked in, they asked the innkeepers to recommend a fun place to eat, not too expensive, and were given directions to a Celtic-themed café in downtown South Bend.

When they arrived at Fiddler's Hearth, they were delighted to see tables set up outside like a sidewalk café. It was a pleasant June evening, not too hot, with a slight breeze stirring the air. Music from a free concert in a nearby park drifted their way. Michelle glanced at the menu. This was nice. It'd been a long time since they'd been out to eat, just the two of them. Why did it take a significant anniversary to get them out on a date?

Only downside was, even though everything on the menu sounded interesting—Smoked Salmon, Irish stew, Shepherd's Pie, Gaelic Sirloin—she wasn't really hungry for anything heavy. Her stomach felt a bit queasy. Was she *that* tense over the things they needed to talk about? Or . . . oh, great. Maybe she was getting her period.

"Think I'll try one of their specials, that bangers-and-mash business." Jared chuckled as he closed his menu. "'When in Rome' and all that. What about you, honey? Want to try something adventurous?"

Michelle shook her head. "Um, think I'll just have the smoked salmon salad. Not feeling like anything too heavy tonight."

Jared gave her a suspicious look. "Honey, if you're trying to go cheap, just because I think the inn is a little overpriced, you shouldn't—"

"No, no, that's not it. The salad looks good. That's what I feel like."

The raspberry iced tea they ordered was soothing, and they held hands while waiting for their food. Michelle studied her husband's face—a darker brown than her own, smooth, no wrinkles. His wire-rim glasses and trim, slightly graying moustache gave him a serious air . . . until he smiled, when a couple of dimples appeared, which made him look boyish. Would she look as good as he did at forty-two? She felt older. Tired.

She saw his eyes light up as a middle-aged white woman with a yellow Lab settled down at one of the sidewalk tables near them. Jared reached out and petted the dog. "That's a nice Lab. They allow dogs here?"

The woman laughed. "As long as we sit outside. God bless sidewalk cafés. Buster hates to be left home alone. Now that the kids are out of the nest, he goes everywhere with me."

Jared turned to Michelle. "Funny. We never got a dog for the kids. Maybe . . ." He looked wistful.

She gawked at him. "Get a dog? Jared Jasper, I like dogs as much as anybody, but did you hear what she said about dogs hating to be home alone? Think about it! During the school year, none of us are home."

He made a face. "Guess you're right . . . oh, here's our food."

They ate slowly, ended the meal with a scoop of Irish Cream ice cream, then walked back to the inn. "Ohh, Jared, look at this garden!" The Oliver Inn was set in a classic garden that included an antique fountain splashing amid a flower bed, an old-fashioned wooden glider under an ivy trellis, and even a porch swing hanging from a huge tree limb. Michelle sat in the swing and patted the seat for Jared to join her. "I'd love a porch swing like this," she mused. "How about a swing instead of a dog? Easier to take care of. Wouldn't have to take it for walks or scoop the poops. A place to relax, sit and talk . . ." *Would make a nice anniversary present.*

"Uh-huh." Jared put his arm around her and nuzzled her neck. "*Mmm.* Sun's gone down. How about going up to the Tippecanoe Room or whatever they call it and getting into that big four-poster bed? No kids, no telephone, no alarm clock, nothing but just us." He stood up and pulled her out of the swing, grinning. "This was a great idea, Gumdrop."

It *had* been a great idea, Michelle groaned in the middle of the night. Until suddenly she'd had to run for the squeaky-clean bathroom where she lost her entire smoked salmon salad dinner—just moments after they'd climbed into the cloud-soft bed.

Jared had stuck his head in the bathroom door. "Honey, are you going to be okay? Was there something wrong with the fish?"

"Just . . . go 'way," she'd gasped, bent over the toilet. Upchucking while stark naked wasn't exactly sexy.

By the time she'd finished throwing up and came shakily back to bed, Jared was propped up on several big fluffy pillows, still bare-chested, glasses on, reading through the big white packet from Pastor Q.

# Chapter 35

MICHELLE AWOKE THE NEXT MORNING in the luxurious bed and stretched, realizing she felt a lot better, so she responded when Jared reached out and drew her body close.

So sweet . . .

They eventually made their way downstairs to the sumptuous breakfast table, set with crystal glassware and fluted china painted with delicate pink roses. The innkeepers made a fuss over them because it was their twentieth anniversary, but Michelle could see Jared trying to keep a straight face. The whole Victorian atmosphere was no doubt a bit more "girly" than his taste. Not to mention a far cry from the usual hurry-scurry Jasper breakfast.

But the caramel pecan French toast and bottomless cups of good coffee won him over.

They still had a two-hour drive to Fort Wayne, so they pulled out by ten thirty, and got to Michelle's parents at half past noon. Bibi, of course, had set out a big lunch—homemade bread, ham and turkey slices, a three-bean salad, veggies and dip, watermelon chunks, and a peach cobbler for dessert. Michelle just nibbled a bit of this and that, saying her supper hadn't agreed with her last night so she was going light today—but when her father heard she'd actually thrown up after their meal, he made her call back to complain. "A restaurant needs to know when you get food poisoning, Micky!"

She called, feeling slightly foolish, and didn't bother to tell her father that the manager said no one else had complained of any trouble last night. Nor did she tell her parents or Jared about the worry nibbling at the edges of her consciousness. Good thing she was having her physical next week. No sense fretting yet.

Tabby was ecstatic about her week at cheerleading camp and chatted for the first hour in the car about the four girls on her

239

"squad" who'd worked together to develop some creative cheer routines. "One of the girls, Kathi—that's Kathi with an 'i'—has her own Facebook profile, and she wants all of us to create a Facebook profile so we can 'friend' each other and stay in touch. Facebook lets you have a profile when you're thirteen, and we're all thirteen. Can I do Facebook? It'll be so cool."

Jared and Michelle glanced at each other, and then chorused from the front seat, "No!" which chased the smile right off Tabby's face.

"Facebook doesn't make the rules for our family," Jared said.

"You're too young, honey," Michelle added. "Too many stories about how stuff posted on Facebook goes viral, goes to people you never intended."

"You guys never let me do anything!" Tabby pouted and curled up in the back seat, giving them the silent treatment the rest of the way home.

Jared just cut his eyes toward Michelle and mouthed, *"Ignore her."*

Charlotte Bergman poked her head into Michelle's office on Monday morning, waggling her eyebrows suggestively. "How was your anniversary?"

"Wonderful . . . if you don't count me getting food poisoning, which chose to make itself known just as we were getting, shall we say, 'romantically involved' in our fairy-tale bedroom at the Oliver Inn."

"You're kidding!" Charlotte's eyes popped. "You're not kidding." Michelle's boss started to laugh, tried to stop herself, then gave up. "You gotta admit, that's funny! Heh, heh, heh. It'll become part of the Jasper family lore for generations to come." The woman disappeared out of the doorway, still snickering.

Drat. Why did she say that? Knowing her boss, her date with the toilet bowl would become part of the "family lore" here at Bridges Family Services too. And she didn't really know if it was food poisoning or not—but it silenced any questions.

For some reason Michelle felt as if she were moving in a fog. She and Jared hadn't discussed the seminary idea on the way to Fort Wayne as she'd anticipated. He'd just handed her the packet he'd read while she was "indisposed" the night before, told her to take her time, they could talk about it later. After all, he said, the application deadline wasn't until August first for the fall semester, so they still had time.

Destin, on the other hand, had given her a look of betrayal Saturday evening when Jared confronted him about selling SlowBurn for Mr. Singer. But at least Jared hadn't forbidden him to do it. "You want to try selling that energy drink?" Jared had said, his tone of voice saying he thought it was a stupid idea. "Then you better work your butt off selling it. Because you still owe us five hundred bucks by the end of the summer." Then he'd jabbed a finger toward Destin's chest. "But if any of the other jobs come through, you take it, and tell Mr. Singer you're done, you hear?"

She'd apologized to Destin later when Jared wasn't around. "I'm sorry, honey. I didn't mean to tell him, it just came out. I wanted him to know you weren't just blowing off the job hunting, that you've actually been working."

Destin had shrugged. "Well, at least he didn't tell me I couldn't do it, so maybe I can do some real selling the next couple days and when I get back from camp."

The week seemed to pass in a blur. Tabby kept busy babysitting for Mrs. Singer, Tavis hung out at the Bentleys with DaShawn more than he was home, and Michelle spent Monday and Tuesday evening while Jared was at work helping Destin get his clothes and gear together for basketball camp—T-shirts, shorts, socks, gym shoes, and toiletries, plus towels, sleeping bag, sheet, and pillow. Which meant she had to tell Estelle that she wouldn't be able to come to prayer time at Grace's house Tuesday night.

Which prompted a phone call from Grace at nine that evening. "Michelle? I . . . just wanted to check in with you about the, um, Hope and Healing group we talked about. You said it starts first Saturday in July—this coming weekend?"

"That's right. Ten o'clock, and we go for nine weeks. Do you need the address of the Lifeline Care Center?"

"I think I have it . . . Yes, I have the brochure you gave me." There was a pause. "Have to admit, I'm kind of nervous about doing this. It's . . . it's hard facing up to what happened so long ago. You know, all the memories and feelings. I worked so hard to bury all that in the past, you know. It's been hard enough to fully accept God's grace and forgiveness, though that's been"—Grace's voice got husky—"been really important these past few months."

"I know." Michelle wished she'd gone to Grace's house that night This was a moment for face to face talk and hugs of encouragement. "But I think you'll be really glad you came to the group. Some things can heal with time, but some things need to be dealt with at a deeper level to truly experience freedom."

Michelle heard sniffling on the other end. Then, "Thanks, Michelle. I'll be there. Pray for me, though!"

Michelle hung up the phone. Her prayer life had gotten a little ragged again. Why was it so hard to hold onto those special times with God? What she needed to do was keep a prayer notebook or something, a list of things and people she wanted to pray for, but maybe also room just to write down her own heart thoughts and prayers.

She'd been hoping Jared would ferry Destin the hour-plus drive to Lewis University south of the city on Wednesday, but he didn't get off work till two o'clock, and by the time he got home it would be three, and the FAQs sheet said all campers had to check in *no later than* four. Destin didn't want to risk being the last one to arrive . . . so once again, Michelle begged time off from work and found herself heading down Lake Shore Drive and out Route 55 to Romeoville.

Jared definitely needed to pick their son up on Saturday, though, because the new Hope and Healing group was starting, and no way could she miss that.

"You're all set, Destin," said the muscular young man at the registration table. "All we need now is your fifty dollar room and key deposit."

Michelle blinked. "What's this? I thought we paid everything already."

"Well, you did. We got your registration fee and the full tuition, but we just need this room deposit—which will get refunded if Destin leaves his dorm room in good shape and turns in his key."

Michelle gave Destin a look that said, *"You better not lose that room key, buster,"* and handed over her credit card.

But as she waved good-bye and drove away, she wished she'd taken the time to pray with Destin before leaving him at camp. Well, she'd pray for him on the way home—and she had plenty of time, since she had to drive through the city during the heaviest rush hour. Could use the time to pray for Grace and Estelle and Ramona too, since she'd missed their prayer time the night before. Had Estelle invited Nicole Singer yet? Neither Estelle nor Grace had mentioned it, so probably not.

Charlotte Bergman wasn't too happy that Michelle was taking *another* half day off work for her doctor's appointment on Friday, but this one had been scheduled for a couple of weeks, so what could she say?

Doctor Marie Callas had been Michelle's primary doctor since before the birth of the twins. But the dark-haired, green-eyed white woman—she looked Irish to Michelle—peered over her reading glasses at Michelle after flipping through her chart. "Mm-hm. It's been quite a while since you've scheduled a physical, young lady."

Michelle allowed a wry smile at the "young lady." She and Dr. Callas were probably around the same age. "I know. Too busy to think about it, I guess."

"Yes, but it's been five years since you've been in, and that was because you got bronchitis. We didn't do a full workup. But you're now . . . what? Forty-one? You really should start having a regular physical every other year until fifty, Michelle, then annually." The doctor flipped through her chart again. "I don't see any mammograms, either. I'll schedule a baseline now, and you should repeat it every year or two. Do it around your birthday. Makes it easier to remember. The good news is, we can probably wait on a colonoscopy and bone density test for a few years, but today let's make sure the rest of you is in good health."

Michelle nodded meekly as the doctor reviewed her recent health history. Joint pain? *No* . . . Blackouts? *No* . . . Headaches? *Yes*

... Seven to eight hours sleep? *Um, sometimes* ... Still menstruating? *Yes, though irregular* ... Smoke? *No* ... Night sweats? *No* ... Regular exercise? *Not really* ... Self breast exams? *Sometimes* ... Any recent complaints? *Often tired, appetite off, occasional nausea* ... Stress? *Huh, I'm a social worker and have three teenagers, goes with the territory* ...

She dutifully gave a urine sample, winced as a nurse drew two vials of blood, and changed into one of those stupid gowns that opened down the back for the "physical" part of the physical. She followed the doctor's finger with her eyes, said "Agggh" as the tongue depressor gagged her, breathed deeply as Dr. Callas moved the stethoscope around her chest and back, and obediently put her feet in the stirrups for a pelvic check and Pap smear.

The doctor thumped here, pushed there, felt everywhere.

Michelle stared at the ceiling. At least she was thorough.

Dr. Callas finally peeled off her plastic gloves and stuck them into a waste container. "All right, young lady. You can get dressed now. I'll be back in a few minutes and we can talk."

Talk? That sounded ominous. Hopefully she'd just get a lecture on taking better care of herself.

Michelle had just finished dressing when the doctor knocked and came in. She pulled up her stool-on-wheels and folded her arms in front of her. "So."

Michelle waited several moments. "Is . . . everything okay?"

The doctor nodded, pursing her lips. "Mmm, you're more or less healthy—in spite of the fact that your stress level is high, you're not getting enough sleep or exercise, not taking care of yourself like you should. But there is one thing . . ."

Michelle held her breath. She knew it.

A small smile tipped the edges of Dr. Callas's mouth. "You're pregnant."

# Chapter 36

S TUNNED, Michelle licked her lips. *Pregnant?*

*No, no, no . . . can't be! Not now . . .*

She tried to swallow. "Are you saying positively? Or maybe?"

Dr. Callas nodded. "Pretty positive. Urine sample and blood test will tell me for sure, but from my pelvic exam, you're probably at least eight weeks along."

*Eight weeks!* Michelle tried to get a breath. She couldn't be pregnant. Couldn't have another baby, not *now*. She was forty-one years old! Destin would be off to college in a year. The twins were thirteen. She had a full-time career! And they needed both incomes for their double mortgage, medical insurance, car loans . . . not to mention still paying off their own college loans.

"I realize a pregnancy is challenging at your age, Michelle," Dr. Callas was saying. "There's a bit more risk after forty, but there's no reason you can't carry this baby to term and give birth to a healthy child. But you *will* need to take better care of yourself. Cut down on your work hours if you can. Pay more attention to your diet and exercise, get more rest. I'll get you started on some prenatal vitamins and write up some basic health guidelines I want you to follow. And, frankly, I'd like to see you in another four weeks, just to keep everything on course, but you'll also want to make an appointment with an obstetrician. I can refer you to an excellent team. What hospital do you prefer?"

Michelle shook her head slowly. Naming a hospital made it *real*.

The doctor stood up and patted her on the shoulder. "That's all right. Take your time." She chuckled. "Good thing it takes nine months to grow a baby. Takes about that long to wrap our minds around bringing the little rascals into the world."

Alone in the examination room, Michelle stared, unseeing, at the health posters on the wall. The thought *had* crossed her mind, but she'd squashed it before it took root. She always used birth control. Yes, her period had been late, but she'd never been regular—though, admittedly, she'd never been *this* late. But she'd been too busy, too stressed, too distracted to keep track or worry about it. She'd worried about other things—a brain tumor (the headaches) . . . some kind of gastric cancer (the nausea) . . . a low-grade virus (general malaise) . . . or even mononucleosis, though she was a bit old for that. In college, stressed-out students were always falling prey to mono, with fatigue, headaches, and nausea being typical symptoms. Well, along with fever and swollen glands, neither of which she'd had, but still.

But it wasn't mono. Or a virus. Or cancer.

Michelle was still in a state of shock when she walked out of the doctor's office half an hour later with a prescription for prenatal vitamins, a long list of instructions for prenatal healthcare, an appointment in four weeks, and the phone numbers of three excellent obstetricians who delivered at St. Francis Hospital. But all her mind could think as she drove to work was, *O God, O God, let Dr. Callas be mistaken!*

Fortunately, she had two clients to visit that afternoon back-to-back to distract her, and when she returned to the office, her desk was piled with a stack of case folders to update and report forms to fill out. The full import of the doctor's diagnosis didn't hit her until she was back in her car heading home.

A baby? Jared would freak. He loved their kids, he was a great dad. But they were done. When the twins were born, bringing the number to three, they'd decided that was it.

Was *supposed* to be it.

A fourth child? Or . . . she suddenly gulped. What if it was twins? Again.

She couldn't tell Jared. Not yet. Hadn't the doctor admitted she wasn't a hundred percent sure? She'd wait for the results of the urine test and blood sample. That was it. No sense getting her husband all worked up about something that might not even be true.

Michelle rehearsed all the way home what she was going to say—and not say—if Jared asked how her doctor's appointment went. But his car was gone, much to her relief. Out running errands or something. Gave her time to catch her breath.

Estelle Bentley called while she was making supper, saying Harry was taking DaShawn miniature golfing, did the twins want to go? "Destin too, if he'd like. We might take Ramona—they're about the same age, aren't they?"

*The same age?* Ramona *was* young, but she'd never realized she was the same age, or maybe even a little younger, than her son. Michelle shuddered, thinking of Ramona naively traveling cross-country with a drug runner, grateful Destin was a boy. Surely not as vulnerable as a young girl . . .

"Destin's at basketball camp, but I'm sure the twins would love to go. I could send Jared if Harry needs backup." Nothing like volunteering her husband without his permission. But right now Michelle needed some space.

"I bet Harry would like that. Why don't you—"

"Actually, why don't *you* have Harry call Jared and ask him personally if he and the twins would like to go? Might make the medicine go down better, if you know what I mean."

Estelle's deep, throaty laugh filled her ear. "Got it. I'll have Harry call."

Jared came in just as Michelle was dishing up the Hamburger Helper to go over the mashed potatoes. "Sorry, Gumdrop. Thought I'd be back before you got home. Had to get the oil changed in the Nissan, took longer than I thought." He kissed the cheek she held up to him as she passed carrying a hot dish between potholders. "Should probably take the Honda in tomorrow for the same thing—oh, rats. Can't. Gotta go pick up Destin, right?"

"Yes, dear," she said, making a face at him. "You're on chauffeur duty this time. I'm starting a new Hope and Healing group at Lifeline." She raised her voice. "Tavis! Tabby! Supper!"

"What time do I have to be there? Tomorrow is first Saturday of the month, men's breakfast meets at eight. Think I can go after?"

Michelle tried to keep her tone lighthearted. There was no way he was going to wiggle out of picking up Destin. "Camp info sheet says pickup is eleven o'clock. But I think there's a game or presentation ceremony in the morning that parents are invited to attend. Would be nice if you could be there for that."

"Yeah." Jared frowned and scratched his head as he sat down. "Hate to miss the men's breakfast though . . . hey, hey, hey!" he hollered as the twins skidded into their chairs. "Where's the fire? This is the dinner table!"

"Sorry, Dad."

They held hands around the table as Jared said the blessing, then busily filled their plates as Michelle passed the food around. "So how was babysitting at Singers' today, Tabby?" she asked. She only half-listened as first Tabby, then Tavis, chattered away about their day with mouths full. Just keep them talking.

But during a lull, Jared cocked an eyebrow at her. "Didn't you have a doctor's appointment today? What'd he say?"

"*She* said you guys have to put up with me for twenty or thirty more years at least. Though she said I *might* live longer if my kids brought me breakfast in bed, if my husband did all the laundry and housecleaning, and—"

"Mo-om." Both twins rolled their eyes.

"Seriously, hon."

She shrugged. "Okay. She said I'm in pretty good shape, but should cut down on stress, get more rest, get more exercise, include more vegetables and fruit in my diet—you know, the usual."

"But what about—"

The phone rang. *Saved by the bell.* Michelle jumped up to answer it, then handed Jared the phone. "For you."

"Jasper here . . . Well, uh, sure, don't think we have any plans tonight." He shot a look at Michelle, who shook her head. He covered the mouthpiece. "Hey, Tavis, Tabby, DaShawn's grandpa is asking if you guys want to go miniature golfing tonight—"

"Yes!" they both yelled.

Michelle smiled. Out of the house. A quiet evening at home for her.

Jared was gone by seven thirty the next morning. Said he'd put in an appearance at the men's breakfast, but leave in time to get to Lewis University by ten. Traffic shouldn't be bad on a Saturday morning.

Michelle poured herself a second cup of coffee and slumped at the kitchen table. She hadn't slept that well. And when she did fall into a restless slumber, she'd dreamed she was being chased by . . . by something, never clear what, but ahead of her was a steep cliff, and she was running straight toward it. Couldn't turn right, couldn't turn left, couldn't turn back . . . but disaster lay straight ahead.

She'd awakened in a sweat. It was still early, not quite six, but she got up, took a shower to fully wake up, and decided to put the coffee on and start the laundry.

Anything to shake that dream.

Should she make breakfast? Jared was gone, the twins still asleep. She didn't really feel like eating, but she had a full day ahead. Needed the strength. Nibbling on a piece of toast, she felt uneasy about not telling her husband all that the doctor had said—but good grief! He'd asked in front of the kids!

The phone rang, jolting her out of her thoughts. "Michelle?" It was Grace next door. "Wondering if I could ride with you this morning to Lifeline. Trying to make sure I actually get there. I've been known to panic and run." She laughed self-consciously.

"Of course—if you don't mind going a little early. The group meets at ten but I try to get there by nine. Meet you out front at eight thirty?"

"Yes . . . yes, fine. See you then."

Knowing Grace was going to be riding with her gave Michelle the jump-start she needed to get dressed, start another load of laundry, leave instructions for the twins, and head out the door at eight thirty.

Grace was waiting beside the Honda. "Thanks," she said, climbing in. "Don't know why this is such a big deal for me. Just is."

Starting the minivan and squeezing past Lincoln Paddock's fancy town car parked in the cul-de-sac, Michelle nodded and smiled. "I know. But you're going to be fine."

Grace chatted nervously as Michelle drove to the crisis pregnancy center—mostly about Ramona. "Kind of weird having someone else in the house. I'm so used to living alone . . . She likes to cook—mostly Mexican food. Good thing I like it . . . She's not real neat, but she's trying. Keeps most of her mess in the guest room . . . I wasn't sure she'd want to go when Estelle invited her to play miniature golf last night, but she did and seemed to have a lot of fun." Grace gave a half-laugh. "Felt like a middle-aged mother waiting up for her to come home . . ." Grace's voice suddenly cracked and she quickly turned her face toward the side window.

Michelle glanced at her neighbor, saw her brush a tear away. "Grace? Are you all right?"

Grace nodded but her chin trembled. "Ramona told me she's 'almost seventeen.' Made me realize that . . ." She paused, making another swipe at her eyes. ". . . if I hadn't aborted my baby, she or he would be a teenager like Ramona right now—well, a few years younger, more like your twins, but still."

"Oh, Grace . . ." Michelle laid a hand on the young woman's knee for a brief moment. Grace was quiet the rest of the way.

They arrived at Lifeline in good time. Introducing Grace to the affable Bernice, Michelle asked the receptionist if she'd be willing to give Grace a tour of the center, then excused herself to gather her thoughts together. Review the list of clients who'd signed up for the group. Review how she wanted to introduce the nine-week course. Mark the scriptures she wanted to read. Pray.

She had already met individually with each of the four women who'd signed up for the new post-abortion support group—well, not exactly "met" with Grace, but Grace had shared enough at Manna House about her situation to know the basic story—and knew that each one was making a choice to attend the group. But that didn't mean it would be easy. Sometimes a woman came thinking there was a quick fix for the "blues" she was experiencing after an abortion. Sometimes the anger—at herself, at others, at God—was so deep it hindered the healing. Sometimes a woman just wanted a safe place to talk about her abortion, to share her story, to know she wasn't alone—especially if she'd kept it a secret from family and friends for years. Sometimes a woman was hoping to be reassured that having the abortion wasn't all that bad, her guilty feelings were irrational, she should just forget it and move on . . . as though that were possible.

"Lord," she breathed quietly, "you know each of these women, know what they need. Fill the room with your Spirit and your peace. Help each one to set aside any hindrance to what you want to do in their lives . . ."

Like her doctor's visit yesterday, which kept trying to invade her thoughts.

Michelle stood up firmly, gathered her notebook, books, and Bible, and headed for the conference room. No, she had to set her own issues aside. A problem to deal with another day. She had to focus on Grace and Hannah and the other two young women.

The first meeting seemed to be going well. Michelle had passed out a notebook and a sheet with some starter questions to think about, and then given the four women time to write answers privately. After a while she opened the meeting with a prayer and an invitation for anyone to share something about her abortion experience—or not. Totally voluntary.

At twenty-nine, Grace was the oldest of the four, still hadn't told her parents about the date rape and abortion she'd had at sixteen. Had been trying to "make it up to God," she said, by making abstinence before marriage a theme of her concert tours. But she felt like a fraud. "I'm only now beginning to understand what my name means—*Grace*. Realizing God covers me with his grace and forgiveness, even when I don't deserve it. Still . . . I have a hard time admitting publicly what I did. Afraid my career will be over."

Hannah's story made the other women angry—raped by an abusive uncle, had an abortion to protect her deeply religious family who couldn't handle the truth, had never told anyone. But even five years later, she felt unable to move on. "I'm so stuck. It's . . . it's a relief to finally be able to tell someone."

Camille Cortez and Shantel Morris had more typical stories— consensual sex with a boyfriend, an unwanted pregnancy, friends who said no big deal, just get an abortion. Now having second thoughts.

Camille twisted a strand of her long brown hair. "*Mi familia*, we are Catholic. I am supposed to get married before I have a baby. But my boyfriend—he disappeared. Huh! Didn't want to be a daddy. What was I supposed to do? But . . . even though I got rid of the baby, somehow it didn't seem right."

Shantel shrugged. "Girl, I didn't want to get an abortion, either. But I can't support no baby by myself. An' it's not like I broke some law. What's done is done, can't feel bad about it the rest of my life. Some of my home girls, they came here to Lifeline to get help when they got pregnant, an' I guess I coulda done that too. But . . . I dunno, can't help feelin' relieved I'm not the one with a kid in a stroller an' another by the hand."

"*Yeah . . . in th' end, ya still got a kid . . .*"

Michelle tensed. Where did *that* thought come from? She'd heard someone say it recently. But she shook it out of her head. She had to focus.

But even as she heard herself read Jesus' promise in the Sermon on the Mount that "Blessed are those who mourn, for they will be comforted," and told the story in the Gospels about the woman who washed the feet of Jesus with her tears because she'd been forgiven so much, the voice in Michelle's head continued to tickle the edges of her consciousness . . .

"*Yeah, but in th' end, ya still got a kid—or two or three or six. Abortion's legal an' it's quick. Seems like th' easy way out ta me. I done it. Why not?*"

The memory clicked. The woman Lottie at Manna House the night she and Grace had gone with Estelle to share about Lifeline said, "*Seems like the easy way out . . .*"

The hour ended. Michelle passed out some questions and scriptures to think about relating to God's character—the One who sees us as we are, the One who loves us as we are, the One who forgives us when we fall—before the next meeting. Then she pasted on a smile, hugged each woman, said she'd see them next week, and excused herself. Slipping away    to the staff restroom, she locked the door and leaned against it, trying to get her breath.

*"Seems like the easy way out . . . Why not?"*

Michelle closed her eyes, hands and forehead pressed against the bathroom door. The idea of having another baby at her age felt like being swept along by an avalanche. Losing their second income. Stuck-at-home like Nicole Singer, left behind professionally by all her peers. Sleepless nights. Colic. Diapers. Potty-training. Preschool. Another eighteen years before she and Jared got to enjoy an empty nest. Eighteen years! She'd be in her late fifties by then!

*Except . . .*

Michelle was breathing hard. She hadn't told anyone about the pregnancy, not even Jared. Only her doctor knew, sworn to confidentiality.

The fetus wasn't viable. No one would ever have to know.

*There's a way out . . .*

# Chapter 37

MICHELLE LURCHED OVER TO THE SINK and turned the water on full force. What was she thinking! This was crazy! It went against everything she believed, everything Lifeline was trying to do, everything she talked about in the Hope and Healing groups. Abortion was not an "easy" way out.

But . . . it would solve so many problems.

She gripped the sink with both hands, head hanging, shoulders shaking as big silent sobs rose up from her gut, pushing a flood of tears down her cheeks. *O God, what am I going to do?*

A knock at the door. "Sister Michelle? One of the twins called. Uh . . . you all right?"

Had Bernice heard her crying? Michelle quickly flushed the unused toilet to make more noise and grabbed a paper towel to blow her nose and dry her face. "Yes, yes . . . I'm fine. Can you take a message? I'll be out in a minute."

But it took another five minutes to get control of herself. Her insides felt as if they were doing a tug-of-war, tearing her apart. *I can't do this, I can't . . .*

Can't do what? Can't go through with a pregnancy? Can't go through with an abortion?

She felt like screaming. *Can't do either!*

But she took several deep breaths and slowly blew them out. She had to open the door and go out there. Had to assure Bernice she was fine. Had to take Grace home.

The phone message Bernice handed her was from Tavis, wanting to know if he and Tabby could ride bikes over to Pottawattomie Park with DaShawn. Michelle asked Bernice if she'd call back and tell them Mom said fine. Bernice gave her a funny look but said, "Sure."

As she and Grace went out to the car, she wondered how was she going to make it home with Grace right there. Michelle felt on the verge of having a hysterical crying fit. On impulse she slid an instrumental CD into the car player and murmured, "Just sit back and listen to the music, Grace. We don't have to chit-chat. Sometimes it's good just to reflect on the things that were said in the group, stay in touch with your feelings." *Yeah, blah, blah, blah . . .*

Jared and Destin weren't home yet when she came in. The twins were still out, having left peanut butter and jelly smears and breadcrumbs all over the counter. But the jars and loaf of bread had been put away. Their version of cleaning up after themselves.

*There's a way out . . .*

No. She had to get busy. Stay busy.

Quickly making a shopping list, she got back in the car and headed for the grocery store. But by the time she was loading bags into the back of the minivan, she started to feel faint and realized she'd only had a piece of toast and a cup of coffee all day. Pulling a banana and a carton of orange juice out of one of the bags, she sat in the car in the store parking lot, trying to eat and crying.

Jared and Destin were home—the twins too—by the time Michelle got back from the store. "Hey, how was camp?" she beamed, bussing Destin on the cheek and sending the twins outside to carry in the groceries.

Destin cast an anxious glance at his father. "Um, great. I got an award for Best Post-Up Moves, and a couple scouts talked to me after the game this morning. Right, Dad?"

Jared shrugged and nodded as he leaned against the kitchen counter, arms folded, eyebrows raised as if reluctantly acknowledging Destin's comment. "Could say that. One of the coaches told me Destin has real defensive potential too, introduced him to a few of the college scouts—Eastern Illinois, Southern Illinois, U of I in Champaign. Just one little problem . . ."

Michelle looked back and forth between her husband and son. "Problem? What problem? Oh no . . . they wouldn't refund your room key deposit." No wonder Jared looked peeved.

"No! It wasn't that, Mom. I turned in the key and they canceled the charge on your credit card." Destin heaved a sigh. "It's just that—"

Jared snorted. "Just that they caught him selling SlowBurn to the other guys in the dorm, gave him a disciplinary warning, and confiscated the cans of SlowBurn he'd brought. They said one more infraction of the rules and he was outta there."

Michelle's eyes widened. "What infraction of the rules? I didn't read anything like that in the rules."

"See, Dad? I didn't know."

"Oh, come on. Think about it, Michelle. They see a kid selling who-knows-what to the other kids. Could be alcohol, could be drugs, could be steroid enhancement—"

"But it's not, Dad! It's just an energy drink! Already told you, I thought basketball camp would be a smart place to sell it. Guys always get real thirsty playin', and need extra energy."

"Well, it wasn't, was it?" Jared pushed away from the counter and pointed a finger at Destin. "You need to find a real job, young man."

Destin sulked. "It's Fourth of July weekend, don'tcha know. Nuthin's open till Tuesday."

"Well, then, find someplace *else* to sell this energy drink. You still got five hundred bucks to cough up." Jared headed downstairs to the family room and Michelle heard the TV flip on.

Destin turned pleading eyes on Michelle. "Mom . . ."

Michelle sighed and shook her head. "I don't know, Destin. Maybe you should just give the stuff back to Mr. Singer, tell him you can't work for him any more. Put all your efforts into getting a regular job. Maybe bagging at the Jewel or Dominick's or something. Anything."

"Not that easy . . ." Destin mumbled, headed for his room, and slammed the door.

Michelle felt like a puppet at church the next morning. Going through the motions. Jerk a string, give a churchy hug to First Lady Donna and all the "church mothers" dressed in white. Jerk a string, stand up, sing and clap with the choir. Jerk another string, open the Bible and follow along as Pastor Q expounded on 2 Chronicles 7:14: *"If my people, who are called by my name, will humble themselves and pray and seek my face and turn from their wicked ways, then I will hear from heaven, and I will forgive their sin and will heal their land"*—his favorite sermon around Independence Day, which happened to fall on Sunday this year. Jerk another string, check in with the women's ministry committee about next Saturday's presentation on *Discerning the Voice of God*. Sister Norma said she'd review the second session and do the introduction to the next video. *Amen, hallelujah.*

At Old Country Buffet after service, all three kids began clamoring to go to the fireworks downtown that evening.

"Thought Chicago did their fireworks on July 3." Jared looked hopeful.

"Changed it back this year!" Tavis hooted. "An' Monday's a holiday too. You got the day off, Dad?"

Jared shook his head. "Taking my holiday at Christmas."

Tabby cuddled up to her Dad's arm. "So it's a good thing the fireworks are tonight so you can go too, right? Please, Daddy?"

Jared laughed and pulled her close. "You got it, baby girl."

Which turned out to be a good thing, Michelle realized. In spite of the tension of the night before, they packed a picnic supper and made plans to go downtown by "L" to avoid parking headaches. By the time they were ready to leave, Tavis had told DaShawn Bentley, who wanted to go too—Harry and Estelle said they weren't up for those big crowds—and before they knew it, Grace and Ramona from next door wanted to tag along as well. Between three adults, five young people goofing off and laughing, the noisy "L," navigating the crowds along the lakefront, and the huge, deafening display of fireworks over Lake Michigan, there wasn't time for real conversation or even thinking, for that matter.

Which was just as well, as far as Michelle was concerned. The voice in her head hadn't bothered her all day. Maybe it was gone.

Except . . . when she crawled into bed at eleven o'clock, and the house had quieted except for Jared's gentle snore, she felt as if a heavy weight was sitting on her chest.

Nothing had changed.

She was still facing the possibility—probability—that she was pregnant.

She still hadn't told her husband.

And the voice was still there, whispering in the darkness . . .

*There's a way out . . .*

The phone rang at eight the next morning.

"Michelle?" It was her boss at Bridges. "I hate to do this to you on a holiday, but we got a call from one of your case homes out in Franklin Park near the airport, foster kid ran away, whole family is upset."

"Franklin Park? The Domingo family?"

"That's the one. You probably know he was supposed to spend the holiday with his birth mom, now she's freaking out too. They really need someone they trust to calm the situation, help them decide next steps. Could you by any chance . . .?"

"Sure. I got this one, Charlotte. " Michelle surprised herself by how quickly she said yes. The office was closed for the holiday and she could sure use a day off. But she also needed time away from conversational potholes at home. She wasn't ready to talk to Jared yet. She just needed to keep busy. By the time she got home, he'd probably be at the tower for his two to ten shift, and the tumbleweed week would be on a roll, giving her at least until next weekend before they came up for air again. By then she should know for sure. By then she'd tell him.

But she forgot just how far she had to drive to get out to Franklin Park—a good forty-five minutes. Not counting bumper-to-bumper traffic. Didn't people stay home on the holiday? Were people leaving town? Coming home? Whatever, Michelle began to feel oppressed by the silence in the car. Too much time alone with her thoughts. The doctor's pronouncement . . . the dream she'd had . . . the feeling of heading toward that steep cliff with nowhere to turn . . . the women in her post-abortion group . . . the voice in her head . . .

*There's a way out . . .*

Michelle turned on the radio, punched the button for 1390. Gospel music. Loud.

As she neared the airport—the drive Jared took every day—she took the ramp onto Route 294 South. Only a couple of miles to her exit . . . yep, there was the sign. *Irving Park Road 1 Mile—*

*Oh, great.* Toll plaza came first. She didn't have an I-PASS on the minivan, didn't use the tollway that often. But she'd been in such a hurry to get out of the house she hadn't checked whether she had enough change for tolls.

Michelle slowed as cars in the Cash Only lane edged toward the tollbooth. She fished in her purse for her wallet. What? No bills? Oh, *crap!* She'd used up her cash last night feeding the vending machine at the "L" station for tickets for the five of them. How much did she need? She glanced out the windshield . . . *Cash Only: $1.50.* And no attendant in the booth, either. She needed coins.

Fishing in her coin purse, she dumped all the change into her lap. Three quarters, four dimes, a nickel, two pennies . . . okay, that was a dollar and twenty-two cents. She still needed, uhh, twenty-eight cents.

The car ahead of her rolled up to the unmanned toll booth, tossed change into the basket, and the gate went up. And down again.

Her turn. She inched up beside the toll basket. *Twenty-eight cents* . . . she needed twenty-eight cents!

Michelle frantically pulled out the little drawer that supposedly held parking money. *Two dimes and two pennies* . . . Almost there.

The car behind her tooted its horn. "Okay!" she yelled.

She was still six cents short. Michelle dumped out her purse in the seat beside her. Sometimes change fell into the bottom . . .

More horns blaring now. Somebody yelling. Sweat trickled down between her shoulder blades. *O God, O God, all I need is six cents* . . . there! A nickel! Maybe she'd counted wrong. Maybe it was enough.

Rolling down her window, Michelle gathered up all her change and dumped it into the basket. Metal hitting plastic. Rolling down into the bottomless pit . . .

She held her breath.

The gate didn't move.

"Hey, lady!" the man in the car behind her yelled. "You gonna sit there all day? Move it!"

Michelle felt like giving him the finger. What was she supposed to do? All she needed was one penny! Why was everything in her life going wrong? Where was God when she needed him, huh? What ever happened to *"I will never leave you nor forsake you"* and *"I will supply all your needs"*?

More horns blared. More voices were yelling. Tears welled up in her eyes. "I'm not asking for much, God!" she said, gritting her teeth. "I just need one rotten penny!"

Her breath was coming short and fast. Maybe she should just step on the gas and crash right through the gate—

And then she saw it.

A penny sitting on the concrete ledge right beside the toll basket.

One dingy, beautiful penny.

Opening the car door, Michelle got out, picked up the penny, and tossed it in.

The yellow-striped gate lifted.

Still shaking, Michelle got off the toll road at her exit, turned in at the first fast-food place she saw, and found a parking space. She needed to pull herself together.

What had happened back there? She'd come close to losing it.

But God came through. Came through with a penny.

Such a little thing . . . but it felt big. Felt huge. "Thank you, Jesus, thank you," she breathed, dabbing at her eyes with a tissue and blowing her nose.

Michelle sat in the fast-food parking lot for a good ten minutes. Her thoughts tumbled, became prayers, back to thoughts again. Was that God? That penny had to have been sitting there . . . who knew how long? But it was there when she needed it.

*Lord, I just need to know you're going to take care of us! I mean, if I'm pregnant, it's going to knock our whole lives off course.*

Huh. Things had already felt "off" for longer than that. Jared's demanding schedule at the airport. Her own long workdays at Bridges and volunteer work at Lifeline. Their responsibilities at church. All good things! But . . . not enough time with the kids. Not enough time with each other. Finances were tight, even with two working parents, and going to get tighter with college looming. And the other elephant in the room: Pastor Q wanting Jared to go to seminary. Okay, deep down she knew Jared wanted to go too . . .

*God, what are we going to do?!*

Wait. God had just answered her desperate prayer back at the tollbooth . . . for a penny. Was God trying to tell her something?

What if . . . what if she asked God to give her a penny every day this week? Just a penny a day! That wasn't asking too much, was it? Not a penny she went hunting for herself. She wouldn't ask anyone for a penny, wouldn't go to the store and get pennies in change. No, she'd ask God for a penny, one that just showed up.

The whole idea felt rather silly. But . . . that's what she was going to do. She wanted to know for sure that God would take care of them, would sort out this whole mess.

She needed a sign.

# Chapter 38

CHARLOTTE BERGMAN POKED HER HEAD into Michelle's office the next morning. "How'd it go yesterday?"

Michelle almost snorted. No way was she going to tell her boss she almost had a meltdown on the 294 Tollway. "The Domingo situation? Going to be okay, I think. Rafael ended up at a friend's house in the city, and the friend's mom had the presence of mind to call Rafael's mother. She picked him up—she was supposed to spend the day with him anyway—and the last I heard she was going to bring him back to the Domingos last night as planned. I made an appointment to go back and talk to Rafael and the Domingos this week, but I think maybe we need to get everyone together here at the office soon, review the situation."

"Sounds good. Guess you earned some time off—oh wait. You took a couple half days last week, right?" Charlotte smirked happily. "Now I don't feel so guilty ruining your holiday."

Michelle wadded up a sheet of paper and threw it at her. "Ha. Never knew you to feel guilty about anything!" She shook her head as her boss disappeared, chuckling to herself. Charlotte Bergman could be hard-nosed, but she was fair, had thick skin, *and* a sense of humor. Probably why she'd lasted so long as director of Bridges Family Services.

Sighing, Michelle toyed with a paper clip. The *real* question was, how was it going *today*? First it'd been Tabby away at cheer camp, then Destin at the Five-Star Basketball Camp last week, and now Tavis . . . which he'd had to remind her about last night. "Mom, are you gonna take me to Lane Tech in the morning?"

She'd had to think fast. Right. Lane Tech Basketball Summer Camp the rest of the week. Except . . . Tavis's camp didn't start till ten and she had to be a work by eight.

"No sweat, Mom, I can just hang out at the school, watch the ninth graders." Soon-to-be freshmen had the first slot in the morning, 8:00 to 10:00. But Michelle didn't feel comfortable letting Tavis hang out at the high school for two unsupervised hours.

Jared had come up with a solution when he got home at eleven last night. Since Destin wasn't working a nine-to-five, *he* could accompany his brother by bus to Lane Tech High School for the 10:00 to 12:00 session, wait for him, and get him back home again. "Boy's got to make himself useful if he's not working," Jared had groused.

At least that took care of both boys for half days this week. Now all they had to figure out was supervision and activities for the rest of the summer. emTabby was babysitting for Mrs. Singer off and on all week again—good for her. Nicole Singer had warned Tabby her part-time job was probably temporary until her husband got his SlowBurn business established, but it was still great experience for a thirteen-year-old. Maybe she could even expand her babysitting services to other families on the block . . . like the Horowitzes? The Jallilis? Maybe even the little boy across the street—Danny, the one with two dads. The guys seemed nice enough, pretty quiet homebodies in fact. No wild parties, always pleasant.

In fact, the only "party house" on Beecham Street was Lincoln Paddock's big house on the cul-de-sac sometimes on weekends. But what could you expect from a bachelor with a big house? She'd heard through the grapevine that he not only owned Lincoln Limo, but was also a junior partner at some prestigious law firm in the city. No wonder he could afford to build one of those "McMansions."

Her desk phone rang, shaking Michelle out of her wandering thoughts. She had to get rolling. Lots to do before she could leave work today. Taking the call, she listened, scratched an address on a notepad, hung up, updated her calendar. Another distressed foster family. Another appointment to work into her already busy week.

Made her request for God to send her a penny today seem pretty silly now.

Michelle wasn't surprised to get a call from Jared just before she left work, saying he'd probably stay over at the airport hotel that night. Summer travelers were cramming the airport, victims of the usual delays and cancellations, camping out in the lounges, waiting for early flights in the morning. The tower was facing a glut of departures in the morning, more than usual. Said he might get an hour or two more sleep before switching to his daytime shift if he didn't have to commute home and back again.

"Okay, honey. By the way, I checked with the boys. Sounded like everything went fine getting Tavis to and from Lane Tech today. I actually think it's a godsend that Destin's free to take him to basketball camp this week."

Jared just grunted on the other end. "Gotta go, hon. See you tomorrow."

Another Tuesday night with an empty bed. Michelle didn't like sleeping without her husband. On the other hand, she felt a twinge of relief not having to worry about too much alone time with Jared that might lead to The Conversation. She wasn't ready yet. In fact, she should probably call Estelle and beg off from the Tuesday night prayer meeting at Grace's house. Just tell them she wasn't feeling well, needed to stay home tonight.

It was true. Not sure whether it was emotional or physical, but she felt exhausted. An early night would feel good. And maybe it'd be good for Grace too, if she weren't there. Grace could share how she experienced her first group meeting at Lifeline if she wanted to without having to tweak it for Michelle's sake.

Destin was jubilant when she got home. "Hey, Mom, guess what? I gave out samples of SlowBurn to some of the kids at the basketball camps this morning, and several of 'em said they'd bring money and buy some six-packs tomorrow."

"You sure that's okay? Remember what happened at the Five-Star Basketball Camp." No way did she want Destin to get in trouble with his own school just before his senior year.

"Not a problem, Mom. I stayed off school property, caught the freshman guys comin' outta the first camp. Didn't have so much luck with the younger camp—you know, parents picking them up and all."

"Mm-hm." Michelle's mind started to wander to what to make for supper.

"An' that's not all." Destin was still grinning. "I think that mom-and-pop grocery store over near Pratt and Western might be one of my customers. The owner said he'd take four six-packs, see if his customers liked it. Had to cut the price a little, 'cause he needs to resell it for a profit—but at least the guy said he'd try it out. If their customers buy it, they'll buy more from me!"

"Yeah, Mom," Tavis butted in. "I helped him by saying how good it was an' all."

"*You* helped him?" Michelle gave Destin a *when-was-this* look.

"Comin' home from his basketball camp, Mom. We got off a couple stops early, gave my pitch to that store. Tryin' to 'redeem the time,' ya know." Destin snickered, pleased with himself. "Only had a six-pack with me for samples, though, so I went back to the store this afternoon with four six-packs." He whipped a check out of his pocket and kissed it. "See? See?"

Michelle had to smile. "Well, good. Put that someplace safe . . . Oh, guess you should cash it this week. Maybe you should open a separate account at the bank."

"No worries, Mom. Got it covered."

The boys disappeared downstairs to turn on the TV until time for supper.

Supper . . . Michelle opened the refrigerator, eyeing the leftover chicken from the weekend. She could chop that up, throw in some veggies, and make a stir-fry over rice. The kids liked that okay. Maybe add an apple-raisin-celery salad. All quick and easy.

Grabbing an apron from the skinny broom closet, Michelle slipped it over her head since she still had on the skirt and top she'd worn to work. Her mom had given her this one a few years back, though she didn't wear it often—Bibi had always been the dedicated apron-wearer in the Robinson kitchen. Chuckling, Michelle started the rice, then gathered a zucchini, a red pepper, a few mushrooms, and a yellow onion, and started to peel and chop.

*Oh, rats, the onion . . .*

She'd meant to put the onions in the refrigerator to cut down on the stinging eyes and drippy nose that seemed to happen every time she cut one up. A tissue . . . she needed a tissue. Fishing in the big apron pockets, she suddenly froze.

No tissue. But her fingers had touched something else.

Heart suddenly thumping, she pulled it out.

A penny.

* * *

Michelle felt distracted most of the evening. *Okaaay.* So she'd found a penny. Just a coincidence? Or had God really listened to her heart cry yesterday for a sign? Still . . . it was just a penny. Probably if she went looking, she'd find pennies in strange places all over the house. Except . . . she hadn't gone looking. It was just like she'd asked God—to give her a penny out of the blue. One she wasn't looking for.

Giggling to herself, she felt like calling Jared to tell him. God had given her a penny! But it wouldn't make sense unless she told him everything. No, no, she had to wait. This weekend, she'd told herself. But she couldn't wait too long. The clock was ticking. The doctor had said she was probably eight weeks last Friday. Every day that went by added to the pressure.

And it still wasn't a "for sure."

But the call came Wednesday on her cell while she was on the way back to the office from her meeting with the Domingos. "Both urine and blood tests are positive, Michelle," Dr. Callas chirped. "Have you started those prenatal vitamins yet? And I want to encourage you to get on the phone and make an appointment with one of the OBs I recommended. If you tell me who you plan to call, I'll put in a good word to work you in because of your age." The doctor chuckled. "There are some advantages to being an older patient."

So. That was it.

She was definitely pregnant.

*Now what?*

The voice in her head slipped in unbidden. *There's a way out . . .*

Michelle punched on the radio—loud—all the way back to the office.

# Chapter 39

MOM, PLEASE!" TABBY JIGGLED IMPATIENTLY in the kitchen while Michelle fried fish for supper that night. "I gotta go shopping *tonight*! I can't wear my sandals like this—" She stuck out her foot, one sandal strap torn away from the sole. "An' it's too hot to wear socks and gym shoes all the time. *Pleeease?*"

"Honey, it's prayer meeting night tonight. Your dad and I—"

"Mom, please! Can't you go late or something? I'll trade doing dishes with Tavis or Destin. We could leave right after supper."

"Hey, hey, hey, Tabby. Chill." Jared came into the kitchen, holding a dress shirt wadded up in one hand. "Your mom just said tonight's already scheduled. It won't kill you to wait till tomorrow." He shooed Tabby out of the kitchen with a playful tweak on her cheek, then turned back to Michelle. "I, on the other hand, have a major problem." Jared shook out the shirt, revealing blotches of red stain. "Uh . . . I splattered ketchup on the front of this at lunch today. Tried to wipe it off, but, well, as you can see . . ."

Michelle feigned horror. "You wore that the rest of your shift? Ha. Guess we'll have to have to send a change of clothes to work with you, like we did for the kids when they were in kindergarten."

"I know, I know." Jared looked sheepish. "It was stupid of me. Just tell me what to do, and I'll do it. Cold water? Hot? What?"

Michelle handed him a spatula. "Just turn the fish over in about a minute. I'll take care of the shirt. Oh, here, you'll need this." She took off the apron and hung it over his head. "Don't want any oil splatters on *that* shirt."

She ran the stained shirt down to the laundry room in the basement. Ketchup splotches . . . not the easiest stains to get out. But a few sessions with cold running water, rubbing in detergent, then sponging the stains with white vinegar looked hopeful. She might as well run it through the wash. Running upstairs, she gathered up several more items from the laundry hamper in their bedroom to make a full load, then started the washing machine.

By the time they finished supper and it was time to leave for church, the wash load was done and she stuck it all in the dryer. But as the dryer started she heard *clink, clink, clink.* What was that? Better not be a ballpoint pen or something. What a mess *that* would be!

"Michelle!" Jared's voice sailed down the stairs. "Are you coming?"

"Just a sec!" She pulled the clothes out of the dryer, shaking them as she did so. Nothing. Reaching in, she felt around the drum . . . and found the culprit.

A penny.

Michelle was so dumbfounded at finding the third penny, she had a hard time paying attention at prayer meeting. Another coincidence? God showing up? She could only imagine how silly the whole thing would sound if she told anyone.

"Sister Michelle! Sister Michelle!" Sister Paulette hustled her way after Pastor Q's devotional as people were gathering into the small prayer groups. "What we gonna do about all those wimmins comin' in late after the video started? They nothin' but rude if you ask me."

Michelle tried to focus. Women's ministry event this Saturday. Right. Which meant moving the Hope and Healing group to one o'clock. Had she mentioned the change in time to the four participants? She'd better call Bernice, get their phone numbers—

"Sister Michelle!" Paulette snapped her fingers in front of Michelle's face. "You in there, girl?"

"Oh. Sorry, Sister Paulette. Um, latecomers . . . don't think we can do much about it except make a point to encourage everyone to come on time. I'll make a note to add that to the announcements."

"Let *me* make that announcement. Maybe we could do like they do at theaters—once the play starts, you ain't goin' in!"

Michelle could just imagine Sister Paulette, standing at the door like a bouncer. *"You late! Too bad. Try next month."* They'd certainly get the message . . . but probably wouldn't ever show up again.

They prayed for the usual requests—jobs and finances, Deacon Brown's wife suffering from cancer, family members in the military, salvation for the lost, violence in the city, wayward sons and daughters. Michelle only half-listened, automatically murmuring, "Mm-hm" and "Yes, Lord" from time to time as if she was right in there. But she was having her own private tug-of-war with God.

*I want to trust you, Lord, but I don't see how you can sort all this out for us . . . I feel trapped, whichever way I go . . . Don't know how we'll ever manage if we add another child to this family—it's too much! . . . I know, I know, I asked you for a sign, but I'm not sure finding three pennies is very convincing . . .*

Still, it was kind of unbelievable.

"You okay, honey?" Jared glanced her way on the way home. "You're pretty quiet tonight."

She nodded but didn't meet his eyes. "I'm fine. Just the usual. Long day."

And Thursday would be another long day. Jared had practically promised Tabby that she'd take her shopping Thursday night. But Michelle dreaded having to go out again after supper two nights in a row.

But that gave her an idea. Stopping by Tabby's bedroom once they got home from church, she proposed a deal: if Tabby would start supper for her dad and brothers tomorrow evening—something easy like quesadillas or tacos they could finish up themselves—Michelle would take her shopping for sandals as soon as she got home from work. Then they could eat later when they got home from the mall. Should work on a Thursday night—Jared didn't have to leave for his night shift until nine or so.

Tabby was ready to go when Michelle drove up to the house at five thirty the next evening. "Got everything for tacos lined up on the counter," Tabby said, jumping into the minivan. "Even fried the hamburger with that taco seasoning, like you showed me. All those dorks gotta do is stuff the taco shells . . . oh, sorry, Mom. I didn't mean Dad." But she grinned, proud of herself.

Michelle was proud of her daughter too. Given the right motivation, Tabby was perfectly capable of moving to the next level of responsibility.

But after looking through two major department stores at Lincolnwood Mall and not finding what she wanted, Tabby wanted to look at some of the smaller stores along the mall. "Fine," Michelle said, heading for a bench. "But my feet are tired. I'm going to sit here for a while. Come get me if you find something you like that won't cost an arm and a leg."

Tabby happily ran off.

Michelle looked at her watch. Seven o'clock already. She'd been hoping Tabby would find something quickly and they could be in and out and back home by this time. She heaved a sigh as the minutes ticked by . . . 7:03 . . . 7:09 . . .

Was she destined to be this tired her whole pregnancy?

*There's a way out . . . no one need ever know . . .*

Michelle stood up quickly. She had to get moving, should go look for Tabby. But her mouth had turned to sawdust, she needed a drink. Spying a water fountain just down the way, she hurried over. As she bent over to drink, something rolled across the floor into her line of sight and bumped into her shoe. Michelle stared at the object lying by her foot. Then, hand shaking, she bent down and picked it up.

A penny.

Goose bumps stood up on her arms. She quickly looked around. No one was close by, but someone must've just dropped it. It wasn't hers. But all she saw were parents with strollers whisking this way and that, a knot of teenagers laughing as they disappeared into one of the stores, a janitor down the way sweeping up litter and dirt with a broom and long-handled dustpan.

What was she going to do, call out, "Did someone drop a penny?"

Her fingers closed around the copper coin.

That made four.

# Chapter 40

ICHELLE WOKE UP THE NEXT MORNING feeling breathless. Would God give her another penny today? Or maybe she should be thinking, *how* would God give her a penny today? After all, the penny in her apron pocket and the one in the dryer could be explained as totally coincidental. But that penny rolling right up to her at the mall . . . had to be God. Had to be.

Not that she really wanted to face the implications of her "penny test." So what if God "proved" he would take care of her? What she really wanted was to *not* be pregnant in the first place. Not now.

But it was too late for that.

Her first moments of wakeful elation were already dissipating under a cloud of dread. She'd have to tell Jared today or tomorrow.

Speaking of Jared, he'd be home soon from his night shift. Hungry and wanting to crash. Throwing on her robe, Michelle scooted barefoot to the kitchen and started the coffee. He didn't usually eat much on Friday morning before hitting the sheets—a toasted bagel with jam and some OJ ought to do it. She'd see that he got settled, then wake the boys before she left for work to be sure they got to Tavis's last day of basketball camp on time.

But Jared seemed grouchier than usual when he came in that morning. He straddled a barstool at the kitchen counter and loosened his shirt collar. "Is the air on? Feels hot in here. 'Bout time we get a break from all this ninety-degree weather we've been having this week."

She set a bagel and glass of juice in front of him. "You okay?"

He snorted. "Yeah. It's just . . . some of the guys in the tower can be such jerks! Just because it was a slow night—huh, slow only in comparison to that glut we had a couple nights ago—some of the guys were goofing off and . . . frankly, I don't know what happened, but suddenly half the screens went down." He shook his head. "Pretty dicey for about twenty, maybe thirty minutes. Had to keep the incomings up in the air for a while and delay the departures. But we managed to get all the planes in and out safely, thank God."

Jared shook his head at her offer of a cup of coffee. "Nah, don't need any more caffeine. Thinking about taking a walk to calm down before I get some shut-eye . . . the kids up yet?"

She shook her head, sipping her own cup of coffee. "Gonna wake the boys before I leave for work. It's Tavis's last day of basketball camp."

Her husband grimaced. "So, how much of that SlowBurn stuff has Destin sold this week? He told me he was going to try to sell to the kids coming to the basketball camps at Lane Tech this week."

Michelle felt annoyed. How would she know? Wasn't Jared checking in with him? "I haven't asked—though he said he sold some to a mom-and-pop store over on Western. Sounded like a good outlet if they decide to stock it."

Her husband snorted. "Oh yeah, I heard. Four six-packs so far. Big deal." Pushing back the barstool, Jared strode down the short hall to the boys' bedroom, opened the door, and flipped on the light. "Destin! Time to get up. I want to see some action today on your so-called job. C'mon, get moving."

Michelle could hear muffled protests from both boys, a few sharp words from Jared, then he came out muttering, "Going for a walk. Be back in half an hour."

She glanced at the clock and then at his half-eaten bagel. She'd be gone in half an hour. Well, Jared was the "at-home" parent today—though he'd be sleeping for most of it—so let him deal with the kids. She couldn't do everything. Or be everywhere.

But his bad mood had rubbed off on her, and she had a headache by the time she walked through the front door at Bridges.

"*Buenos días*, Michelle!" Mercedes sang out. "How you doing this fine morning?" Without waiting for a reply, the receptionist handed her some messages. "Had a couple calls for you already this morning. Looks like a fun day."

Michelle glanced through the little yellow slips. *Liz Turner, DCFS, pls return call ASAP.* Wanted to dump another wayward kid on them, no doubt. . . . *Annamarie Domingo.* Oh, brother, what now? Had Rafael run away again? . . . *Brianna Lewis.* Michelle racked her brain. Brianna Lewis, Brianna . . . oh, right! Jeffrey Coleman's mother. Last she'd heard things had been going well with Jeffrey's supervision and oversight from Ray Stevens, their college-age Family Friend volunteer.

Well, she'd make these calls, then head out on her already scheduled appointments.

It was going to be a long day.

Her last appointment of the day canceled, so Michelle headed back to the office. Maybe she'd have a chance to fill out her reports and not have to take paperwork home over the weekend for a change. And so far, no penny today. She'd been at home, at Bridges Family Services, in the car, at a group home, in the homes of two foster families . . . and no penny from heaven.

Well, so what. The whole penny test was pretty silly anyhow. At least she'd feel silly telling anybody about it. Pastor Q would probably say, "All the promises you need are right there in the Bible, Sister Michelle."

Yeah, like she didn't know. After years of leading the Hope and Healing groups at Lifeline, she was a veritable fountain of promises from the Word. But somehow those promises felt pretty hollow when faced with what felt like two impossible choices . . .

Go through with a pregnancy at age forty-one that would turn their whole lives upside down? Ruin any chance she had to get her life under control?

Or have an abortion that would leave her feeling guilty the rest of her life?

Michelle pulled into a parking space in the small lot next to Bridges, but just sat in the car for a few more minutes, not ready to go in. Not ready for the workday to end, either, when she'd have to go home and face Jared. She'd told herself she'd tell him this weekend. But the wall of resistance was still there. As if hoping for some magic "fix" to get her out of this mess.

Her cell phone rang. She fished it out of her purse. Caller ID said *Jared Jasper.* What was Jared calling her for at three in the afternoon? Probably woke up hungry and the refrigerator was almost bare. Well, it was Friday . . . everything ran low by Friday. She'd shop tomorrow.

Sending the call to voicemail, she tossed the phone back in her purse and got out of the car. Didn't feel like talking to Jared right this moment. Whatever it was could wait.

But a few moments later as she dumped her briefcase and purse on the desk in her office, her phone rang again. *Jared again.* Sighing, she tapped the Talk button. "Hey, hon, what's up?"

"Michelle!" Jared's voice was a gasp. In the background Michelle could hear traffic. And crying. Sounded like Tabby.

"Jared! What—!"

"I'm on my way to St. Francis Hospital. I've got Tabby in the car with me. You need to come right away. The police called—Destin and Tavis . . ." Her husband's voice broke.

Michelle grabbed her purse and started running for the front door, phone to her ear. "The hospital?! The police? What happened? What's wrong?"

Mercedes gave her a worried look as she ran past the reception desk but Michelle just shot out the door, trying to hold the phone to her ear and fish for car keys in her purse at the same time.

"Gunshot. Which one . . . maybe both . . . I don't know. Police said they were taken by ambulance to St. Francis in Evanston."

*Oh, no . . . No, no, no, no . . . O God! Not her boys.*

"Just hurry, Michelle! I'll meet you in the emergency room."

Wheeling into the emergency room's circular driveway, Michelle screeched to a stop and left the car sitting there as she ran for the sliding door. Jared met her just inside the door. "They've taken Tavis into surgery. All they've told me so far is that he has a gunshot wound in the side. Said it's serious but not . . ." He swallowed. "Supposedly not life-threatening."

"Oh, thank God!" Michelle's heart was till pounding. "But . . . Destin? Where's Destin? Is he hurt? Jared—"

"Mommy!" Tabby ran into her mother's arms and buried her head in her shoulder. "Oh, Mommy, I'm so scared."

"I know, honey. Shh, shh . . . I need to hear about Destin."

Taking off his wire rims, Jared mopped his face with a handkerchief. "They said he got shot in the leg. He's still in there . . ." He jerked his chin in the direction of the double doors marked *Authorized Personnel Only.*

"I want to see my son." Michelle started for the double doors.

"Honey, wait!" Jared grabbed her arm.

She pulled away. "I want to see Destin!"

Jared grabbed her again. "Michelle, stop. Right now the police are talking to him. They said they'd come get us as soon as they're done. Just . . . just come over here, sit down a minute."

*The police* . . . Was Destin in some kind of trouble? Did they think he knew who'd shot them? Could the police tell them what happened? For a long moment, Michelle stood rooted in place, staring at the doors leading into the restricted area, wanting to barge through and find her son. But finally she followed Jared back to the rows of chairs and sank into the closest one.

"But . . . why? Where did it happen? Didn't the boys come home after basketball camp?"

Jared sat down beside her. "I—I don't know. I was asleep. I assumed they'd come home and check in with me . . . But first thing I knew, Tabby came running into the bedroom with the phone, said it was the police!"

Tabby was curled up in a chair, hugging her knees, and crying again.

Questions tumbled around in Michelle's head like rocks in a rock tumbler, driving her nuts. Why hadn't the boys come straight home? Where did this happen? At school? On the way home? Were they out somewhere trying to sell more of that energy drink? Did someone try to rob them? Why would anyone shoot two innocent kids?

Finally a trim Asian woman in a doctor's white coat came out through the double doors with two uniformed cops, one white, one black. Michelle and Jared stood up. "Mr. and Mrs. Jasper?" the woman asked. They nodded. She shook hands with a firm grip. "I'm Doctor Louise Wang. This is Officer Lester and Officer Hill. Let's find someplace we can talk."

The doctor led the way through the swinging doors and into a small conference room. Tabby gripped Michelle's hand tightly as they all found chairs. "Please," Michelle begged, "how is Destin? Can we see him?"

Dr. Wang nodded. "Of course. He took a bullet in the thigh, which is no fun, but he should consider himself lucky. We've stopped the bleeding and he's stable, so we'll do surgery as soon as possible to remove the bullet and repair damage."

"And Tavis? When can we . . .?" The words came out in a croak.

"They'll let you know as soon as he's out of surgery," the doctor said kindly.

Jared turned to the uniforms. "What can you tell us? What happened? Why were our sons shot?"

The white cop let his partner do most of the talking. "Far as we can tell, this was a case of your boys being in the wrong place at the wrong time—but not exactly random."

Michelle's mouth went dry. "What do you mean, 'not random'?"

"Well, according to your older boy in there—Destin, right?—he and his brother approached a bunch of kids on a street corner trying to sell them this, uh, energy drink—"

"We never heard of it," shrugged the other cop. "But we did retrieve his backpack with the cans inside, and it seems to be what he says it is."

"That's right," Jared butted in. "Kid got himself a summer job selling for some energy drink company. What's wrong with that?"

Officer Hill held up his hands, palms out. "Nothing, Mr. Jasper. He just didn't pick a smart place to do it. Our best guess is, some of the gangbangers in that area thought the boys were some new bloods muscling in on their territory. They—"

"They thought our kids were selling drugs?" Jared's face was a storm cloud.

"That's what it looks like. Won't know for sure till we catch the perps. But according to witnesses, a couple guys ran out of a nearby alley and started shooting. Kids split all over the place, all except your two boys, who probably didn't know what was happening. But the paramedics who brought them in told us they were lucky, said these two are going to make it."

"Going to make it . . ." The words rang in Michelle's ears. *Oh yes, please God, let them make it.*

They talked for a few more minutes with the police, who took down contact information for both Jared and Michelle and said they'd be in touch. Then the doctor led them into the large room with beds for emergency patients on three sides—half of them occupied—separated only by white curtains. Dr. Wang held the curtain back from one of the bays. "Destin? Your parents and sister are here."

Michelle caught her breath. Destin lay on the gurney, broad brown chest shirtless, hooked up to an IV pole. His bare right leg lay outside the top sheet, thigh wrapped in gauze, tinged red with blood seeping up through the layers from below. "Mom! Dad! Tabby!" Tears welled up in his dark eyes. He reached for their hands, his forehead creased with worry and fear as they crowded around both sides of the gurney. "How's Tavis? They won't tell me anything, just that they took him to surgery."

"That's all we know too, son." Jared was having a hard time staying in control.

"No, no," Michelle added hastily, gripping his hand. "They say it's not life-threatening, that he's going to make it." Was she assuring Destin, or herself?

Jared cleared his throat as if he was going to say something but Destin blurted, "I'm sorry, I'm so sorry! It's all my fault! If I hadn't taken Tavis along . . ."

"Shh, shh," crooned Michelle.

But Jared prodded, "Tell us what happened, son. Where did this happen?"

Destin's story pretty much confirmed the police version. "It was my last chance to sell SlowBurn to the kids doing the basketball camps at Lane Tech, but a lot of the guys who told me they liked it and would bring money, said they forgot or whatever. Then this one kid said he knew where a lot of guys hung out over near

Hamlin Park, maybe they'd buy some. So we went with him over to that neighborhood—"

Michelle heard Jared suck in his breath. They never would've let Destin go into that neighborhood by himself, much less with Tavis.

"—an' next thing we knew, there were gunshots, and . . . and Tavis went down, and . . . and . . ." Destin's shoulders were shaking.

Michelle gave Jared a look. *Don't push him anymore!*

They heard the curtains being pushed back all the way. "Mr. and Mrs. Jasper?" said a male voice. Two young medical personnel in blue scrubs. "They're ready for Destin in surgery to remove that bullet. We'll be assisting Dr. Thomas. You can go up to the family waiting room on the surgical floor, and we'll come get you when he's in recovery."

Michelle stood aside with Jared and Tabby, watching as the side rails were raised and the gurney wheeled out of the bay with her oldest son. And somewhere in the hospital, her baby was undergoing an even more serious surgery.

A flush of helpless anger coursed through her veins. *Is this how you take good care of us, God? Like this? Both my boys? How am I supposed to trust you now?*

Dazed, she felt Jared's arm on her elbow guiding her out of the room and toward the elevators that would take them to the surgical floor. As the doors closed on them she heard Jared mutter angrily, "I blame that Singer fellow down the street. None of this would've happened if he hadn't recruited Destin to sell his stupid product!"

# Chapter 41

THE SURGEON WHO OPERATED ON TAVIS came to the family waiting room, looking pleased. "Bullet didn't hit any vital organs. He lost quite a bit of blood, had to have a transfusion, but the bullet exited nicely out the back. We had to repair some muscle and his kidney was bruised, so we'll keep him here for several days, and he'll need to take it *very* easy the rest of the summer. But I think he should be ready to go back to school by the time school starts. As soon as he wakes up from the anesthesia, you can go to recovery and see him."

Michelle thanked the surgeon profusely. *Good news . . . good news . . .* So why did she still feel so awful?

Tavis seemed confused when he saw his parents. "Wha . . . what happened?"

Jared kept it brief. But Michelle had a hard time listening to the story. Every repetition felt like driving a nail into her skull.

Destin's surgeon, Dr. Thomas, found them in the recovery room with Tavis and motioned them outside. The surgery to remove the bullet in his thigh had gone smoothly, he said, and with the right physical therapy, he should make a full recovery. "The good news is that the bullet missed his femoral artery—would have been serious business if it hadn't. Nicked a bone, but that's going to heal. Going to be painful for some time, though. He's going to need to stay here a few days till we can get him up and walking. He's going to need crutches for a while, and then it'll be several months of physical therapy—and whatever else you want to add on to 'doctor's orders,' like making his bed or whatever, ha ha . . ." The surgeon chuckled at his little joke. "But barring any unforeseen complications, he might even be able to play basketball again. In time."

Michelle wasn't in any mood for jokes. Still, she thanked the surgeon, excused herself, and went back to Tavis's bedside.

A patient advocate stopped by, said they were trying to get both boys assigned to the same room to make it easy on the family. But it was after eight o'clock by the time the boys got settled in a room. Michelle and Tabby went looking for something to eat—the cafeteria was closed—and found some sandwiches in a vending machine. Jared was watching the sports channel with Destin on the TV that hung between the two beds. Tavis had fallen asleep.

At one point Jared slipped out to call Pastor Quentin to let the church know what happened and to ask for prayer. Michelle thought she ought to make some calls too—she was supposed to lead the women's ministry monthly event tomorrow morning, as well as the second session of the new Hope and Healing group at Lifeline! She'd have to cancel. Couldn't do it. But for some reason she couldn't work up the energy to talk to anyone. What was wrong with her? The prognosis for both boys was good. She should be thankful. But the reality of what had happened still rattled its chains in her face like Marley's ghost haunting old Scrooge.

Both of her sons had been *shot.* They could be dead.

She should be grateful. She wanted to be grateful.

But the thoughts roaring in her ears threatened to come out in a scream: *How could you let this happen, God?*

Michelle sat slumped in a chair, holding onto Tavis's hand as he slept. On top of all this, she was supposed to tell Jared that she was *pregnant*? No, no, she couldn't do that to him. Bad news on top of bad news. Maybe . . . maybe she should just go ahead, get an abortion, be done with it. God would forgive her, wouldn't he? Isn't that what she told the women in her Hope and Healing groups? That there's no sin so grievous that God can't forgive. That God doesn't want them to live burdened by guilt the rest of their lives. Wasn't that what Grace Meredith said she'd needed to hear? That she didn't need to "buy" God's forgiveness by all her good works. That grace and mercy were hallmarks of God's forgiveness.

Wouldn't that apply to her too?

"Honey?" Michelle felt Jared gently shaking her shoulder. Her eyes flew open. She must've dozed off in the chair. "Honey, it's almost eleven. I'm going to spend the night here with the boys. But I think you should take Tabby home, get some rest. You two can come back tomorrow morning."

Michelle was about to protest, but one look at her daughter changed her mind. She needed to take care of Tabby too. "Okay." She gathered her things. "I'll be back," she whispered as she kissed both boys.

For some reason her gaze swept the room. But she already knew she wouldn't find a penny. The day was over and God hadn't come through. In more ways than one.

Tabby was quiet as they walked to the car, which Jared had parked in the parking garage. "You okay, sweetie?" Michelle asked as they drove down the ramps.

"Guess so." Tabby lapsed into silence as they headed home. Then . . . "I'm supposed to babysit for Mrs. Singer tomorrow. But I'm gonna call and cancel. I wanna go back to the hospital."

"I'm sure they'll understand, honey." But Michelle felt a check in her spirit. Had Tabby heard Jared's angry comment in the elevator blaming Greg Singer? "Uh, maybe you shouldn't say anything to the Singers about why the boys got shot."

Tabby gave her mom a funny look but said, "Okay."

They were almost to Beecham Street when Michelle's cell phone rang. "Can you get that, sweetie? Maybe it's Daddy."

Tabby dug around in her mother's purse and pulled out the phone. "It's not Daddy, Mom. It's just a number."

"Then forget it." If it were a real call, whoever it was would leave a voicemail. She'd deal with it later. Or not.

But Tabby had already answered. "Hello?" She listened, then turned to her mom, wide-eyed. "It's that little girl, Mom! Candy! . . . What, Candy? Say that again?"

Candy Blackwell? Why was a seven-year-old calling her at eleven at night? Michelle looked questioningly at her daughter, who had the phone pressed to her ear. *O God, I can't deal with anything else right now . . .*

"Uh-huh . . . uh-huh . . . okay, okay, just hold on, Candy." Tabby pushed the Mute button. "Mom! Candy's crying, says their apartment burned up, and she and her mama and little brother don't know what to do! She said you said she could call you anytime . . . Mom! Stop! Don't just keep driving! She wants you to come!"

Michelle jerked the wheel and pulled over to the side of the street. "Tabby!" she hissed, breathing hard. "Your brothers just got shot! They're in the hospital. We need to get home and get some rest. I can't deal with work stuff right now." She gripped the steering wheel as if hanging on for dear life.

"Mom!" Tabby's face was pure shock. "It's not work stuff! It's . . . it's *Candy*."

The Blackwells' street was a tangle of emergency vehicles and fire hoses, so Michelle had to park a block away. This was probably the craziest thing she'd ever done. Jared would have a fit if he knew where she was. Tonight especially.

Holding tight to Tabby's hand, she walked quickly toward the now-familiar apartment building. Except half the building was eerily dark. Windows were broken out on the third floor along the front, but firemen had already unscrewed one of the big fire hoses from the fire hydrant across the street and were hauling it back toward the largest fire truck. The fire must be out. Residents of the building in assorted stages of dressed and undressed were standing in clumps here and there along the sidewalk.

Michelle scanned the crowd. "Do you see them?"

"Not yet," Tabby said anxiously.

A police officer walked by carrying a large roll of yellow "crime scene" tape.     "Excuse me . . . sir? We're looking for one of our, uh, friends who lives in this building. Was anyone hurt? Have they taken anyone to the hospital?"

The police officer shook his head. "Far as we know, everyone got out. Ambulance is standing by, but the firemen did a thorough search of the whole building, didn't find anybody. You might check that bunch over there." He jerked a thumb at the people milling around on the sidewalk. "Red Cross should be here soon to help these folks find some shelter tonight."

Michelle felt a tug on her arm. "Mom!" Tabby hissed. "I see her!"

Tabby started running across the dusty excuse for a front lawn toward a little girl standing near a group of adults. "Candy!" she yelled.

With a screech, the little girl threw herself into Tabby's arms. "Tabby! Miz Jasper! You came!"

Tabby gently peeled the little girl's arms from the stranglehold around her neck and set her down. "What's this you got?"

The little girl was clutching something in the crook of one arm. She shyly held it out. "I saved it from the fire. I keep it under my pillow."

Tabby's music box.

Tabby took the music box with the shepherd on top and wound it up. The tinkling strains of "The Lord Is My Shepherd" caressed the tense night air.

"Are you okay, Candy?" Michelle asked. "Where's your mom and little brother?"

Candy turned and pointed. Pookey was riding on his mother's hip—thumb in mouth, dressed only in a diaper and shirt—while the wiry woman, hair awry, gestured wildly with her free hand, talking loudly at one of the police officers.

Candy lowered her voice. "Mama think Otto set the fire. He say Mama gonna be sorry she kick him out . . . an' our apartment got burned up worst of anybody's."

"Oh, Candy." Michelle wrapped the girl in another hug. "I'm so glad you're safe."

"Oh! I gots somethin' else too." Candy darted away, but a moment later she was back, lugging a backpack, which she unzipped and lifted out a heavy jar. "I been savin' these for ever an' ever . . . even Mama don' know about it. 'Cause I wanted to buy a princess bike. They gots 'em at Walmart. But . . . I think Mama needs it more."

The little girl shook the glass jar, which tinkled and rattled, and then held it up so Michelle could see inside by the glow of the streetlights. *Pennies*. Hundreds of pennies. Candy pushed the jar into Michelle's hands. "Please, Miz Jasper, can you take this to one of those places that counts pennies and makes 'em into dollars? Maybe it'd help Mama find another place for us to live."

Michelle couldn't find her voice.

But Candy was busy fishing inside a pocket on her shorts. "Here, you can have this one, Miz Jasper. I saved it just for you— you know, for helping me with all those other ones." Grinning, she held up a shiny new penny, waiting for Michelle to take it.

"Mom?" Tabby leaned in close. "Mom? Why are you crying?"

# Chapter 42

TABBY WAS FINALLY ASLEEP.

They had stayed with the Blackwells until the Red Cross vans arrived to take them to an extended-stay motel for a few days until more permanent arrangements could be made. The Salvation Army soup truck had also showed up with hot soup and cold drinks.

*God bless the Red Cross and the Salvation Army,* Michelle thought as she'd watched the displaced residents crowd around the soup truck and then board vans to take them to various shelters for the night. Even the neighbors in this rough part of the city had come out into the night with blankets and disposable diapers and bags of clothes and shoes.

By the time they got back to the car, she was exhausted and had to fight sleep every mile of the long ride home.

Now, shutting Tabby's bedroom door quietly after one last peek, Michelle carried Candy's jar of pennies into the master bedroom and set it on her dresser. Lighting several tea light candles in glass holders on the dresser top, she also lined up the pennies God had given her during the past week—just four because she no longer had the one from the tollbooth. But she still had the one from her apron pocket . . . the clothes dryer . . . the mall . . . and Candy's shiny penny.

Yes, the pennies God had given her—Michelle knew it now. Knew beyond a shadow of a doubt that God was assuring her of his love and care.

Turning off the bedside lamps, she lay down on the bed staring at the display on her dresser. "O Lord," she whispered, watching as the pennies in the jar seemed to dance and shimmer in the flickering candlelight. "You are so faithful! So faithful! Can you forgive me? Forgive me for not trusting you. For . . . for letting fear take the place of faith, for trying to convince myself there was an easy way out of this pregnancy."

Tears once again slid down her cheeks. But this time the tears mingled with a strange and comforting peace.

As the tea lights burned out one by one, Michelle slept.

Her cell phone rang at 7 a.m. Michelle was instantly awake. The boys . . .

But it was Norma. "Michelle! Girl, I got a call from First Lady Donna last night that your boys got shot. Oh, honey, tell me it ain't so!"

Michelle slid out of bed and groped for her robe and slippers with her free hand. "They're all right, Norma. I mean, they will be. Both of them got wounded . . . but God spared them. Jared's at the hospital, stayed overnight." She stumbled toward the kitchen. "Tabby and I came home late to get some sleep, but we'll be going back this morning."

*This morning.* Second Saturday of July. Women's ministry event.

"Norma, I need to ask a huge favor. Can you and the other committee members handle the second video and discussion this morning? I . . . I need to go back to the hospital and be with my boys."

"Girl, you don't even need to ask. Just got off the phone with Sister Shareese. She called, already wanting to know what she could do this morning. I think the prayer chain went viral last night. But I had to hear for myself your babies are okay." Michelle could hear Norma start to choke up. "Oh, Michelle, I can't believe it. Not Destin and Tavis! How—"

"I can't go into that right now, Norma. Promise I'll fill you in later. Just . . . pray, okay? I have a bunch of calls to make."

"Okay. Love you bunches."

Michelle started coffee, then realized the smell of dripping coffee made her feel queasy. She turned off the coffeemaker and turned on the teakettle.

*Lifeline* . . . she needed to call and cancel the post-abortion group this morning. Hated to do it, it was only their second time. But she had no choice. Hopefully the four women would understand. Retrieving her briefcase where she'd dumped it on the dining room table last night, she dug out the Hope and Healing folder with its list of participants and phone numbers. But she hesitated, not sure she had the emotional strength to make calls to these particular women . . . not after toying with the "easy way out" all week.

*Bernice.* Bernice would do it. The Lifeline receptionist didn't usually come in until eight thirty. Did she have her home number? If she gave Bernice the names and phone numbers . . .

Ten minutes later she hung up the phone with Bernice, who promised to call the list and just say Mrs. Jasper had a family emergency, but to plan on meeting next week unless they heard differently. All except one participant . . . Grace Meredith.

Michelle really should call Grace herself.

And Estelle Bentley.

She owed it to both of them.

Not only that . . . but she wanted to. Of all the people in the neighborhood, Estelle and Grace had become not just neighbors but prayer sisters. She'd missed the last two Tuesday prayer times—helping Destin pack for camp last week, and then . . . to be honest, she'd avoided going this week because she hadn't wanted to admit the struggle she was going through, didn't want to tell anyone yet about the pregnancy. Just in case.

Deep down, Michelle suspected that Estelle and Grace had probably been praying for her this week, even without knowing why.

Something else she needed to do this morning before Tabby woke up. Some overdue quiet time alone with God . . . maybe listening more than talking this time.

Jared looked haggard when Michelle and Tabby walked into the hospital room that morning. "Didn't get much sleep last night," he admitted. A curtain was pulled around Tavis's bed. "Tavis had a lot of pain during the night. They finally sedated him so he could sleep. Destin got a few hours though."

"Hey, Mom. Hey, Tabby." Destin was sitting up in bed, sucking on a straw poked into a plastic container of juice, his breakfast tray mostly demolished, the TV monitor on and the bedside controls for sound turned low. "Pastor Q was here already this morning."

"That's nice." She gave Destin a kiss. Not surprised that the pastor would be their first visitor.

Tabby down sat on the edge of Destin's bed next to his good leg, but he still winced. "Sorry," she said. "But move that TV control over here so I can hear too."

Michelle crept behind the room-dividing curtain and watched Tavis sleep for several minutes. She'd thought she was ready to come back to the hospital and sit with her boys, to be cheerful and positive. But her youngest looked so small lying there, his smooth skin the color of coffee beans standing out against the white sheets, his skinny middle swaddled in bandages. An IV was taped to his wrist, monitors attached here and there.

What if they had lost him? Or Destin?

Each of their children was a gift from God. *Precious, precious.* And now there was another to think about . . . a new life. *Another gift from God?*

She certainly hadn't been thinking about her pregnancy that way. Had it taken almost losing both her sons to change her heart about the life she was carrying right now?

Leaning over and kissing Tavis gently on the forehead, Michelle went back to the others. "Have you had anything to eat, honey?" she asked her husband. "We're here now, you could go."

He pushed himself out of the chair gratefully. "Yeah, thanks. Guess I'll do that."

But as he headed for the door she changed her mind. "Wait. I'll come with you." She needed time with Jared as much as she needed time with her sons. Time alone. Michelle gave her cell phone to Tabby. "Text Dad's phone if Tavis wakes up, okay?"

They sat in the hospital cafeteria as he ate his plate of scrambled eggs, hash browns, and sausage. Should she tell him now? She could say, *"Jared, there's something I need to tell you . . ."* But just then he laid down his fork and sighed, his plate only half eaten. "Did you know Destin took money out of his college fund to buy cases and cases of that SlowBurn drink?"

Michelle's mouth dropped open. "What? No. I thought . . . I don't know what I thought. I knew he didn't have any money, so I just figured it was on consignment or something."

"Yeah, me too." Jared took a sip of his lukewarm coffee, made a face, and set it down. "He seemed real upset in the middle of the night, said he didn't know what to do now, didn't know how he was going to pay us back for his basketball camp. I told him to forget it. But he said that's not all . . . that's when he told me. Believe me, Michelle, I was really pissed! Had to go walk up and down the hall just to let off steam. Huh. I was ready to rip that boy up one side and down the other, Singer too. But when I came back, he'd actually fallen asleep. Good thing, I guess. Spent most of the night doing a lot of thinking . . ."

Jared got up, dumped his coffee, and got a hot refill. When he asked if she wanted some, Michelle shook her head. The smell made her feel queasy. They walked out of the cafeteria and found a lounge with a private corner.

"It's tempting to blame all this on Singer. But the more I thought about it, Michelle, the more I realized . . ." Jared's mouth twitched, as if his emotions were close to the surface. "I realized I'm also at fault here. Been riding that boy all summer about getting a job. But like you said, he *was* trying. Thing is, I just hung him out there, didn't give him any direction, didn't come alongside . . ." Jared's voice broke and he shook his head. "Funny thing, it wasn't until Pastor Q showed up this morning, making his hospital rounds, stopping by with a prayer and a word of encouragement, that it hit me. I've been trying to be like Pastor Q. Ready to do the work of the Lord at the drop of a hat! I admire the man, Michelle. He's a good man, a good pastor . . . but he and Donna don't have kids at home anymore." Jared's eyes brimmed. "I do. Three beautiful kids who need me. And most of the time I'm not even there." The tears slid down his cheeks and he fished for his handkerchief.

"Oh, Jared." Michelle scooted over and put her arms around her husband and just held him for a few minutes as they sat in the mostly empty lounge.

Finally he blew his nose and sighed. "I don't know what the answer is, Michelle. But I need to be spending more time with my kids. Maybe *especially* now that they're teenagers. Because we can't take them for granted." He looked at her soberly. "We could've lost both our boys yesterday. But we didn't. God spared them. Maybe to give me another chance to take my job as a parent more seriously."

"Me too." The words came out in a whisper. She tried to swallow past the lump in her throat. "But that parenting job just got a lot bigger."

Jared looked at her with a little frown. "What do you mean?"

Michelle took both his hands in hers. "We're going to have another baby."

# Chapter 43

MICHELLE HAD TO HAND IT TO JARED. He handled his shock better than she had. "Wow," he said. "Oh, wow." Then, "You're sure?"

She nodded.

"When?"

"End of January or early February. Thereabouts."

"That . . . puts a wrinkle in things, doesn't it?"

She almost laughed.

"Wow," he said again. "Four kids." And then he choked up. "It's God's mercy we've still got the three we already have. Makes adding number four not such a big deal, right?" He put one of his strong arms around Michelle and pulled her close. "We'll make it somehow, Gumdrop. We'll make it . . ."

Jared's cell beeped. A text from Tabby: *Tavis awake Being a jerk Pls come back.*

They held hands as they walked back to the boys' room. "Let's not tell the kids yet, okay?" Michelle said. "We need some time to figure things out."

There wouldn't have been any time to tell the kids anyway. The whole rest of the day passed in an antiseptic blur as nurses and aides came in to take vitals, got Destin out of bed for a few painful steps, brought meals on trays . . . and visitors.

Harry and Estelle Bentley were the first after Pastor Q. "We won't stay long, honey," Estelle said, wrapping Michelle in a big hug as Harry shook Jared's hand. "Just want you to know you been on my heart all week, knew God wanted me to pray about something . . ."

"Thank you," Michelle whispered. Praying for her all week, she said. And Estelle still didn't even know about the pregnancy.

"Don't you worry about meals, now. Harry an' I been cookin' up a storm all mornin' since we got your call. Grace too—though she got a concert comin' up. An' Nicole Singer offered to make a meal or two as well."

"Nicole Singer?" Michelle was startled. She sent a quick glance in Jared's direction, but he and Harry were talking with the two boys.

Estelle nodded, kept her voice low. "Remember when you said we ought to pray for the Singers a couple weeks ago? Well, I ran into her on the street and on the spur of the moment asked if she'd like to join us for prayer. You didn't come last Tuesday but she actually showed up."

"Really?"

"She didn't say much that night, but I had a sense she needed some serious prayer, so I actually stopped by to see her a couple days later. She opened up a bit more, I was able to pray with her. I'll leave it to her to share what's going on when she's ready, but one thing for sure . . . that young lady needs some praying sister-friends."

Estelle was true to her word. The Jaspers found a cooler with several meals' worth of dishes on their front porch when they got home from the hospital that evening. And the next day the Bentleys showed up at the hospital again on their way home from church, this time with DaShawn. "You two gettin' a break from babysittin' these here hooligans?" Harry asked gruffly, winking at the boys as DaShawn bumped fists with Destin and Tavis.

"Well, we did go home to get some sleep last night, but we've been here since eight this morning," Jared explained. Even Michelle had been surprised when he'd suggested they skip church and come back to the hospital that morning. "Don't want the boys to be here alone any more than they have to."

Harry pulled a chessboard and a bag of chess pieces out of a backpack he carried. "Well, I been lookin' for a captive audience to play some chess with me. So why don't you two tired souls go hang out at the lake or something for an hour or two. Go on. Get out of here. We're good. Right, Destin?"

"I never played chess before, Mr. Harry," Destin said, looking worried.

"Perfect. I'll teach ya. Maybe I'll win a game or two before you get too smart. DaShawn here beats me every time *we* play. It's hard on my ego."

Ten minutes later, as Michelle and Jared slipped out of the hospital room, Harry was explaining chess moves to Destin, DaShawn was playing Crazy Eights with Tavis with a deck of cards, and Estelle had pulled out some needles and yarn and was teaching Tabby how to knit.

"How did they know we need some time to talk?" Jared asked as they pulled out of the parking garage and headed for the South Boulevard Beach on Lake Michigan, which was just a mile away.

Michelle chuckled. "Some sixth sense from God, I think."

Unlike the free Chicago beaches, Evanston required a beach token or daily fee, but Jared and Michelle weren't really dressed for the beach anyway. They found a bench in the shade on the little parkway facing the lake and sat, Jared's arms stretched out on the back of the bench, Michelle leaning against him, neither of them speaking for a while. A few thunderheads seemed to be forming to the far south, but overhead small, puffy clouds still played hide-and-seek with a relentless sun.

Michelle finally broke their silence. "What are we going to do, Jared? How are we going to manage adding a baby to our family? I mean, if I have to quit work, be home with a baby . . ."

"It definitely boggles the mind."

They sat a minute or two more in silence. Then Jared leaned forward and rested his elbows on his knees. "There's a couple things we could do. Refinance the house, for one. Reduce our monthly payments. And we're almost done making payments on the minivan. That'll help. But I've also been thinking. There's a supervisor position open at the tower training new controllers. It'd mean a jump in salary and I could probably finagle regular hours . . . what do you think?"

She touched his arm. "Oh, Jared. I know you enjoy being an ATC. You turned down the supervisor position once before, remember?"

"Yep. But that was then. Might be a good thing now. No guarantee I'll get it, of course, but won't hurt to apply."

"I can probably work at Bridges till November or December, but after that . . . I stayed home with the other three. Don't want to stick this one in childcare too soon." Michelle tried not to think what that would do to her career track as a caseworker.

Again a long stretch of silence. Then Jared took a big breath. "But you know it's not just our jobs. I've been thinking it's time I stepped down from the deacon board, give some of the other men in the church an opportunity to serve."

Michelle was touched. *And seminary?*

As if reading her mind, Jared said. "I need to tell Pastor Q that seminary is out of the question right now. Maybe in a few years, I can do online courses or something. But God's been telling me my first priority right now is my kids. And my wife." Jared drew her into a hug and kissed the top of her head. "I'm . . . I'm so sorry I've been so busy, Michelle. Realized last night we haven't even had a date night for ages. Might be fun to put *that* on the calendar again like we used to."

She rolled her eyes. "Not so easy with an infant."

He chuckled. "Yeah, but we've got . . . what? Five or six months till Baby Jasper makes his or her debut."

Michelle snorted. "Let's just hope it's not *his and her* like last time."

"Oh, dear Lord, Michelle! You don't think . . ."

They talked, brainstormed ideas, prayed a bit, even cried a little . . . and suddenly jumped when Jared looked at his watch and realized two hours had passed. "Help! The Bentleys will think we took advantage of their offer and are headed for Mexico."

But Michelle's heart was a little lighter as they headed back to the hospital. She and Jared were talking. They were planning. They were praying . . . together.

She should tell him about the pennies.

Destin was released on Monday afternoon. Jared had called his supervisor that morning, said he needed to take a few sick days for a family emergency. Michelle did the same—though she did tell her boss the reason she couldn't come in that week was both her boys had been wounded by gunfire on their way home from basketball camp.

News about the pregnancy would have to wait till later.

"Those were *your* kids?" Charlotte Bergman gasped into the phone. "I read about that shooting in the paper, but . . . Oh, Michelle, I had no idea it was your boys." The woman let loose with a few choice swear words. "I tell ya, these gang wars have gotta stop. Too many innocent people get caught in the crossfire."

*Too many kids, period,* Michelle thought as she hung up. On her job, she often wondered how many gang members were "innocent kids" once—kids like Pookey—but got sucked into gangs because of absent fathers, soul-crushing poverty, lack of jobs, lack of hope. Needing someplace to belong.

She'd never worried about gangs with her kids . . . but look at Tavis, thinking it was cool to adopt gang culture with those baggy, low-slung pants, wanting to be accepted by other kids. Was that how stuff like that started?

Wait. She had a sudden horrible thought. Was that how Tavis looked standing around the street corner with Destin last Friday? Like some little gangbanger wannabe?

*No, no, no* . . . she couldn't go there. Her kids had made some stupid choices that day, but what a kid wore wasn't the real culprit. Parents too busy or too stressed or too broken themselves to be parents in a world sucking young people into destructive paths. *That's* where it started.

*O God, help us make the right choices here!* she prayed as she drove Destin and his crutches home that afternoon to get him settled. Jared was still at the hospital with Tavis, who had a few more days before the doctors were willing to release him. Later that evening, she and Jared would trade places.

"Guess I won't be getting my driver's license any time soon," Destin said glumly. "Not with these." He jerked a thumb in the direction of the crutches in the back seat.

"Hey, it's going to be okay." Michelle gave her son an affectionate pat on the knee. "The doc said you're going to make a full recovery—it's just going to take a little time. Bet you'll be driving before you know it." Probably before he'd be able to play basketball, but she didn't say it.

She knew he was eager to get home, but there was something important she needed to do on the way. "Hey, Destin, mind if we stop at the bank for a minute? Shouldn't take long." Pulling into the parking lot of a branch bank on Western Avenue just south of their neighborhood, Michelle reached into the backseat of the minivan and retrieved Candy's jar of pennies.

# Chapter 44

MICHELLE PUSHED THE GROCERY CART through the aisles at the local Jewel store faster than usual. Too bad she couldn't shop on Tuesdays all the time—much less crowded than on Saturday afternoon. But even with the meals that had been showing up at their house from some of the neighbors, they were out of basics like bread and milk and Dr. Pepper. *Hmph.* Something wasn't quite right when Dr. Pepper had become a "basic," but Destin had picked up on Jared's habit too.

She'd spent the morning with Tavis at the hospital, then Jared had relieved her so she could get some errands done—including delivering Candy's eleven dollars and seventy-seven cents to the extended-stay motel where the Red Cross had housed the Blackwells. Candy had beamed when she handed the money to her mother. Renatta Blackwell—Michelle had finally learned her first name—had actually seemed touched by her daughter's gift, had even grudgingly asked for one of Michelle's cards. "Might need some help from that place you work for," she'd admitted.

Michelle grabbed some apples, bananas, lettuce, and carrots from the produce section, then hustled to the checkout stations. She didn't want to be gone too long. At least Tabby was at home with Destin, who was hobbling around the house on crutches. Should she be thankful the double shooting had happened in summertime so Tabby could help out with her brothers? Even the fact that the Singers didn't seem to need her anymore for babysitting had turned out to be a blessing. Odd, the things one ended up being grateful for in the midst of a crisis.

"Mrs. Jasper . . . Michelle?"

A familiar voice made Michelle turn around as she was unloading her cart onto the moving belt. Rebecca Horowitz, her three kids in tow, had stopped in the aisle behind her, though it looked as if she were just starting her shopping. "Oh . . . hi, Rebecca." She gave a little laugh. "Funny to keep meeting like this—second time at the grocery store, right?"

Rebecca, dressed as usual in her snood and long skirt, nodded, but her face was full of concern. "I . . . I heard about your boys, uh, getting injured." The Jewish woman cast a nervous glance at her children, who didn't seem to be paying attention anyway. "I'm so sorry. Is there anything we can do?"

Michelle shook her head. "Thanks, but we're doing okay. Uh, how did you hear?"

"Oh, the little boy across the street—Nathan—sometimes comes over to play with Jacob and Ruthie when they're outside. He said Tabby—that's your daughter, right?—was supposed to babysit but had to go to the hospital to see her brothers. I hope you don't mind. Isaac and I said a prayer for you at Shabbat."

Michelle was touched. "Thank you, Rebecca. I . . . we appreciate the prayers. It could have been much worse."

Rebecca seemed to be studying her closely and a little smile tipped her mouth. She leaned close to Michelle. "You are going to think I am very nosy, I'm afraid, but . . . are you pregnant by any chance?"

Michelle was taken aback. No way had she started to show. She was only nine weeks, for heaven's sake! But no use denying it. She nodded. "As a matter of fact. Still in shock . . . at my age, you know. But we haven't told anyone yet, not even our kids, so I'd appreciate it if you wouldn't say anything to anyone." She looked at Rebecca curiously. "How in the world did you guess?"

Rebecca grinned. "I'm a midwife. God has given me a sixth sense about these things. But actually, it's not so mysterious. Your face . . . a little fuller. Your skin . . . a certain sheen. And you are touching your belly in a protective way. But I promise"—she put a finger to her lips—"won't tell a soul."

*That* was strange. But Michelle couldn't help smiling as she drove home. Her skin had a sheen?

Jared called as she was putting groceries away. "The doctor came by, said Tavis might be able to come home tomorrow. So I'm thinking about staying here this evening, but going in to work on my regular day shift tomorrow. I want to get that application in for the supervisor position as soon as possible."

So. He really was serious. "Sounds good. I'll come to the hospital in the morning and stay till they release him. See you tonight . . . Love you."

Michelle put away the last bag of groceries, then pulled a casserole dish of enchiladas out of the freezer to thaw for supper. She'd missed the last two prayer times with Grace and Estelle. But now she was going to be home tonight instead of at the hospital. Maybe she could run next door for a little while after supper. After all, Tabby would let her know if Destin needed her and she could be home in less than a minute.

But what if Nicole Singer showed up too? That might be kind of awkward. Jared told her that Greg Singer had showed up at the house last night while she was at the hospital to say he was sorry to hear about the boys—and Jared had kind of lost it about the SlowBurn business. Didn't sound as if they'd worked it out about Singer reimbursing Destin for all that product he'd bought. If Nicole were there tonight, it might put a damper on what Michelle could share with the others.

As it turned out, she needn't have worried. Nicole didn't show up, and Ramona was holed up in the guest bedroom, talking with her parents in Los Angeles. "It took a lot of coaxing to get her to call," Grace murmured. "She's embarrassed to admit how foolish she was to run away with Max and get involved with that whole drug trafficking thing and end up here in Chicago. But I told her if I was her mother, I'd be worried sick and she needed to call, let them know she's all right." Grace smiled sheepishly. "I've turned into a downright nag."

They prayed for Ramona's phone call first thing, then Grace said, "Please, tell me how Tavis and his brother are. I can't believe they both got shot! I—I still remember how sweet Tavis was to shovel my walks for me last winter. *And* rescue Oreo when you-know-who accidentally let him out."

*You-know-who* . . . probably Grace's ex-fiancé. Michelle thought the singer's new love—her agent, the very charming Jeff

Newman—would've popped the question by now, but . . . maybe they were waiting until Grace had dealt more thoroughly with stuff from her past. Which made Michelle sorry she'd had to cancel the Hope and Healing group on Saturday. But it was what it was.

Taking a deep breath, Michelle tried to bring Grace and Estelle up to date with a short version of the whole complicated mess . . . but as her new friends listened, genuine love and concern on their faces, everything started to spill out—including finding out she was pregnant.

Both sets of eyes went wide. "Mercy, mercy," Estelle murmured.

"We . . . we haven't told the kids yet, so please don't say anything. In fact, I only told Jared this weekend, because . . . because . . ." And, tears streaming down her face, she confessed the struggle she'd had with coming to terms with the pregnancy, even tempted to terminate the pregnancy. "I'm so sorry, Grace," she said, taking the box of tissues Estelle handed her, "I know that probably disillusions you about the Hope and Healing group I'm supposed to be leading. But, yes, I came dangerously close to believing the lie that an abortion would be the easy way out."

Grace moved to her side on the couch and wrapped her arms around her, holding Michelle tight. "No, no," she whispered. "Now I know you truly understand."

The prayer time with Grace and Estelle Tuesday night somehow fortified Michelle for the days that followed. She had asked them to especially pray for her and Jared as they took a hard look at their schedules and responsibilities and finances to find ways they needed to reshuffle their lives.

She'd taken the whole week off from Bridges, even though Jared felt he had to go back to work for his remaining three shifts that week. Tavis was released late Wednesday afternoon, and she'd been playing nursemaid the rest of the week, keeping up with medications and dressings and trying to keep both boys entertained. She and Jared still had a lot of decisions to make, but at least he had turned in his application for a new position at the

O'Hare Airport tower and said he planned to talk to Pastor Q on Sunday about stepping down from the deacon board and that he needed to put the whole idea of seminary on hold. Indefinitely.

But what sacrifices would she be required to make?

Jared agreed she should go ahead with her Hope and Healing group on Saturday, said it would give him some good time to "just be" with the boys—something he hadn't done for a long time. When she left, Destin was trying to teach Jared and Tavis how to play chess.

*Huh.* Good luck with that.

Michelle had just planned to do the session they'd missed last week, but all four women said they were willing to stay a little longer if they could also move on to the next session on "relief and denial." *That* prompted a lot of discussion and honest sharing: about the relief an abortion brought, to not be pregnant anymore, and how much they'd wanted to deny that it was any big deal, deny that it was human life—*their child*—they'd aborted. The hardest thing to deal with was the clash between relief and denial with the nagging regret and even anger that had also followed.

After sharing some relevant scriptures, Michelle mostly listened. It was all she could do to finish the session. *That could so easily be me . . .*

By the time Sunday morning rolled around, both boys were so bored staying home they begged to go to church. Michelle dreaded parading Destin and Tavis into church and the fuss people would make, but she had to admit it felt so good to all be sitting together in the "Jaspers' pew." Even Jared. Stepping down from the deacon board wasn't official yet, but Jared told Pastor Q that sitting with his family that morning was symbolic for him. Something he needed to do not only for his wife and children, but for himself.

Michelle squeezed her husband's hand as the choir stood up to sing. After the usual rousing gospel praise number, she was surprised to see Shareese Watson, her reddish-brown weave freshly coiffed, come down out of the choir and take the handheld mike from the choir director. As the keyboard launched into the gentle strains of an old hymn and the choir hummed, Shareese began to sing . . .

*'Tis so sweet to trust in Jesus*
*Just to take him at his word*
*Just to rest upon his promise*
*Just to know, "Thus saith the Lord"* . . .

Michelle was surprised at how clear and strong the young woman's voice was. Didn't know the girl could sing like that! The rest of the choir joined with Shareese as she came to the chorus . . .

*Jesus, Jesus, how I trust him!*
*How I've proved him o'er and o'er!*
*Jesus, Jesus, precious Jesus!*
*Oh, for grace to trust Him more.*

A lump formed in Michelle's throat, remembering the five pennies lined up on her dresser. Her silly penny test . . . yet God had honored it. Given her those little reminders that he *did* care and that he *would* take care of them. And the promise seemed to fill the whole sanctuary that morning as Shareese closed her eyes and put her heart into the last verse . . .

*I'm so glad I learned to trust thee,*
*Precious Jesus, Savior, Friend.*
*And I know that thou art with me,*
*Wilt be with me to the end.*

The whole congregation joined in with Shareese and the choir on the chorus, but Michelle's heart was still stuck on the last verse: *And I know that thou art with me, Wilt be with me to the end.*

As Shareese made her way back into the soprano section of the choir, Michelle had a revelation. *Shareese Watson* . . . that's who should take over the women's ministry at Northside. Yes she was young, but she was enthusiastic and had a lot of ideas. When Michelle had come in that morning, several women told her how much they were appreciating the video series. "Too bad you missed it. Best thing we've done in a month a' Sundays," Sister Paulette had declared before bustling off.

Shareese's idea. Shareese's initiative.

Michelle grinned as she thought about her first step to simplify her schedule. One less thing to organize and worry about. And it was going to be fine. It was going to go forward. Might even be better with Shareese's zeal at the helm. Though hopefully Norma and the other committee members would hang in there. Even fresh wind needed a few good rudders.

"You boys ready to go home?" she asked Destin and Tavis as they waited for Jared to finish speaking to Pastor Q after the service.

"Home?" Tavis looked shocked. "But we always go out to Old Country Buffet after church. I'm starving."

"Me too." Destin was demonstrating his dexterity with the crutches for a few admiring preschoolers in the foyer.

Tabby rolled her eyes. "Showoff."

Jared didn't take long speaking to the pastor. He gave Michelle as nod as if to say it went okay. As they made their way out of the church and headed for the minivan, Michelle held Jared back a few steps and whispered in his ear. He looked at her. "You sure?"

So it was over soft-serve ice cream sundaes, loaded with bananas and candy chips and hot chocolate fudge, that Jared cleared his throat. "Hey, guys, listen up. Your mom and I have something important to tell you . . ."

Destin and Tavis listened to their mother's announcement open-mouthed, ice cream forgotten. "A *baby*?" they chorused in unison, faces registering mock-horror.

But Tabby gave a fist pump and yelled, "Yesss! 'Bout time I got me a little sister. Can I name her?"

Michelle didn't bother to tell her daughter it could just as well be another brother. Leave well enough alone for now. Boy or girl, she was sure of only one thing:

*She could trust God to work it out, and he would be with them to the end.*

# Acknowledgements

**In memory of Lee Hough**
**Our exceptional agent and friend at Alive Communications**

Special thanks to **Tish Suk,** whose own "penny test" and testimony of God's faithfulness inspired an essential part of this story. Tish, this story is for you!

Much appreciation to **Brenda Shuler,** a post-abortion counselor at Bridges of Hope and Life Network in Colorado Springs, Colorado, who not only served as a resource for this story, but graciously read the manuscript and gave us helpful feedback. Brenda, you and Clarence are such an encouragement to us with the way God is using your "Building Lasting Relationships" marriage seminars, and we also treasure your heart investment in racial and cultural diversity.

Many thanks to **Jennifer Stair,** who has edited many of the novels that make up the "Yada Yada world" and remembers details about our characters that we've forgotten! Thanks, Jen, for dropping everything to edit *Penny Wise* in spite of your busy schedule.

Thanks, too, to **Janelle Schneider** (fellow author and friend), **Michelle Redding, Lelia Austin**, and **Krista Johnson** for your willingness to proofread the edited manuscript on a tight deadline, as well as offering many helpful questions and comments. Add another star to your crowns!

To our son **Julian,** Director of Experience Design at the Adler Planetarium in Chicago, thanks for being a sounding board for cover and design ideas! And special thanks to grandson, **Elijah,** age seven, who found a glaring typo on the cover!

*A disclaimer:* None of the above are responsible for any mistakes, goofs, or typos that slipped past. Those we take full credit for ourselves!

Last but not least, to our faithful readers . . . we so appreciate the reviews you leave on Amazon.com, B&N.com, ChristianBook. com, and other online bookstores—they help more than you know. And thanks *always* for your letters, emails, FB, and Twitter posts of encouragement! It's because of you that we keep writing.

*Neta and Dave*

# Book Club Discussion Questions for
# *Penny Wise*

1. In *Penny Wise,* the Jaspers are the third family we meet on Beecham Street in the Windy City neighborhood. (We met Grace Meredith in *Grounded* and Harry and Estelle Bentley in *Derailed.*) What were some of your first impressions of the Jasper family?

2. What do you see as the strengths in Michelle and Jared Jasper's marriage? What do you see as the weaknesses in their relationship? Give examples of both.

3. Michelle and Jared are not just "pew warmers"—they are faithful, committed church members, the kind of people pastors can count on to be there every Sunday and during the week, ready to serve. At what point did you begin to suspect that this is not always a good thing?

4. If Harry and Estelle Bentley moved into *your* neighborhood—purchasing a home that had been foreclosed by the bank—how would you feel about their efforts to get to know all the neighbors up and down the street, even though they are the newcomers?

5. How do you feel about how Jared and Michelle handled the situation with Destin, who wanted to go to an elite basketball camp early in the summer, *before* he had a chance to work and earn the money to pay for it? How would you have handled it? What particular circumstances would influence your decision?

6. Michelle encountered a wide variety of at-risk families in her job as a social worker for Bridges Family Services. What was

your gut reaction to some of these cases? Was there a person or situation that touched you in particular? Why?

7. Social workers can only do so much. How might local churches come alongside to help in some of these situations? Neighbors? Friends and family? You?

8. Did you have any sympathy for Michelle's temptation to act against her conscience (and everything she stood for as a volunteer at the Lifeline Care Center) when she faced a personal crisis? Why or why not?

9. Are you aware of any post-abortion support groups in your area? What would be the hindrances to someone seeking out this resource? If you or someone you know has had an abortion, in what ways do you think such a support group would be helpful?

10. Who do you think was to blame for the scary mess Destin and Tavis got themselves into? How do you feel about Greg Singer's role in what happened? (You will get to know Greg and Nicole Singer in the *next* Windy City Neighbors novel, *Pound Foolish*—see the excerpt at the end of this book!)

11. Have you ever "tested" the Lord, putting out a "fleece" in a similar way to the story of Gideon in the Old Testament? What did you think of Michelle's "penny test"? Did it speak to you in any special way? If so, how?

12. Like many of us, Michelle and Jared "let the urgent crowd out the important." What do you think of the changes Jared and Michelle plan to make in their personal and family lives? What else might you suggest to them to deal with their "over busyness" and distraction from what's "important"?

13. Do *you* need to step back and evaluate if you are over-busy—at work, at church, at home? Is it hard for you to say No when asked to take on more? Do you keep busy to avoid an unpleasant situation or relationship? What important things or relationships might you be neglecting?

# Chapter 1

From the moment Nicole Singer saw the long black Lincoln sliding toward her down Greenleaf, she knew it was the same vehicle that had almost hit her and her two children a few minutes before as they dashed across Western Avenue in the rain. She gripped Nathan's and Becky's hands, lifted her head a little higher, and picked up the pace, ignoring the approaching stretch limo and the large drops that were making their way through the branches of the overhanging elms.

The black Lincoln eased over to her side of the street—the wrong side of the street, though there wasn't much traffic in this quiet neighborhood—and slowed to a stop as it came even with her. A dark rear window hummed down. "Excuse me," a man said.

Nicole kept walking, looking straight ahead to the far end of the sidewalk.

The car began backing up to keep pace with her. "Excuse me. Do you live on Beecham Street?"

Her six- and eight-year-olds were lagging, twisting to look at the speaker. "Mom, it's the McMansion man," Becky said in a stage whisper.

Nicole relented and looked.

The man in the limo chuckled, an easy smile spreading across his handsome boyish face. "She's right, you know . . . big house across the end of the block? I suppose you could call it a McMansion, but to me it's just home. I'm Lincoln Paddock, by the way. And I'm really sorry my driver gave you a start back there on Western. I don't know why we were going so fast. I'm not in any kind of a hurry. Here . . ." He swung open the door to the plush limo. "I'm so sorry, and the least I can do is offer you a ride and get you out of this rain."

Nicole hesitated. But Nathan tugged on her hand. "Can we Mom? We've never ridden in a real stretch limo." At least her son knew what to call it. She hesitated, but Becky began to whimper. "Please, Mommy. I'm gettin' cold."

Nicole stepped across the parkway grass toward the curb. "Well, I wouldn't want to put you out, Mr. Paddock."

"Just Lincoln, just call me Lincoln. But it's no problem giving you a ride. Please." He stepped out and held the door open like a gentleman ushering them into his coach. He was tall, taller than Nicole and a real hunk under his black business suit. Nicole felt herself blush at taking note. How would she like it if that was his first note of her?

Both kids had claimed the long side lounge seat, stretching out each way with their heads together in the middle. "Look, Mom. A TV in the car and a little kitchen with things to drink."

She could have walked all the way to the front and taken that seat, but it didn't seem dignified, all bent over from the waist, so she sat down on the far side of the back seat. "Kids, get your feet off the seats . . . now." They complied just as their neighbor closed the door and sat down beside her.

"Don't worry about it. The seats are leather and wipe right off with a damp cloth. Here, kids, let me find something for you to watch." He pressed buttons on the controller until a cartoon came up on the flat screen.

The car began to move, the driver proceeding without being told.

Paddock turned to her. "Guess we've never met. But I've seen you in the neighborhood with your kids. So you are . . .?"

"Nicole, Nicole Singer."

He extended his hand, and she shook it awkwardly. "Nicole. That's nice. Do they call you Nikki?"

She shrugged. Her husband, Greg, was really the only one who used that pet name for her, but it had been a while.

"After we almost ran you over, I thought I recognized you, so I told Robbie to go around the block until we found you. But . . ." he chuckled, "what I wanna to know is, what you three were doing this far from home in the rain."

Nicole was going to brush off his question by saying it wasn't that far and it hadn't been raining when they started out, but Nathan seemed to have two-track hearing. "We were at Indian Boundaries."

"Not *Boundaries*, dum-dum, Boundary, Indian Boundary Park," corrected Becky, proving she, too, was tuned in to more than the cartoon.

"Oh, I know where that is," said Paddock. "No wonder you were rushing back across Western."

"Yes, we probably should have driven. You can never tell how fast rain'll come up with this spring weather." Nicole grabbed her damp blouse at the corners of the shoulders and lifted it away from clinging to her like a second skin, only to realize her actions drew Paddock's attention.

"Mom, can we have something to drink?"

"Honey, we'll be home soon. You can wait."

Paddock chuckled again. "That's okay, but the bar's dry. We haven't restocked it for awhile." He pushed a button. "Robbie, head on up to Howard and swing by McDonalds to get these kids something." He turned and glanced out the back window. "There's another McDonald's back there a couple blocks, but turnin' this thing around is like a battleship in a canal."

"But he . . ." Nicole let her eyes go wide. "He can get it through a McDonald's drive-thru?"

Paddock's chuckle was becoming characteristic. "Not a chance. We'll stop across the street, and he'll run our order over. I usually take one of our smaller limos. You can't even jockey it around in our cul-de-sac. Robbie'll have to back it out of Beecham."

"Oh, I don't want you to go to any trouble on our account. The kids don't need anything, and we can walk."

"It's no problem, Nikki. We've got plenty of time, and he was taking me home anyway." Lincoln Paddock looked at the children. "So why aren't a couple of bright kids like you in school today?"

His questions seemed far too personal, but when the kids didn't answer, she said, "We homeschool."

"Homeschool? That means you do your own lessons and, and . . ."

"And we get to go on fieldtrips," Nathan offered, still staring at the cartoon.

"And your fieldtrip today was . . .?"

"The zoo."

"Really? I didn't know there was a zoo in that park."

Nicole hastened to say, "Oh, it's not really a zoo anymore. Just a few goats and chickens." Then in case he got the idea that homeschoolers took "fieldtrips" to nowhere, she added, "The kids have been studying hard, so this was more of a break than a real fieldtrip."

"Yeah," Nathan said. "So when can we go to a real zoo, Mom?"

"Oh, you like zoos? Maybe one of these days, I could take you down to Lincoln Park Zoo where they've got lots of animals. Would you kids like that?"

"Could we, Mom? Could we?" The cartoon had lost their attention.

Nicole's mouth fell open. What was with this guy? "Um . . . maybe some day . . . when Daddy's home." It seemed high time she bring her husband into the conversation. On the other hand, there was something enchanting about this ride in the back of a limo with a handsome stranger . . .

Look for *POUND FOOLISH* in October 2014

CPSIA information can be obtained at www.ICGtesting.com
Printed in the USA
LVOW08s1126290614

392202LV00001B/214/P

9 780982 054468